DAUGHTER OF THE DEAD

REMNANTS OF RAGE

BOOK ONE

K. JAMILA

Editing: Grey Moth Editing & Kayla Morton
Proofreading: Tiffany Thomas
Map: Dewi Hargreaves
Cover Illustration: Mitra Katsuyoshi
Cover Typography: Silver Grace
Interior Art: Kim Cavrak | spiritofebllience

K. Jamila

Mine Would Be You
Golden Hour of You and Me
Tomorrow I'll Love You

Praise for Daughter of the Dead

"*Daughter of the Dead* is an absorbing tale of power, magic, heartache, and anger. A rich and deadly read full of vivid world-building, dazzling action, and complex characters. K. Jamila has crafted a gem for lovers of the morally grey, tortured heroine."
     —**Jessica J. Ayala, author of *The Dusk and Dawn* series**

"*Daughter of the Dead* is a breathtaking spin on fantasy that will leave you wracking your brain trying to untangle the threads of the story while simultaneously getting so lost in the intricate world you forget where you are. Unique magic, family turmoil, political intrigue, and multifaceted (and might I add, *badass*) female characters, *Daughter of the Dead* has everything you could ever want in a fantasy read. K. Jamila's debut into fantasy feels like she's coming home to where she's always been meant to be."
     —**Kaitlyn Swanson, author of *Queen of Blood and Stardust* series**

"*Daughter of the Dead* is what epic fantasy readers dream of! The intricate and intriguing world building paired with deep, flawed characters and constant secrets keep you on the edge of your seat, yearning for more!"
     —**Nicole Platania, author of *The Curse of Ophelia* series**

Author's Note

This book contains subject matter that might be difficult for readers, such as depictions of grief and loss, mentions of animal harm (off-page), mentions of suicide (off-page), self-harm, depression, anxiety, blood/gore, death, violence, torture (both physical and emotional), and other possible triggering content.

Dedication

For anyone who has had their wings clipped—you will fly again and cast shadows on those that tried to break you.

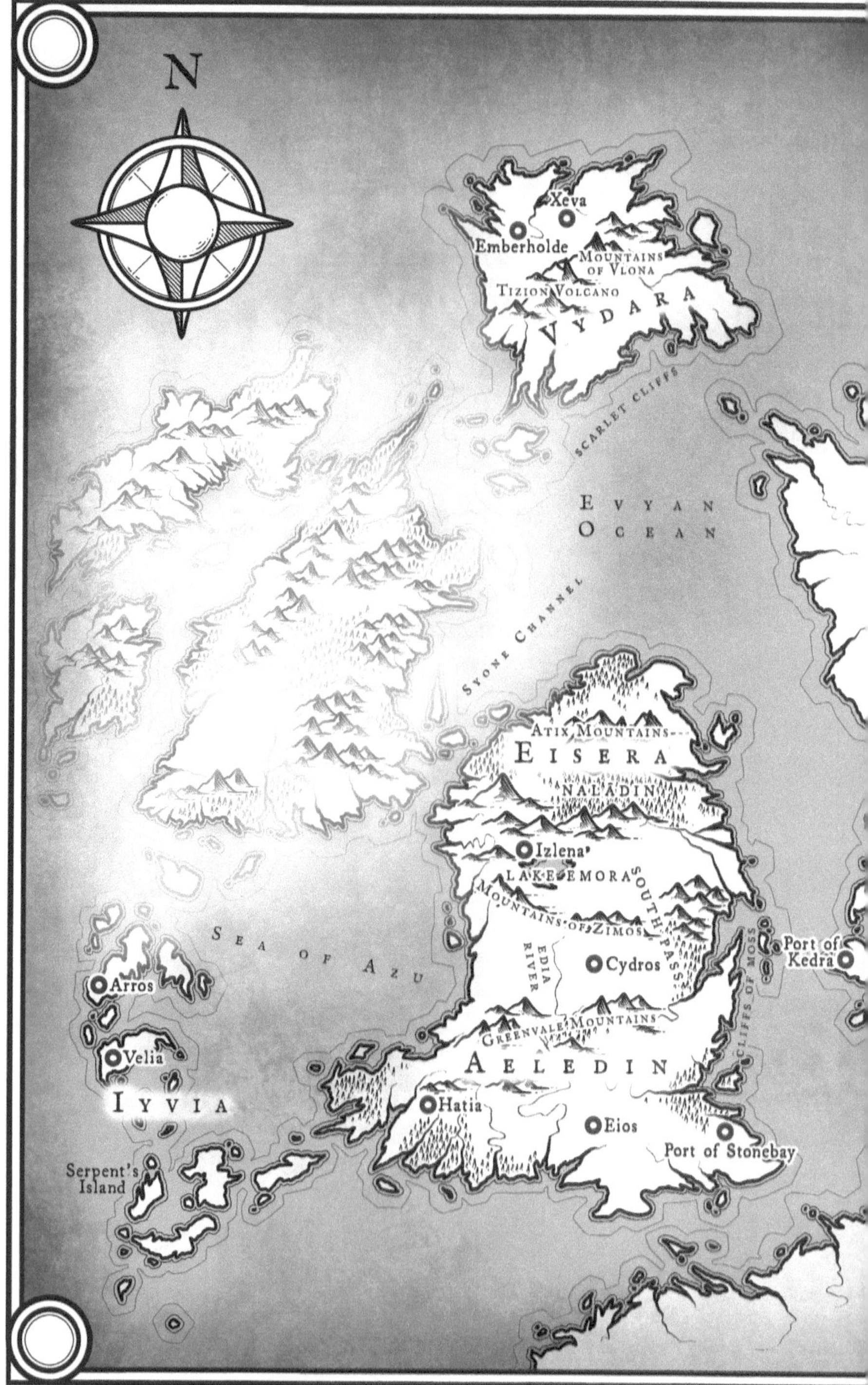

N
VYDARA
Xeva
Emberholde
Mountains of Vlona
Tizion Volcano
Scarlet Cliffs
Evyan Ocean
Syone Channel
Atix Mountains
EISERA
Naladin
Izlena
Lake Emora
Mountains of Zimos
South Pass
Edia River
Cydros
Cliffs of Moss
Port of Kedra
Sea of Azu
Arros
Velia
Greenvale Mountains
AELEDIN
Iyvia
Hatia
Eios
Port of Stonebay
Serpent's Island

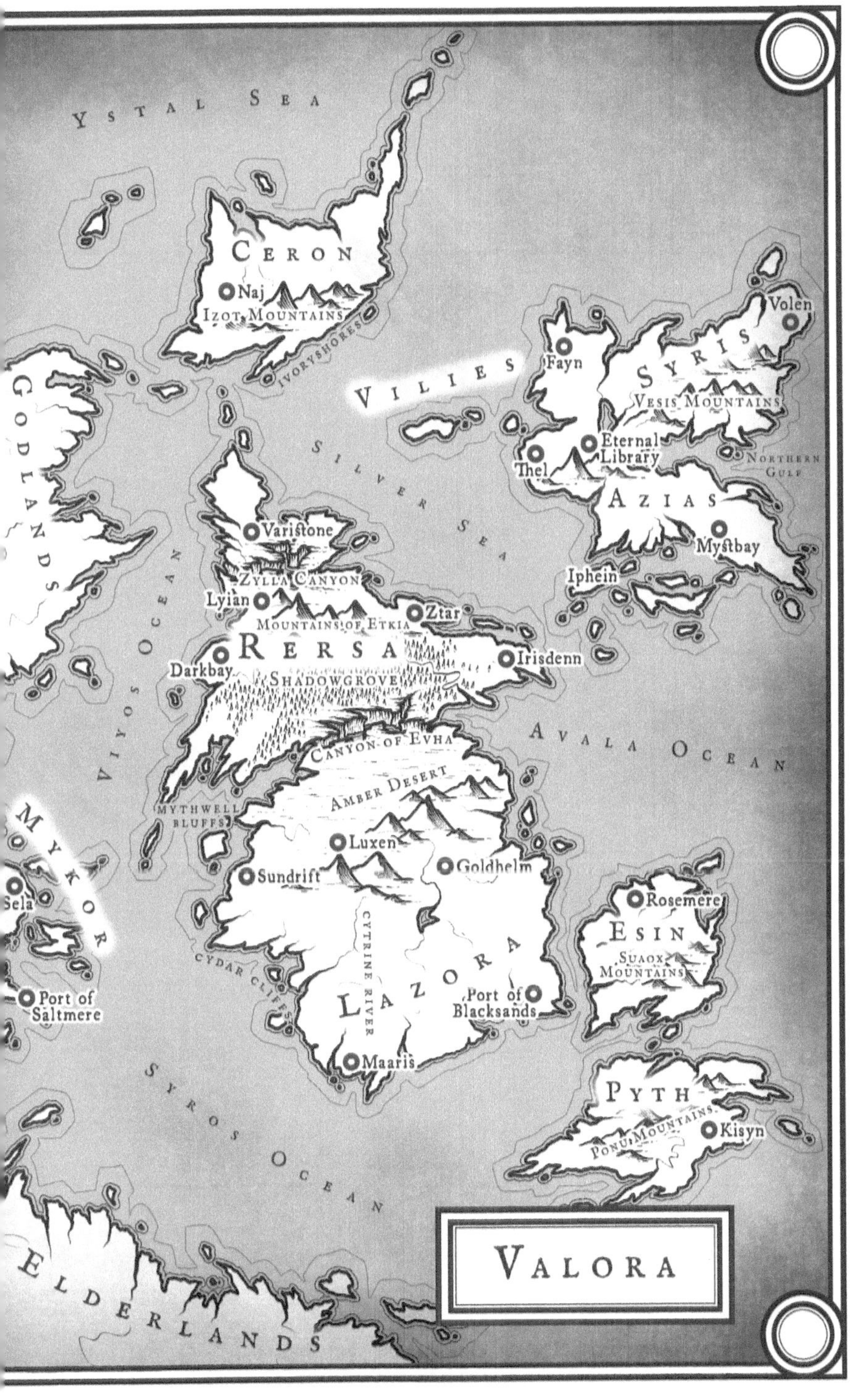

YSTAL SEA
CERON
Naj
IZOT MOUNTAINS
IVORYSHORES
VILIES
Fayn
SYRIS
Volen
VESIS MOUNTAINS
NORTHERN GULF
Thel
Eternal Library
SILVER SEA
AZIAS
Mystbay
Iphein
GODLANDS
Varistone
ZYLLA CANYON
Lyian
Ztar
MOUNTAINS OF ETKIA
RERSA
Darkbay
Irisdenn
SHADOWGROVE
VIYOS OCEAN
AVALA OCEAN
CANYON OF EVHA
Amber Desert
MYTHWELL BLUFFS
Luxen
MYKOR
Sundrift
Goldhelm
Sela
Rosemere
ESIN
SUAOX MOUNTAINS
CYDAR CLIFFS
CYTRINE RIVER
LAZORA
Port of Saltmere
Port of Blacksands
Maaris
SYROS OCEAN
PYTH
PONU MOUNTAINS
Kisyn
ELDERLANDS
VALORA

Appendix

The Gods

The Elementals
Emaris, *Samara,* God of Earth
Enya, *Fyrebird,* God of Fire
Zaphine, *Sea Serpent,* God of Water
Ihara, *Acul,* God of Air

The Naturalist
Senka, *Nitehound,* God of Shadows
Nalara, *Goldentail,* God of Light
Okien, *Snake,* God of Healing
Cayval, *Dove,* God of Spirit

Valora

Eisera

MAY THE VINES PROTECT YOU, MAY THE WILLOWS GUIDE YOU.

Kingdom of the Earth Elementals. Home to the Aether point, Nalādin.

Aydin Slater, King
Gena Slater, Queen
Amala Slater, Heir
Killian Zroň, Heir

Vydara

MAY THE FLAMES LIGHT THE PATH FOR YOUR SOUL TO FOLLOW.

Kingdom of the Fire Elementals.

Zazu Stvan, Lord
Anika Stvan, Lady
Nyoko Stvan, Heir

Aeledin

A HOME FOR ONE, IS A HOME FOR ALL.

Human territory, ruled but the Chamber of Five.

Rheya Liot, High Commander.
Live Fallow, Commander of the People
Vinnia Howe, Commander of the Guard
Wayde Ver, Headmaster
Osie Zol, High Creator

Iyvia

LET THE WATER WASH AWAY THE PAST, LET THE SEA GUIDE YOUR PATH.

Isles of the Western Water Elementals.

~~Zvon Savali, Reyn~~
Syrena Savali, Reyna
Torin Erevi, Reyna's Spear

Mykor

THE SEA WILL SHAPE YOUR DESTINY, AS IT SHAPES THE SHORES.

Isles of the Central Water Elementals.

Farah Ven, Reyna

Ceron

Be as unyielding as the ice, but remember to let yourself thaw.

Kingdom of the Northern Water Elementals.

Yenna Rydal, Reyna

Rersa

Do not fear the darkness, become a part of the shadows.

Kingdom of the Shadow Naturalists. Home to the Aether point, the Canyon of Evha.

Desmond Zūne, High Shade
~~Nomara Zūne, High Lady~~
Elaia Zūne, Heir
~~Shaye Zūne, middle daughter~~
~~Rayn Zūne, youngest daughter~~
Zahra Savu, Betrothed to Elaia
Rohan Boyd, Shield

Lazora

The light will shine even after the darkest of nights.

Kingdom of the Light Naturalist. Home to the Aether point, the Amber Sands.

Mylla Kovaci, Empress
Tobiah Kovaci, The Blade
Samuel Kovaci, Prince
Madeira Kovaci, Princess
Rosanna Kovaci, Princess

Vilies

Where there is pain, there is also rebirth.

Kingdom of the Healers. Home to the Eternal Library and the primary school for the Magistrate of the Second Star.

Okara Shae, Master of Vilies
Ceclia Baron, Headmaster
Erik Tor, The People's Advisors

Syris

The Mind is only as vulnerable as you let it be.

Kingdom of the Spirit Naturalists.

Mireya Vahl, Queen
Mikel Vahl, King
Isla Vahl, Princess
Nova Aarin

Azias

WHEN THE AIR THINS, THAT IS WHEN YOU MUST FIND THE STRENGTH TO BREATHE.

Kingdom of the Air Elementals.

Haya Farr, Queen
Niklas Farr, King
Vittoria Farr, Heir

Esin

YOU ARE OF YOUR OWN MAKING, NO ONE ELSE'S.

A human territory. Home to a melting pot of Athera.

Pyth

A republic of the Fire Elementals.

Godlands

A place of honor that cannot be visited without approval or invitation. A place of respect and

rest for the Gods of Valora, their Scions, and their favored.

Elderlands

Home to the Eight Elders of Valora. Ancient entities meant to manage and mind the Aether.

~~Witchlands~~

Stricken from existence. Essentially destroyed and uninhabitable after the massacre.

PART ONE

REBIRTH

Nova was suffocating.

Soil caked her nails, staining them black. Her hands clawed through the dirt, searching for the relief of oxygen. With every move, every grasp toward freedom, the dark soil kept coming. Panic was inevitable—nothing was as important as breathing again. In the cage of her ribs, lungs compacted and expanded, choking on their pleas for oxygen that went ignored.

In the hazy recesses of her brain, the voices were hushed. *"We have done all we can do. Sacrificed what we were able, given what we could."*

Nova pushed upward with determination.

"This is as far as we go."

It was endless, the pain coursing through her veins, the exhaustion tugging at her muscles. Yet, she fought.

"We have done our service to the Gods, to the Arcana."

Something told her she was close to escaping the suffocation. Maybe it was hope, a notion she wasn't quite familiar with. Maybe it was pure determination. Whatever the cause, Nova pushed on.

Air—fresh air—wound around her fingers.

"It is her time."

Her chest heaved as she crashed through the earth trying to hold her hostage, gulping down the air as it enveloped her face. Halfway in the dirt and halfway out, she fell back under the dark sky. It was silent in her head and all around her. Cool air danced over her skin that was mottled with dirt. No suns or stars in the sky above, only a sliver of the moon.

Nova heaved, expelling the dirt still choking her. No amount of air felt sufficient. Water leaked from her eyes, trailing down her cheeks. There was nothing near her—no homes, no lights from a nearby city, no grand stone buildings or even fallen fortresses. It was dark, aside from the light of the moon.

With shaky hands, she pulled herself from the soil, watching it fill in the space where she had previously been. Images flashed in her mind, but she couldn't make anything of them. They were fractured and blurred—snapshots of places she did not recognize, people without familiar faces. A life that did not feel like her own.

Nova pressed her palms to her temple. But the pain was a thorn, burrowing deeper every moment. Crawling to her knees, she looked around. In her immediate proximity, there was nothing of note. Small wilting flowers pushed through the soil, but she noticed a pattern. They grew only in certain spots, leaving sections of the ground blank. In the distance, it continued, but she noticed further away, the flowers were blooming—manicured —compared to the wildflowers barely surviving. There were tiny stone carvings dotted around the soil, the spots where the flowers did not touch.

Another image winked in her mind—clear this time—of a fortress, a castle that felt vaguely familiar, shrouded in between ice-tipped peaks.

Nova swallowed, spitting dirt to the side. Fear bloomed in her gut, unfurling petal by petal as she moved over the ground.

Upon closer inspection, her throat closed.

The inscription read, *'May the Dove guide your spirit.'* It churned her stomach, the dirt on her skin suddenly feeling poisonous. Nova read another and another, willing it to be some illusion her oxygen-deprived mind had made up. But it wasn't.

It was a graveyard.

Back at the pit she dug herself out of, her fingers curled into the edge, staring at the soil that took her place, hoping she might find some answers. She was buried. Someone had buried her. Packed soil on top of her and left her there.

Yet, here she was.

All she got was that one clear image. Mountains shrouded in snow and ice. A fortress tucked between them. Repeated over and over like a beacon. She had no idea what memory that place held, yet it remained the only thing she had.

Nova swallowed and stood. On shaky legs and with an unsound mind, she started walking.

In the distance, like mist in the clouds, like dew evaporating on an early morning, voices echoed:

It is time.

It is her time.

Chapter 1

The Executioner

Seven Years Later

NOVA EXISTED ONLY TO STEAL THE LIFE FROM OTHERS.

She woke. She breathed. She killed. She slept. She did not *live*.

For her, life and death often felt the same. Her life offered her no joy, no peace, no love. Her life *was* death. At least in death, there was no life to have, no life to be wasted. Death, from her understanding, was oblivion.

There was no freedom in the life that Nova lived.

There was freedom in becoming nothing.

The stained glass was cool against her skin. Below, the waves crashed against the icy cliffs, black under the midnight sky. Frost crackled over the window, and cold air seeped in through the opening, drifting through the room. Even up high, she felt the ocean mist dancing over her skin.

Flexing her hand, her blood warmed underneath her skin, dispelling the goosebumps that had taken purchase, so there wasn't much of a chill at all. Outside, the sky was dark. Black. Not a single star to be seen. She sighed, closing her eyes.

She loved the stars, but they never showed up when she needed them.

There was no blood on her hands yet tonight. When she

looked at them, her skin was clean. But it wouldn't last. It never did.

And she knew it was pointless to hope for the stars to show up for her—but she did.

Instead, she found shapeless streaks of clouds in the midnight sky.

Useless and disappointing.

The steady beat of blood from the hall alerted her, forcing her to focus. Their minds were guarded as they'd taught her to do. As everyone was taught to do in the Kingdom of Syris. The knock on the door rang out.

The door opened, and Jonah moved stoically. There was not a doubt in her mind that shame was flickering in his eyes. Even in the dim light, the scar on the side of his face was plain to see. Nova stood, the black dress swishing around her legs with the movement.

Jonah stepped forward. His presence was familiar, and his blood flowed calmly. "Princess—"

Nova shot him a look. They had been doing this for years, and yet he still would not break the habit. She was no princess. She was no daughter of theirs.

"*Princess*, don't do this."

She twitched her nose. "You haven't even told me what I'm doing yet, Jonah."

Over the years she'd spent here, she lost count of how many violent quests she had fulfilled. How many executions she had carried out. From the time she arrived from the dirt after her sixteenth year until now, just past her twenty-fourth, this had been her life.

All at the hands of Queen Mireya and King Mikel Vahl. They had taken her in when she showed up on the steps eight years ago, dirt and mud streaked over her face. Ever since, she'd been here. Under their watch, their thumb. Their orders.

They had their ways of keeping her in line, namely through

the use of people like Jonah. People that she would become responsible for.

Before Jonah, there had been another. They were killed when Nova tried to escape after two years. It had been Jonah ever since. Her cared in his own way, but at times like this, he begged her to stand against the Vahls's orders—unwittingly adding another burden to her shoulders. She could not be the person he wanted her to be. Not now. Maybe not ever. Not when the price was so high.

Stupid, it was. Caring about the person who was responsible for your well-being and who was consequently the person that suffered because of it. She stared at him for a moment longer before turning back toward the window.

"What do they want?" Her words were gentle enough to be carried away by the breeze.

"Two in the prison. They're ready for you."

Nova nodded but couldn't bring herself to look away. In the darkness, against the snow-capped mountains, she saw the shadow of a bird caught in the moonlight and wondered what it must be like. To be free.

The increase of his heart told her of his approach. Jonah stood before her, brushing her arm as he went before quickly pulling it back. Nova's heartbeat increased. His touch, though friendly, remained an uncomfortable pulse on her skin.

"We can find another way."

"You know we cannot." She caught her reflection in the glass, her light-gray eyes icy and stern. *There was no other way. Not without consequences.* So, what was the point? He held strong for a moment, but his shoulders fell.

"They have forgiven you."

But I have not. She swallowed, guilt rushing through her veins as images of Jonah's family flashed in her mind. Of how they'd been tied up and bound, waiting to greet Jonah after she'd disobeyed a direct order. His husband and himself had been bruised, beaten. A simple act of defiance, and destruction was wrought. Because of her.

"I'm not going to argue any further," she said. Time was ticking. The Vahls were only so patient. "We must go, Jonah."

He swallowed the sadness that she knew was well and truly pity and nodded. Pity was useless; she just wasn't as powerful as she needed to be. *One day.* Nova pressed her fingers against the connector of the gold hand chain she wore and watched as it transformed. The titanium chain reshaped at the tips of her fingers, shifting and growing into claws. Shimmering gems from its previous form remained in the weapon, sparkling in the light.

Underneath, her skin was still clean.

For now.

TWO GUARDS TRAILED behind them as they walked through the gray stone hallways. Underground, goldstone lined the halls, flickering to life and casting shadows as they passed. Nova fortified her mind as they approached. She ran her fingers over the links of her bracelet, a delicate chain wrapped around each of her fingers, and traced the central gem and each link, pressing the tip of her finger against the claws. Nova drew a drop of blood and pressed it on the locking mechanism. The lock clicked as it absorbed the blood, and the door slid open, revealing her parents.

Who weren't her parents at all.

Nova's fingers curled, the blood of the Vahls calling to her as it always did. A low hum that only she could hear. It would've been so easy to manipulate if she chose. But choices had consequences. Behind her, she was aware of Jonah, the quickening of his pulse. Exhaling, she settled herself, ignoring the urge to make a choice that would only result in more consequences.

She stepped in, the door slamming behind her and Jonah, and flexed her hands. Beyond her parents, another wall separated them from the two prisoners visible through the clear window. They both had coverings over their faces as they sat, tied tightly to the chairs.

"Nova," Mireya said coolly, though the gesture of her hand to *come* was colder. The queen's fair skin was pristine. Her eyes were narrow and full of ice, her cheekbones sharp. Queen Mireya was a razor-edged manipulator; despite her cold exterior, she could easily turn her icy features warm when it suited her.

Nova twisted her nose, hesitating, a small show of disobedience before she approached.

"Mother. Father." The words were venom, a poison instead of an anecdote.

They insisted on Nova calling them as such. A petty, lazy way of keeping her in line. When she first arrived, they claimed it would fell confusion from the citizens—they could spin a simple lie for her absence. She quickly learned that wasn't the case. It was all for show, as it often was.

King Mikel's pale brown skin flickered under the dim light, appearing as though the cold had leached all the warmth away. His regality had a haughtiness to it, as if pride had painstakingly formed his features piece by piece. Those cool gray eyes, as cold as the mountains in the deep winter, watched her carefully as Mireya approached as prey might do.

Mikel strode forward, out of the shadows of the room. Before he could speak, she did. "Who are they?"

His eyes sharpened. "Who they are is not important. What is important is that they do not leave here alive."

Nothing new then—another day, another death.

Nova ground her teeth but turned her eyes to the prisoners. From their seated positions, few details could be uncovered. One was shorter than the other, likely younger. They were tied with aetherchains—chains made by Creators that had been imbued with blackclover and hemlock made essentially to leech the abilities of Athera, weakening them. And their hands, despite being tied, kept reaching for each other.

Mireya was poking at the edges of her brain, her power shielding itself as a gentle tug instead of a leech. To anyone else, it might've gone unnoticed. But Nova was quite attuned to their various methods. Still, it sent a twinge of annoyance down her spine. As if she needed to be reminded that she was always being watched. Mireya was always prodding, just to ensure she could.

"What did they do?"

Mireya was bored, barely sparing a glance. "They've been in the dungeons for some time now. Their time has come."

Nova raised a brow. They never kept prisoners that long—at least that she was aware of. "Why?"

"Why doesn't matter. What matters is their life is over. You will take it from them."

She narrowed her eyes. They were hiding something. She was sure of it. Though it was useless, she pressed the barriers of their own minds. As expected, she found them impenetrable.

Anger boiled under the surface, and her blood ran hot. She felt every vein, every heartbeat searching for an outlet. Exhaling, her muscles relaxed, her hands unclenching. Mikel's eyes latched on to her hands, her veins darker than they had been. Her veins pulsating under the black of her gown.

"Be careful with that, dear. You understand the consequences," he said, eyes flicking behind her to Jonah.

Their blood thrummed, called out to her, and though she was powerful, here, she was powerless. Nova did not care for many people—there weren't many here worth caring for—but Jonah was one of them.

"Enough," Mireya snapped, motioning her forward. "Find out what they know, and make them bleed"—she handed her a vial—"and collect a bit a blood from each of them."

So many times, Nova wanted to ask about the vials. Sometimes they wanted their blood, and sometimes they did not.

And while she didn't expect they'd ever give her an answer, she wasn't sure she wanted to take the chance of knowing.

With that, the clear door opened for her to step through. Immediately, the prisoners' heartbeats quickened. Nova could feel the panic in their blood, the way it moved through their veins under pressure. There was a distinct quality to their blood, a weight that humans didn't have. They were Athera. She approached the left most prisoner first, the one she believed was older, and tugged the covering off her head.

Hooded golden-brown eyes met hers. They were angry, sure, but on another day, they might've been warm. She was thin, gaunt almost. In another life, her skin might have been warmer, but it was dull.

"What did you come here for?"

The woman shook her head, black hair that was damp—either from blood or water—stuck to her face in strands. Her eyes kept drifting to the other prisoner. She tucked that information away.

"If you make this easy, it'll be quick." Nova raised a brow, arms crossed. This was the worst part—interrogating people when the Vahls could do it themselves. But everything she did or did not do had a consequence.

The woman still refused. With a twist of her left hand, she felt for the woman's blood and watched as her throat muscles started to constrict. The woman's eyes widened as she fought to move but found she could not. Nova had momentarily stopped the flow of her blood. And she reached for the other, when finally, against a constricted throat, the woman spoke.

"Stop," she croaked.

Nova let her blood flow freely again. Bending down, she tapped a sharp talon against her temple. "Smart choice. Now talk."

"We've been here for so long...too long. We originally came for refuge." The woman's heartbeat increased. Annoyance danced down her spine. *What was the point of lying when you were already dead?*

"Lying is useless here." Nova cut off blood flow to their extremities with a twitch of her finger. She knew it had settled when her fingers started twitching, the uncomfortable numbness taking over.

She took a good look at the prisoner. There were rings on her fingers. Simple upon first glance but were intricate in further detail. Silver and gold metals twined together, decorated with onyx and moonstone. Her posture was straight, despite the weakness Nova felt in her blood. But there was something proud, even now, that was not the same hunger that someone seeking refuge had. There was a sharpness in the woman's eyes, a strength that could not be taught, in her blood.

Nova asked again.

And again: "We came for refuge."

There was a sudden scratching sensation in her head. The Vahls. Nova pulled back her defenses with a sigh. She wasn't a fool. She knew she couldn't show them how strong she'd become, how good she was at keeping them out. At some point, like now, there had to be a false sense of weakness, a spot they could creep in and keep her in line. It kept her safe in some ways and left her in danger in others. Even now, she barely let them in.

"Enough. If she won't talk, get the information yourself. And kill them."

She fought the urge to remind them they could do that themselves. But control was their version of power.

She cut them off quickly, pushing them out. It wasn't something every Spirit Naturalist possessed, the ability to speak clearly in others' minds. It was difficult and took years of training, but the Vahls were as powerful as they were awful. Unfortunately.

Nova stepped closer, slowing the woman's blood down, and with a twitch of her hand, expanded her blood vessels slowly, like tiny pressure bombs exploding under her skin. Not enough to be truly painful. Yet.

"You're going to kill me no matter what I say. I have nothing else to tell. That's the truth—"

"It is not." Nova bent, eye-to-eye with her. "But you haven't yet felt pain, have you?" She hated when they fought. It forced her to become exactly who the Vahls wanted her to be. Violent. Monstrous.

Realization bloomed in the woman's eyes. Everything until now had been uncomfortable, eerie, abnormal—but not painful. With the taloned fingernail, Nova broke her skin, and, in an instant, her blood boiled. A wail left the prisoners lips by no conscious choice.

Hot blood spilled out of every crevice from the woman, streaming over Nova's skin and dripping onto the floor. A numbness prickled over Nova's skin as she blocked out the sensation, the emotions. It didn't matter what she felt—she'd rather feel nothing at all.

She cupped the woman's face. Contact wasn't necessary, but it made for easier access, a stronger connection. Her power seeped out like an early morning mist and infiltrated the woman's mind. It was weak—from the aetherchains or the blood manipulation, it didn't matter. The thick shadowed walls around her mind fell easily, leaving nothing but wisps in their wake.

It didn't matter whether her mind was fortified or not.

It would never have been enough.

Nova slipped past like a ghost in a haunted hall. It was like skipping down a deserted hallway with doors decorating each wall. Everyone's mind looked different. This one was simple.

"Please, please! I'll talk."

Nova ignored her and pushed on. The first image was of the second prisoner next to her. A young woman, no more than nineteen years, and Nova felt her heart lurch. The following images flashed quickly: a brief image of a canyon of darkness, the castle tucked into the icy mountains. A brief image of a figure covered in blood with tear streaks of red—Nova assumed that was meant for her. There were stories, rumors. *The*

Cardinal, some called her. She'd just never come face-to-face with them.

What did you come for? Her voice was a loud boom in the woman's mind, and Nova felt her tremble under her hands.

"I was escaping, trying to keep us safe. I came here for the truth," the woman gasped. "This kingdom, this place—something—" She coughed, blood spilling from her tear ducts. "Something is wrong. The land is not right, the people..."

She realized then this was a pointless show of control.

The Vahls knew this woman didn't hold any vital information. They just wanted Nova to bloody her hands again.

With her hands still pressed to the woman's skin, she saw glimpses of family. Memories of kids running, playing. A mother. A wife. Withdrawing her hands, she created space. It wasn't often she stumbled across information like that—let it infiltrate her—but when it did, she remembered everything.

"Nova. Enough!"

The intrusion was swift and violent. It left a pounding behind. She met the woman's eyes, and her despair was palpable. Not for herself. For the girl next to her. The blood kept streaming.

She infiltrated her mind again. *"What is her name?"* The weight of what she was doing began to settle. The death she was about to inflict. At the very least, she could carry the person's name with her.

The woman's voice was filled with fury. "Does it matter? You'll kill her anyway." The scent of blood was palpable in the room, and Nova felt every drop of it.

"It will be painless."

"You," the woman spat, blood splattering on the ground, "are a coward. She's only a girl—she's *my* girl—please. *Please,* do not take her. Do not hurt her."

Nova didn't confirm or deny. It was over. There was no way out of this; there never was. She had no choice. She was watched and stalked at every turn. Every action had a reaction. Mostly, to

Jonah and his family, sometimes to servants in the halls, sometimes to herself. There was always an ever-present threat of suffering if she disobeyed.

Guilt sat heavy in her throat, threatening to choke her.

But she *could* make the end painless, which would likely only result in punishment to her. It was a risk. It wasn't often she did so, but when she did, it never ended pleasantly for her.

Not daring a look backward, she approached the younger one first. She did not uncover her face as she placed her hands on her cheeks. The girl let out a quiet gasp. But that was all. Infiltrating her mind, she was met with no barrier. She found memories, happy memories, ones she tried not to see, and called them forward. Quickly, she blocked out her nerve endings, numbing her.

Nova slit her throat in one fell swoop. And she waited until her heart stopped before removing her hands, ensuring that she felt no pain at all. Blood dripped onto the floor in a steady, grating noise. Nova collected enough to fill a vial. Approaching the woman again, Nova saw tears mixing with the blood, coating her teeth in a pink film.

Her eyes had the fury of a burning star. "Coward."

For her, she did the same. Nova held eye contact with her golden eyes as she pulled the memories forward, and her hands were covered in blood. She saw the moment they resonated and the pain fell to the wayside. The anger never faded.

With a sharp talon, Nova slit the woman's throat.

Moments later, there was only one beating heart left in the room.

Chapter 2

WAVES OF MIDNIGHT

Nova left bloody footprints behind upon her exit.

She could still hear the steady drip of the dead prisoners' blood on the stone floor. Could feel the phantom beat of their hearts that were now silent. Mikel stopped her in the doorway, hand out to collect the vials. Behind him stood Jonah.

They will not hurt him, she repeated. Over and over. Willing it to be true.

Seconds felt like hours as they stood there, facing off. Mireya's eyes narrowed. "Jonah, you may go."

Jonah's skin blanched, his eyes distraught. Exhaling, Nova imperceptibly dipped her chin. There was nothing he could do. For a moment, he didn't move, the air thick with tension. Finally, he retreated. She let herself breathe again.

The Vahls eyes were harsh and unforgiving.

"Come."

She followed them down the hallway to another floor, deep under the mountains, where despite the goldstone and stone walls, the cold dark seeped in. White stone walls turned to gray and then to black as she followed them down the curving steps.

There were other rooms in the hall, but she was led to the only one she'd ever been in. The one that belonged to her.

Two sets of doors slid open. Aetherchains were draped along the walls, and even off her skin, she felt herself growing weaker. Nausea pooled in her stomach at the sight of the single chair in the dark room.

"Sit." Mikel's stare was blisteringly cold.

One of the guards approached, waiting for her to do as told. She lowered herself into the chair. With a deep breath, she slowed her heartbeat and tried to convince herself she was safe.

She tried to send herself into the place where she felt nothing. A place where she was nothing more than a body of blood and bone.

All this because they *knew* she had not caused the prisoners pain. All because she made a tiny show of disobedience. It was her way of remaining whole. Yet every time she did it, the Vahls tried to take more pieces of her.

The chains were heavy despite their delicate appearance. Around her throat, the chain tightened with every breath, thick and choking. She never took her eyes off her parents as the chains were draped over her wrists and wound around her ankles. She was tired, chest heaving with exertion, though she'd done nothing. Mireya's lip twitched—barely, but enough for Nova to know—

The pain had just begun.

Upon entering her room, Nova slumped. Her shoulders fell and her hands shook as she locked the door. Outside the sky was still dark and void of stars, but dawn couldn't have been far off.

Hours. She'd spent hours down there with them. And they made the hours feel like days.

Everything hurt. Her body. Her mind.

Like countless times before, she headed toward her bathing chambers, turning the faucet until warm water poured from the shower head. She collapsed next to the shower walls, undoing her dress. Her titanium talons were gone, and dried blood caked her hands. The body she could handle. Nova could scrub it clean until there wasn't a speck left. She could ignore the bruises and the beaten muscles and the scars they'd left behind.

The mind was not as simple. She couldn't take out her brain and scrub it clean of the Vahls's punishment. Or undo the death she'd inflicted. Or the memories she had that weren't hers.

Most days, she felt like a shell. Made of skin and bone and memories of other people. A place where a soul should be but was empty. Life and death had lost meaning to her over the years because more often than not, she had a hard time ascertaining the difference. But days like this, she was reminded of how painful it was being alive. How painful they could make it.

Stepping under the spray, she watched the hot water run from pink to clear.

Her mind twisted, replaying images of blood and scars and bodies. *It's not real. Not all of it was real.* The Vahls liked to create scenarios for her to live through. Some where she felt the fingertips of death herself. Others where she inflicted it. Sometimes, they made it hard to remember what she had done and what she hadn't.

Nausea rose, and she expelled whatever was in her stomach. Exhaling, she grabbed the soap, cleaning the blood from under her fingernails first before wiping it over the rest of her body. Not once but three times until she felt sufficiently clean.

The shower wall was cool against her forehead as the water turned her curls heavy and damp. Her eyes fluttered closed, and she was bombarded. This was the worst of it—the moments right after when it was all fresh. When it was hard to remember what was real or not. What was her own life and what were glimpses of someone else's. When Nova took away the pain, she ended up *ingesting* the memories of those she killed. Happy memories— laughter, euphoria, love. She'd gotten good at shoving them into a box within her head. And the Vahls became adept at dragging them out.

It was like having teeth pulled. They would pull them forward, make her watch someone live a life they no longer had. They would do it until she was drowning in guilt.

Other times, the Vahls would force her to live in a time loop. They'd twist her mind and convince her she'd been tied to that chair for days, or weeks, or months—when it was only hours. They'd blur the torture from her mind and then do it again. And again. Until she bled. Nova hated bleeding in front of them.

Nova's skin stung, and the remnants of pain sent a tremor down her spine. It squeezed her wrists around the tiny scars that had never faded from the restraints. It stole her breath and sent stabs of pain all over her skin. She counted to ten until she could draw in a full breath, the water running cold. Pain shot up her leg when she stepped out, reverberating in her nerve endings as it ran its course.

She toweled off before slathering her body in a thick salve. It smoothed over the bruises, calmed the wounds, and gave her a semblance of control. After dressing, she wrapped herself in a blanket as she moved toward the balcony and stepped into the retreating darkness. She sat, leaned up against the railing, and looked out over the sea.

The Froststone Castle was tucked high into the northernmost mountains of Syris. Her room was in one of the higher, more isolated towers. From here, she could see the mountain peaks shrouded by the mist, the snow traversing over the sharp points. Salt spray from the ocean waves found her skin even up high, cooling the parts of her that were burning up in patches, pain flaring sporadically.

Nova didn't possess control over the water. It wasn't

necessarily something she yearned for, but sometimes, she felt it should've been a part of her. Maybe it was the countless times she'd done just this—sat here and wished for a way out. Her eyes fluttered closed as she listened to the sound of the waves, and peace found her like it always did when faced with the water.

It was funny how the things people weren't could bring them peace. How something that wasn't hers could feel like hers. She stared at the swirling waves of midnight and wished she could float on them, let them lead her wherever they chose.

Maybe then she could be free.

Chapter 3

Monsters of Reality

Nova exhaled as he paced in circles behind the privacy screen. She was being poked and prodded and made up for the meal later. She supposed it was because she usually didn't eat with the Vahls. Maybe they wanted her to look presentable. *Pointless.* She shook her head.

While his pacing was somewhat annoying, she'd rather have it than not. It'd been three days since she last saw Jonah. Her pain and bruises had faded, but the marks around her wrists were still red. And around her throat, though that one blended in with the scar she carried. One of her attendants inspected the marks before dropping her arm. When she was younger, she'd been determined to learn their names, to learn about their lives, until she realized she was not a person to them—they were here on orders from the Vahls.

That had been six years ago. The less she cared, the fewer ways they could hurt her.

"I cannot stop worrying. The last time they requested you at the evening meal was months ago. Before they sent you into Pyth."

Ah, Pyth. She hated thinking of that assignment. It'd been humid and sticky. She hadn't expected a young boy to be there, sleeping next to the man she was supposed to kill. Even now, she recalled the fear in the boy's eyes when she instructed him to turn and run, so he did not have to watch as she killed his father. The boy was brought back here, and she never saw him again. She tried not to think about it—the consequences of her actions. They were getting harder to ignore the longer she did her parents' bidding.

She waved her hand. "I'm sure it's regarding the Assembly of the Athera." As she said it, her veins flashed red—a blood flare.

It happened when her emotions were too unruly, too close to the surface with no outlet. Disgusted looks came over the attendants' faces, and she met their eyes with an unflinching stare. It was not her fault they forgot what she was.

"Precisely, but why would they want to see you for that? They never—"

"Jonah," she said. She could practically taste his worry. Somedays it was endearing. Other days, it was annoying. At the end of the day, she would still be the one to suffer the most pain—not Jonah. This life, the life she lived under their hands, was hers alone. "Why are you so worried? It is nothing new. This is *nothing* new."

His usually warm brown eyes swam with something she could not read. "I-I have a bad feeling."

Nova raised a brow, feeling for his pulse. But it was steady. She sighed. "A feeling is nothing to worry about."

A breeze came through the balcony doors, dancing over her barely veiled skin as she let herself be moved around the room. She couldn't stand the feeling of their hands on her skin, like sharp leeches, so she blocked it out as best she could and closed her eyes.

They are just hands, and they are not hurting you. In and out, she breathed. Over and over again. Every second that passed wore her patience thin. Rage flared when an unkind hand squeezed the spot above her knee.

"Are you finished?" A gentle tone of violence accompanied her words.

The attendant met her eyes, hiding the fear that flared. "Almost."

As soon as the gown was pulled over her head, a barrier between their hands and her skin, she exhaled. The silver long sleeves muted her veins, but a sheer overlay accentuated the brown of her skin. Clear stones shone like ice on the stitching, accentuating the low dip of the dress down her chest.

"You may go," she said the moment the last button was snapped.

"But…"

"I'll finish the rest." There was no room for argument, and they dipped their heads. Maybe they'd tell her parents, maybe they wouldn't. "Jonah." As the attendants exited, he stepped fully into the room.

She waited until she could no longer sense their heartbeats. "You're all right?"

He took a seat in the armchair by the bookcase. "Yes, so is my family."

That singular incident with his family hung over her head. Every time she disobeyed, every time she misstepped, she worried whether his husband and kids would suffer, too. So far, they hadn't. But he knew when she asked about him, she was asking about them, too.

"Maybe the Assembly is changing. Maybe it's an announcement of some sort."

He crossed his leg, draped in his own formal wear. "Maybe."

Nova recalled the words of the women she killed. About this place, this kingdom. "They're keeping something from me." She stepped onto the balcony, the suns doing little to combat the chill.

Mikel and Mireya were powerful. Annoyingly so. She'd tried to infiltrate their minds as they did hers, but they were well fortified. Guarded beyond measure. She knew they had secrets hidden in their minds. She just wasn't strong enough to find them.

"Something is wrong, Jonah. Something is always wrong, but..." Her eyes tracked the foggy clouds above.

Jonah joined her on the balcony, enough space between them so they didn't touch. He held out his palm, something wrapped tightly in the center. "From Loren." His husband. "And the kids."

Nova started to protest, but Jonah clicked his tongue.

"Take it Nova," he said, grabbing her hand and placing it there himself. "It is the least I can do."

She swore guilt flashed in his eyes. But what would he have to feel guilty over? Unwrapping it, she found the almond pastry she loved so much. Her heart swelled. "Thank you."

She broke off a piece of the triangle-shaped pastry—a very small piece—and handed it to him. His eyes crinkled, momentarily carefree. "That's all?"

Taking a bite, she nodded. "Yes. You've more back home. Be thankful I'm sharing at all." A small smile played on her lips, one that only appeared every so often, usually with Jonah.

He was the closest thing she had to a friend. Even then, there was pressure that his safety, his family, and his life depended on her ability to follow orders.

Even standing next to him, Nova was utterly alone.

FROSTSTONE WAS BEAUTIFUL. On the outside, the castle walls were sheer faces of gray stone, made to blend into the mountains. Streaks of obsidian and gold were etched into the walls. When the sunrays or the reflection of the snow struck, the castle became a beacon. Curved walkways connected the various towers decorated with stained glass windows. White vines wound themselves around the stone, dotted with the winter daylilies, some of the only flowers to grow here.

Nova glanced out the sheer windows of the bridge to the central hall. Despite the disdain she had for this place, the sheer vastness of it was alluring. Below, the bridge was suspended between two small peaks, nothing below but the sharp edges of the mountains. In the summer, the windows would open, allowing air to pass through. Jonah walked beside her, two guards a few paces behind. They entered, and the glass doors shut behind them. The central hall was stunning, with detailed molding decorating the tall vaulted ceilings and art along the walls.

Reaching out as far as she could, she felt the heartbeats of the Vahls. All three of them.

"Isla is with them." Her sister. In the same way her King and Queen were her parents.

"Why would that be?"

"Likely nothing of importance. She's a reminder for me," she said, and he dipped his chin.

Isla, like Jonah, was a tool to keep her in line. Isla was five years younger than her, but she'd been born *weak*. There was nothing wrong with her medically. At least, there had been nothing for the healers to heal.

Her parents, despite the love they had for Isla, often held her safety over Nova's head. *Because of course, they did.* "This way, whatever they ask of me, you and your family are not the only ones at risk. So is she."

"She doesn't concern herself with your well-being. Why do you with hers?"

Nova kept her eyes forward, if only because she didn't have an answer. For the first few years, Isla had been kind, welcoming even. A little girl who wanted a big sister. Everything had changed when Nova woke up in the basement room, tied in chains. Isla had been the one to take her there. The girl had taken claws to the inside of Nova's head until she was weak and did what her parents wanted.

Jonah eyed her. "I'm sorry for prying."

"No apologies, Jonah." She swallowed down the nausea and kept her voice clipped. It didn't really matter what was true and what was not. Not anymore. It was not as though it would make her different, better.

She would do what they said. She always did.

On and on they walked. Past the art that hung on the otherwise bare walls, over the polished stone floors, through the curved hallways, until they came upon the dining hall. Nova slowed her heart rate. The pressure on her chest diminished as she did and with a deep breath, she stepped forward.

The stone doors were already open, gray light pouring in from the floor-to-ceiling windows. A few attendants lined the wall, and the smell of food permeated the large ornate room. Mikel and Mireya sat side by side at the head of the table. Isla was to their right, her back to the windows.

Nova ignored the eerie feeling of their eyes on her as she sat, Jonah beside her. As collateral.

"Nice of you to join us," Mireya said, taking a long pull of the purple wine, a delicacy from Esin. The wispy sleeves of the midnight-blue blouse fluttered as she leaned forward, her sharp nails clinking against the wine glass.

Isla's lips curled across from Nova, a haughty look on her face. Every time she saw Isla, she looked more and more like her parents. A perfect mix of the two—the cool tone of her father's pale brown skin and the sharpness of her mother's.

What a shame. To look like the monsters of reality.

"What's the occasion?"

Mikel met her eyes with a bored stare. "The Assembly of the Athera is fast approaching. We leave in six days' time."

Nova raised a brow. She already knew this. Why repeat it? "Yes." Under the table, her fingers worried with her bracelet and the sleeves of the silver gown.

Just barely, she felt a tiny jump in Mireya's heart rate.

Excitement. And that rarely happened. Often times, she wondered if the queen was even human.

"We will be the first to arrive. We have an assignment for you."

Isla stared at her sister as if she knew the punchline. Beside her, Jonah's heart raced, as it often did since he was perpetually on edge, but Nova kept her eyes on the king and queen.

"You are going to kill the Elders."

CHAPTER 4

THE ELDERS

"Excuse me?"

Beside her, Jonah choked on his water. His heart rate careened. The room stilled, frozen in time.

"You will kill the Elders upon our arrival, before the others show."

Bleeding suns, she couldn't be serious. Her blood was so still, her heart so slow, she barely breathed.

Mireya's ice blue eyes were mocking. Nova stared at her, unable to look away from the woman who, somehow, surprised her time and time again. Mikel might have been the king, but that meant nothing in terms of Mireya's power. Nova knew that as much power as he held, Mireya held the same, if not more. She was the mastermind of the kingdom.

"The Elders," Nova stated, her skin still buzzing.

Mireya was out of her mind. In what world did this make any sense? For Gods' sake. She couldn't kill the Elders. They were essential to Valora. They managed the Aether under Valora's surface and delegated over the Aether points among other things, but most importantly, kept the kingdoms at peace, or at least in neutrality.

"They've been around for centuries, Mireya, and you want me to kill them?"

Implemented almost five hundred years ago, during the Massacre of the Witches, the Elders were sacred. Originally nine—but now eight—powerful Athera were chosen to serve as guides. They became managers of the Aether—the magic that ran through the world and under its surface—and also the people of Valora. They maintained their home on the most southern continent, simply known as the Elderlands. Out of the five Aetherpoints, the Elderlands were one of the strongest, one where the Aether was closest to the surface, where the rawness of it could be seen deep in the ice, glowing silver miles below. The Elders managed it, kept watch, and protected it. She couldn't *kill* the Elders.

Because...what would happen if she did? What would become of Valora? Of the Aether itself? Would kingdoms fight to control it? Would they wield it in ways the world had not seen?

"I cannot kill them, Mireya."

Across the table, Isla laughed in that unnerving giggle she so often let loose. "Oh, but you will, my dear girl." Mireya cocked her head.

Gods, she hated when Mireya called her that. It sounded like a curse from her mouth, and an unsettling sting crawled down her spine.

Under the table, Nova clenched and unclenched her palms, the veins hot and dark. This wasn't... They couldn't. "That will be unforgivable."

Mikel scoffed, a precise smile on his face. "Exactly."

This was different. It was not about protecting their secrets or killing those that threatened them. This was a statement.

"Can the Elders *be* killed?" They weren't Gods, but they were...closer than any other Athera were. They did not age. They did not grow sick. Could they die?

"They bleed, do they not?" was all Mireya said. And Nova controlled blood. That was all she needed.

"And what about me?"

Mireya raised a brow. "What about you?"

"What will happen to me?" She was in disbelief. What life could she have if others found out? Would anything she'd done ever be enough? If she did this, was there anything she would *not* do? "I cannot—I will not do this."

The king and queen shared a look. Mikel looked directly at her when he spoke. "You will not?"

She shook her head. Unblinking.

"Are you sure about that?"

On the table, Mireya slid a folder toward her. Within it, Nova saw her own handwriting—poorly sketched drawings and detailed plans of possible escape routes. Details of how she may get out unseen. Details of how to disappear.

Her eyes widened as she turned to Jonah, her heart twisting in her chest. He was the only one who'd seen them—by accident, too. She'd been too slow in hiding them, but she never expected he would give them up. Her hands shook as she stared at him. She knew she'd been responsible for his suffering, but...they were past that. So she thought. But this?

Giving it to Mireya...showing that Nova was not simply existing, showing that she dreamed of escaping. Mireya would use that against her. It ruined any chance of her leaving and meant, should she deny their order, they would ensure her suffering lasted far longer than it usually did.

"Nova, I—" His words were cut off as he and Isla started writhing in pain.

Her heart raced, but she was numb.

Their hands pressed against their temples, and tears dripped from Isla's eyes and onto the table. She could feel it, the pain they were in. It clawed at her with invisible talons, pounded with angry fists at her own mind. Before she could, they took grip of her mind, too. In the haze of their pain, her guard had slipped. And now, she couldn't move, could barely breathe. If blood had been spilled, she'd be able to break through, but without it and without control over her own, she was helpless to watch them.

"Stop," Nova said, barely a whisper. A strangled shout escaped Isla's lips. It echoed on the glass windows and reverberated against Nova's mind. Her breath came in quiet pants as she tried to unwrap Mireya's power from her mind. "Stop." Another whispered plea and stabbing pain. This time Jonah cried out, head falling forward, and all Nova could think of was his family. "Stop!"

And then, it stopped. The echoes of their pain dissolved. The tight grip on Nova's mind was gone. Isla wiped her tears with a quiet chortle, interrupted by sobs that still passed her lips.

Swallowing, she turned her eyes to Mireya, who watched Isla with only a hint of concern.

"My apologies, love. Are you all right?"

Isla waved her hand, dabbing her tears with a cloth Mikel had handed her. "Yes, Mom, I'm fine. I was prepared." Her hair, a dark chocolate cherry, stuck in wispy strands to her damp face. But her eyes were almost amiable as she looked at Mireya. Though, Nova supposed this twisted type of affection was all Isla had ever known.

But beside her, Jonah did not wake. Panic and anger crawled through her as one. How could he?

Still, she asked, "What did you do to him?"

Mireya waved her hand. "He'll wake shortly."

The queen stood, stalking over to her daughter. The flared edges of her pants whispered against the floor. Her hand was draped in jewels that looked like ice dripping from her pale skin. She watched quietly as she smoothed down Isla's frizzy hairs. From across the table, she stared at Nova, her lips quirking.

"I assume there will be no more protest from you?" She hummed when Nova said nothing. "Strange that you would decide this now. Decide that the Elders have some level of importance to you. And for what? So you could hold on to whatever morality you believe you have left? So you can maintain some fragment of autonomy?" A cold, haunting laugh echoed in the room. "You do not have any."

Nova clenched her jaw, blood rushing at the callous truth.

"You have killed countless people at our instruction. That does not change now. Understood?" Mireya's hand sat precariously on Isla's neck. The beat of her heart was steady. Isla was not afraid, knowing whatever her mother did, it was for control.

"No." No. Nova would *not* do this for nothing. They'd already seen what she wanted. Fine. They would give it to her. She would die, or she would be free.

Mireya's eyes flared. "Excuse me?"

"No. I won't do this. Not for nothing." Anger flowed hot and violent under her skin. Each of their pulses were in the palm of her hand, including Jonah's. Weak, but still there. "I want something."

The queen stared at her, eyes unflinching.

"I want out," she said softly. "I want out of here. I want my freedom." She stood, the sharp edges of her titanium nails digging into the table. All her previous attempts at escape had been foiled, ending in pain. For so long, she'd given up. Resigned to suffer her fate. But no more. "I will no longer do your bidding. I will no longer be your executioner. If I do this...I am done."

Mireya's lips curled into a cold smile. She could feel the sharp bite of it from here, like frost encompassing a window bit by bit. "You are sure that's what you want? All you want?"

The queens eyes danced over to her left.

Her heart dropped, nausea heavy in her stomach as she looked over at Jonah. He was draped over the table, light wisps of pain curled at the edges of his mind.

In hindsight, turning over her plans was nothing. But they were *hers*. They were private. And he'd let her think they were friends—or close to it. Still, how could she have been so quick to fight for her own freedom and not his?

But how could she not? If there was a chance, even a minute

possibility for Nova to disappear into the world without the weight of Mikel and Mireya...she had to take it.

And she would not be ashamed.

She met the amused gaze of Mireya. It was knowing and cruel. And she didn't care. "That is what I want."

After a moment and a shared look between the king and queen, Mireya raised her glass to her. "Deal. However, there is one stipulation. You will bring us vials that contain each of the Elders' blood. No vials, no freedom."

Her brows furrowed. *Their blood?* "Understood."

"Good. Mikel? The rest of the plan." Mireya waved her hand and returned to her seat. Beside her, Jonah woke with a scratchy cough, trying to suck in air. His wide, fearful eyes met Nova's as he found his breath again.

She couldn't bear to look at him for longer than a second.

It was as she always thought. No matter how often he was by her side, she was still alone.

Mikel downed the rest of his wine, tapping his fingers on the table. At some point, food had been served, but only Isla was eating. The king pressed his thumb on the underside of the table. At the center, a section of the table raised and transformed into a map of Valora.

"We leave in six days, and we will dock at the eastern port, not the central, in case any others should arrive early. As per our intel, that is not the case. We have mapped out the Manor for the past two years from top to bottom. There will be a map for you in your room." Mikel glanced at her. "You will study it. You will memorize it. You have two days to scope out the Manor, the attendants, and where the Elders rest. Night three is when you will strike."

This was wrong. She knew that. Thinking her freedom was more important than the lives of the Elders, but she had a task. It had to be completed. Shoving aside any hopes or dreams of being able to make her own choices, she focused on what was to come. The lives of the Elders were private. Kingdoms were not invited or allowed at any time other than the Assemblies. Beyond that, the Elderlands were a place of legend.

"How?"

At the quick glance between them, she knew. This would not be a slit throat. Or a destruction of someone's mind.

"Make it so the others know the Witches have returned."

She found it hard to breathe with dread wrapped around her throat. If the world ever found out, she would never be free.

"Oh, Gods," Jonah whispered beside her, and the words ricocheted around the room.

They were proud of themselves, the king and queen. Nova's existence had been kept a secret for eight years—longer. Deciding to spread rumors of the Witches was calculated. There had not been a single mention of them since the massacre centuries ago. Why now? Why her?

"Do you understand?"

She wanted to fall to her knees on the cliffs edge and beg the Gods that never answered for a reason. Why was this the only path to freedom? Why wasn't she brave enough to make one herself? *Why is this the life I was given?*

Returning from the dirt in the ground had brought her no more peace. She went from one death to another. Anger and resentment pricked at her eyes and dug at her skin with sharp talons from the inside. She met their eyes with hardened resolve. The eyes that once had been welcoming, tricking her into believing that she'd found safety. Instead, she'd found shackles. Chains attaching her to Jonah and Isla. Chains attaching her to the king and queen.

All that was left was an anchor to the last remnants of her morality.

And yet, she felt the links weakening day by day. "I understand."

CHAPTER 5

A RAGEFUL WITCH

Nausea rolled in Nova's stomach.

It wasn't the waves—she found the steady rocking of the ship underfoot comforting. The queasiness had been a constant friend beside her while she studied the large rendering of the Manor, sitting like a rock in her gut while her clothes were packed. And had been with her since they boarded the ship twelve days ago. They had passed from the Northern Gulf to the Avala Ocean, the days dwindling until their arrival.

Two days remained until they arrived at the Elderlands.

Five until she had to kill the Elders.

They promised her freedom. But would they give it to her? Was killing them even worth it?

Jonah stood beside her. She wished he wasn't. But this was his job. "Loren and the kids drew this for you."

She slanted her gaze toward him as he pulled a piece of parchment out of his pants. Loren, his husband, and his children had suffered because of her, too. Did they know Jonah had not forgiven her as they seemed to? She took it with her right hand, the sunlight shimmering off the rings on her fingers. On her left, her talons were there, covering her hand. She felt vulnerable without them.

There was a picture drawn of the Froststone castle and the mountains. Of the Ystal Sea she often looked out on. It was beautiful. Colors were strewn about the pages even though most of the time, they all existed in a world of gray.

Her hand tightened on the page. No one ever made her anything. "They didn't have to do this."

He huffed, amused. "They do what they want."

"As do you," she said, looking back over the water.

"Nova...you must know, I am sorry—"

Her hand curled over the railing. "I don't want an empty apology. You made a decision to protect those you care about, those you love." Bitterness was a nasty thing. Would anyone ever care for her? *Love* her? For who she was, not whom they might want her to be?

"I care—"

Her lip curled. "Enough, Jonah."

Really, he had every right. He owed her nothing. What he did was a reminder they were not friends and never had been. She was a means to an end. As was he. She didn't confide in him. She did not tell him things. She had kept him at arm's length, so why should he have done any different?

She stared at the picture, her heart warming despite herself as she looked at it. There was no use in wishing she was different; she wasn't. Probably never would be. But it was nice that sometimes, they saw her as something else. Something human. *I wish I could feel that.*

But knowing what she had done...she wished they had never cared for her at all.

Turning to look at him, she saw a past version of him. One with bruises mottled over his skin, black and blue and yellow. A version of him that flinched at every sound, that tracked every footstep. A version that curled in upon himself when others were around. The fear that had never left his eyes from whatever the Vahls had done to him. She remembered learning they had done the same to Loren. How they made the kids watch and then erased the memory from their heads. But not from Jonah's. Not from Loren's.

She should've known better than to hope he would've forgiven her.

She squeezed her eyes shut so that when she opened them again, she would only see the real Jonah. Not those tortured memories.

Jonah exhaled. "I am sorry."

"Apologies do not change our actions, Jonah. What is past, is past." *I was a fool to think you cared about me.* "There's nothing else to say," she said, her words almost lost to the water crashing against the ship.

Around them, there was a constant hum of busywork. The captain kept watch from the bow while the sailors were down below, ensuring the ship maintained order. They were either pirates or for-hire sailors, surely paid to keep quiet about the early arrival. But they were more for show than anything.

Long ago, the Water Elementals worked hand in hand with the Creators—those not quite human and not quite Athera—to mold the Aether into mechanisms to power the ships. Creators had the ability to mold and influence the Aether without imbuing any specific power into the final product, allowing it to be used by all, not just those that contained the same magic.

Away from the shores of Syris, the suns were bright, and seabirds dived from the blue sky into the deep water, hunting for fish.

Jonah stood still beside her. "I could not let them touch Loren or the kids again. But you cannot keep letting them destroy you. I cannot keep watching them destroy you."

Letting. As if she hadn't tried to leave. As if he hadn't given them her plans to try. Now as long as she did what she was ordered, she would be gone.

"There is nothing left to destroy, Jonah." She shook her head, curls blowing in the wind behind her.

She didn't mean it in the sense that they had destroyed her

from the ground up. Even though they had. But in the sense that she'd never been anything else. From the moment she'd arrived on their doorstep—the Froststone castle being the only memory she had—she was going to be nothing more than a pawn.

Nova had never even had a chance to be anything more than an executioner.

And it wasn't that she didn't understand conflict and power. It wasn't always the blood spilled that dug into her like a knife. It wasn't that when people saw her in the dungeons, they instinctively knew she brought death with her. It was that she never got a chance to learn what else she might've enjoyed. What she might have liked to do with her life. Though, she probably should've known the first time she looked in the mirror and saw the jagged scar on her throat.

"I am what they have made me. I will never be anything more." She shrugged as if it caused her no pain.

His heart raced with anger; she could see it in his eyes. Before she could stop him, his hands were on her shoulders, the touch reverberating to her bones. Without choice, small shakes traveled up and down her body. It was as if a distress signal was blaring in her head. Her blood ran hot and cold. Burning and chilling her the longer the touch remained on her skin.

"That is not true." He shook her. "You are not what they have done to you."

"Get off me," she said—pleaded. "Get off me."

It was as if he was frozen, infuriated with the king and queen, and for once, letting it show. He knew how much touch pained her—physically and emotionally. How it forced her to relive memories of that room and being chained to that chair. Still, he did not let go.

Pain pounded at her. She tried to count down from ten, but she could feel the visual attack of her memories. Of having to try and fight through which memories were real or not.

All because of his touch.

*Nine, eight...*She breathed in and out. "Jonah, *please*," she begged, her eyes squeezed shut. *Seven, six...*She felt for the essence of his blood with her hand. She didn't want to control him that way, but she would. If he didn't stop, she would. She felt its frantic pulse in her fingertips. *Five, four...*

Jonah stopped.

Her diaphragm relaxed as she exhaled. She let his blood go, her hand shaking. Blood dripped from her left palm where the talons had dug in. When she opened her eyes, she found him with shaking hands.

"Nova, I-I am so sorry," he whispered with a shaky voice. Remorse was visible, his eyes wet with unshed tears.

She took a few steps back, placing space between them. She couldn't—couldn't feel her own heart. Couldn't feel the blood rushing through her veins. All she could feel was the burning remnants of the touch on her arms.

How desperately she needed it off.

She pressed the mechanism on her bracelet, retracting the talons, turning the metal red. "It's okay, it's okay," she repeated over and over and over.

"I didn't—"

"Enough." Her voice was detached, resolute. Sadness flickered in his eyes, but he dipped his head. On the drawing, her blood had stained the edges, a small tear in the corner.

She stalked away with the drawing clenched tight in her hands, her blood ruining it.

Like it ruined everything.

IN THE SAFETY of her room, with two small windows letting in the sunlight, she sat on the floor. Trying to control her godsdamn breathing. She'd found the technique in an old book written by an air scholar. To be expected from them, it instructed everyone to work on their breathing.

Well, it wasn't godsdamn working. She forced her eyes shut again. When she failed to calm herself, she stood, stalking back and forth. If she kept at it, she'd wear a hole in the floor by the time they arrived. Back and forth she went. What was the point? Trying to work on her breathing. What a shit idea. Nova couldn't erase the response she had to being touched. Not yet, at least.

Gods, she was angry. She was angry more than she wasn't.

Nova felt rage on a daily basis, budding beneath her fingertips, like winter flowers on the vines.

For as long as she'd remembered, that was all she was. A rageful Witch. And if she ever forgot it, the Vahls would take the time to remind her with a pointless killing, a relentless hunt for someone they deemed threatening. She huffed. Maybe it was wrong to admit, but at least it gave her an outlet. A place to let all the rage flow.

What was she supposed to do with it the rest of the time?

Contain it? Let it burn until it left her in flames?

It was all useless.

She stopped in front of the small ornate mirror on the wall. The scars around her wrists were dark red and pulsing. Almost hot to the touch. She knew what she was.

A Witch.

There was no denying it. No other Athera had these abilities. No one else could control blood. Except for the Witches that had been massacred centuries ago. She was the first.

A fact that was carefully, pointedly hidden, by the Vahls and by herself. Besides them, only the people she killed ever realized it, right before their hearts stopped beating. She believed Jonah suspected, but that was all it was—suspicions. However, it didn't explain her ability to access the mind as Spirit Naturalists did unless her true parents had been Spirit Naturalists and somehow, it, too, passed down to her. It wasn't as if she could find out. She had no idea who her parents were, and she couldn't ask the Vahls.

The one time she had, she was left chained to that chair for three days. It was of the lesser sentences they forced upon her, but one of the first.

Beyond that, there were only two other places that might have that information, on powers mixing. The Eternal Library in Vilies and the Emerald Library in Eisera. And the Vahls had never allowed her to go to either.

But this—this task of killing the Elders in such a way that would let the rest of the world know there was a Witch walking on the surface—was another strategy she wasn't privy to. What did they gain from it? The world believed—or, at very least, was taught—that the Witches had been blood thirsty and hungry for power. That they were able to control the Aether unlike anyone else. That they killed without remorse. But what did they get from revealing her? Alliances? A Witch hunt? Fear?

Yet none of it was enough to make her rethink it. She wanted out. They could start a Witch hunt if they wanted. She would be long gone.

All she had to do was survive. And then, she would be free.

Free to get herself far, far away from Syris.

ON THE HORIZON, the frozen tundra of the Elderlands approached. Sharp rays of light glinted off the ice sheets. Streaks of red and orange bled against the sky, bouncing off the Second Star. Not quite a sun or a moon; no one truly knew the purpose. Where the suns or the moon were, the Second Star followed.

The ship navigated through the icebergs in the frigid water, approaching the dock. With one hand on the railing, she watched the sea. In the ripples of the boat, colorful fins shimmered under the surface. Fish jumped out and left tiny ripples behind as they dove under.

At the bow, Mikel and Mireya stood together. The queen's red hair was like a teardrop from the sky above. Nova scrunched her nose. *More like a drop of poison.* Bitter air wound around the ship and through its passengers as they approached. As if the queen could sense Nova's eyes, she turned, fixing her cold, lifeless gaze on her, a haughty, calculating smirk on her face as she did.

Nova thought that if the end of the world stared Mireya in the face, she'd greet it with that smile. That she'd wear it to her grave.

Still, Nova held her ground until the queen faced forward.

"You should run," she said quietly, the wind carrying her voice.

"Run?" Jonah stepped into her line of sight. The picture he gifted her was tucked into the right pocket of her long furred coat.

"Leave Syris. Take Loren and the kids and run." This was their goodbye. Their final one.

Jonah wouldn't be joining them. No one was allowed on the Elderlands but world leaders and their heirs. A few guards were welcome to stay with the ships at the docks, but they never even breathed the same air as those in the Manor. The Assemblies were private.

After they docked, Jonah would be heading back on the smaller ship that had been trailing them, where any unnecessary crew would depart. He would be free of them for a few days, but that was all.

He nodded frantically. "Of course. I know."

"No. Not eventually. You need to leave immediately." She turned to him, a blazing force. It was the very least she could do.

She would not be coming back. She would not get another chance. He'd hurt her, but they had hurt him. The relationship she thought they had formed was broken, but she did not want him dead.

"We will," he said, but his voice faltered.

Nova's eyes flashed as bright as the world around them. "Promise me you will go."

Jonah had tried once before, but the Vahls had eyes everywhere, and the consequences—his family—were not worth the risk. But now...he had a chance, and she needed him to take it.

Whatever he saw in her eyes was enough. She didn't ask for much, didn't ask for anything. But she was asking for this. "Okay. Okay. We will go."

Around them, a whistle sounded, announcing their arrival to the dock.

"Thank you, Jonah."

His eyes watered, but he blinked them away. This would be the last time she ever saw him if all went to plan. Part of her hoped it would be. If it meant she was free and if it meant he would be safe. They wouldn't be able to hurt each other anymore.

Nova would miss him. Despite what he'd done, he'd been by her side for years. She would miss that.

He said nothing. They stood together in careful silence as the ship docked.

Side by side until they couldn't be.

Chapter 6

Scarlet Snow

THE MOMENT NOVA STEPPED FOOT ON THE Elderlands, her head exploded.

She collapsed to her knees on the frozen tundra, palms pressed into her temples as the icy cold seeped into her. It felt like her skull was being hammered, everything touched by shattering pain. A quiet, elongated scream left her lips. She'd felt pain before, was used to it, but this…

"Make it stop," she growled, blinking her tear-filled eyes open to glare at Mikel and Mireya.

But their faces were filled with confusion.

Another wave of pain washed over her. It was agony, and it was everywhere. It felt like her heart was trying to run from the pain but had nowhere to go. The blinding sun rays danced on her skin. The contrasting heat and frigid air was overwhelming as she felt the heartbeat of everyone around her and the essence of their blood. And she could *feel* their emotions and hear their thoughts floating around their bodies like autonomous entities, like a million strings tying together.

Nova couldn't make it stop. She couldn't make the pain stop. Her head was a jumbled mess of thoughts and feelings that weren't her own.

"Get up," Mireya snarled, her hand wrapped tight on her arm. "This is unacceptable."

She tried to stand on unsteady feet with the queen's forceful touch, but she fell back to her knees. In the haze, she knew there would be consequences for this. She felt the burning touch of Mireya's hand and almost screeched. Nova could feel the blood but was too weak to grab it. With only her nails, she clawed at the queen. A single drop beaded on the queen's pale skin, and it was all Nova needed.

She took control over the blood flowing from Miraya and twisted her hand. She felt the pulse and the heat, and she drew it out. Through blurry eyes, she watched dark blood drip on the snow and watched Mireya's face twist in pain.

With the queen at eye level, she stared at her. "Make it stop." Squeezing her hand, she turned the queen's blood into a rope and pulled tight, choking her.

Mireya fell forward, hands grasping at her throat. "Mikel," she coughed, "the chains."

A bolt to the temple loosened her grip and Nova let out a painful whimper. Felt a kick to the legs as the queen fought to stand. A heavy weight fell over her, wrapped around her wrists and her neck, and somehow, someway, the chains worked. Not fully, but the pain lessened, and Nova could finally inhale.

For the first time in her life, she was thankful for aetherchains.

Everything receded, and she could finally, *finally*, feel the beat of her own heart. Until her face was turned sideways with a stinging slap.

"Get up. Now."

She spat blood onto the snow. It dripped from her nose and lip where she'd scratched herself. Nova could feel the eyes on her, but she didn't look away from the Vahls who'd never looked quite so furious.

Mireya stepped up, face-to-face with Nova. Her eyes were as

sharp as knives. "Look around. Count how many unfamiliar faces you see."

She didn't have to look. She knew there were four sailors that had seen the whole thing, if their frantic heart beats were any indication. Underfoot, the snow was scattered with blood, and in the distance, the suns shone off a sweeping, grand building ahead—the Manor.

The queen's lip curled. "They will die now. By your hand."

Anger boiled under Nova's skin. "Why? You want the world to know anyway. Why kill them?" She spat again, a drop of blood still on her lip as she stared at Mireya. She knew why. She just wanted her to say it.

"Because I ordered it so," Mireya snarled.

Everything she did resulted in someone's death. What a godsdamned burden.

"And the bodies?"

"They will return to Syris with your friend, who can join them as he is or as they will be." Mireya straightened her back. "Make it quick," Mireya said, strolling to Mikel, who gently strummed his fingers over Mireya's throat. "Inform the captain." With a nod, Mikel headed toward the ship. Nova knew it was to pay off the captain to ignore the dead bodies that would be joining him on his journey back.

A quick survey of the four scared faces was all she needed. They hadn't heard anything. If they had, they'd be running. As if that would stop her.

It was what she had to do if she didn't want to suffer. If she didn't want Jonah to suffer.

She exhaled and grabbed control of all four of their blood streams—heavier under the weight of the chains. She hated them for watching. Hated the Vahls for making her do this. Surprise flickered over their faces as their blood became a sentient thing. One *not* in their control. With her anger, she twisted her hands, forcing their bodies to contort as mewls of pain escaped their lips. She swept her arms back and watched as blood began to stream.

From their ears and their eyes and their noses, the blood dripped, turning the snow scarlet.

Pain battered against the weight of the chains. Exhaustion gripped Nova's soul, and she fell to her knees yet again. She spared one more glance in time to see Jonah turn to look at her. She felt the sadness emitting deep from his chest, slinking like a shadow in the crevices of his mind. From the distance, she couldn't see what was reflected in those eyes of his.

Was it kindness? A harbored hatred? Forgiveness? She supposed it didn't matter because she'd never see his eyes again.

Goodbye, Jonah.

WHEN NOVA AWOKE, she was in a room that looked like pure ice.

The walls were gray but with a sheen that made the stone akin to frozen water. Grand pillars sat in the corners of the room, delicate molding lined the ceilings, and large curved windows showcased the dangerous and beautiful frozen tundra outside. Above, goldstone illuminated the delicate chandelier, casting shadows over the room.

She blinked until the blur faded, taking stock of her surroundings. Immediately, she knew the few weapons she carried were gone, save for the bracelet around her wrist—inconspicuous as it was meant to be. But the small circular blades she usually sheathed on her left thigh were missing and the daggers gone from her right. The chains were still on, thicker now, because she was tied down to the bed.

The pain was still there, muted. Her abilities dimmed and under control.

What had happened? Why did the Elderlands bring her to her knees? There were so many questions and nowhere to get the answers. She kicked her leg out, hitting the post of the bed and jangling the chain.

Taking a deep breath, she centered herself. As hard as she wanted to try, there was no getting out of these. Not a second before Mireya and Mikel allowed her to. Which, given the scratch on the queen's face and the choking, might be a while.

She was an idiot.

Throwing her head back, she stared at the intricate ceiling. Etched into it were scenes from Valora's history. Myths and legends of battles, of the Gods, of the Aether. The most intricate carvings were the Gods. And to her surprise, the dragons—the Gods of the Witches were included.

In the books she'd read and the art she'd seen, if the Witches were shown, it was only as the world remembered them. Murderous, godless women who practiced dark magic and were deserving of the massacre that eradicated them from Valora. She had never heard anything that suggested they were anything but monsters. But above, tucked in the corner, was an elaborate carving of a Dragon—a sharp-edged wing and a peek of a narrowed eye.

And there she sat, tied to a bed underneath the God of her ancestors. What a *disgrace*.

Somewhere to her left, a door slammed open. The angry clicks on the floor obviously belonged to Mireya. Nova took a deep breath. Gods knew she'd need it.

The bed dipped, and Mireya's face appeared.

"Good, you are awake." She reached into the pocket of her trousers and pulled out a key.

First her ankles were freed, then the heavy chain over her waist removed. Mireya left the ones around her wrists and tied them in the center, keeping them visible, and the one wrapped tight around her throat remained as she pulled herself into a sitting position.

A necklace of black and blue bruises wound around the queen's throat. Her eyes were bloodshot. If Nova had only pulled quicker, harder...whatever. It was good enough. *For now.*

"Mikel," Mireya said with a snap of her fingers.

He approached, unfolding a version of the map that was drawn on parchment and laying it before her. She zoned out as they discussed the details of the Manor. She already knew every last detail of this map.

They were treating her like an amateur. As if she hadn't been killing people for the last eight years for them. She bit her tongue. An amateur she was not.

"On our third evening, a ship will return to the eastern shores after the suns have set. You will board with us only after the Elders are dead, and from there, you may go free. We will retreat for a day or two, arriving at the agreed upon date of the other monarchs."

She was unimpressed. It seemed lazy for Mireya, which probably meant the queen was hiding something. "And the people of the Manor? They will have seen you. Seen me."

Mikel snickered behind them. A sound of a young boy, not that of an aged king. "That is not your concern." She did her best to not to roll her eyes. Mikel was rarely anything but a gnat.

"Anything else?" She wanted to ask them everything. What was the purpose of this? What did they gain? Anything else but a thirst for power? Still, she bit her tongue, scared that if she questioned them, the deal would shatter.

Mireya dragged her sharp nail down Nova's face and onto the scar on her throat. The touch was discomforting, sending a sharp chill down her spine.

"Leave no scars, but make them bleed." She placed something in Nova's palm. "And here—the vials. Do not forget, Nova. Or you will not be free."

She dipped her head, closing her fingers around the vials. She waited for them to leave or to tie her back up but instead, Mireya tugged off the glove on her other hand. "Mikel, come."

As quickly as she could, she ensured the walls were solidified around her mind. It wouldn't last long, but it would keep the pain at bay. Mikel put the chains back around her ankles, connected in the center like her hands instead of around the bed posts.

Quickly, Mireya pressed her palms against her temples, and the world went dark.

In her mind, memories, real or fake, flashed in her head. Of her throat being slit by a faceless ghost. Of being back under the dirt only to suffocate. And Jonah dying at her hands. Over and over again, Mireya made her relive those moments, those fears. Her neck throbbed, her mind convinced she was bleeding out again, and her lungs fought for air that she had.

On and on it went, stringing her out on emotional and physical pain until her limbs gave out. Until her vocal cords were raw. Until all the fight died out.

CHAPTER 7

A WITCH OF THE BLOOD

THE DAYS PASSED QUICKLY.

The first frosts of winter had begun in the Elderlands, their long nights upon them, in which the suns only remained in the sky for a mere four hours. It should've felt endless, but given that for a period of each day she spent with the king and queen, the time passed exceptionally fast.

It took her at least an hour to recover from the torment they inflicted. And in the mornings, she exercised, pushing herself up and down until her arms gave out or until she was sore in the legs, as best she could, given the circumstances. But the rest of her days had been spent perusing the Manor.

The Elders' quarters were central on the lowest level. Guards stood attentive at the doors and stairwells, but she'd watched long enough to learn when they switched off. So, she spent time admiring the Manor itself, made to be an extension of the frozen tundra it sat on. All white stone with accents of various blues and greens to match the clear skies above or the lights that appeared in the sky on certain days.

The great hall was made of windows, including the domed ceiling above. From there, the entire rise and fall of the suns could be seen, along with the moon and every star of Valora. She found herself there every day, just to stare at the sky above.

Within the manor, the intricate carvings and ceilings continued in every room. From the guest quarters to the bathing chambers to the hallways to the kitchens and the stairwells. Even the arsenal room, where every visitor was required to pass through. There wasn't enough time to study them all. The Manor was vast and so was Valora's history.

She'd found the origin story of the Gods, of the Naturalists and the Elementals. Of the Witches, who fell somewhere between the two types of magic. Carvings depicted the sea serpent of the Water Elementals to the nitehounds of the Shadow Naturalist. All of them were painstakingly carved, along with depictions of wars and skirmishes throughout history. In the entrance hall, a map of Valora made up the whole ceiling, complete with cities and capitals, though the most western side was out of focus.

She could've spent her entire life tracking every facet here.

Instead, as darkness fell on the third night, she found herself in her room, staring at the dragon carved into the corner. The vials were laid out on her bed, all eight of them. Her curls were braided away from her face, while the sleeves of her silver blouse fell past her hands, hiding her scars and the bracelet around her wrist. She paced, her trousers brushing over the stone floor, past her belongings, which were stuffed into a single bag, waiting. Day in and day out, she'd thought about the choice she was making, weighing the Elders' lives against her freedom.

All that stood between her and freedom was death. Delivering death did not scare her.

She sat on the edge and turned her eyes up to the dragon.

What would they think of me? She imagined that dragons did not take orders from anyone. She also imagined they would not rest until they were free—if they ever found themselves chained. Maybe they'd look at her with shame or maybe with a speculative pride.

She'd briefly wondered if there was another way. But if the Elders did not die, she might.

Maybe it was foolish to put her life above the Elders'. But she wanted a chance. A chance to be someone else.

To put all she was and all she had done behind her.

It probably wouldn't matter, but she wanted the choice.

Because she'd never had it before.

Nova's footsteps were featherlight as she slunk between the shadows. There weren't many guards in the Manor, it was—or was supposed to be—a peaceful place. Mostly, it was attendants slipping from room to room. In the meeting hall, she paused, taking note of the stars and the position of the moon to track the time. She should arrive at the stairwell with enough time to slip down between the guard changes.

She was a silent wraith as she traversed. They were deceptively intricate despite the overwhelming shape of the Manor being quite simple. The entrance to the Elders' quarters weren't far from the meeting room. A few doors and connected halls took her right to where she needed to be. Light emitted from the goldstones, casting shadows over the art encased in jewels along the walls.

She felt the fear, the anticipation following her in the shadows. A ghost threatening to pull her in. Her mind spun in the darkness and cleared in the light. *This is what I have to do.*

With two doors still in her way, she calmed herself and reached out. The wispy edges of her power slinked and were met with a single steady heartbeat. Their mind was semi-fortified, but Nova left it alone. Instead, her powers waited at the edges in case she needed it. She wasn't apt at manipulation, not like the king and queen. She could do it, but it always felt *just* out of reach.

Silently, she crept through. Only one door between them. In and out. Kill them and disappear. Nothing more, nothing less.

Her worries became gnats, and she swatted them away. Her life was at stake and nothing more. Of all the things she'd done, all the people she'd killed, this had to be a level of insanity that she'd yet to reach. Time slowed.

The guard tapped their foot, impatiently she assumed, waiting for the midnight chime to free them. The manor held a bell that chimed twice. At midday and at midnight. Eventually, it came. She heard the clicking of the locks to the stairwell. It was a risk leaving only one door between them as there was no telling which the guard would take.

Luck was not on her side.

The guard slid in the door, eyes widening as their eyes landed on her.

Of course, she sighed. Before the guard could move, she slipped behind him, her hands hovering near his head and allowed the slinky power to enter their mind. They were weak, tired. She took full advantaged.

She whispered, "You did not see me. No one was here." In his mind, she found the memory—it was quick, just a glance of her in the room—and repeated the words until it fragmented, likely to appear as nothing more than a dream.

"I did not see you. No one was here," the guard repeated, monotone.

She silently backed out of the room through the door they'd come through, all the while whispering the words over again. She shut the door and waited for their heartbeat to retreat. Alone at last. Moving quickly, she approached the door to the stairwell. It was a simple door, given where it led to, and she picked every lock with a pin from her hair in seconds.

An upside to the time Mireya had chained her up in the frigid waters of Ystal with nothing but a dull needle.

Ahead, the staircase was grandiose, its polished bright stone contrasting with the dark walls. Goldstones were spaced along the winding, circular stairway and stealthily, she trekked downward. The pain that had been a soft under current was pounding at the bounds of the atherachains.

Her hand gripped the only one remaining, around her throat. It was digging into her skin, but she wouldn't remove it. Not yet. She couldn't risk being overwhelmed with magic again.

Voices echoed in the hallway as she approached the bottom of the staircase. The door that greeted her was lavish, made entirely of marbled stone with gleaming circular handles. More art was etched into the stone along with various gemstones. This was the only part of the Manor unmapped. She had no idea what to expect when she opened this door.

For all she knew, they could be sitting in a circle holding hands.

As best she could through the chain's weight, she reached for their heartbeats. One by one she loosely mapped out how close they might be to the door. She latched onto the blood closest to her, enough to have a loose hold, and started to pick the lock.

She tipped her head up and said a silent prayer to whatever Gods were listening. She pulled the door open as soft as possible, and thanks to whoever built this brilliant place, it barely made a sound.

With a quick glance, she surveyed the room. *Entrance hall, hallways on both sides. One straight ahead. Five heartbeats on the right. Two to the left.*

With a final deep breath, she went forward, following the blood she tracked. The entrance hall was empty, and the other heartbeats did not quicken, did not move closer. She moved swiftly, practically dancing over the floors, and found the first Elder. They sat in a small room with their back to the door and a single light illuminating the space. Quietly, she shut the door and stepped into the shadows.

The Elder's head raised, but that was all. She held control of their blood, stopping them.

"What is this?" Their voice...their *voice*. It was not a single sound but an echo, as if multiple people spoke all at once. "Who are you?"

Circling, she stepped in front of them. She found the Elder of the Shadow Naturalist. The veins in his hands were black before she'd all but frozen him in place.

Maybe she should've felt something. Anything. "It doesn't matter."

The Elder was composed, though his eyes were as black as the shadows. She squeezed her hand and watched as bruises formed instantaneously on his pale skin, his blood vessels bursting under the surface. Another quick tug, and she watched as the blood started to seep out. Slowly, it trailed down his skin. Upon further investigation, she noticed silver threads running through the red —she'd never seen that before. Confusion bloomed, but she grabbed a vile from the pouch under her blouse.

It was a slow process, and he watched her with an eerie level of focus. And acceptance. "A Witch." He cocked his head. Much like the voices, it felt as though multiple people were watching her. "A Witch of the Blood, no less. I had—"

She didn't care to hear more. The blood pooled out quicker now, and she watched him choke on it. Shadows withered at his fingertips, but they couldn't fight against her control. She held his eyes the entire time, watching until they fluttered closed.

Guilt rose in the pit of her stomach, but she choked it down. The Elders were peaceful pacifists, and they did not deserve this. But people met fates they did not deserve all the time.

It was the way the world worked. She would not be the one to change it.

Even if she wanted to.

As quickly as she came, she left, tucking the vial away, leaving the bleeding shadow Elder behind. Through the darkness, she slipped toward the five heartbeats. All of them were clustered at the end of the hall. As she treaded over the rug, she flexed her fingers, feeling each distinct heartbeat.

That was the thing about blood. It was similar, for the most part, in everyone. The same amount in every body. But she knew blood. Had known it her whole life, at least what she could remember. Every chance she could, she studied it with focus and intent.

Different antigens separated the blood into distinct types and categories. But even then, there were variants. Blood in those that were ill was weaker, easier to manipulate. Athera blood had a different weight, a different *feel* to it than humans. Some even carried blood where, on a molecular level, the cells were shaped differently. And when she was able to touch the blood, to manipulate it in the physical world, not just under their skin, she could learn so much more.

But for now, knowing the distinct five was enough.

One down, seven to go.

She slipped in with full control, finding all five of them sitting near the hearth where a fire blazed. Their heads snapped to her, eyes widening at her entrance as she once again froze them in place. Sweat dripped down her nose and spine.

All four Elemental Elders stared at her, while the Light Naturalist's eyes narrowed. In the dim room, it seemed as if her eyes were pure gold.

"What is this?"

"How?"

Their voices echoed like before. The sound denser now that there were five. They resonated over her skin, a scratch on her spine that made her lip curl. They were calling to attention what she was doing, the lengths she was going to, the lines she was willing to cross. Anger sat on her shoulders like an unwanted friend.

"Enough," she growled. Their blood pumped against her fingertips as she prowled in, grabbing the vials.

"What is this?" The fire Elder's voice was irate, and the flame in the hearth flickered with it.

She studied them. It was strange how wise they felt when, in front of her eyes, they looked no older than Mireya or Mikel.

"It is the end."

She repeated her motions from earlier. Watched bruises bloom like flowers on the pale skin of the fire and air Elders. Patches spread over the brown skin of the earth Elder, while the only sign of the vessels bursting in the water and light Elders were the drops of red tainting the whites of their eyes.

"What do you know about endings—"

She started with him. Pulling her hand and watching the blood drip out of the fire elder, making sure to collect his silver threaded blood. Every life she'd taken flashed before her eyes, a number too high to count. "I know enough."

She felt the eyes of another on her back. The earth Elder's green eyes were piercing.

"We had heard rumblings," the Elder said, the echoes grating in her ear. "Rumblings of the Witches return." The others hummed in agreement, the noise a constant crack on her nervous system.

"The Witches haven't. It's only me," she said, spilling the blood of two more, watching as the vials filled.

"Only you?" Somehow, the earth Elder found it within her to laugh. "Only you. It is only you that is doing this, then?"

Nova met her eyes. "Only me."

"Unlikely. The Witches do not travel alone." The voice was older this time.

If only that were true. She snorted, twisting her hand so blood spilled out of every crevice of the Elder. Nova was alone. Had been for her whole life. The Elder's annoying musings wouldn't make that any less true. Still, the words settled in her stomach like a rock. Why her? Why *was* she alone?

She shook it away. She didn't have time for this. Without the grating voice of the earth Elder, the last one bled as well, and Nova had six full vials of blood with two left to collect. With a sparing glance, she took them in. Their heads dangled back, streams of blood painting their cheeks and neck, dripping from their eyes, pooling on the ground below.

Every room she entered, death followed.

There were splatters of blood on her hands and her blouse, but she paid them no mind as she approached the remaining heartbeats.

Except they were waiting for her. Instantly, her head ached, more pain thrashed at the barriers of the chain around her throat, and her mind felt like a mess of fog. It didn't infiltrate the walls she had, but it was working overtime to break them down. The wisps of this power, the spirit Elder she assumed, felt like nails scratching over broken stone.

She felt their pulse in her fingertips, locating them somewhere to her right. Franticly, she shoved her hand out, and the pain receded. She gasped for breath, trying to find her footing again.

"Foolish girl," they said.

She blinked her eyes opened with both hands outstretched, both of them held in place away from her. The spirit Elder stood to her right, her eyes an angry lightning storm.

She knew she was weakening. The chain was eating at the well of her abilities. This needed to end—and end quickly. The healer looked at her with almost-kind eyes. She couldn't stand it.

This was a wholly selfish act. She didn't deserve kindness or understanding or empathy. No matter how badly she may have wanted it, that didn't change the truth. She wasn't *worthy* of it.

With a forceful push, Nova moved the Elders backward until they hit the wall, and she held them there. Her right arm trembled, and the spirit Elder fought and clawed at her mind. With a heaving breath, she pulled, blood spilling from the healer who just kept looking at her. Like she knew something Nova didn't. Keeping the spirit Elder in place, she collected the blood of the healer before spinning, using both hands to hold the spirit Elder at bay.

Their eyes met.

"Finally."

Nova's brows furrowed. The voices echoed, but it was different than moments ago. A different tone. She didn't understand the voices as it was, but she certainly didn't understand that.

Let me in.

The voices were a high-pitched scratch against her ears and heavy pressure digging into her head. Why were they doing this? Panic crept in. Her time was running out.

"No." Nova gritted her teeth, exhaustion boiling within her. She was tired of people in her head, manipulating her mind. She did not want the Elder to see the broken parts of her.

"Let me in." *Let me in.*

It echoed and pounded at her head until she couldn't hold them off. It was forcefully strong—stronger than the Vahls. A million voices at once attacking her ears and her mind. Nausea rose in her stomach as she fell to her knees, landing in the blood of the dead.

In the haze, she felt the Elder enter her mind, flinching. Though the Elder did not go searching. Did not pull memories forward.

"Thank you." The Elder spoke the words both out loud and within her head.

Her tired eyes landed on the Elder. "What?" she sputtered out. They were *thanking* her? For what? There was blood trailed over this place—all her doing. How was this happening? *What* was happening?

"I have been trapped here for so long. Decades. Centuries. With no way out. I assume when the body dies, I will be free."

Her extremities trembled in shock or fear, maybe both. She stood, never taking her eyes off the Elder. She wasn't sure if she was being tricked, but she was intrigued.

"Who are you?" Though she could've communicated silently, she thought best to conserve what little energy she did have.

"My name has been long forgotten, diminished over time. And it does not matter." The Elder cocked her head, studying Nova with an intense focus. *"The rest are dead?"*

"Yes."

"*Good.*" The Elder stepped closer, and she stood as still as stone as her hands approached her face. "*Listen to me. This will have consequences. At first they will be slight, minute. A rumble underfoot, storms stronger than normal, a world lost. Without us, there is no one ensuring the health of the Aether. The world will be unbalanced.*"

This was, in every sense of the word, Nova's fault. Maybe it was not her plan, not her evilness that led her to this action, but she was the one carrying it out. She inhaled, but the air was sharp, like swallowing blades.

When the world changed, Nova would know *she* was the catalyst.

The Elder continued, "*Beyond that, you must not let them get their hands on the blood you have spilled today.*"

Nova didn't need to be a mind reader to know she meant Mikel and Mireya.

"*They will damage the world irrevocably. I have seen their plans through others' eyes. Have seen what they want the world to become. Have seen what will become of the realms.*" The Elder twitched in pain as Nova's mind spun. The realms? Beyond this one and Thāna...what else was there? Nova felt her eyes prick. Were there any consequences this decision would not yield?

The Elder's next words were strained. "*You must leave here. Take the blood, and get rid of it. The blood spilled will be of no use, too long dead, too long exposed. But the blood in those vials...they* must *never touch it. Do you understand?*"

The words hammered at her head. She was in pain. "Why do I care what they do with the world?" she asked, trying to shake off the weight.

In truth, the world was not kind to her. Why should it deserve her own? This was her chance at freedom. The world could wait. The world could suffer.

A pitying look spread over the Elders wise face. "*You think they will let you have a life that is not theirs to control? You think they will let anyone you care for live freely?*"

"My life is already theirs."

"Only if you continue to let it be." The Elder pressed her fingers against her cheeks, pulling her close. *"They are false. They are sick. You must find the truth before it all turns to lies. You must find the rot. A Witch of the Blood. I never thought this day would come."* Nova swore the Elder almost smiled. *"You are not like them. Do not let them ruin you."*

She wanted to tell her they already had, but she said nothing. And something shifted. The hands at the edge of her mind turned sharp again, angry. The Elders eyes changed, practically glowing.

"You must end this and go." The Elder howled in pain. *"Quickly."*

She didn't think twice. A quick push sent them flailing backward, too weak to do any real damage, but with a forceful pull, the blood slowly trickled out. Except their blood was not like the others. It was black, threaded with silver. And it was not smooth. It did not flow.

She watched as the Elder choked, tried to fight it, and failed.

With shaky hands, she collected it anyway, closing the final vial. She looked around, blood-soaked and weak with exhaustion. The vials clinked together in the pouch tied at her waist.

Regardless of her choice, she needed to leave. The darkness wouldn't last much longer. But something ate at her. Telling her to listen to the voice that had spoken into her head moments ago. All the words of the Elders felt like thorns in her skin. And though it was only the spirit Elder who had spoken to her as such, she could practically hear all of them in her head. Floating like wraiths and whispering words she didn't understand over and over.

The rot. The realms. The destruction.

Her panic became violent.

Do not let them ruin you—but they already had. If she took the vials, they would *never* stop looking for her. She couldn't— she couldn't live with that. *Don't be stupid,* she sighed, *just do as your told. Just keep doing as your told. The vials for freedom.* It was the only way. The only *sure* path she had.

Even if it angered her, an anger as violent as the sea when it greeted those who did not respect it, it was her path. It was the only one that was still in reach.

As she moved, she tried—painfully—to convince herself it was true. Why should she care about what they wanted with the world? Her freedom was in her hands. The world was not her responsibility. *The world is not my responsibility.* She swallowed down the bile in her throat, ignoring the burn of that reality.

Nova found a sink within the chambers and washed the blood from her shoes before exiting. She stuck to the shadows and avoided eyes of any guards. The instructions had been to meet the Vahls in their room one last time. But what if she went in there and they kept her? Tricked her into staying? They had promised a small boat from their ship but nothing more. What if that, too, was a trick? Every possibility circled in her head.

And she kept coming back to one.

She couldn't save the world, but she could save herself.

Slowing, she felt for their blood as she approached, careful not to make a sound as she unclipped the bag with the vials and ever so carefully placed it on the floor. It was either the best or the worst thing she'd done for herself. She only hesitated for a second before she ran.

She practically floated over the floor, wanting only to escape. Wanting only to be free. All of it came back at once. The effort exerted, the deaths she'd delivered. Nova heaved for breath and fought to keep her muscles from clenching.

Her blood was tired, heart pumping harder than it should've. *She* was tired.

Upon exiting, cold air wrapped around her, nipping at her cheeks. But she ran. Through the snow and toward the smell of the sea, trying to outrun the smell of death.

Nova had killed the Elders.

She was free.

And it was that, that sent her sprawling in the snow.

CHAPTER 8

PRINCESS OF THE SHADOWS

"WAKE UP."

The slap of a hand was a burning coal against cold skin. Nova blinked open her heavy eyes. Exhaustion weighed on her back. A groan escaped her lips, pain shattering the edges of her mind. Rolling over, she pushed herself up, her arms relying on muscle memory, and she spit out blood. It stained the snow beneath her.

Above, it was dark. Though the suns would not rise for at least a few hours, the black sky began to give way to deep indigo.

"Frankly, you don't have time for this." The voice was detached. Nova fixed her eyes on the woman crouched beside her. She didn't appear to be much older than herself. A hood kept a majority of her face in the shadows.

"Come, you need to go."

"Who are you?" She rubbed her hands in the snow, attempting to get the speckled blood off her skin.

"Get up." The girl wrapped a gloved hand around Nova's bicep, her skin reacting instantly. She ripped her arm away, stumbling. Weakened still, Nova felt for her heartbeat, the blood, and held it in her palm, ready to strike.

"*Who* are you?" Nova snarled.

"Not your enemy."

"Not what I asked."

At the girl's feet, shadows swirled in contrived motions. Not shadows born of the darkness, but instead, shadows born from the girl's fingertips.

"If I tell you, will you come with me?" The shadows crawled up her legs, sentient beings. Nova dipped her chin. "My name is Elaia. And I am not your enemy. You need to *leave.*"

She'd heard the name before, but she couldn't place it. It was there, hiding behind the fog of pain and fatigue. Still, she reached out with what she had, circling the edges of Elaia's brain, looking for a weakness. Instead she was met with a wall of darkness.

"Get out of my head," Elaia snarled, stepping toward Nova. She pulled her hood back, exposing half of her face. Black hair danced along her collarbone and eyes as golden brown as the suns glinting off the sea shone in the darkness.

Elaia was dressed like the shadows themselves.

"Given the blood all over your clothes, I would bet your time is precious. The choice is yours. I can help you to the docks, or I can walk away and let you get swallowed by the snow."

Nova took a step, and her head spun. *Bleeding suns,* she exhaled. She'd never used her powers against aetherchains like that. Never continuously fought against something that was made to weaken her. It was taking a toll. More than the torture and training the Vahls had inflicted. Nova could fight through the agonizing pain and sleepless days. This was pulling from an empty well.

Given her options, the choice was clear.

"Fine."

Elaia turned and started plodding through the snow. Nova had exited the Manor with no plan. She hadn't even bothered to find the road that traversed underneath the grand statutes all the way to the docks. Under the cover of fading darkness, Elaia silently led the way.

She watched the way the shadows moved with her. They danced under her footsteps, slunk around her legs, and slithered over her fingers. There was a confident authority about the woman. It was silent, simmering under the surface. Even now, she could tell that much.

Suddenly, the name clicked. Elaia. The Princess of the Shadows. Her father was Desmond Zūne, the High Shade of Rersa. One of the eastern continents, less than a week's travel from Syris, depending on the seas and the fortitude of the ships.

Recently, according to the Vahls, Elaia had been in the west, in Aeledin, serving as an emissary for her father. It wasn't strange that she was here, given the upcoming assembly that Nova supposed would no longer be happening. But why was she *already* here?

"No one was supposed to be here."

Elaia tossed a weary look over her shoulder. "Obviously."

Suspicion lived in Nova like a coiled snake, always wound tight and waiting to strike. With the dregs of power she had left, she felt Elaia's blood. It was slight but within reach. She stopped, the cold keeping her on her toes.

"Explain."

With an exasperated sigh, Elaia hung her head. "You could at least ask me nicely." Nova raised a brow. "I arrived early on behalf of my father. The seas happened to be on my side." With quick scrutiny over Nova's bloody form, her nose twitched. "Though I wish they weren't."

A wave of dizziness washed over Nova, exhaustion battering at her like waves in a storm.

"Can we go now? Before you decide to pass out and I have to drag you?"

The thought of another's hand on her skin was enough. Nova stalked forward again, picking up her slow pace. She'd never felt her own blood feel so heavy. Every step felt like the effort of twenty. She was also convinced the chain was tightening as she breathed. The Manor was a beacon behind them, casting shadows over the snow from the towers on each corner and reflecting off the statues. Ahead was pure darkness.

Elaia led them through the snow, though she noticed as she placed her feet exactly where she'd already stepped, that the Princess did so carefully. Landing on crunchy ice that did not leave distinct foot prints. *Smart girl.* Nova swallowed, her skin dry and tight from dehydration.

Then, the alarms sounded. An earsplitting sound ricocheted off the ice around them. Underfoot, the earth rumbled, and the girls tumbled down. Nova pushed herself up to find the Manor had more secrets than she'd believed. Walls of stone and ice rose from carefully crafted cracks in the ground around the manor, decorated with large goldstones that shot through the darkness as guards spread along the surface.

"We need to hurry." Elaia rose, the shadows dancing around them.

Everything became background noise as they ran, the alarms were deafening, and Nova felt liquid trickling from her ear.

Somehow, they must have used the surroundings to amplify the noise, used the ice as a weapon itself. Over the slight hill, finally, she saw where the world split. Where the ice stopped and the sea began. Upon approach, Elaia banked left, off to the side of the main docks. Away from where Mikel and Mireya would've had her ship waiting.

But Nova followed.

Her adrenaline wore thin as they bounded down the road. There were ports where the preparations for each arriving country had started. But Elaia kept going down a long skinny dock surrounded by the dark sea. Tucked in the shadows was a small ship. There was no hull, nowhere to hide down below, but the wheel was protected as best it could be.

There goes my chances of survival. Nova coughed, spitting into the gently rocking sea.

"Get in."

Nova knew this was rash—beyond stupid, really. But it was this or them. As physically tired as she was, she was just as exhausted from being used as a pawn. By the time they realized she wasn't coming and found the vials, she would be long gone. And by the time they got back to Syris, hopefully Jonah would be, too.

"I'm not going to harm you," Elaia said, her voice soft. Like one might talk to a wounded animal. Nova imagined the blood on her skin and her exhausted, most likely blood-shot eyes might give that effect. "You need to go, and I need to protect myself. So please, get in."

So, she did. The ship was small, but there were mechanisms here, too. Elaia leaned over, pointing at them. "You have to row until enough water is gathered for the wheel to pull from. It will power itself. You only have to steer. If at any point it stops, start rowing, and it will start again." Her golden eyes looked out beyond Nova. "When the suns rise, go west."

Elaia moved quickly, untying the boat from the dock and throwing it next to Nova's legs. Nova took the oars up, adjusting to the rocking of the sea.

"Good luck." Elaia stood on the edge of the dock, light from the Manor haloed around her.

With one last effort, she reached out to the princess's mind, only to be met with shadows once more. It was no use anyway. She was too drained.

Nova said nothing. Instead, she watched as she rowed out. Watched Elaia manipulate the shadows to cover her in darkness as she floated off into the sea.

At the mercy of the waves.

THE SEAS WERE RELENTLESS. Moments after the suns rose, she saw the cluster of clouds on the horizon. Gray and ominous, rolling without bounds in her direction. Soon enough, the light disappeared behind them, the suns hidden in the sky, and she could only hope she was still moving in the right direction.

Underneath, the waves crashed against the ship, bucking it whichever way it felt.

She'd emptied her stomach multiple times, though there was nothing left to empty. Her skin was tight with dehydration. She had not rested, had not slept, had not given her body the chance to recharge.

Not that it would do her any good. *In and out. Deep breaths.* She inhaled, rain plastering her curls to her head. Her clothes stuck to her uncomfortably so. Her head was spinning, her eyes fighting to keep open.

It was only a matter of time before she passed out, could feel it in her blood. Nova hunkered down as best she could on the small boat, forcing herself under the shelter that shielded the wheel.

Above her, the sky grew dark, as dark as the shadows. *Storms, stronger than normal.*

There were no suns.

There were no birds.

There was nothing but the crashing waves and thunderous rain from the sky. There was nothing she could do. She would either make it through the storm alive. Or she wouldn't.

Honestly, it didn't very much matter to her which it was.

Chapter 9

A Heavy Dance

Elaia knew death better than anyone. Knew the consequences of it, the gaping emptiness, and cannibalistic grief it left in its wake. After the loss of both her younger sisters and her mother, Elaia had become well-versed in the aftermath of it.

And though different, she found herself surrounded by it once more.

When people died, the air took on a certain quality. A timid yet choking feel. Like there wasn't enough oxygen to breathe, and even if there was, you'd be unable to do so. As she sat surrounded by the leaders of Valora, the air felt like that again. Elaia drew her finger over her brows, pressing them into her temples.

What had she done?

What had she done?

The Elders were dead. Those that managed the Aether were dead. There had been a time, centuries ago, when the Aether flowed autonomously. After many wars, the Elders were implemented as a way to control who gained access to the Aether and that all uses were approved. They ensured that under the surface, it flowed as the world's heated core did.

They had been without them before...but could they be

without them again? Familiarity made people lazy. What would the world become without its familiar confines?

And on top of that, this was her first assembly on behalf of her father. It was supposed to be a rite of passage. Instead— because of the woman collapsed in the snow, splattered in blood —it was shadowed by death.

Everything in her life was shadowed by death.

Elaia took a deep breath, settling herself.

Right now, the full extent of the consequences of the Elders' death could be hypothesized. Mythics, a subset of the Magistrate of the Second Star, had studied the Elders and the possible ramifications. The Elders weren't human, but they weren't Gods, nor were they Scions, but something in between. They did not age nor grow sick. They simply existed and had for centuries.

Mythics believed, in the event of the Elders' death, the Aether may flare under the surface of Valora and manifest in various ways —storms, power flares, an interruption in the flow of the Aether. But those were all just theories.

More immediately, the death of the Elders would lead to the gentle peace between kingdoms fraying. The Creators of Valora would no longer need to seek approval for their inventions. The Aether points would no longer be protected beyond the rules of their home country.

Soon, the whole of Valora would be dealing with the fallout. For now, every leader sat around the stone table, sharing unsure glances with one another.

Elaia studied them all.

They all wore crowns or customary jewels of their homes, of their people. Each and every one of them were draped in intricate, detailed clothing indicative of where they came from. She noted who with whom—alliances that were more symbolic than anything. The Eastern Alliance—those of Rersa, Azias, and Syris. The Alliance of Zaphine—those of Ceron, Mykor, and Iyvia. Though Iyvia was not present at this assembly as Zvon Savali, the Reyn, had recently passed.

The alliances were for show. They often meant nothing beyond trade and private agreements between the countries. Beyond them, there were those that would rather keep to themselves.

Elaia forced her shoulders to settle as she looked around the main hall, a circular room with windows spanning every wall. Light reflected off the snow outside, brightening the room. Guards stood at the entrances, a bit wide-eyed and empty. Grieving or dissociating maybe. It was their job to protect the Elders—not that they had ever needed to before—and they had failed.

"They're dead? Truly dead?" Yenna, the Reyna of Ceron, the Northern Waterlands, and one of the three rulers of the Water Elementals, broke the extended silence.

Queen Mireya Vahl of Spirit answered, "You are welcome to go down and look, Yenna, if you desire to see pools of blood."

Yenna gave the queen a severe stare. The two of them never got along. No Water Elemental cared much for anything the Vahls did or said.

"How long are we going to sit here and discuss this? They're dead. Instead of questioning the truth of that or not, we should find the person who killed them." Mikel Vahl paced around the long stone table. "The *Witch* who killed them," he corrected with vitriol.

The word sent a chill through the air. "Do not spread tales of the Witches without proof, Mikel," said Lady Anika of Vydara. Under the light, the colors in her gown made her appear as living flames.

"What else could it be? You have heard the whispers of the Cardinal—she haunts your people as she does ours." Mikel stared at them, willing anyone to disagree. "The blood tears, the *blood*. Who—what—else could it be?"

Anika waved a hand. "The Cardinal is a story told to scare children."

"Maybe for you. But they have visited our shores."

"Our first priority should be returning home, preparing our homes, our councils. Consulting the Mythics about the effects of this loss."

"And cause hysteria?"

"So, you plan to leave your people in the dark?"

"You plan to start a Witch hunt—how is that any better?"

"Warn them about what? Even we do not fully comprehend the consequences of this."

She lost track of who was talking. Of who was arguing. It didn't matter.

Elaia, admittedly, was bored. This was useless. Already tensions were raised with no Elders to calm them. There was peace in Valora and had been for some time now, but would it last?

"Enough." Queen Mireya stood, her lifeless blue eyes tracking over everyone. "What you do within the borders of your own country does not need to be fought over. But we must find them—"

"The Witch," Haya said, the Air Naturalist Queen of Azias. The words were soft yet danced on the air she twisted.

Another beat of silence fell. This time no one argued.

A gleam reflected in Mireya's eyes. "The Witch," she spoke, "must be found.

"To be clear, you all want to start a Witch hunt based on the centuries-old information?" asked Okara Shea, Master of Vilies and the healers.

"The information we have is enough. All those centuries ago, the Witches did as they pleased. Spilled the blood of those they felt threatened them, which was *everyone*. Or have you forgotten, Okara? Forgotten that, at the time, they cursed and killed every leader in Valora? That they could manipulate the Aether to their liking?"

"That's a rumor, and you know it." Okara rolled her shoulders. "They have been dead for over four hundred years. What makes you think they have suddenly returned?"

Mireya rose a brow. "Do you have a better theory? An explanation for the blood? For any of it? Who else would be capable of killing the Elders? Who else could haunt all of our shores?"

Elaia felt the urge to scream.

This was the world now. Abstract fears and arguments that would go unheard and unmediated. The Witches had been gone for almost five centuries—massacred because of their abilities that were decidedly unnatural. Uncontrollable. Everyone, to this day, was taught the story of the Witches. Of how they made people bleed. Of how they controlled people.

Some believed that the stories had been twisted, to be made more violent than they were—people like her mother. And others believed that the Witches were inherently evil, that no moral being could possess another person's blood. Because if one Witch could do this...what could the return of them look like? At its core, Elaia recognized what this was—fear.

Because despite the girl—the Witch—being covered in blood, she had not seemed evil to her. But she supposed things, people, were not always as they seemed.

"At very least," Mireya said, tapping her nails on the desk, "you should return home. Tell who you must—of the Elders, of the Witch. Prepare how you see fit." When no one spoke, Mireya surveyed the room, eyes lingering on Elaia for a second longer. "I suggest we schedule a new assembly, one not darkened by death."

Anika and Mylla Kovaci, the Empress of Lazora, both stood abruptly, though it was Anika who spoke once more. "You may all do as you please. We will not attend."

"Nor will we," Mylla said cooly.

Elaia's shadows danced by her feet, impatience nipping her skin. Already the cracks had appeared underfoot. Without the Elders, the respectful comradery would crumble.

Either the world would stay as it was, or it would fall.

It was only a matter of time.

Elaia rested her hands on the railing of the *Nomara,* the ship named after mother. The moment she had stepped on board, she instructed the crew to retreat before sending word to her father what had happened by the quick silver-winged messenger birds. Under foot, the boat was smooth and steady as they headed west, back to Rersa.

The seas were calm for now, but Elaia knew how quickly they could change. How in a blink of an eye, they might decide to toss its passengers. She thought of the Witch rowing away in that tiny shell of a boat.

"Princess," Rohan, her most trusted guard, spoke behind her, "you should eat."

Elaia sighed. As far as the eye could see were shades of blue. Deep cerulean from the sea below and the bright blue of the sky above. Fluffy clouds were speckled haphazardly, doing nothing to shield them from the rays of the suns. They latched on to the black of her gown, sleeveless and light as it was, and the heat penetrated, warming her.

With a slow hand, she traced the ink on her forearm all the way up to her elbow, moving up and down the swirls she'd had since she was sixteen. Every native of Rersa, Shadow Naturalist or not, received the ink of their family name.

"Strange, isn't it, that when the world starts to fall apart, we're still expected to carry on as normal." She glanced at the guard standing steady beside her.

"It is. But life requires sustenance, even when it's hard."

Her nose scrunched. "I can't stomach any more fish, Rohan."

"Your father would want you to eat."

She stopped herself from rolling her eyes. None of them knew what her father wanted anymore. Desmond, the High Shade, was too busy sinking under the burden of his own grief. It was all up to Elaia, as if her grief was less important than his. She loved him, but why was she expected to be strong when he got to be weak? It was so typical of men. To expect women to carry on while they fell. To keep dancing with bloody feet and a broken heart.

Womanhood itself was a dance. Constantly adapting to what others demanded. From footsteps that were nimble and swift, careful enough to not shatter a fragile surface, to spinning leisurely, all to capture one's attention, to charm them. And to knowing when to spin so swiftly, they'd never see you coming. So Elaia danced. Every step was an uphill battle against the loss battering her fragile heart. Her feet ached, and her shoulders were heavy. Still, Elaia danced. She pushed her shoulders back and carried on without so much as a moment to breathe.

Rohan studied her with dark eyes. His dark beard was peppered with gray, matching the short cut of his hair. The ink from his tattoo crawled up the side of his neck and disappeared beneath his shirt. "Besides, they broke into the food stores below, now that the trip has been cut short."

A smile danced on her lips. "No more fish?"

"Not for tonight," Rohan said. "Now come. We can discuss your plans for when we dock."

Elaia unwrapped her hand from the railing and followed. Rohan had been with her for as long as she could remember. She was positive he was there when she was born, waiting outside the room, and from that day on, he'd never left her side. They walked over the wooden flooring to the captain's quarters at the stern of the boat. Around them, deck hands wove the water into the mechanisms, spurring the boat on and cutting through smooth seas at a quick pace.

She pushed open the doors to her quarters, greeted by dark teakwood and the permeating smell of saltwater. Tucked away to the left, a desk was nailed into the floorboards, piles of organized materials spread over the surface, and a dark wooden table sat a few feet away, a spread of food laid out on top. A partition wall cloaked her neatly made bed, pressed against the opposite wall. At the very rear, a large window let the sunlight in, and the breeze sneaked through, dancing through Elaia's short black hair.

She took a seat along the bench around the table, pulling her leg up to rest on and grabbing the nearest piece of bread. "Sit. You won't do me any good pacing the room."

Rohan rolled his eyes but pulled out a chair opposite her, but not before grabbing a folder off her desk. Reaching up, she tugged the crown out of her hair. The weightless silver band was simple, inlaid with onyx gemstones all the way around. Sometimes, it felt heavier than it should've.

"What are the latest reports? From Aeledin and Rersa?" Elaia asked, dipping her bread in the light salty broth until it was soaked.

Since the disappearance of Nomara and her youngest sister, Rayn, and the subsequent death of her middle sister, Shaye, she split her time between the two. Aeledin was governed by the humans and their chamber of five, and Rersa, the Empire of Shadow, where her father resided. Her true home.

Rohan opened the folder and began laying out parchment between them. Bringing her free hand up, shadows weaved between her fingertips until she instructed them to the parchment. When the darkness covered the tan colored paper, the writing appeared, practically glowing. She scanned every report top to bottom.

The reports from Aeledin were bare. She'd been working with the Chamber on the occasional riot after they had requested the help of the Nightguard. While there, one of the Chamber members, Liev Fallow, had reported sightings of dead Scions—descendants of the Gods. Elaia looked into this with him—discovered dead Scions of her own. It was a high crime in any country, but there were very few issues and none so isolated. But even stranger was that when she or Liev tried to show others, the dead Scions were gone. Almost like they'd never existed.

Unsurprisingly, there was nothing in the report of them.

The usual scrawl of Zahra, her betrothed, was on the Rersa

reports, which continued to be strange. Sightings of the Nightguard manning the coasts and the ports and all the governing cities without request. It also stated her father had been hard to find—often he disappeared into the canyon and returned late at night, forgoing his duties. It was part of the reason she'd come to the assembly.

"My father is," she started, exhaling. "I don't know what my father is, but it's not who he once was."

Rohan looked over the reports before leaning back. "Well, I suppose he is different. I doubt he'll ever be the same."

And it was true. But she wasn't the same either, and still, she persisted. "He's losing his grip, Rohan. Over himself. Over the throne." Her father, in her opinion, had come to the end of his rule. The grief was too heavy to bear, the loneliness something he could not wade through. And with the unknown future looming over them...she was not confident he could protect them. Protect Rersa. But she could. "I think it's time a different Zūne sat the throne," she said, meeting Rohan's eyes.

It was something she hadn't let herself admit—that she wanted the Obsidian Throne. Before she'd been scared of threatening her father, but now, she was more scared of what might happen if she didn't.

Rohan blinked. If he was surprised, he didn't show it. "That is a decision you cannot take back, Princess."

"I wouldn't."

"If you believe you're ready, you know I'll stand with you," he said, calmly. "But it will change things, Elaia. Between you and your father. If the decision is not his...it will change everything."

Elaia rolled her eyes. "I shouldn't have to wait for him to decide I'm ready. I've decided. That's enough." Her father had barely ruled the last three years at all. Why should he continue to sit the throne because he was too afraid to give it up? She was afraid of what would happen if he didn't.

He held her gaze. "Anything from Liev?"

"Over the Scions you don't even believe I've seen?" She knew what Rohan and Zahra thought. That she had read one too many of her mother's stories or too many tales, that she was imagining them, dreaming of them. So she'd stopped mentioning it.

"If you believe you have, then—"

She interrupted, "No, Rohan. Nothing in the report."

He dipped his head. "I'll leave you for now. You look..."

"Exhausted?" Elaia's lips quirked.

"Something like that."

Sometimes it threw her off how quickly he could go from stoic and calculated to gentle and compassionate when it came to her. Rohan stood and bowed his head. "We'll train again tomorrow. I'll have tea sent to you before your meeting with Vittoria."

"Thank you." Elaia sat back as he silently slipped out, leaving her alone.

It was dangerous at times, leaving her to stew in the silence, in the thoughts that swirled through her head. To wade through the dense fog that made it impossible to see the path. Her shoulders fell under the weight, and she heaved out an exhale. The day was not done, not yet. She had agreed to meet with Vittoria Farr, the heir of Azias, and then, she could rest.

Elaia watched the princess's ship anchor in the deep seas. Often, because only so many were allowed on the Elderlands, council members or heirs who hadn't come waited offshore in the depths of the Syros Ocean.

The beams extended from each ship, meeting in the middle to make a bridge. She took deep breath. Though it wasn't his job to comfort her, Rohan placed a hand on the small of her back. A brief, steadying touch.

Vittoria appeared, her pure blonde hair streaked with white

and silver-colored strands throughout, brightening her appearance. Elaia often found her disarming. The bright, soft hair, and the hooded doe eyes made Vittoria look inconspicuous. Something she was not.

"Vittoria," Elaia said, extending a hand as the princess approached. The ships held steady, the water calm beneath them.

She smiled crookedly. "How lovely to see you again, Elaia."

Elaia sighed. "What can I do for you?"

"Nothing of great importance. I heard about the Elders. Tragic, isn't it?" Vittoria's orange-brown eyes narrowed with a tilt of her head.

"Valora will certainly never be the same." *In so many ways...* Elaia kept her shoulders back. She hated this partnership more than anything. But it was vital. To prepare for what would be unleashed, working with Vittoria was a sacrifice she had to make.

"No." The princess smiled. "I suppose it won't." With a wave of her hand, Vittoria held out her palm, her guard quietly placing an envelope in the center. "Anyway, I only wanted to personally invite you to Eisera's coronation. And my official engagement to the prince."

A sly smile took over her face. Genuine or not, Elaia wasn't sure. But there was a warmth on her face that wasn't there moments ago. *Or it's all just an act...*By her side, Elaia tapped her finger against her thigh no less than seven times.

"Yes, it'll be very exciting. You must come." The princess's fingers found the necklace that served as her engagement present —intricate silver woven together like vines, decorated with emerald and iridescent stones. "They said the Witch left tears of blood, like the Cardinal. I suppose the Vahls will let us know what she looks like soon enough. What do you make of all this? The Elders? The Witch?"

Elaia raised a brow. "Does it matter what I think?"

"It matters what you do." Vittoria cocked her head, like a bird.

"I will do as I'm told and as I see fit." She clenched her jaw. "Is that all, Vittoria?"

She hummed. "I also wanted to ensure you received our latest request?"

For more members of her Nightguard, as per their alliance. "The request will be honored. As it always is."

Finally, Vittoria dropped the doe-eyed act. Her eyes narrowed, as sharp as a hawks. She studied the Princess of Shadow. "Good. You're not a stupid girl, Elaia. Always making the smart decisions."

The air became tense, tight. She was unsure if it was Vittoria's doing, whether or not the princess had the air wrapped around her finger, or if it was just a reaction of a hostile environment.

When in fact, this was one of her stupider decisions. An alliance she'd agreed to without her father. The Nightguard for more trade routes, for more security. She still had to tell him.

"I am so glad we could work out a deal. Especially now with the Elders dead. We only want to protect ourselves. Our loved ones." Vittoria's eyes turned icy. "Right?"

Even thinly veiled, Elaia could pick out a threat. She pressed the onyx ear peace twice, her guards rounding the deck of the ship with two Air Elementals with them.

"Of course. But perhaps you should keep a better eye on your own first."

Vittoria's lips twitched in annoyance, eyeing the two guards now on the deck. They seemed to have climbed up from the sea, stealing the air of the crew members to walk undetected. But she knew. She had been waiting. King and Queen Farr had patience, something their daughter lacked. She was also used to getting her way.

"Thank you for the invitation, Vittoria. I'll be in attendance. For now, I must return home."

Vittoria tipped her chin, her icy-blue gown clinging to her fair skin in the breeze. "I shall see you soon, Your Highness."

As quickly as she had come, Vittoria retreated back to her

ship. The smallest amount of pressure lifted from Elaia's shoulders, and the air literally lightened. Across the gap, the two stared off at each other, Elaia unwilling to back down first.

Air Athera were tricky. Sometimes Elaia thought they were more like the Naturalists than anything. They were peaceful on the surface and as written in much of the history books. But they were like splinters. Stuck under your skin before the pain could even register. And they were disciplined. Almost all of them were required to train at the air academy high up on the Floating Isle of Azias. From then on, no matter what path they chose, whether that was the army, or the government, or even the scientists, they were all powerful. All the force and strength of the Elementals, but they were sly and cunning.

And Elaia hated that she was in this alliance with them. Mostly, she just hated Vittoria. With a sigh, she stood until the princess's ship became a blur. In the light of the setting suns, Elaia returned to her rooms, the exhaustion and disbelief rearing their heads again, her thoughts once again returning to what had happened.

A Witch. Gods, she wanted to laugh. A *Witch*.

And a Witch who killed the Elders. *Who could've ever predicted this?*

Her mother could've.

The thought hit her hard and fast, like a blade of fire piercing her heart. Her mother was obsessed with the Witches, what had happened to them, if they would return. Namora spent hours in the library, hours poring over the massacre, studying every word she had access to. Even when they went into the small towns, Nomara snuck them into those tiny shops—*mystic shops,* her mother would call them—to listen to them spout prophecies or tales. Claiming they could read the stars and predict the Witches return. Elaia and her sisters were there for it all. Because her mother believed truth was often hidden within what was written.

Elaia had never feared the Witches; she simply wanted to understand them. Though, it was hard to understand something that didn't exist. And as she got older, she cared less about things that she couldn't control or study, so she stopped paying much mind to Nomara's stories. Something she wished she could rectify now.

Maybe the stars predicted this.

Maybe the shadows had. Because shadows talked, too.

Others, namely the Elementals, believed they were nothing more than an envoy of darkness, and there were things they would never understand. She knew this was only the beginning. Darkness was coming and not the kind she could control. Only the kind she could brace for. She'd felt the shadows in her home in Aeledin, slinking under the doors, whispering along the walls like wraiths.

She wove a wispy shadow through her fingers and watched it dance around her wrist. Shadows didn't always share the things they knew, no matter how much she begged them to. But they were a constant—her constant—in a world where, more often than not, Elaia felt alone.

As if the sea could feel the pain emitting from deep within Elaia's chest, large swells rocked the boat. A loud snap as the waters racked the wood. A rumble under foot, a quake. Others would've been discomforted by the movement. Thrown off balance.

But Elaia barely noticed.

Her life had been off-balance since the moment her mother and sister disappeared three years ago. Since the moment she found Shaye no longer breathing in her chambers.

It would take a miracle for her to ever feel steady again.

CHAPTER 10

CLOAKING NIGHTMARES

ELAIA WOKE UP IN A ROOM OF SHADOWS.

They were pressing in on her from every angle, winding around her arms and legs and locking her to the bed. Her head swam. Images of her mom and sisters the last time she saw each of them—there one moment and gone the next. They appeared in other ways, too, not memories, but nightmares—nightmares of them lost in the Shadowlands. Locked in a dungeon beaten and bloody. Them screaming for help, only for it to go unheard. Her mind had a knack for conjuring answers where she didn't have them. And she remembered the grief that sank into her father like a ghost, eating away all the parts of him she'd once loved.

Her throat was raw and scratchy as she blinked her eyes open. Shadows were wrapped around her neck—something her subconscious had discovered would wake her up. Elaia shot up, heaving for air. Water dripped from her eyes, residual effects from the lack of air, and drops of sweat beaded on her shoulders.

Years. It had been years since she saw them. But the nightmares remained.

She'd tried everything from teas and herbs, to working with healers that believed in 'healing the mind,' to breathing techniques and stretches. She even tried chugging coffee to try and keep awake through the night.

Nothing worked.

She downed the water on the table beside her bed and placed her feet on the floor. Elaia matched the rocking of the ship, inhaling and exhaling with the motion until the shadows curled in on themselves and disappeared. The sky outside was black but dotted with stars now that the storm had passed.

At her desk, she flipped through the files, leaving most of them to the side. Only in the darkness did she pull out her mother's plans. Nomara had been more diplomatic than Elaia or her father. But she was also more secretive. Studying things her father had deemed unimportant, a waste of time. Things that didn't have answers.

Desmond was a factual person. It was how he raised them, how he led. Nomara was a free spirit—she was mystical, intrigued by the unknown. It was why they had worked so well together. But when they disappeared, much of her research had been tossed to Elaia, her father unable to bear it. Elaia was left to muse over messy scrawlings and half-thoughts on the Athera, on the Witches, on the Gods. But it was the most she had left of her mother. She hadn't read them in full since she received them. Most nights, Elaia just sat here with them, tracing her finger over her mother's handwriting.

There was one page that consisted of only fairytales and stories. Stories Nomara had read to Elaia and her sisters, Rayn and Shaye. Stories of the sprites dancing through the woods, or fearful tales of wraiths haunting in the night. Elaia turned to the page that was dotted with her dried tear stains.

That familiar feeling pricked at her eyes again.

Where have you all gone? Why did you leave me here? She bit her lip and tried to force the tears back. She hated the feeling of missing someone more than anything. It tore a well wide open like a gaping hole and tainted everything it touched.

She rubbed a palm over her chest where the pain radiated

from and closed the folders. There was no use. She would find no answers.

In the silence, she could imagine her mother's voice. *We have not left you. We are always with you.* But it never lasted long since it was no longer real.

Elaia dressed in leggings and a plain cotton shirt before making her way outside, dipping her head to the guard. Goldstones casted shadows from the wooden panels and the low hum of the wheels powering the *Nomara*. She crossed the deck and knocked on the door of another quarter. Rohan appeared, still demure from sleep.

He knew why she was here. The reason never changed.

"Give me a moment." Rohan gave her a fleeting look of concern before disappearing again.

She crossed her arms. The sea air was cool against her warm skin. But the phantoms of the shadows still teased at her nerves. He reappeared, and they silently made their way to a clear, central spot on the deck. Rohan didn't give her a second, swinging first with a thin dagger. She defended, spinning on her heels.

Immediately, her body relaxed. This was a fight she could see.

Shadows danced on her fingertips. With her right hand, she drew the short sharp dagger from her thigh. With quick steady steps, Rohan attacked again, wielding powerful blows one by one. Elaia defended, moving as swift as a dancer. She saw her opening and attacked. Wisps of shadows wound around his wrists.

Rohan smirked. His own shadows joined, large and imposing where her own were like snakes in the grass. They wound around her face, blocking her eyesight, and curled around her legs. She could feel where he was, her shadows still holding on, and sensed the hit coming. Narrowly avoiding the strike, she crouched, kicking out and catching him from below. He stumbled but recovered as he always did, his shadows practically dragging her to him.

They continued sparring. Quick and aggressive. Shadows pulling limbs and spilling secrets. It became mindless. Second nature. Her mind went comfortably numb. They danced over the deck, avoiding the masts, moving over the quarterdeck and back down.

Rohan was an uncompromising fighter—he had to be. But he was masterful. His shadows were heavy, suffocating, but Rohan was swift. Elaia was skilled, avoiding many of his hits, but she knew the ones that landed would turn her skin black and blue. Her shadows twirled behind him, waiting for her. After dodging yet another blow, she went low, spinning over the deck to come up behind him in the dark. Her dagger poised at his jugular, shadows constricting his wrists.

"Careful, Your Highness. You may have the killing blow, but which shadows guard your back?" Rohan said, lethally calm. His breathing barely elevated.

She became aware of his heavy shadows surrounding her. Worse, she felt them wind around her neck, waiting to strike. A lazy showing. Exhaustion pounded at her head, disappointment biting at her heels.

They released one another and stepped back. Beads of sweat rolled down her spine as she surveyed her guard. And her friend.

Rohan sat on the stairs leading to the quarterdeck, calmly wiping his blade. He watched her carefully. Like a wounded animal. "Tell me what you could've done."

She leaned on the railing. "Rohan, please. Not tonight."

"Yes tonight." He joined her, looking over the blackness of the night. "Talk it out."

"There's no good answer. I was more concerned with containing you than guarding myself."

Rohan seared her with a look. "That cannot happen, Elaia."

Her head fell, wisps of her hair brushing her cheeks. "I know that." And she did.

But the grief was a heavy thing. The responsibility saddled to her shoulders threatened to drown her. They were unwanted friends. At times, they felt like her only friends. They took turns battering her, berating her. She felt like a ship in a storm surrounded only by dark clouds. It was moments like these where she wondered if leaving herself unprotected was such a bad thing.

Glancing up, she tracked the stars and the constellations. Unable to stop wondering if her mom and sisters were somewhere she could not go if she still breathed, if her heart still beat.

"Elaia..." Rohan started, but she shook her head.

"You can't say anything I haven't heard before." She turned to look at him, her voice as cold as steel. "So, please. Don't."

He dipped his head. She exhaled, ignoring the prickle of guilt. He'd been her punching bag both physically and emotionally more times than she could count. And yet, he stood by her side.

"We dock in the morning. I'll see you at sunrise." Pushing off the railing, Elaia walked back to her room. Her pain and grief didn't matter. There was work to be done.

They may have left her physically—Nomara and her sisters— but they were still with her, somewhere safe in her heart. But her father, he was still here. Her country, her people, Zahra. They were still here.

So, Elaia would persist.

CHAPTER 11

MAY THE REIGN BE TRUE

More realistically, never thought she would have to be. Some naïve, childish part of her was convinced her brother was going to live forever. Death had a way of surprising people. It slunk under the water, sentient, wading in the calm seas, waiting for the right moment to change the current.

Two weeks ago, the tide Syrena was accustomed to had disappeared.

Everything had changed. She'd been as unsteady as the waves around the Isles of Iyvia. A series of islands deep in the sea that were now under her rule. Where the palace sat, her people were waiting for her arrival. To accept the title of Reyna.

Instead, she stood in the lagoon, waist deep in the Sea of Azu. The tips of her hair were damp, and saltwater misted her skin.

She took deep breaths, holding the oxygen in as her hands drifted over the water. With her eyes tightly closed, she could almost convince herself that her brother was still here. That he was waiting for her on the Serpents Island with a bowl of salted mango all for her. That they would sail smoothly over the waters she'd grown up with and sit under the suns.

"Syrena."

Her focus broke, her daydream shattering. Because he wasn't waiting for her.

Her brother was gone. Today, Zvon should've been attending the assembly in the Elderlands.

Instead, he was dead. Instead, she would be crowned.

Blinking her eyes open, she turned to see Torin, her advisor, waiting at the doors of her chamber. "It is time."

Behind her stood attendants waiting for Syrena to enter the room. With a dip of her head she stepped out of the water and onto soft white sand, her anklets tinkling with her gentle steps. Under the bright suns, her jewelry glimmered, reflecting a rainbow of colors onto the sand. The doors to her room were open, letting the sea breeze float through.

There were no grandiose homes on Iyvia. No towering fortresses. Instead, the royals and citizens lived in salâs—homes that were designed to easily open to the island air, decorated with stones and shells, palm fronds, and green tropical leaves. They were made with light teakwood and often vaulted or domed ceilings. The wood was painted to fit the family or the royal, stained blue to match the sea or shades of green to match the jungles within. On the royal islands or the Serpents Islands, each chamber had access to a private lagoon and docks to travel throughout the islands.

Syrena entered her room. The suncatcher made of shells chimed in the breeze.

Torin's eyes were reserved. She never could tell what her advisor was thinking, but the past week, Torin's solid strength had become unnerving. It made Syrena uneasy, unsure of herself, unsure of whether Torin liked her or not, whether Torin cared for her or not. Torin protected her, sure. But in her weakness, left to fend for herself, obligation suddenly did not feel sufficient.

Torin had known Syrena and Zvon their whole lives. She had promised to serve the Savali's, and she had. For Syrena, she was a teacher and a confidant. It had been Torin's job to train Syrena, teach her, advise her—and she had.

But was it an obligation she was filling to appease the dead King?

Trust had always been a fickle thing, but now, as Reyna, there was no room for that. Trust had to be stronger than stone.

"Come." Velyen, the younger attendant, motioned for Syrena.

Torin dipped her head. "I'll wait in the hall."

Syrena followed the attendants into the bathing chambers. The tub was filled with fresh water, waterlilies and rose petals floating on the surface. She rolled her shoulders, relinquishing control to the attendants and trying to find the tranquility she'd felt in the lagoon as she sank into their care. The warm water and soap cleared the salty residue from her skin, and her long platinum tresses were washed and combed. Their hands were gentle and firm through the bath and after, spreading a balm over her skin.

She watched them in the mirror. Her dressing robe was light, barely touching her deep brown skin as they continued their care. Colorful beads were placed on framing strands of her hair. Her eyes were lined with dark kohl to accentuate her lashes and white kohl on her waterline, drawing attention to the cerulean blue of her eyes. Shimmering dust was brushed over her cheek and collar bones, reflecting under the light.

When Syrena looked in the mirror, for a moment, she saw what other people might. What her people might. A beautiful, resilient girl, ready to take the throne. Syrena saw only sadness in her eyes. She felt only loss.

The older attendant, Ira, stepped in front of her. Ira was caring, gentle. She couldn't speak—or didn't, Syrena wasn't quite sure—so she waited for her to sign with her wrinkled hands. Ira's gray hair was braided away from her face, her warm brown skin recently tanned from the suns, and she smiled comfortingly at her.

"You are a strong girl. But you must believe you are."

"Thank you," Syrena signed with shaking hands.

"Your brother would be proud. Remember that." Ira smiled before departing with the others, leaving her to dress.

Syrena sighed, walking to her dressing room—a room filled with colorful gowns and matching sets. Various sandals lined the floor, and straight ahead, the rest of her jewelry cluttered the surface of a dresser in piles of gold and silver. She knew that some of it came from the parents she'd never known, some from the markets on the islands.

Her favorites now were the ones her brother had left her. The rest had come from a friend, a *lover*, whose name was painful to think about. Though the small *x* scar they shared would be on her skin forever.

She swallowed, running her hand over the fabrics. In her grief, Syrena had not dressed in anything but loose dresses and her swimwear. And now, she had to parade around in a role that still belonged to her brother.

He would not want you to be lost. She turned her face to the ceiling, willing the tear not to fall. *He would want you to be strong. To be sure.*

With a decisive hand, Syrena selected a gown that weaved bright aquamarine and teal together flawlessly. The fabric was practically weightless as she slipped it on. It draped over her feet in one smooth motion, the thick straps squared between her neck and shoulder. It plunged between her breasts and left most of her back exposed. But every inch of her skin was accentuated by the colors. Her hair had been pulled up, wispy pieces framing her face while the beads jingled with her movement.

A necklace of shells sat tight around her throat, and the other, the one she was sure she would never take off, dangled lower, settling on her chest—a carved silver lily, inlaid with a dark pearl at its center. A necklace that her brother had carved himself and worn before her.

In the mirror, she saw herself as they would. As the Reyna.

The only thing missing now was the crown.

Syrena's heart thundered in her chest as she strode through the doors of the throne room. Light streamed through the glass ceiling, colors dancing over the light stone from the sea glass inlaid in windows. Members of the council stood at the end of the aisle, all eyes on her. Behind them and in front of her was a sea of people. All awaiting her.

The heels of her sandals clicked over the aisle of stone, echoing in the silence. Stone pillars decorated with sea glass were placed squarely in the room, one in each quarter. Torin trailed behind her, watching. Guards stood at the foot of the throne, hands behind their backs.

Syrena stalked past with her head high. In private she could crumble to the weight of heavy tears. She could fall to her knees and scream into the sea as long and as loud as she wanted.

In public, she would not falter. Not under the weight of their expectant stares. Not under the pressure that would fall on her shoulders with the crown on her head. Syrena would not give them a reason to doubt her.

She would not disappoint those who'd sat on the throne before her.

With light footsteps, she strode up the steps and paused before the throne. The back was curved like a shell and inlaid with pearls and sea glass. She turned, surveying those watching her. Along with the council, these were leaders of the community—people with the island's best interests at heart.

Syrena inhaled and sank into the throne. It was a relief to have something to physically support her. From here on, she was in many senses of the world, on her own.

"The crown," Torin said, her voice commanding.

Behind the throne, the doors leading to the archives opened, and two guards appeared, holding one glass box each. They stopped diagonally to the throne.

The Regent—Makyai Jone, the Rey or Reyna's right hand—stepped forward and faced the room. Syrena had known him her entire twenty-seven years. He had served her brother without falter. She hoped he would do the same for her.

"Today, we crown the beloved sister of the late Reyn, Zvon Savali. Though we are saddened by his loss and we will greatly miss the friendship and leadership he gave to us in this room, on the shores of our islands, and in the seas. Today is a day to celebrate. Today is the day that Princess Syrena Savali becomes Reyna."

Cheers rang out from the crowd as the light splayed over where Syrena sat. She dipped her head to them, grateful for their initial support.

Within, she couldn't help but wonder was it true? Or did they think her unworthy?

"Princess Syrena Savali has earned our respect and our support. She has sailed beside us, dived beneath the seas to learn the ways of her islands and those that came before her. She has aided us when we needed, supported us when we have fallen, and laughed beside us in times of joy. Today, we celebrate the start of her reign."

The weight on her shoulders grew heavier with every breath. Their eyes bore into her with all the focus of a hawk. Makyai beckoned his hand, opening the glass boxes. He pulled the ring and the spear that was currently compacted into a small handheld rod.

Syrena rose, adrenaline coursing through her veins. Anxiety thrummed against her bones.

"Your hand, Syrena." Makyai spoke quietly enough for only her to hear, and she held out her right hand.

The ring, a white gold signet inlaid with an aquamarine stone, was slipped onto the middle finger of her right hand. Under the sunlight streaming in, the stone reflected the light, beautifully so.

Next came the weapon, though she was positive her brother never used it more than once. Same as the ring, the compacted spear was wrapped in white gold with pearls and various green stones placed in an intricate pattern.

Next came the crown. The base of it was thin, seemingly breakable, but it wasn't. Around the base, they had welded the white gold into the shape of kelp leaves and carved the outline of waterlily flowers into them, small pearls placed all around.

"May the Reyna's rule be long." Makyai lowered the crown, his voice ricocheting around the room.

Her people repeated the words, the echo reverberating around the room. Syrena felt the words sink into her skin. She felt the hopes and the doubt of those who spoke. If she tried hard enough, she could hear the waves crashing on the shores as if they were welcoming her.

"May the Reyna's rule be peaceful."

He lowered the crown. She felt the cool metal against her skin. The weight of the world.

This was it.

"May the Reyna's rule be true."

SYRENA SAT at the head of the table.

Torin was on her left and Makyai on her right. The remaining council members were spread around the table. The main dining hall imitated the throne room with glass ceilings and large windows that allowed the suns to stream in. The windows were open, allowing the salt air to drift in.

Around her, the council murmured amongst themselves while she tried to process it all. Reyna. Who was *she* to be Reyna?

Of course she knew how, hypothetically. Her brother made sure of that. Zvon never wanted kids or to marry. So, he'd ensured the council he would raise her as he would his own heir, so that in the event of his passing, the crown would pass to her. The council had agreed with a stipulation that if she failed to prove worthy of the throne, they could raise a challenger of their choosing within the first year of her rule.

While she never quite wanted the crown, more so because she was a little girl who never wanted her brother to die, she hated failure just as much. She'd been an impeccable student—the top of her class in school and later in university. She'd participated in council meetings since she was a young girl. She'd traveled with her brother across Valora and offered insight when he encouraged her. She was impeccable then, and she would be impeccable now.

Syrena would not fail him, and she would not give them a reason to challenge her.

She knew how to lead.

What Syrena didn't know was how she was supposed to do it —to do anything—without her brother. Zvon Savali was a good man, and he was a *great* king. And the two were not always synonymous. There had been the world with him in it, and now, there was this...this world without him.

Everything was different. There would be no more long walks around the islands, laughing at jokes only the two of them knew. No more boat rides under the suns spent in silence with the waves as their music. No more hugs. No more shared meals. Her brother would be nothing more than a memory floating beside her in the halls.

There was just...no more.

She heard the words he so often repeated to her. *Remember, Syrena, you hold magic in the palm of your hands.* They were as gentle as the morning sea. Still, they broke her heart. She'd never hear them again.

Despite herself, her eyes pricked, and her throat tightened. She could sense the tears building, rising to the surface. Turning, she gazed out the windows, focused on the palm trees swaying in the breeze. Tried to listen for the crashing waves. She stared at the bright flowers blooming on the leafy bushes and birds floating from the sky to the sea. Anything to feel grounded again. To feel like the world wasn't going to crack underfoot.

But then, it did.

They felt it more than they heard it. A rumble under their feet. Plates on the table shook, and the window panes rattled. It was strong, traveling up her limbs and rattling her core.

"A quake?" Makyai inquired, holding the glasses steady on the table.

"No, no." Syrena shook her head. "This feels different. Captain?"

The head of the naval forces, Calix Ravai, dipped her head and crept out of the room. Syrena rose, the rest following suit. "Make sure the citizens are okay. Inspect the islands and find out if there is any surface damage." She strode out of the dining hall and down the corridor until she felt fresh air.

Panic shook her fingers, and her balance felt off. Her brain spun. But she would *not* falter. She took three inhales, accepted what she could not change, and steeled her spine.

She would be strong.

She *was* strong.

Beyond, the waves were swelling. Not enough for a tsunami or major concern but enough to send a prick over her skin. Part of her wanted to retreat, part of her expected her brother to appear, but it was only her. Syrena stepped off the path and dropped to where the ocean met the shore, pressing her hands to the water.

What was happening? She'd felt quakes before, had seen them happen under the surface of the oceans. It was a shifting. Depending on the size, tsunamis might ensue, stone might shatter, or there would merely be a gentle shaking.

She couldn't explain the resounding rumble coming from the below. Couldn't explain how there had been a slight shift in the sound of the ocean waves. Even from inside, even without touching the water, Syrena had heard it. An echo across the water. Almost as if it was in pain.

The ocean talked but only to those who listened.

The water washed over her hands, soaking her gown. She tapped the pearl in her ear. "Torin?"

"Heard."

"We need to dive." She needed to visualize it. To see it. To make sense of it.

"Understood."

The salt water wove between her fingers, practically crawled up her arms, and the sticky salt felt like home. It always would. And she needed to protect it. This, Syrena could do. Be in action. Find a problem and find a solution. She strode toward the arched pathways connecting the stone halls of the Island where Torin stood.

In silence, they walked toward the private chambers, the room tucked behind the throne room and the archives. Light stone gradually shifted to dark blue, inlaid with sea glass. At the end of the hall, Syrena pricked her finger on the needle and let a drop of blood fall into the water-filled stone tray. The blood dissipated until the water was drained and the door clicked open. Upon entering, a guard provided a vile—a mixture of black kelp and extract from the underwater sage.

Water Athera had lungs that functioned at a higher capacity, and their skin adjusted to drastic temperatures, but the serum provided a bit of extra time, along with the masks made out of black kelp that Syrena and Torin fastened on.

Stepping into the private chamber, Syrena pulled on a slippery, reflective wet suit and zipped it up to her neck, throwing her gown on the floor to be collected later. In the center of the room was a platform, a lift that would take them past the underwater city and closer to the sea floor. It had first been built long before her time by Earth Elementals, but during her brother's reign, they had worked to improve its function.

Syrena removed her crown and placed it on the console that mapped disturbances under the sea and stood square on the platform.

"Ready?" Torin asked, eyes firm and steady. Right now, she found that comforting.

"Ready." She sighed but looked forward.

What an introduction to becoming Reyna.

Syrena was cradled by the water.

A few trusted people floated behind her. The deep sea was calm. But below, there was a rift in the sand. The fracture was considerable—at least a mile across the sea floor. Around them, glowfish provided rays of light since the suns did not reach this far below the surface.

Alone, Syrena swam down, manipulating the water to her will. The fissure went farther and deeper than she could see moments ago. It disappeared into the darkness behind the rays of light.

Torin sent a message via pattern through the pearl in Syrena's ear. She spun in the water, facing her advisor who signed, "You are too close." Even under water, Torin's gaze was sharp.

She pressed the pearl, sending her acknowledgment. From the fissure, bubbles floated up, and with the ray of the glowfish, she saw the fleeting reflection of the Aether below the surface. Silver and gleaming, it flowed through like a stream of water. As she moved closer, she noticed little bubbles floating like oil might.

Twirling, Syrena found the Master of the Seas floating behind her. "Commander Ikina, please join me," Syrena signed. Ikina floated beside her. "Have you ever seen this before?'

"Which part?"

She huffed. What a mess. "Either."

"No. Quakes appear differently. A mere crack in the surface, if it's even visible to the eye. Similar to a crack in the stone of a dining table. This looks as though something pried the sea floor open and didn't bother to smooth the edges." Commander Ikina cocked her head, the few bubbles rising past them. "As for those... never."

Syrena took her dagger out of the holster strapped across her thigh. With the blade, she sliced a bubble. Something dark leeched out, floating in the water before dissipating in the darkness.

"Hm." Despite Torin's orders, she swam closer, approaching the tear.

Annoyance flared. She closed her eyes, taking a breath. Torin was doing her job, but it didn't make it any less grating. She eyed the thread of silver swirling within. She'd never seen the Aether before. Not many had. It was closest to the surface at the various Aether points in Valora and managed by the Elders.

Honestly...she expected something more. Something imposing. The Aether seemed surprisingly gentle.

Though she wasn't stupid enough to touch it and find out. That and Torin might tear her head off.

"We will need to inform Professor Caro. He will need to get his team down here. This needs to be collected and studied. Immediately."

"Yes, Your Grace."

Syrena did not bother to correct her, no matter how much the term scratched uncomfortably on her spine. *This is my life now. I have to adjust.* She watched a few more bubbles pass before swimming away. The Reyna navigated her way through the glowfish, felt the water flow through her knotted hair and around her fingers.

Under the sea, it didn't seem so scary.

Becoming Reyna. Wearing a crown.

Amongst the ocean currents, among the fish and creatures swimming along the ocean floor. Among the peaceful whales and the vibrant coral reefs and the ruthless predators. Underwater, ironically, Syrena could breathe.

Better than she could on land, better than with her feet on the ground.

She was the sea. Salt water was in her veins.

Governing over her people would come with time. Learning the ins and outs of what this required, she would learn. But this, protecting the sea, that came second nature.

For now, if that was all, that would be enough.

PART TWO

CHAPTER 12

KINGDOM OF EISERA

Nova was beaten and bruised.

And badly dehydrated.

Salt water crawled its way out of her throat, her stomach heaving as it tried to expel it all. She fisted her hands, coarse sand scratching her palms.

Land. She was on *land*. Thank the Gods.

She was dizzy and tired and deathly ill. Or at least it seemed that way. She imagined this was what being on the verge of death would feel like.

Above, the suns were burning her already burned skin. A whimper of pain seeped out of her mouth as she inched out of the white water. She took a quick inventory of her body the moment she was fully on the sand.

Pain sparked over every inch of her body. Her skin was blistered, and a few of her ribs were bruised or broken. She couldn't tell. There was a stinging pain on the side of her neck. She was almost positive one of her ankles was shattered. She tried her best to shut off the part of her brain that reminded her of the pain. To compartmentalize it.

Like she'd learned to do.

Nova crawled, vomiting salt water with every move.

Eventually, she turned over onto her back, panting under the suns. Their light was blinding, but when she closed her eyes, she saw the sea crashing over her, eating her alive. Black spots danced behind her eyes.

Shit. She needed to figure out where she was.

Was she far from the Vahls? Or were they close by, waiting to strike?

Was she safe? Was she free?

Nova took a deep breath, slowed her pulse with the energy she had, and listened. There were the waves against the shore, the wind whistling above, and the cawing of birds. She'd visited the countries closest to Syris enough to recognize the birds—studied them relentlessly. Syris didn't have much animal life as it was, so she studied it when she could.

With that, she knew she wasn't anywhere near her home. Maybe Rersa or Lazora, but she doubted it. She'd listened to Elaia when she said to go west, but with the storm...she hadn't been so sure. But now, she was.

She threw her head back on the sand.

Nova wavered, her vision fracturing, the world falling away and refocusing in spurts. Every few moments, the pain woke her back up and sent her heart racing.

A shadow fell over her, blocking the suns as she fell back into the limitlessness of her head.

INCESSANT PAIN FORCED HER AWAKE. A sound she didn't recognize echoed around the room, ricocheting back to her ears. Her blood burned, and her head wouldn't stop aching. It felt like it was filled with a heavy weight, histories and things she'd never seen before, things she didn't understand. And her skin was so sore, even the air caused it pain.

"Hey, hey. You're all right. Take a deep breath," a calm voice broke through the dark haze. She could feel a heartbeat, but she couldn't make anything else out. "You have to sit down. You're injured."

There was a brush of something against her skin. "Don't— don't touch me." Her voice was shaky but firm, her skin immediately revolting.

"Okay, I'm sorry. I won't touch you. But you have to lay down."

She tried to focus on what she could smell, feel. Something soft under her hands. The smell of soil and rain and grass. Syris didn't smell like that. It was devoid of smell. But this place—it smelled like life.

She was in too much pain to care. "Make it stop." *Make it stop. Make it stop.*

Nova couldn't tell how many times she repeated the words out loud or in her head. All she knew was that it hurt. And she was so tired of hurting. There was nothing she knew more than pain—all the various forms it came in, all the ways someone could be hurt. And most days, she could turn it off, force her brain to shut down and get through it.

But right now?

She didn't want to hurt anymore.

Through scattered blinks, she saw something green. Leaves or plants, she wasn't sure, but they took over the whole room, leaving a gentle warmth behind. A touch that didn't make her want to crawl away. She let herself fade into the darkness that swarmed around her.

She let pain win.

WHEN NOVA AWOKE for the second time, she was warm. And her throat was no longer scratchy and parched.

She sat up, her head spinning and ribs aching.

"Careful there."

Alarms went off in Nova's head. Where was she? The room was dim, curtains drawn over the windows, and a single goldstone on the wall, casting shadows over the floor. Candles were lit on a table a few feet over and plants decorated every surface, filling the room with the smell of soil and flowers. There was a blanket over her legs, and her scraps of clothes were long gone. Instead, she was draped in a simple cotton.

In the dark corner, there was someone there—the voice, she presumed. "Who are you?"

A man rose in front of her. He was tall and leanly muscled. Warm brown skin was illuminated by the dim lights, and she could just make the sharp cut of his jaw and the cropped dark curls on his head.

"You need to lay back."

Nova shook her head, practically snarling as he took another step. "*Who* are you?"

In the light, she could see the green of his eyes, sharp and focused. "My name is Cyrus. I found you on the sand and brought you here."

His words were calm, his heartbeat steady. Something about him felt honorable, proud. His clothes were clean. The white linen shirt was without a single wrinkle, and his trousers were pressed.

"How long have I been here?"

"Two days. But you've slept through them."

She blanched. Two days? How many days had she lost? How many spent at sea and now this? Was she far enough away from the painful claws of those who had caged her? By the pain radiating warmly from her abdomen and ankle and generally, her entire body, she had no idea how many more she might lose.

Cyrus approached, grabbing a glass off a table. "Here," he said, gently. "You need to drink."

Nova stared, taking the glass but not yet drinking. Despite the watching eyes, she took only a drop of water on her tongue. She had ingested poisons before—for her own knowledge and because she hadn't had a choice. When she detected nothing, she drank the whole cup.

His lips twitched. "I'm going to go get Asha."

"Who's Asha?"

"She's a healer I brought here to help."

Nova hummed but sat back. Regardless of the fact that these people hadn't killed her in two days, she didn't feel safe. What if this was a trick? What if it was really the Vahls making her believe she was on her way to freedom when she wasn't? Was this real or not?

Stop. Breathe. What can I feel?

Based on the tight wrappings around her ankle and her ribs, escaping wasn't an option. At least, not yet. There was nothing in the room that hinted at her location. There were herbs in glass jars and stone, parchment with haphazard scrawlings, and suncatchers hanging from the ceiling.

Nova sighed. If she could manage enough weight on her ankle, maybe she could get to the window. Kicking her legs around with a sharp breath, she felt the hardwood underfoot. With a gentle touch, she pressed her left foot against the floor, only to be met with an instant shot of pain.

"By the Gods," she mumbled. She'd worked through pain before. She could do this. Another press and shot of pain, but she didn't lift it, even as spots appeared in front of her eyes.

The door opened. "Ah, ah. I wouldn't do that if I were you," a new, almost abrasive voice said.

Looking up, she was greeted with whom she assumed was Asha. Even now, she could sense the years of wisdom radiating off the woman. Her dark brown skin shone under the light, and her short white curls bounced with every step. She was short but stood tall, and only a few wrinkles marred her skin.

"I've had to set that ankle twice. If you break it again, I'll cut it off myself."

Cyrus snorted from his spot behind her, his arms crossed as he leaned on the doorframe.

Asha turned. "Be useful. Go fetch the food from the kitchen."

Instead of responding, he dipped his head with a half-smile and shut the door behind him.

Nova blinked. "Do you speak like this to everyone?"

"When I feel like it." Asha approached her, her hand cupping Nova's chin before she could stop it.

She instinctively ripped her head back. "Don't."

"You're going to have to let me look at you. Close your eyes," Asha said, and after a moment, Nova listened. She felt the woman's fingers grab her chin again, softer. "Better or worse?"

Nausea rose in her gut. With her eyes closed, she was bombarded by memories crawling out of the hole she'd tried to shove them in. "Worse." She blinked open her eyes and let Asha study her.

"You have a laceration on the side of your neck, though it's not as bad as it was. Same with the one on your calf. You've two broken ribs, one bruised. The ankle, obviously. The blisters from the suns have already diminished. Aside from that, a few shallow scrapes and a minor concussion," Asha said, stepping back and grabbing something from her table. "You're still dehydrated, and you haven't eaten anything but the broth I fed you. I'd highly advise you don't try to escape until we can get you settled." Asha handed her the tin. "Here. It's a salve for pain; you can put it on yourself now. And I've been fastening crutches together to help you walk. What's your name?"

"Nova," she said, unable to keep from wondering *why* these people were helping her. Did they gain something from it? She spread the salve over the cuts and her ribs. "Where am I?"

The healer spared a quick look toward the door. "You're in Eisera."

The Kingdom of Earth. By all means, here, she should've been free of the Vahls. "Why are you helping me?"

Asha took a seat on the chair that was tucked under the desk. "Well, you were half-dead when I showed up at his request. Seemed inappropriate to leave you that way."

Nova averted her eyes. She should've felt relief at being here, at being free of the Vahls. But she remembered seeing the dark clouds of the approaching storm at sea. She'd buckled down as best she could. But she didn't pray, didn't call out to the Gods that didn't answer her. She was free, but she didn't feel that way.

Because right here, right now, she *was* free. So why didn't it feel so? This was what she wanted, what she had killed for. Why didn't she feel any different?.

Was freedom more than her proximity to the Vahls? Was it something she would ever be able to truly grasp?

Maybe only death would grant her true freedom.

It would've been an escape—from all the memories that plagued her, the pain that she could not erase, the lives she had taken.

Death, for her, wasn't scary.

Maybe for people like her, death was freedom.

She swallowed, ignoring the way Asha's sharp eyes watched her. A knock on the door drew their attention. Cyrus entered with an overflowing tray. She watched him move around the room, placing the kettle on the desk by Asha, moving each dish onto a table. She felt his heartbeat, calm and steady, slower than many others. Healthy. She was willing to bet he had at least three weapons tucked away somewhere on his person.

Upon closer inspection, she could see more of him. The way his nose was slightly crooked, the dark stubble on his chin and jaw, the dark spots serving as freckles on his brown skin. There was a scar on his left cheek. As he moved around the room, she noted the way his muscles moved smoothly under this clothes. He was confident and sure. Well-trained. There were silver rings on his right hand and swirls of dark ink on his left.

"Can you manage on your own?" Asha interrupted the silence. She nodded.

Cyrus handed her a plate with a bowl of stew and bread, another cup of water placed on the table beside her. He was the only one of them not eating. A brief memory of being carried flashed sporadically in her head. Nothing clear. Just a snapshot of his jaw and the motion of movement. And green eyes. The same green she had seen before darkness had greeted her.

Cyrus gave her a guarded, kind look. "How is she?"

"Fine. Or she will be. She's healing well."

Nova furrowed her brows. "I'm right here." They continued to talk as if she weren't.

"Is there anything you need that I don't have?"

Asha listed off various plants and herbs, to which Cyrus only nodded. "I'll be right back."

"Whatever. We'll be here."

He snorted but dipped his head, sending a piercing gaze her way. It made her heart jump. "Glad to see you're up."

She just watched, barely tipping her head in response as he exited the room. She tracked his heartbeat until she couldn't any further.

Nova turned her attention to the food, overwhelmed by the sheer aroma of it. *Gods*, she was starving. It probably was nothing but a simple soup, but she didn't care, the bread—the *bread!* She was famished. In the haze, she practically forgot about the old woman. Nova could feel her eyes on her.

"What?"

Asha smirked. "Nothing. It's just when I showed up here, I couldn't have predicted this. A Witch."

Well, shit.

Chapter 13

Illusion of Freedom

"I'm not." Nova stared at the healer, choking down the nausea that crawled up her throat.

Immediately, she reached for Asha's blood. She wouldn't make it far with her ankle, but she could escape. Put herself back together in the woods if she had to.

"I suggest not running," Asha mused, reaching for the kettle and pouring steaming water into two mugs, the smell of pomegranate and cinnamon permeating the space. Asha handed her a mug, extra herbs floating on the surface. "I think we should make a deal not to lie to each other."

"How would that benefit me? You could turn me in. You could kill me the moment my eyes drop if you wanted to." Nova's voice was cold, and any kindness from before was gone.

"If I wanted to kill you, I would've done that while you were asleep," Asha said, pulling something out from the desk. "And truthfully, I'm not sure I could have. Not in such short time, at least." A clear dish was placed on the table with a red substance moving around.

Asha took a small magnifying glass and leaned over it. "This is your blood. I hadn't thought anything of it at first; as you could guess, I've seen quite a bit of it. But nothing—*nothing*—like this."

She held it up in the light, and Nova could see it moving. Slowly, barely. But it wasn't coagulating.

"Your wounds shouldn't be partially healed yet. You should be facing infection, continued bleeding. You're not." She twisted the dish. "See that? How it moves? No Athera I've ever healed has blood like this. I've read about this. Once. Twice. Scrutinized blood. But even the scarce Witches I've healed, their blood is just...blood."

Other Witches? There were others?

"Yours is still alive. Dying, yes, but slowly. When you first showed up, your cuts were deep. You should've been bleeding more than you were. But your blood was almost stitching itself together to stop the bleeding. Almost like a healer's, but different. This can only be one thing. You can only be one thing. A Blood Witch." Asha leaned back, crossing her hands over her stomach, watching Nova like this was the most normal thing in the world.

Wasn't she scared?

"Sounds like a myth."

Asha sucked her teeth, a scratchy laugh breaking through. "You're not a stupid girl. I can see that. You're not a weak one, either. Not if your nightmares were any indication. So, you can deny it, but there's no use."

Nova felt cornered. This is what she didn't want. People knowing what she was. It made her feel exposed, trapped.

"So, how about that deal? I'm sure you'll be able to sense a lie, right?"

Nova weighed the options. She could use it to her advantage if she asked the right questions. Learn anything she could before she left.

"Fine." She exhaled. "No lies." Asha waited. "How do you know Cyrus?"

Asha crossed her leg. "He's a friend. Some of the smaller towns don't have many healers or access to remedies. I call on him for help, and he provides it."

"And you help him in return?" The healer nodded. "Did I... did he have anything of mine when he brought me here?"

Asha shook her head. "You had nothing." She stood and went to poke the fire burning in the corner of the room. "Now, drink your tea."

She furrowed her brows. "That's it?"

"For now. Cyrus will watch over you this evening. By tomorrow or the next day, I should be able to repair your ribs. They seem to be the only things not healing at an accelerated rate." Asha tossed her a fleeting look. Nova realized she wasn't *just* a healer. She was an Athera. A Naturalist. "And I'm not going to turn you in. I don't believe in the lies we've been told about the Witches. Even now, centuries later, I've seen the occasional Witch hunt. And they're nothing but violence, born of fear and tales that have been too far spun. Unless you give me a reason," Asha said, shrugging, "I gain nothing from it. You certainly don't."

A beat of silence. *Was it too good to be true?* Could she trust Asha? Did she have a choice? "Okay."

Asha left the room, leaving her to mull in the quiet with only the crackling fire to join her.

Despite the healer's words and her deal and that for centuries, the healers had been known to uphold a code of honesty, a code to the patient, Nova hesitated.

Trust was not something she felt nor extended to people because trust was always broken. There was no tangible reason she should believe Asha. As far as she knew, most kingdoms had a standing rule that if a Witch was found or thought to be found, they were to be killed. If that existed here, maybe Asha was simply biding her time. Nova would have to be prepared. For anything.

Exhaustion rattled her bones. She was so godsdamned tired.

Tired of running along the edge of a cliff, waiting to see what might push her over the edge.

Nova was just tired.

Nova walked through a graveyard littered with bones, two burning red suns above in the sky. She walked over gnarled roots of oak and willow trees, blood spilled on the forest floor. Shadows danced at the edges of her vision. And her head—her head ached in pain. Battered by blurred voices echoing painfully in her eardrums. An echoing laugh followed her through the trees and sent goosebumps over her spine.

It was then she saw the blood dripping down her hands. Onto the leaves below.

Drip.

Drip.

Dr—

Nova sprung over the side of the bed, heaving.

"Another dream?" Cyrus spoke, sliding a bucket to her. Nothing came out, but nausea sat heavy in her stomach.

"Another?"

"You had multiple when you first arrived." He handed her a cup of a tea, the dish warming her palms. For a second, she thought blood coated them. Until she blinked and the blood was gone. "I'm surprised you don't remember. You thrashed and called out multiple times. Some in fear, some in warning."

She hummed, taking a sip of her tea. Further rested, she paid attention to her body as a whole. There were remnants of the pain she felt on the Elderlands. She wasn't sure it ever went away. It felt like something was trying to claw out of her head, shredding the walls she'd built to protect herself from the inside out. Looking down, she studied the cut on her calf. Long and deep, honestly, it should still be bleeding. But the scab was thick. She'd never paid much attention to cuts she received from Mikel and Mireya.

Most of their injuries were internal or blunt force. They preferred to make her bleed from the inside.

"Would you like to discuss—"

"No."

Cyrus raised his brows. "Understood. I'm going to grab Asha so we can fix your ribs." She sipped her tea, sitting in pain until they returned. Rays of light seeped in through the window, and a breeze drifted through the room, smelling of damp soil and rain.

Asha entered and said, "Let's take care of these breaks."

"Finally. I'd like to breathe without pain."

"Keep that attitude up, and I'll make it so you never so much as blink without pain," Asha said, lethally composed. Her dark-brown eyes, as dark as the hallways of a library, were piercing.

Nova quite liked the indestructible old woman. "Understood."

"Lay back." Asha turned, motioning to Cyrus. "You'll need to stay."

"Why?" She looked between the two, apprehensive.

"Your ribs will be painful, but you will manage. If you want that ankle healed, you'll need to be held down. It's been reset multiple times, and you have a torn ligament. You'll be in unbearable pain." Asha turned to him. "Come here."

"No."

Asha rolled her eyes. "By all means, if you'd like to tough it out, be my guest. I'll have him wait until you pass out."

"Do I have a say in the matter?" Nova flexed her ankle, sharp pain shooting up her leg.

Honestly, she'd been partial to believing Asha wasn't healing her ankle only to keep her here. She'd battled through pain, pushed herself beyond her limits, but even she knew her ankle was badly broken. Anytime she tried to place weight on it, she almost passed out.

But the thought of being held down was just as bad.

"I thought you were supposed to be healing me," she said. "How painful can it be?"

Asha's white curls draped over her forehead. "You've never been healed before?"

Looking up at the ceiling, Nova felt the echoes of every cut, every scar, physical or not. "No."

The healer hummed, rubbing a balm over her palms. "I can't say how much. Everyone is different," she murmured, giving Nova a sidelong look. "But I imagine you've felt your fair share of pain." Brown eyes lingered on the scar on Nova's throat.

Instead of responding, she turned her face to the ceiling. Whatever it was, she would get through it. She sighed as Cyrus approached, taking up space behind her, his hands hovering over her shoulders. There was a brief memory of being carried, a strong determined face looking down upon her. Nova steeled herself and stilled.

The first touch of Asha's hand was as alarming as ever. Harrowing tingles spread over her skin as her shirt was rolled up to reveal the wrappings around her ribs. *In and out. Just breathe.* The wrappings were cut.

"Ready?"

"As I'll ever be." She focused on herself, slowing her heartrate. Moments later, she felt the larger, cooler hands of Cyrus on her shoulders. Her pulse jumped, and she swallowed thickly.

"Are you all right?" he spoke softly, only for her ears.

Looking up, she saw the gentle green of his eyes. Like leaves in the summer sun. Moss on a sun bleached rock. She nodded. Their hands pressed harder, and his ensuring her shoulders were pinned was enough to bring about the nausea.

But it was Asha's hands that sent a spark up her spine. "Let's begin."

The touch was gentle, at first a simple press over the bruised ribs. Heat radiated over her skin, as if standing too close to a fire. Asha's hands firmly pressed on her as Cyrus's did. And it burrowed, like a knife twisting over and over again. It was a strange sensation, a painful thread weaving around her bones and her ribcage.

The pain was searing. She could feel the individual fragments of each break or bruise. Her blood rushed to the area, unused to this feeling, as if trying to protect her. Asha's power felt golden, like the sun's rays in the morning, searching to eradicate the darkness. Despite herself, Nova thrashed as it continued pulsing through her. She dug her nails into her palm, trying to keep herself still.

"Not much longer, Nova." Asha pressed harder, each fingertip digging into her skin.

It wound tightly around her ribs, squeezing, pulling, tearing. Sweat beaded over her skin as she fought to stay still. There was a final push, black spots dancing behind her eyes, and then, as quickly as it came, it was gone.

But their hands stayed in place and breathing did not come easy. Asha took a moment to press a cool cloth against her skin. "They'll be sore for a day or two longer, but the break is healed." There was caution in her eyes. "Ready for your ankle?"

Looking up, she found Cyrus looking down at her. Sure and steady. "Okay."

But this time, as soon as that heat burrowed under her skin, black dots swam behind her eyes. All the pain coming together as one.

And for Nova, it ended as soon as it began.

When she awoke, the room was dim, and outside, the suns had fallen behind the trees. Cyrus was asleep in the armchair tucked into the corner, and Asha sat by her bed.

"Finally."

Nova snorted, pushing herself up. She pressed a hand to her ribs; only a flicker of pain returned, and when she flexed her ankle, she could do so with only minimal pain. Asha moved quickly, handing her a tray of food and water.

"I'll need to heal it once more, but until then, keeping it wrapped will suffice."

"A bit of a scam that healing causes so much pain," she said, taking a long sip. Her curls were frizzy and misshapen; her clothes, though clean, were wrinkled, and she smelled like the medicinal balm.

"If it came easy, it wouldn't be worth the effort."

"You have your opinion. I have mine."

Asha cocked her head, flickering her eyes between Cyrus and herself. "I felt something when I was healing you," she said, lowering her voice. "Something calling for help."

A chill went up her spine. What could she have felt? Memories? Her dreams? The things she'd done? Or would Asha find broken parts of herself Nova couldn't see?

"I would rather not discuss my long history of pain."

The healer rolled her eyes. "That's not—it was something else. I know pain. I recognize it in all its forms. It felt like repressed memories. Though I'd have to feel it again to understand how what I felt in you differs."

She stared into the bowl of soup. She cared not for what she had forgotten. No. She was afraid of learning what else had been done to her. "I don't have a desire to bring forward memories my mind chose to repress."

"Things have a way of making themselves seen, whether you want them to or not."

She sighed. There were things, pieces of herself and her life, she had no knowledge of, like the years before she woke up in the dirt. There were things she didn't know were real or not. Memories tortured out or into her in the basement of Froststone. The thought of them was enough to haunt her in the night, to follow her around like a ghost. She couldn't imagine what they might be in the light.

If they broke through, she would face them. But she would not search for them.

All she wanted was to disappear.

Asha met her eyes. "I could help you. Whenever you decide to ask for it."

"Thank you. I'll remember that." She was torn between trusting and untrusting this woman. She wanted to believe Asha was good, honorable, as healers were supposed to be. And yet, she was unsure.

Asha patted the bed beside her. "I'm going to leave you. You should eat and rest. If he wakes, tell him there's food for him on the desk."

Nova dipped her head, looking him over as he slept. The flames from the hearth cast shadows over his dark skin like a painting. She reveled in the silence of the room. Only the sounds of the trees in the breeze outside and the fires snaps echoed throughout.

She closed her eyes, willing sleep to come to fight the exhaustion battering her inside and out. There was a moment that she felt sleep arrive, the soft edges of it, as though it was welcoming her. And she let it.

IT WAS SOMETIME in the darkness of the night that more nightmares dragged her from sleep. Her heart pounded in her chest, and her nails dug into her palm. Her throat was scratchy, as though she'd been screaming. Cyrus was no longer in the room; it was only her and the flickering light of a candle.

Nova crawled out of bed on unsteady feet, approaching the small basin of water beneath the mirror.

As soon as she faced it, an echoing pain shot through her head.

Ah. Her legs buckled as the echo became louder. The pain sharper.

"They are false. They are sick. You must find the truth before it all turns to lies. Or you will never be free."

The words of the dead Elder were not just a memory; it was as if the Elder was in her head, shouting at the edges of her mind. And when she looked up, it wasn't only her reflection she saw.

No. It was the face of each Elder she had killed, blurred and iridescent as they stared at her.

Their mouths moved with no sound. Instead it pounded and repeated in her head, like shattering glass. *"The truth of the world has gone rotten. The truth of the world has gone rotten. If you run, we will follow. You cannot turn away, you cannot turn away."*

"Oh, Gods. Get out, get out, get out," she murmured, horror wrapping around her like the wind. The words repeated.

The truth of the world has gone rotten.

If you run, we will follow.

Her eyes would not shut. Tears ran in rivulets down her cheeks, some dark with blood. Her chest ached, as though there were claws within her, tearing her apart.

The voices grew louder. The shapes in the mirror grew closer. Suffocating. She could feel them surround her. *"You cannot turn away. You cannot run. We will follow."*

She wasn't safe in her sleep nor in the moments of reality. All she had wanted was her godsdamned freedom. To have the chance to be something, *someone,* that existed outside of what the Vahls had made her. But it was all a lie. Her *freedom* of landing on Eisera was an illusion. She wasn't free. She wasn't safe.

She collapsed to her knees, hand gripping at her throat.

Freedom didn't feel like much of an option anymore. Because if she left, would they truly follow? Haunt her until she went mad? Would they demand from her until she gave in?

Placing her hand on the floor, she tried to ground herself, but there was no blood to be controlled, nothing that would help.

She'd escaped one crown only to end up at the mercy of the dead.

She sobbed until her tears ran dry, until her blood stopped falling. And in the reflection of the blood beneath her, she saw the Elders once again.

Her life was not her own. It never had been.

It probably never would be.

CHAPTER 14

PLAGUE OF THE DEAD

NOVA DID NOT SLEEP.

Not since the Elders began to infect her reflections. When she tried to sleep, it would not come. Dreams plagued her. Shapeless darkness and lethal words kept her from resting. And in daylight, in every reflection, they would appear.

Exhaustion was all Nova knew.

She wanted, so badly, to go. To run. But even the thought of attempting escape had her mind shattering with pain. Her freedom was no longer up to her.

Nova laid there, on what had to be the third or fourth morning, and stared aimlessly at the ceiling. She could hear Asha and Cyrus in the other room. She could feel their heartbeats, and sometimes, she swore she could feel the heartbeats of the Elders who haunted her now.

Though she was sure it was a side effect of her exhaustion.

It was endless. Dark and violent and devouring.

And all of a sudden, she felt it creep over her again, like dark clouds in the sky. *No, no. Please. It's enough—*

Her eyes would not open. Her mind would not stop. And her body would not move.

The darkness fluttered behind her eyelids and pulsed in her head.

A dark, aimless shape stared back at her. When she moved, it moved. When she breathed, it breathed.

It was a mirror. "Say it..." it whispered, with no mouth or teeth or eyes. "Say it. Say it. Say it."

But her mouth was stitched together, and no words would fall. She clawed at her head, and the mirrored shape did the same. "Say it, what you fear. What you know. Say it..."

And she screamed, "My life is theirs. My life is theirs. My life is theirs."

Somewhere between waking and sleep, tears fell from her eyes that would not open.

If she was free, what of her belonged to whom?

She wasn't sure what stopped it—no more tears to fall, no more parts of her to hurt—but eventually, it ended. It left her with nausea heavy in her gut.

It was obvious she would not be leaving here. Not yet, at least. Her freedom had not yet been earned. So how was she going to appease the dead? They didn't speak to her straight, didn't tell her what they wanted. They just...haunted her.

You cannot run. We will follow.

The truth of the world has gone rotten.

She pulled herself into a seated position with her head on her knees. *Focus.* She was in Eisera, home to the other major library of Valora—the Emerald Library. Could that be the way?

She swore, within her, some of the exhaustion peeled back like a film, as though it was repelled by her thought. If she could get to the Emerald Library, she could find the archives. Find whatever bloody rot and falsities the dead demanded of her. Find the truth they were so insistent had been buried. Maybe find out more about the Witches in the meantime.

Another layer of weight removed from her shoulders. Was that them? The dead? Silently telling her that she was on the right track? Another smaller pressure relieved. Of course, the dead would find a way to communicate with her. After all, she'd been the one to kill them.

Gods, what is happening to me? Nova buried her fingers into her curls, pressing her palms against her eyes. The consequence of her decision was worse than she could've imagined.

There would be no peace, no rest—not until she did what the dead demanded.

NOVA SAT IN THE ROOM, unblinking and unmoving for hours. The suns had risen, light leaking into the room.

Eventually, Cyrus appeared in the doorway, his curls slightly damp. "You're up. How are you feeling?"

She trailed her eyes over him, unable to help herself. "I'm all right," she said. Could he sense the lie?

"How about some fresh air?"

She stared at him for a moment, wondering again what they wanted from her. Would they let her go? Could she use them to get to the library?

She stood, placing her foot on the ground gingerly, thrilled when she was only met with a dull ache. "Where's Asha?"

"She's resting in the other room. She'll most likely return home this evening." He held the door for her as she padded down the halls.

Plants hung from pots in the ceilings and sat upon every table she saw. The walls were painted in shades of green and brown and yellow in various patterns, making it look like art itself. She noted the rooms as they passed—a bathing room, a bedroom, and what looked like a small library.

They approached the ebony wooden door, etched with designs and finished with a delicate glass doorknob. Though it appeared to be a simple home, it was stunning, filled with knickknacks and beautiful things. He pulled the door open and stepped into the suns.

Nova couldn't help but let her eyes linger. Under the sun's rays, he was striking.

His deep brown skin was warm and smooth. From above, sun rays danced delicately over every exposed inch. A simple cream linen top was draped over his chest and arms, tucked into dark brown pants. The cut of his muscles were defined under the suns and light reflected off the silver of his rings. Short dark-brown curls danced in the soft breeze, but his eyes—Gods, his eyes. Shades of fresh moss and the deep forest swirled together, flecked with golden bronze.

She wasn't often enticed by beautiful things; she found them to be the most threatening. Froststone, the Vahls, the ocean. All beautiful. All deadly.

But he was a vision. And even she was not immune to glaring beauty.

There was a smirk pulling at his lips, but he said nothing.

She rolled her eyes. With her strength back, despite her lack of sleep, she was able to feel his blood. Though to her surprise, his head was well-guarded. An intricate fortress with no way in. Those that did not interact with Spirit Naturalists on a regular basis usually had weaker guards. Nova eyed him for a second, but then turned to the world around her.

The smell of rain lingered in the air, and the scent of damp soil and flowers overwhelmed her senses. It was wondrous. Large oak trees towered over the home with gnarled roots and limbs, their twisted branches winding through the woods. Heavy green leaves casted shadows from the suns that peeked through the foliage. At their base, blooming daffodils were dotted colorfully against shades of brown and green.

Following, Nova took the time to study him, too. He walked softly, springy. As if he was a part of the ground beneath him. He led them beyond the stone path and onto firm soil. The trees welcomed him, the suns cutting through the trees glistening over his skin. On his left arm, movement caught her eye, and she watched, intrigued, as vines wound around his skin and his fingers, serving as living, breathing jewelry. It confirmed what she already believed—he was an Earth Elemental.

Eventually, they reached a bench along the dirt path under the canopy of trees. In the silence, she swore she could hear the trickle of water somewhere. "So, you found me?"

Cyrus sat beside her on the rounded bench. "I did."

"And you carried me here?"

"I did."

"Why? Is it the whole damsel in distress thing?

He laughed at that, a gentle sound. "Not at all. Was I supposed to leave you bleeding and injured?"

Nova shrugged, because honestly, she probably would have. "A project then?"

"Are you determined to find some underlying scheme of mine? Would you like me to apologize for saving your life?" His lips twitched, fighting a smile.

"No," she said, watching birds flit through the trees, their calls the music of the forest.

"All right then." Cyrus turned those forest eyes on her.

He studied her, a smile playing at his lips but a sharp glint in his eyes. Looking for an indication of who she was maybe? She wasn't sure.

She hummed, studying him right back. "And Asha?"

Cyrus laughed again. "She's a good healer. One of the best. I stumbled across her years ago. She's a little nuts, but she's a good one."

She let the silence return. Butterflies floated over the flowers, and the grass twitched with bugs she couldn't see.

"Where were you sailing to?"

She swallowed. *Go west*, the princess had told her. And that worked for her. All she wanted was to escape the Vahls, not that she would tell him that. No, this was her chance to find out if he could help her escape the dead. She'd been preparing her lies.

"Here, sort of. I was studying in Vilies, at the Eternal Library, and I...left unexpectedly and aimed here, to continue my studies in the Emerald Library."

She needed him to believe her weak, innocent even. Anything that kept him from looking at her too closely. Luck that it had been the shores of Eisera that she washed up on. The Emerald Library was the second largest library in Valora, second only to the Eternal Library in Vilies, the neighboring country of Syris. As far as she knew, both held miles upon miles of books kept by members of the Magistrate within their extensive archives.

She only hoped she could find what the Elders wanted from her.

"You're a scribe?"

Nova shrugged, keeping her heart calm. "A recent choice, I admit. It's been a hard two years, passing their tests and the interviews. They're a lot harder on the late comers."

Cyrus smiled. "I've heard. The Emerald Library is stunning."

"You've seen it?"

"A few times," he said, and Nova twitched her fingers, feeling the pulse of his blood. "I could bring you there. It's in Izlena."

The capital. She needed his help, but she was on edge. Who was he? And *why* was he helping her? Was she paranoid? Anxious?

Nova sighed. It didn't matter. This was what she needed. "How? I would appreciate it very much."

"I work for the Slaters indirectly. I'm one of the head engineers for Izlena. I help maintain the infrastructure. But I grew up with them, studied in the library as a kid and even now." He glanced at her. "The Creators that reside here spend a lot of time there, and I work closely with them."

His heartbeat was steady, not that of a liar, and right now, there was no reason to believe otherwise. "So *you* spend a lot of time there."

"Precisely." Cyrus smiled. "Once you're healed, we'll leave for the city. If I remember correctly, they'll need to confirm your records, and then, you'll have all the access you need."

Bleeding suns. She'd forgotten about the bloody records. A sharp pain pricked her neck. The weight of the Elders returned. Even so, the two desires fought against each other—freedom and truth. But with them in her head, there was no freedom without the truth.

They were intertwined, threads she couldn't untangle.

"Thank you," she said, dipping her head. "If your work calls you in the city, why do you stay out here? Wherever here is."

"Cydros. The only thing between us and Izlena are the mountains." The wind whistled through the trees. "I like the silence. The distance, I guess. A lot of my job requires me to work with the world around me. To understand it. Out here, there's no one to interrupt that. And it's better than working underground."

The suns danced over him, and he tipped his head to meet it. The vines sat still and calm. Looking at him, it was obvious. Of course, there was a sense of home within any Athera's element but some more than others. Cyrus felt like a vital part of the earth. More so than any other Earth Elemental she'd met.

"That makes sense." She eyed him. "I can't imagine growing up somewhere like this."

The entire world was alive around her. The world didn't have a heartbeat or blood, but there was something about it that felt similar. Obviously, she knew the soil and trees and plants were all living things, but she'd never *felt* it like this. All around her. Syris was the opposite of this—dead and lifeless.

"I've never seen anything like it. I've been to many of the eastern continents but..." She thought of all the times she'd traveled, only to drain the blood of someone she was ordered to. "None like this."

"I'm probably biased, but it is my favorite place in the world," Cyrus spoke melodically. "I grew up running along these mountains and under these trees. Before I was ever taught to control the earth, I learned from it. Listened to it. And I did it here." He glanced at her. "Wait until you see the rest. This is only a little piece of it."

She nodded, almost jealous, that he had a home like this, and the movement made her head spin. Sighing, she pressed her fingers to her temple. She was weak. She could try to deny it or fight it all she wanted, but she was tired, her body beaten. "Sorry, my head—this is awful."

"Here let's go back. Maybe Asha has something to help." Cyrus extended his hand but quickly extended the vines beyond that. "You can hold onto these if you want."

"I'm all right." Her legs were shaky, but she was determined.

Her strength had to come back eventually, even if she forced it. They moved slowly toward the house. Smoke climbed out of the chimney and into the sky, the smell of wood burning permeating the air. As they entered, Asha greeted them from the kitchen, stirring something on the stove.

Candles were lit throughout, a clean smell mixing with the burning wood and whatever she was making. "I see you've made yourself at home." Cyrus leaned on the wall as Nova collapsed into a chair at the carved wooden table.

Asha clicked her tongue. "What else did you expect?"

"Nothing. Nothing at all. Can I help?" The healer only nodded and began instructing him in his own space.

She could barely move. The ache in her head was traveling down her spine and into every crevice of her body. There was a movement beside her, and she blinked the haze out of her eyes to see the old crone watching her with a narrowed gaze.

"There's nothing you can do for these?" she asked, indicating her head.

Asha frowned, a frizzy gray curl flopping over her forehead. She lowered her voice when she said, "Not if you won't let me in. I can take the ache away temporarily, but it's more than that."

Well *that* wasn't an option. Nova hadn't told her or given any indication of her affinity for spirit. Aside from the general fear of uncovering memories, she did not want her entire life exposed. There were time periods she had no memory of herself, and the memories she did have...those weren't for anyone else to see.

"Can you give me anything? Tea? Tonic?"

Asha sighed. "Come with me," she mumbled before going down the hall, waiting for Nova to follow. She felt Cyrus's eyes on her as she left, but he said nothing. Asha shut the door behind her and began rummaging through various jars and container.

"Listen here, wherever you go, you be careful."

"Asha—"

"No. Listen. Whether you remain here in Eisera or go somewhere else, you be careful. I don't know your story. I don't care to. It's your own. But you are a Witch. And you need to watch your back."

Nova's face was stoic. Unphased. As if she hadn't been watching her own back for years. No one else was. She was all she had. And she intended to keep it that way.

"I'm not a fool, Asha, no matter what you might think."

"I don't think you a fool. That's the problem." Asha stepped closer, looking down at her, even though the healer stood shorter. "You're smart. Strong. I could feel it when I healed you. But you have much to learn. About who you are, about the world. Understand?"

More shit for her to learn. More truths buried. But she didn't care. Maybe she didn't *want* to know the truth. Then, she would have to face it. And face herself.

"I understand, Asha." She sighed. What good would understanding do? It wouldn't change her. It wouldn't erase her past. It was pointless.

"Good. I'm leaving tonight. Believe it or not, some of us have lives we have to get back to. But I've packed you extra clothes in here," she said, pointing to a small bag, "along with the pomades for your hair. But here, this is all I can think of that might help." She plopped a small container of herbs into her hand.

It shouldn't have surprised her—the healers kindness—but it

did. Asha had no obligation to her, yet she was willing to help. "Thank you, Asha. For everything," she said, keeping her eyes downturned. Asha didn't need to see her exposed.

Asha said nothing, only headed back toward the kitchen.

With a sigh, Nova faced the mirror. Instantly, the Elders appeared beside her. Their faces were blurred, ghosts in the night. But their eyes were clear. Alone in the room, with only her ghosts, she felt a painful prick behind her eyes, tears threatening to fall. She blinked and, for a moment, saw blood on her hands and all over the small counter she rested on. All the blood she'd spilled. All the lives *she* had haunted.

Maybe it was only fair. For the others, she was death when she landed upon their door steps. A sickness they couldn't fight, a sickness they couldn't heal.

After all this time, maybe it was only fair that now she, a bringer of death, was plagued by the dead.

CHAPTER 15

HOLLOW WELL

"HAVE YOU RIDDEN BEFORE?" CYRUS'S VOICE WAS LIKE the wind curving through the trees.

Nova eyed the horses. She'd tried riding once. It didn't go well. Horses—animals—in Syris were fearful and irate. Unsettled. They'd been kind to her because she was kind to them.

But that was the extent of her experience.

It also wasn't the default method of transportation. Many of the royals traveled by way of the inventions of the Creators and the Athera, including the Vahls. In the east, it was carriages or coaches powered by the air tunneling mechanisms. In the west, the fire mechanisms, where a single spark could power the machine for hours. Horses were not her forte.

"No, I haven't. I wanted to learn when I began my studies but ran out of time." She turned her eyes to Cyrus. "You prefer traveling by horse?"

"I do. They're useful in my work as well, traversing the terrain, but I love them. There's something calming about them —to me, at least. So unless I have to, I prefer riding." He surveyed the horses and briefly, her. "You can ride with me. Though, I assumed you would prefer to ride on your own."

The thought of sitting in proximity to him, to his skin and hands—a chill danced over her spine. She pressed her lips together. "I'm a quick learner; I'll ride."

Cyrus's lips quirked. "Good. It's not a long journey. A friend will meet us at the south pass tonight, and we'll reach Izlena by tomorrow evening. There's an inn we can stay in tonight." He walked toward the two grazing horses. "We'll keep it at a walk. Try not to fight the motion of the animal. Just move with them. You'll catch on quickly."

She studied the two horses—the first a tall stallion, its coat a shimmering ebony with two white socks and a pointed shape on its forehead. The animal was beautiful, its mane long and thick, and it had warm gentle eyes.

"What's his name?" Nova approached slowly, her hand outstretched. The horse's pulse was calm.

"Ghost." The stallion snorted, holding his head high at that.

"Fitting." Nova clicked her tongue as he nuzzled her palm. Animals, when she did get to interact with them, always looked at her with nothing but kindness. "And the mare?"

Just as tall as Ghost, probably both at least six feet. The mare was a strawberry roan, with three white socks and a flowing mane. Her big brown eyes were locked onto Nova, looking past the surface and into her soul. Nova hoped the horse saw something worthy.

"That's Rouge."

Rouge lifted her head at Nova's approach, looking down at her. Her ears stayed perked, one flickering in the wind. After a moment, her soft nose found Nova's outstretched palm.

"She was named after the red sun." The bleeding sun. Every two months, the suns aligned perfectly, casting a red shadow down onto the world. It was fitting. Rouge's tail swished out, hitting Ghost.

"They seem attached," she mused.

Cyrus smiled. "They are." He proceeded to check the saddle

and the reins, brushing a soft hand over each of their necks as he went. They watched him with soft eyes and swishing tails. "Come on. I'll assist you."

Nova was grateful for the leggings Asha had given her and the supple overcoat, blocking the cool wind. Though, she felt bare with no weapons of her own. She was used to an array of small daggers hidden against her skin.

She approached, running her hand over the worn leather of the saddle. He glanced at her and said, "Left foot up in the stirrup, and I'll give you a lift."

With a nod, she steadied her hands and lifted her leg high, a small ache traveling through her ankle. She prepared for the touch of his hands by slowing her heart rate and inhaling. Nova exhaled as his hands cupped her other leg and lifted, allowing her to swing over. In her chest, her heart skyrocketed before she could control it, Rouge adjusting her hooves beneath her. Cyrus was on Ghost before she could even blink. He gave her a quick rundown on how to hold the reins, steering, and keeping her heels steady in the stirrups.

After a few moments, he met her eyes. "Ready?"

She dipped her head, and they spurred forward. Before disappearing into the forest, she looked back at the small home. Eventually, the foliage blocked everything from view, and she faced forward, settling into the steady gait of the horse. Rays of the suns permeated through the thick leaves as they walked on the dirt path. Nova bent down slowly, her hand roving over Rouge's neck, feeling the steady beat of her heart.

To her surprise, the horse flicked her ear at her whispered coos. Feeling steadier than moments before, Nova straightened and looked straight ahead into the dark woods.

AS THEY RODE, the suns continued their path in the sky.

Cyrus sat at ease in the saddle, confidence dripping off him like water off icicles in the suns. She couldn't help but stare at the vines that wound around his wrist and fingers. Was it subconscious? Or were the plants sentient and simply attached to him?

The two horses were enamored, and Ghost kept them side by side. They moved through Cydros in comfortable silence. Within the city, the trees were trimmed and gardens tended. There were streets of smooth stone and pavement with homes situated on quieter roads. The town center was built into a section of the forest of orangewood trees; the orangewoods were similar to redwoods but more varied in color. Shops and buildings were built into and amongst the large trunks, from the ground all the way to the large branches, where leaves provided cover for their neighboring streets. Flowers from the trees fell into the creek that bordered the town.

In another life, maybe she would've stopped to appreciate it. In another life, she wasn't being haunted by the dead or running from those that raised her. It was a beautiful place, but there was no time for beauty in her life. With every step forward, she felt the Elders swirling in her mind, sitting heavy upon her shoulders.

You cannot run. We will follow.

And they did, as though they were hiding within the woods, just out of sight.

Eventually, they veered off the path and into the forest, where the only sounds were the chirping of various birds, the trickling of a nearby stream, and the clicks of crickets in the grass. Ahead, willow trees appeared, their wispy, sweeping branches creating a canopy above them, allowing light to filter in.

It was incredible how the forest changed right in front of her. On the ground, flowers bloomed—tulips and daffodils and tiny little lilac flowers she'd never seen before. She could sense the forest around her as she breathed in and out. Underneath, the soil was firm yet supple, the occasional print in the mud of another woodland creature. Eisera was beyond beautiful.

"This may seem strange, but I can't understand why you helped me," she said. He gave her an inquisitive look. She wasn't sure what possessed her to open her mouth, but here she was. "You could've left me there. Your kindness wasn't needed; my life wasn't your responsibility."

Part of it was that she couldn't fathom anyone looking at her and seeing something worth saving. Another was that it could've put him in danger. She could've been violent in her exhausted state. Even now, she still could. She wouldn't hesitate if her life was threatened.

Killing had consequences—her nightmares made sure of that —but she wouldn't shy away from it. If he became a threat, it would be his blood on the forest floor.

She was also suspicious, even if she had no reason to be.

Cyrus sighed, his forest green eyes meeting hers, more vibrant than the leaves overhead. "No, it wasn't. But if someone only does something because it's their responsibility, what kind of person would they be? It's not the things you do that make you who you are. It's not the tasks you fulfill because they're required or expected. To me, it has always been about what you do when no one is looking. And kindness is never a mistake."

She wanted to hate him for it. What was it like to be so settled in your life and your place that kindness was the first thing that came to mind? That kindness didn't need to be sacrificed in place of something else? Like survival? She turned away, hiding the sneer she felt growing. Kindness was fickle and fleeting. Anger bloomed like one of the daffodils on the ground. She knew it wasn't fair.

What did he ever do to me?

Nothing. Except save her life. Her anger was poorly directed with no outlet. She was so used to being angry all the time— usually at Mikel or Mireya. Or her own life. Blood boiled under her fingertips, and her heart raced. *Pull it together. Do not let them see you bleed.*

But there was only so much rage someone could suppress. Especially a jealousy-fueled one. Her fingers felt tight and achy. She could feel his blood, his mind...if she just...

A sharp sting on her thigh pulled her out of the red haze. *What the...*

Rouge's tail swung wildly, slapping her thigh again, softer this time. Ahead, her ear flicked. Nova snorted at the horse's antics, but the anger returned to a hum. Not something threatening to explode. In thanks, she scratched the neck of the red roan horse, feeling the smooth coat under her palm.

To her left, she felt the gentle gaze of Cyrus. When she made eye contact, his gaze was focused, inquisitive. Forcing her lips into a reserved smile, she built back her calm façade. Even so, she needed to be careful.

What would he do if he caught even a glimpse of the monster she felt she could be? If he could see all the rage that vibrated under the surface of her skin? Some days, she didn't feel anything like the woman raised in Syris, that it wasn't who she was. But most days, she felt that was *exactly* who she was.

And she wasn't sure the pain of trying to smooth all her jagged edges to figure it out was worth it.

Darkness came quickly. Above, the sun's rays receded to make way for the moon to rise. Pain radiated all over Nova's hips and lower back from the saddle. Exhaustion wore at her bones. Even healed, the effects of injury lingered, draining the energy from her core. Through the break in the trees, she could see the stars twinkling above, falling into their constellations, and something within her settled.

If nothing else, the stars were out.

Cyrus's voice drew her attention. "Look," he whispered, pointing into the all-encompassing darkness. Minute, iridescent lights flickered in the shadows. One by one, they lit up the forest. "Moonflowers."

An unexpected warmth bloomed in her chest. They were beautiful. Specks of light in the blackest night. Stars growing up from the soil. They stilled, watching the flowers blink in and out of the darkness. There was nothing comparable to this in Syris. That place was an icy wasteland. This place was alive in every sense of the word.

"Come on, let's go. My friend, Dray, works in foreign affairs. He'll be the one to accompany our journey tomorrow. He's waiting at the inn for us."

Nova sucked in a breath at the sharp pain but gritted her teeth and sank into the saddle. As the suns had descended, they continued weaving through the woods. Tall peaks appeared through the breaks in the leaves, scraping the clouds, and a cool breeze swept around them. In the falling darkness, moonflowers sporadically blinked in her peripheral.

Lanterns appeared as they veered onto a path entering the small town of Idya, where she felt an influx of pulses. Eventually, they slowed to a stop in front of an inn. Cyrus dismounted and made his way to her, but before he could help or think of touching her, Nova removed her heels from the stirrups and swung her leg over, landing firmly on the ground.

There was someone sitting on the entrance steps. She felt the steady pressure of their blood as Cyrus untied their bags and handed over the reins to a stable hand. As they approached, the figure rose.

"Cyrus, took you long enough."

They shook hands before falling into a familiar embrace. "Thanks for waiting, Dray. This is Nova. She's traveling to the Emerald Library tomorrow."

Dray smiled warmly, his whole face lighting up. His cheeks

were full, but his face was sharp; his nose was bent at the bridge, and there was a tiny scar through one of his eyebrows. Waves of brown hair fell to his chin, where there was a tiny indent. Like his mother had pressed her thumb there one too many times.

"Nice to meet you, Nova."

"You, too."

"Sorry you're stuck traveling with this one," he said, motioning to Cyrus, who crossed his arms. There was an obvious ease between them, a comradery that felt miles deep.

She shrugged. "Hasn't been so bad."

"Good. Well, come on. Let's get settled for the night." Dray led the way, opening the inn's large doors for both of them.

His heartbeat was slow—faster than Cyrus's but still slower than average—and his blood was strong. As they entered, the smell of food wafted under her nose, her stomach grumbling after a day of travel on mere snacks. A small desk greeted them at the base of the stairs, the innkeepers eyes passing over them. Ahead of her, Dray and Cyrus shared quiet words, the keys to the room spinning on Dray's finger.

She couldn't explain the anxiousness crawling over her skin or the dread traveling up her spine. It was probably misplaced paranoia, but for the first time since leaving the Elderlands, Nova reached out with the wispy edges of her power and prodded Dray's mind. It was guarded, but some of her strength had returned, and she burrowed her way in.

Oh. It was different. It was heavier. His thoughts pounded—images of his life, of passing faces, all flashed in an instant. But that wasn't all. She had always been able to pick out what people were feeling, but it wasn't clear. But now...she could feel exactly what they felt—the multitudes of their emotions and where they stemmed from. Clear as day.

Like strands of a story. Threads tethering and threads broken.

By the Gods.

His whole life was right there. A tangled web at the tip of her fingers.

And then, it deepened. Nova felt as though she was floating through their entire past at once. Usually, the mind was concealed, like a library of sorts. The brain would organize memories unknowingly in a personal hierarchy. But she had to search for them. There was no *searching* here.

If she cared to look, she could've known everything about him in a single moment. An orb-like creation was at his center, pulsing in waves of color and energy. Instead of being able to enter like a snake and influence him...she was almost positive she could've crushed him from the inside. Dug her invisible claws into his mind and turned him to vapors. Erased his very existence.

She remembered her surroundings and regained focus. Luckily, they were both still deep in quiet conversation. As they approached a room, she drew back. What had happened to her? What were these powers...these *threads*? More importantly, why? Why were her abilities changing? What in the world did it all mean?

She exhaled, more taken out of her than expected. The door opened into a large suite—a simple couch and chairs in the front room and a hall leading to the beds.

Cyrus placed their bags down as Dray took a seat in the chair, turning his honey eyes on her. "They only had one room available. The couch turns into a bed as well. But it's wherever you're comfortable."

"I'll sleep out here," she said, settling onto the couch, maintaining distance between the two of them. "Thank you both for helping me."

"We're happy to do so," Dray said, studying her. The gaze was kind but focused, and his blood was steady but warm in her palm.

That was the other thing—Athera couldn't hide from her. Not that they had any reason to, but the blood gave it away. Each Elemental and Naturalist had a different chemistry in their blood, something specific that made it stand out. Fire Elementals, for example, ran hot. The temperature of their blood higher than others. Dray was a Fire Elemental. It didn't mean anything one way or another; it was merely an observation.

"I'm sure you're tired," Cyrus said. "We'll leave you to get settled and return with some food from downstairs. Is that all right?"

She exhaled. Thank the Gods. "Yes, please. That would be great." She needed a minute alone, a minute to just be.

He dipped his head and clapped Dray on the back. "Come on." They stood, Cyrus giving her a parting glance, and left her alone.

The moment the door closed, her shoulders fell inward. Her whole body ached. This morning, she had started to feel like her old self. She could feel the continuity of her body, the steady beat and flow of her blood. Her nerves and muscles. But now, all of the aches and pains had come back. And it was bone deep.

Forcing herself up, she entered the bathing chambers and splashed soap and water on her face. What was she doing?

In and out.

Was this the stupidest choice she could've made?

In and out.

Would anything even come of this? Or was she only delaying her own freedom? And then, in the mirror, the Elders flashed again, sending her heart careening. This was the only choice she had.

She allowed herself one more breath before exiting, grabbing a blanket from the basket under the tiny window and curling up on the couch. The tiny flames in the lanterns flickered dimly in the room as she stared at the ceiling. The room was small, but it felt large, circling her, threatening to close in on her with every breath.

She thought about sleeping, but when she closed her eyes, all she saw was the Elders. Their bodies strewn on the floor. Their words and faces haunted in her head.

She couldn't—her brain wouldn't let her rest. The façade she wore was tiring, and the choices she was making no longer felt like her own. At some point, Cyrus and Dray returned, and she made sure to appear to be sleeping so they left her be. She heard the clattering of a plate on the table but felt their heartbeats move further away.

Nova should've been chasing her freedom, reveling in escaping the Vahls; instead, she felt like a pawn with the voices of the dead haunting her. She should've felt full, happy—but all she felt was hollow.

Chapter 16

Izlena

Nova didn't sleep. Not one minute.

The fresh air was a welcome reprieve after the stuffy room, and the breeze cooled the edges of exhaustion threatening to crush her.

She inhaled, swallowing the evergreen oxygen like it was water. Above, under the early morning suns, the mountains towered high, visible even under the thick foliage. They hadn't been walking long, less than an hour, snacking on more bread and apples from the inn's kitchen. The horses trotted along, side by side on the thick path. Shortly, they approached the base of the mountains. It looked unassuming, a sheer rock face that rose into the sky.

Dray and Cyrus approached, Nova waiting behind them. Underneath, Rouge flicked an ear and swished her tail. Nova appeased her, scratching the mare's neck as she watched Cyrus dismount. He approached the base of the mountain and grounded himself. Nova couldn't get over quite how large the mountains were, how incredibly grand. How different they were than the ones she'd grown up with. They were beautiful, one of the most beautiful things Nova had ever seen, and—

And then, the ground shook.

Pebbles jumped, pattering against the pathway. Nova's eyes widened as she watched Cyrus make a sweeping motion with his arms, and the base of the smallest peak began to split in two. Sections at a time, the rock cleared, making way to a dark, sweeping tunnel. The light reflected off gemstones within, casting streams of color over the ground of the entrance. Earth Elementals were notoriously powerful, a quiet grounded strength, but she'd never seen this.

His eyes met her own as he mounted Ghost. "Ready?"

She felt the urge to run again. To turn and disappear. *You must find the truth before it all turns to lies. Or you will never be free.* But the Elders were everywhere and all around her. Forcing her to feel the invisible string tied around her throat.

Nova sighed. "Ready."

Nova was walking on a rainbow.

The gemstones in the tunnel reflected the light, casting streaks of sapphire and ruby and orange and violet, painting the stone ground. She had never given much thought to rainbows before. They were fleeting, only appearing when the sun and the misty rain overlapped in perfect harmony. An arc of colors gone before she ever had a chance to admire them.

She understood the magic now.

They kept a quick pace, the hooves of the horses echoing. Goldstones and lanterns were scattered along the walls, continuing the illumination long after the natural light dimmed. As they continued, the simple tunnel revealed hidden intricacies. Carvings were etched into the stone of trees and canyons, rivers and cliffs, ocean shores and mountain peaks—what she assumed was the landscape of Eisera.

Not long after entering, they came across a fork presenting

three different options. Darker, twisting tunnels were visible in two of them, but one was straight ahead with three guards draped in deep green with silver accents standing sentinel. Dray led the way with the guards clearing the path to allow them through, dipping their heads as they passed. Behind them, the sound of rock and stone had Nova looking back only to see them completely block the tunnel entrance.

Her eyes were glued to the carvings, especially the forest as it wound up and over the walls and the curved ceiling

"That's Nalādin." Cyrus maneuvered Ghost closer to her side.

"The sentient forest?" Nova asked, her studies returning to her.

The forest was one of the five known Aether points in Valora, though the forest was a mystery. Very little was written about it. Overtime, it'd become more myth than reality.

Cyrus gave her a soft smile. "The very one. It's in the north."

"It's incredible," she murmured.

"It is. And they're always adding to it. Nalādin never remains quiet for long, so things are always changing. Artists are constantly in the tunnels trying to capture it." He pointed out certain spots where gems were used to highlight the forest. Emerald stones to decorate the leaves and sapphires and rubies for flowers blooming at the tree trunks. "Nalādin is a mystery to all of us. An everchanging place. You never know what you're going to find. In the forest or within yourself," Cyrus said, his voice soft like a gentle breeze.

His cool composure remained confusing to her. Unruffled and steadfast. She'd spent little time with him, but even still, he unnerved her. He was too nice, too balanced for it to be anything but an act. Aggression and vitriol were easy to see. Especially since Nova recognized it from both sides. What it was like to receive it and what it was like to *be*.

Kindness put Nova on edge, teetering on a fog-covered cliff, wondering which way was true.

She felt the lingering prick of his gaze and pushed her

shoulders back, feeling the blood of those around her. With a deep breath, her breathing slowed. The various pulses and beats were a comfort to her. Something she could control if she needed.

The sound of rumbling filled her ears again, and light filtered in from ahead. Underneath, Rouge picked up the pace, settling into a slow trot, though never leaving Ghost's side. Nova let out a small puff of air. Her horse was sick with love. *Unreal.* Light streamed in ahead, bright and blinding already. The tunnel widened, and before she knew it, the suns were shining down on them.

If she thought the entrance and tunnel were beautiful, then *this* was breathtaking.

"Welcome to Izlena." Cyrus's voice was barely an echo.

It was as if the entire world opened before her. Green as far as the eye could see. Mountains stood tall and strong against the distant sky. They seemed to form a barrier—around the city perhaps. The wind whistled as they stood high up at the entrance of the tunnel, and birds soared overhead before diving into the sea of green.

Gods, it was incredible. Syris was frigid and barren. Not that ice didn't have its own type of beauty—it did. But Syris was lifeless. The silence was loud and deafening. The soil was hard and frozen, the weather incessantly gray.

This place was full of life.

Around her, trees rustled in the breeze, and the face of the mountain below was covered with trees and flowers. The suns were bright and high in the sky. Paths were carved into the mountain, weaving up and down, disappearing into the woods.

"Where is the city?"

Cyrus pointed to the center below. "See that ridge?"

"Barely."

His eyes warmed as they took it in. This was his home. Nova wondered what that felt like. "You'll see as we approach."

"Lead the way."

THE JOURNEY DOWN WAS LONG, but it passed swiftly. Nova was entranced by all of it. The trees were taller than she'd ever seen before. There were various types among the forest, but it was the giant red-tinted trunks that seemed to disappear into the sky that she took a liking to—those and the willow trees.

Flowers speckled the forest with color, some flowers sprouting up from the soil at the touch of the suns and sinking back in when the rays left them in the dark. And she swore in her peripheral, there were tiny little beings jumping between the trees, following them. A jingle of laughter echoed through the woods.

"What are those?"

Cyrus smiled. "Sprites."

Nova's eyebrows jumped. "Actual sprites?" She'd only read about them or heard of them in passing tales.

"Forest Sprites. They, like the others, usually stay out of sight, but they're delighted by visitors."

She saw another—the size of her hand, if not smaller. This one was currently sliding down the frond of a willow tree, its small wings fluttering in the air. Nova usually had a hard time appreciating beauty. Her life, her parents, had made sure of that. Being here was strange. It was harder to not become awestruck by everything around her.

From the life teeming at every turn.

Nova was used to death. Not the fullness of life.

They traveled in peace, with Dray and Cyrus pointing out various things to her. Flowers or bugs that were native to Eisera. Trees that only grew during certain times of the years or flowers that bloomed only in the perfect conditions. As they traversed, her head began to pound, an ache building gradually.

Why now? Why again? I'm doing what you asked! All at once her head shattered, pain bursting all around. Was this the Elders?

Or something different? Nova dropped the reins, her hands shaking, and all the pulsing blood she'd held dropped away. Instead, she was bombarded with threads—like the Elderlands. Emotions, feelings, memories—images she didn't understand—attacked her, demanding her attention.

Rouge was unsteady, unsettled by the frantic movements Nova made as she writhed on top.

"Dray, stop!" Cyrus shouted, pulling Ghost to a halt. Nova lost her balance and began to slip. Instead of hitting the ground, it rose up to meet her, stopping her fall.

And there was more. More than just the threads. She could *feel* the life pulsing through the ground beneath her. Pulsing through the roots of the trees and flowers. *Gods, what was this?*

The voices of the Elders were loud but distant. *The truth of the world has gone rotten.*

She curled in on herself. *Get out, get out!* It was no use.

Cyrus appeared, leaning over her, Dray not far behind, their shadows blocking out the suns. "What is happening?"

She bit her tongue, tasting blood. "Herbs. In my bag. From Asha." She blinked her eyes open, black spots dancing in her vision. She hated this—being weak in front of them. The eyes were heavy on her skin. "Go," she said, a whimper of pain escaping her lips. Embarrassment struck like tiny flames.

Weak little Witch. Her parents voices echoed in her thoughts. She rolled her head, trying to shake them away.

As Cyrus returned with the herbs, the same Sprite from the willow tree danced in front of her eyes. *Is this real?* Nova blinked, but the Sprite remained. It fluttered above her, pale wings of lilac and rose moving rapidly with a plant in its minuscule grasp. Nova felt small drafts as the Sprite came closer, placing the plant on her lips. After a brief hesitation, she took it, chewing the strange plant.

If it killed her...well, that solved that.

Hopefully, it would help. Her stomach rolled under the pain, and her limbs felt shaky, but slowly, the pain subsided. After a moment, she could exhale. The pain dissipated enough for her to sit up and open her eyes without pain. When she did, the Sprite was gone.

"Are you all right?" Cyrus asked.

Beyond him, Dray stared at her, an empty concern in his gaze. She swallowed, her nails digging into her palm. Her weakness was probably palpable. It made her sick. She turned her eyes above, to the leaves and the sky.

"Nova, what happened?"

"Headaches."

He raised a brow. "That's all?"

She swallowed, trying to quell her stomach. "I don't know. It's new. I don't know what it is. It just hurts."

His face softened, and she hated it. "Dray, would you give us a minute?" he asked, leaving only the two of them. The next words were not spoken out loud. *"Hey. You're okay."* His voice rang in her head, dulling the ache somehow. He wasn't speaking to her, per se, not like her parents, but more that, he had pushed a thought out, and the edges of her power had caught it.

Nova swallowed. When—*how*—had he caught her? What did she do wrong? Was she not perfect enough? Not careful enough? Not good enough? She was supposed to be invisible. That was what the Vahls taught her.

But he saw her.

"Spirit is a peculiar thing. Hard to catch. Harder to be sure. Do you think it's causing the headaches?"

She tried to sit up. "I don't—" She didn't know what to say. She couldn't exactly say that her head had been exploding since she touched the Elderlands, and she couldn't ask for aetherchains without raising suspicion.

"Forget I asked. Let's try getting you up."

"That helps," she said, swallowing. It didn't make sense, but it did. Maybe it gave her mind something else to focus on.

Questions floated in his green eyes, but he said nothing more and simply helped her stand. He was careful about touching her.

In the chaos, her overcoat had fallen loose, and her sleeves had been pushed up, revealing the scars around her wrist from use of the chains. She saw the exact moment his eyes landed on them. She waited for pity to swim, but it didn't come. He merely held her coat for her.

"I think you should ride with me," he said gently, ensuring the coat was on, barely brushing her. In her palm, his heart beat quickly twice before settling. "I'll do my best to keep some distance." His hand was on her elbow, burning through her layers as he guided her toward Ghost. "I'm sorry."

Nova stared at him and took a step back.

She felt weak. And stupid. *So godsdamned stupid.* She was stronger than this. This was pathetic. All the pain she had endured, all the scars on her skin, and this—*this*—brought her to her knees. That could not happen. Not anymore.

Because if she was not strong, she would crumble.

Nova took a breath. Sharing this horse would not be easy, not with the touch of someone else on her skin. But based on the shakiness of her body, she had no choice. Rouge flicked her ears and gently nudged Nova's shoulder. They locked eyes, and she swore there was a warmth in the horse's gaze. An understanding.

"Come on." Cyrus tied Rouge and Ghost together before returning. Ghost remained calm when Nova patted his neck. "Ready?" She nodded, and before she knew it, she was seated on the horse. "Relax. Let your legs drape, and you'll find your balance."

Cyrus pulled himself up with ease, seating himself behind her. His arms came around to grip the reins, and her loose grip on Ghost's mane tightened.

"Okay?" he asked quietly.

Nova swallowed, feeling the breeze on her skin, ignoring how much she wanted to crawl out of it. "Yes."

Quickly, they caught up to Dray, who was waiting patiently ahead. Rouge walked beside them, her big warm eyes landing on Nova every once in a while. She made sure to focus on the world around her. If she didn't, she would think too long and too hard about Cyrus's body brushing against her own.

It made her think of all the times she was blindfolded in that room and made to feel like her skin was on fire or frozen or chapped. It made her think of all the times the Vahls made her think that dead had crawled to her, had made her think they were touching her skin, leaving dirt and decay behind—

Enough.

But unease sat on top of her skin like mist from an early rain.

The whole world felt unsteady beneath her as they walked forward.

She felt the warmth of the suns and tried to count Ghost's hoofbeats on the ground. Sounds grew louder amongst the forest. But she couldn't control the panic. Her heart pounded, and she couldn't breathe.

"You must breathe, Nova."

But all she could feel was *him.* Everywhere. Nova couldn't feel her own skin, couldn't hear her own thoughts. "I can't—" she rumbled. She tried shutting her eyes, but it didn't help. Memories flashed, her senses heightened, and she couldn't find a thread of logic. There was only fear. "I need to get off."

"I need you to listen to me."

Anger bloomed like a flower. "Cyrus—"

"You are going to listen to me, understood?" His voice was firm. His blood was calm. "You are going to breathe. In and out. Now."

His blood was right there. If she could focus, she could force him away. But the touch...it made her skin crawl. Turned her thoughts into a jumbled mess she couldn't read. Even as he adjusted, moving himself away as best he could, nausea still rose, and her stomach still turned. Her control was slipping, her heart pounding, blood pumping through her veins in a violent rush.

"In. And out," Cyrus demanded.

"You don't...I can't—"

"You will. Now do it."

She clenched her teeth, but she listened. It was all she could do—breathe. And that tiny, pestering little voice in her head wouldn't stop, reminding her she was weak and she was showing it. Reminding Nova she had showed her weakness to him more than almost anyone, more times than she could admit.

Nova should've been better at suffocating her pain instead of flaunting it.

Cyrus repeated the words as they walked, slow and steady—the pace and his voice. "I'm going to touch your hands. Only for a moment." Nova swallowed but let him. His touch was feather light, and it was gone as soon as she felt Ghost's coat underneath her. "Count his steps, feel his strength. Focus on him, the way his movements change with the terrain."

She counted his steps, felt the muscle underneath his coat, the way it rippled throughout his body. She moved one hand up until she felt his mane, and she let her hand sway with the rocking motion of his head. Back and forth, in and out. Slowly, some of her control returned. Cyrus's blood was in her palm, so was Dray's, so was Rouge's, so was Ghost's. They flickered in and out, but she had them. If she needed them.

"Good, good," Cyrus murmured, and she *finally* took a deep breath, letting the oxygen fill her lungs before she let it go.

She couldn't understand him. Why was he so gentle when she deserved less? When she looked in the mirror, she saw a woman with no life in her eyes with no reason why. And weakness—all she ever saw was weakness.

What did he see? What *could* he see, when all she saw was nothing?

His voice broke through her thoughts. "What do you think so far of Eisera?"

"Are you trying to distract me now?"

A small chuckle reverberated behind her. And still, she flinched. "I am."

"It's beautiful." She straightened her shoulders, trying to

shake it off. But the weight of her weakness was not something easily shaken. "What was it like? Growing up here?"

"It's the thing I'm most grateful for. It often feels like the forest raised me as much as anything. Growing up under the trees, in the shores and the ocean, in the lakes—I don't know how to describe it, but it's a lesson in itself. As an Earth Elemental, our sessions were always outside, you know? Learning how the world worked before we learned to control it."

"But you split time between Izlena and Willowgrove? You said you grew up with the Slaters, right?"

His body stiffened. It would've been imperceptible if she wasn't pressed unwillingly against him.

"Right. My parents both served the Slaters, my mother a historian and a former professor in one of Izlena's secondary schools, while my father served the Silverguard. I was in school with the Slaters from age five to sixteen. After that, things changed—deciding whether to continue with school or select a trade, like infrastructure. Things like that. But I spent a lot of time in Willowgrove and the library with those of the Magistrate. Because I was so close with them, I learned a lot about what was required of them, so there's a lot of useless information in my head that I don't need as a normal citizen." She could hear the slight smile in his voice. "But yeah, there wasn't a day we didn't walk into Willowgrove without dirt on our faces."

He didn't overshare, but he gave her just enough to create this weird, warm aura. She wasn't sure what to do with it.

"When did you meet Dray?"

He laughed. "I met Dray when I was ten maybe? He was born in Vydara but came here around his ninth year. I'd been in the mountains near a pond, and all of a sudden, there was a smoking figure running past me to the water. Dray had accidently set himself on fire trying to control his magic and used the lake to put it out."

Everything sounded so normal. Peaceful. She didn't have a

single memory like that. One that she could laugh at or smile about. She was jealous.

"See those flowers?" Cyrus pointed left at the green and violet flowers. "Those are zinnias, my mother's favorites. On her birthday, my father would fill our house with them and tuck them behind her ear and in her hair."

She could hear the smile in his voice, and despite her rigid stance, she felt the air settle and drape around her. His voice became the breeze, brushing coolly along her nerves. It was soft, like a balm.

If only she could let it soothe all of her fraying edges.

Nova felt the undercurrent of mistrust. She wasn't sure she would ever be free of it. All of it since she'd landed here felt too good to be true. Asha's kindness, Cyrus' warmth...she had no tangible proof that they were any better than her parents. She knew all too well how people could hide behind a mask.

But for a moment, she let herself believe it. It was naïve.

Hoping people might be better than they had been.

Even if they were, the moment she could, their blood would be back in her palm. Hers to control if the need arose. As they rode, Cyrus continued telling her stories, unaware of the war raging within her. Nova focused on the things she could see, things she knew were real. The world around her, the flowers and the trees. The steady rocking of Ghost underneath and his mane in her palms and the sound of hooves on the soft soil.

Those were real.

But for a moment, she thought Cyrus might be, too.

And for a moment, she *almost* forgot they were touching.

CHAPTER 17

EMERALD LIBRARY

THE REST OF THE JOURNEY WENT WITHOUT ERROR.

They traversed down from the mountains toward the capital, Izlena. The city, a shimmering suncatcher amongst the gray and greens of the mountains, spread out into the valley with buildings of sandstone and marble and wood, all built into the base of the mountains and beyond. From above, she'd been able to see the rivers branching from the peaks that flowed through the trees and how the mountain range extended far beyond the valley on either side, fading into the horizon.

The suns hovered above the mountain peaks, the very tops shrouded in the clouds, while the rest of the world was painted in shades of red and orange. Willowgrove, the castle, was a spot of bright stone tucked into the junction of the mountain range. It spread high, its tallest towers scratching the sky and low into the valley. Bridges connected sections of the fortress and spanned the gap from mountain rage to mountain range, with grand staircases and a waterfall that emptied into a crystal blue lake.

There was no way to take it all in, but she tried as they dismounted and tied up the horses. The large trees and their thick foliage only allowed for streaks of the fading sunlight to appear through the cracks and onto the path where they stood.

Dray approached, running his hand over Rouge's hind quarters. She huffed a heavy sigh and swatted him with her tail. "How are you feeling?"

"Okay," she said, trying to laugh. "It feels a bit dramatic now, but...I'm fine."

He shrugged. "It happens. I'm happy you're feeling better."

She looked between the two. "Where are we? I thought we were going to the library."

"We are," Cyrus said, a smile playing on his lips and motioned for her to follow.

She was still a bit dizzy, but she forced herself to move forward. The traveling was taxing, mentally and physically. For a second, she imagined she was back on her balcony with only the sound and mist of the waves below. Sure, her bedroom also served as a cage, but there was peace in her solitude.

She felt the eyes of Cyrus and Dray on her every few steps. Whether that was to make sure she was still standing or for some other reason...she was too tired to care. With the quiet, she took the time to try and infiltrate his head. She had to be careful since he knew she was a Spirit Naturalist, but she *needed* to know what her magic had become.

Could she control it? How did it differ? How was it similar? If she couldn't understand something, if she couldn't control it— she would fear it. There was no time for fear anymore.

Everyone's mind was different, their walls indicative of themselves in some ways.

Cyrus's was a forest of tall, towering trees with leaves intertwined and a barrier of trunks. There was no easy way in, but if she could find a weak spot—a soft spot—she could get in. Minds were a maze, a labyrinth to who someone was. But if she was patient enough, she would find a way in.

If there was anything she learned from her parents, it was that there was *always* a way in. Nova carefully and slowly worked around his mind, prodding the edges until finally, it gave. Just a little, but enough and she believed, imperceptibly. There were layers to this, but the threads shimmered in bright silver.

Nova jumped, metaphorically that is, and selected a thread. It felt like flying; she was speeding down a path, images flashing by in quick succession. If she wasn't acutely aware of herself, it would've taken her breath away. If she wanted to, she could've looked at herself through his eyes, his memories—but she blocked that out. What if she saw something she didn't like? She'd been haunted too many times by other people's ideas of her. She didn't need to add anyone else to it.

Relief seeped into her. Her magic was still hers, just changing. The time would come when she could fully understand the threads, it just wasn't now.

They walked in silence, eventually curving around the lake to move behind the rushing waterfall where they came upon a tunnel, the entrance dampened by mist. Vines grew along the walls and the ceiling, the dirt turned to stone with goldstone on the wall, and flowers along the vines. They walked under a domed part of the tunnel where fading light from the suns streamed in and the rushing water could be heard. Other tunnels branched off the main tunnel, winding into darkness, but they continued, approaching a beautiful marble door with detailed carvings and groves.

Nova wasn't sure whether to smile in amazement or laugh in disbelief. This was a place plucked from the old days, a place only Gods could've made.

Cyrus placed his hand on the door, the vines unraveling from his skin and molding to the keyhole. A series of sounds emitted from the door until they opened before them. The Emerald Library was covered in green. Vines hung from the ceilings, suspended in the air from bookshelf to bookshelf before they attached to the wood and wound around the shelves until they touched the floor. The shelves shimmered with emerald stones and were decorated with rolling ladders.

Members of the Magistrate moved throughout the many rows that went as far back as she could see.

"Follow me," Cyrus said, leading her down the central row.

Lanterns hung from the ceiling and the rounded walls. Windows that led to nowhere were adorned with colorful glass, and the floor was a warm stone with more emeralds.

Dray leaned in. "Impressive, isn't it?" He laughed when she remained speechless.

Impressive wasn't the word.

As the first rows came to an end, they stepped on a circular part of the floor. With a firm press of Cyrus's foot into the ground and a smoothing hand motion, the floor dropped, leaving Dray above. It was quick but controlled, and when it came to a stop, the smell of old books became prominent. Above, it was mixed into the air and the smell of the vines, but here, it was only parchment.

"How large is the library?" she asked, trying to make a mental map.

"It's extensive. The upper level extends further back and out, into the mountains." He looked over his shoulder at her. "Down here, things are more separated. Sections of rooms dedicated to studying and restricted archives. There are sleeping quarters both here and above."

They approached a circular desk made of stone, lit with goldstone that sent rainbows over the floor. Nova felt two heartbeats through the dim light. One, a Mythic, she guessed, was draped in plain green-dyed linen.

The other was no Mythic.

Leathers of deep green complimented her warm brown skin. Weapons were sheathed at her thigh and bicep. Jewels decorated her fingers and ears. Her curly umber hair was braided back with clips of silver and green and flowers made of metal with necklaces to match. Her eyes were blue and gray, like the icy shores of the north.

"Cyrus, what a coincidence," she exclaimed, moving forward

to embrace him. But there was a strange tension between them. Something palpable, something off. Her eyes landed on Nova. "Who's this?"

Cyrus motioned toward her. "This is Nova. Nova, this is Princess Amala Slater."

Understanding dawned on her quickly. This was one of the heirs to the throne. One of the ones he grew up with. "Your Highness," Nova said, dipping her head. "It's a pleasure to meet you."

"And you. Are you a new scribe?"

"She was traveling from Vilies but got caught in a storm. I happened to find the wreckage and offered to bring her here myself," Cyrus said.

"From Vilies? A long journey. I'm glad you made it." The princess studied her, her eyes sharp. Nerves pricked at the base of her neck. Would the world be looking for her yet? Or was she paranoid? "I try to make it a point to meet all new scribes but not quite the very same day. I hope I haven't overwhelmed you."

"Not at all. It's an honor." Of course, that was a lie.

She'd rather be left alone to find what she needed, what the Elders wanted, and disappear. She cared not for heirs or *honor*. The ones she knew were not honorable at all. She expected no different.

"And this," Cyrus said, pointing to the Mythic, "is Lucie. They're one of the Headmasters. Lucie will confirm the records, and then, we'll get you settled." He shared a look with Amala but quickly averted his gaze.

Nova remained calm, but within, anxiety thrummed, begging to be released. Lucie began rummaging through the circular desk until they found a large and wide tome, most likely the records. They were kept by hand and organized by date. A million tiny tabs stuck out of the pages in various colors.

"When did you begin your training?"

"Two years ago at the start of the eleventh month."

Lucie selected the tab they were looking for and opened the

book directly to the page. Nova couldn't see the scrawl from here but could see it was tiny and detailed. She avoided looking at Cyrus and Amala and took a careful breath.

"Full name?"

The question frustrated her. She was never given a last name. Didn't know her parents and didn't claim the Vahls. She was just Nova. But that wasn't enough.

"Nova Aarin."

As Lucie started checking the names, Nova pressed in. The headmaster's mind was weakly guarded with fog. As before, the threads appeared, this time twinkling like stars in the night sky. Thoughts and images pounded as before, their emotions banging at the walls of Nova's mind. As she had so many times before, she found a weak spot as Lucie looked at her and the page, and whispered into their mind: *Nova Aarin. Twenty-four years. Originates from Syris. Student of the Eternal Library. Private room.*

As she did, Nova felt as Lucie saw what was in front of them. She could feel the memories forming and being stored away, so she grabbed ahold of those, too. Nova twisted, like plucking strings to make a tune, she willed it to sink it. To believe what she said as truth. If it didn't, she would draw unneeded attention to herself. Attention she wanted nothing to do with.

Lucie gnawed at their lip, and Nova twisted a bit more, manipulated the picture and mentally spoke the words like a prayer. She needed Lucie to *believe* her name was there. Strong enough so they would be confident introducing her to the others. A bead of sweat ran down her neck.

"Ah, there you are." They smiled over their shoulder. "I'll send a confirmation to Vilies. Is there anyone you would like to send a message to?"

There was no one. But she could stop the message from being sent, to keep anyone from knowing who or where she was. She wanted to disappear completely when this was over. "Please, thank you."

"Great. Your room will be on the upper floor. Would you two like to show her around, or shall I?" Lucie addressed the question to Amala and Cyrus, closing the large archival book. "You both probably know it as well as the rest of us."

They fell into step as she was led back to the upper floor, rising the same way they descended, and headed straight down the main hall. The stained glass slowly lessened, but the vines hung to the walls and creeped over framed artwork and mounted goldstone. After a series of twists and turns, Cyrus showed her the kitchen, the multiple bathing chambers, a large sitting room, and eventually, her own room. It was small, as were the rest of the chambers they passed by. Some, like this one, were private, while others slept two or three at maximum. But it had a bed and a lock on the door.

That was enough for her.

"Here you are," he said, standing under the arched doorway as she entered.

"Thank you." Nova spun, placing her single bag on the desk, and exhaled before looking between the two of them. She met Cyrus's eyes. "For everything, I mean."

Under the dim light, his eyes warmed. "Of course."

Amala cleared her throat, stepping up. "Nova, I'd like to have Cyrus remain here with you for the time being." Nova swallowed, fighting to control her unease. Did the princess suspect her? "Only as a precaution. I'm not sure if you're aware of what's transpired, but there was an incident on the Elderlands, and my parents have decided to proceed cautiously. I don't believe you to be a threat, but it would be more comfortable for me if he remained here with you."

Nova wasn't stupid. Just because it was offered as a choice didn't mean she was dumb enough to believe that. She prodded at Amala's mind, finding a guard of stone. "Of course, if that's what you need. I have no objection."

Amala's eyes tapered just so as she tipped her head back. "Wonderful. Cyrus, please show her the utmost hospitality. I'll have some of your things brought down from Willowgrove." She looked between them, her eyes lingering on Cyrus this time. Nova couldn't help but wonder what had transpired between them. He said they were friends but the tension was thick. The longer they stood, the heavier it grew. "I'll leave you both to it. Nova, it was lovely to meet you, and I hope you find the library to your liking. I'm sure I'll see you again. Cyrus," she said, dipping her head before disappearing down the hall.

Nova said nothing until the princess's blood was no longer in her palm. She locked eyes with Cyrus. "Does this mean I'm unallowed to leave?"

"Not at all. She's just"—he exhaled—"taking precautions."

"And you're okay with it?"

"I'm not going to argue with her. And it's not a task worth fighting about." He leaned on the doorframe, crossing his arms.

His shirt sleeves were rolled up to his elbows, veins running down to his ring-decorated hands. Dark ink covered most of what she could see of his left side. His broad shoulders practically took up the whole door frame.

Whether she wanted to or not, she knew exactly what it felt like, being pressed against him. How strong and steady he was. She didn't want him here. She didn't want to be watched or studied. But it wasn't really up to her anymore.

"It won't be so bad. I'll help you get acclimated and navigate the library. And I can show you Izlena. But it's nothing more than that. Eventually, it'll calm down, and I'll be out of your way."

She sighed. Now she had to maintain this image he had of her. The façade she'd cloaked over herself. Knowing it was him that would be watching her—she was hyperaware of the fact that he'd seen all her weaknesses. But he'd also been kind, whether it was warranted or not. She would just have to be careful.

All she needed was the truth, and then, she would leave. Never to be seen again.

The pulse of his blood brought her back to reality. She was jealous of how steady it always was.

"Fine."

He rose a brow, a laugh playing on his lips. Because again, it wasn't like she had an *actual* choice. "I'll leave you to it. Get some rest, Nova."

She dipped her chin. "Goodnight."

Nova could figure the rest out later. Right now, she needed to figure everything else out first. Cyrus exited with a lingering glance, and as soon as his footsteps faded, she locked the door. Nova wanted to collapse on the bed. Her head ached, and exhaustion battered her.

Instead, she tied her curls back and got down on the floor.

And she pushed herself up repeatedly until her arms gave out.

CHAPTER 18

LITTLE FIREFLY

DOCKING ON THE SHORES OF RERSA ALWAYS FELT different than anywhere else.

Maybe because in the literal sense of the word, it was Elaia's home. Where she was born, where she was raised, where she got hurt and got back up, where she fell in love and got her heart broken, and where she started to grow into herself.

It was also a place of pain, a reminder of what she'd lost.

And what she stood to lose.

If the rumblings underfoot were any indication, the world was reacting to the Elders' death. At least, based on the predictions of Mythics and the stories told by the priests of Rersa her whole childhood. And if the note in her pocket was any indication, there was still much to lose.

The shadow will continue to haunt—as long as you maintain your promises.

Rohan stood beside her, but her eyes were focused ahead. Between the guards awaiting her, was Zahra. The longest friend she'd ever had and the brightest light she'd ever known. Zahra was not just a friend, but the person she loved.

"You've missed her," Rohan stated from beside her.

Elaia let out a breath. "I always miss her."

It'd been months since she'd seen her. Elaia had been in Aeledin, and Zahra had remained here to take over her duties.

Zahra stood in a gown of silver that clung to her bronze skin. Thick dark hair flowed past her shoulders, and her eyes—a brilliant auburn, a color Elaia couldn't erase from her memory if she tried—stared at her with a warmth she could feel even now.

A pulse of light flared from Zahra's palms, and beside Elaia, Rohan nudged her shoulder. "Seems as though she's missed you, too."

Zahra wasn't born in Rersa; she wasn't a Shadow Elemental. In fact, she was the exact opposite. But she'd come here as a young girl, and they'd been inseparable ever since. At first, they were the best of friends, and then, Elaia was sure she'd never love anyone like her again.

Rersa was their home. But it had also been where they fell apart. Elaia had trouble reconciling who she had been with who she was...and who she would be in the future. Before, she'd been a girl who had sisters and a mother. Someone who smiled more, bore fewer burdens, even if they were self-inflicted.

Now, she worried about who else could be taken from her, including Zahra. That was the problem with being here. This place seemed to take as much as it gave. Lately, she'd been fearful that this was where she would lose Zahra as well.

For a while, she'd done everything in her power to push Zahra away. Even though Zahra was her betrothed, the girl she was promised to, Elaia couldn't risk losing someone else.

She wasn't willing—*capable*—of losing Zahra.

The thing about the two of them though, they always found their way back to each other. No matter what. And seeing her for the first time in months felt equally like coming home.

Beyond them, past the shoreline, the canyons of Rersa had risen up to greet them. Caverns of obsidian and shimmering steel blue shone under the setting suns above, only partially hidden behind the clouds. In the daylight, rays of sun would touch the rim of the canyons that towered above them, but they could only reach so far. Below, there would be pockets of pure blackness and caverns of shadows, only to be interrupted by lanterns. The northern port was private, used only by the High Shade—her father—herself, and selected council members. Other than that, these canyons were mostly untouched by the citizens of Rersa.

Elaia knew them like the back of her hand. She had bounded through narrow channels and secret tunnels with only the shadows to guide her more times than she could count, learning the land by moonlight and darkness. These canyons, the Canyons of Zylla, were a home to so much of her, especially her past. This was where her skin was inked upon her sixteenth year with the traditional swirls of her family name. It was where she taught Rayn and Shaye how to *feel* the shadows.

It was where all the dreams she'd let die were laid to rest.

They were home, yet they existed now only in her nightmares.

"Princess," Zahra murmured as Elaia and Rohan approached, dipping her head. Her auburn eyes tracked over her, and every inch of Elaia's skin came to life in response. "Your father is expecting you."

"Lead the way."

As Zahra turned, Elaia stepped up beside her. In the swish of their gowns, Zahra's pinky finger wound around Elaia's, something they always did.

The full cadre of guards waited a few feet back, watching them from horseback. Beside them were shadow hounds, distant Scions of the Gods, Senka and Tasyn, the Nitehounds. The Gods most shadow Athera prayed to. Elaia's own hound, Akiro, bounded up to greet her with his long legs and black fur rippling over lean muscle. He nudged his head into Elaia's palms and fell into step.

"Your Highness," said one of the guards, dipping his head and bringing his fist to the emblem of Rersa.

She sighed. "Let us not keep the High Shade waiting any longer." Elaia pressed her nails into the pads of her fingers seven times each as they approached. The moment they were atop of their horses, they were all cloaked in shadows, draped over them like clothes.

As they entered the canyon, there were shapes along the edges, dark shapes under the light of the moon. Elaia furrowed her brow. They continued along every edge, along every crevice. She shared a look with Rohan who watched, confused. The canyons weren't guarded. Never before. So why now?

She took a breath. Her father's doing. As for the reason? She would find out soon.

Elaia took one last look at the crescent shaped moon in the sky before disappearing into darkness.

VARISTONE WAS A FORTRESS. And yet, it was as beautiful—if not more so—than any palace she'd ever been. It was decorated with stained glass windows and swirled marble and stone along every surface. Built into the canyons themselves, the castle stood tall and burrowed deep into the land. Parts of it towered high above, appearing as nothing more than a palace, but it left much to be discovered underneath.

They walked in a single file formation up a winding staircase with a steep fall to the canyon floor below. Members of the Nightguard, castle attendants, stable hands, gardeners, and the like, all mulling about in their respective places. But the Canyon connected them all.

Behind her, Elaia felt Zahra holding on gently to her gown, something she used to always do as a way to stay connected. In some places, water trickled down from above and disappeared into the rock.

In a few centuries, who knew what would become of that trickle.

Everything was always changing here. And yet, nothing was different.

The ineradicable storm-gray doors of her father's chambers towered over her just as they had when she was a girl made of glass. She rolled her shoulders back. Two guards dressed in the traditional black leathers pulled open the large doors. Only Elaia, Rohan, and Zahra entered.

The room was domed with high ceilings. Grooves were inlaid with the traditional stones of Rersa, reflecting light from the lanterns and the hearth. At the center was the large stone map of Valora carved out of canyon rock and one of Rersa beside it. Incense burned from the table by the sitting chairs and shelves of rock towered high, filled with volumes and records.

The High Shade, Desmond Zūne, her father, sat to the right, bent over his desk. Immediately, she recognized the smell of his favorite tea, the one her mother used to make whenever anyone was restless. A dagger of sadness pierced her skin. If she looked too hard, she would see her mother all over this room.

"Elaia. Welcome home."

The familiarity of her father's voice fell over her like a worn blanket. For a moment, she could do nothing but look at him. Desmond Zūne was neither large nor small, but lean, honed, and strong. There was an arresting air about him, even in his grief and times of quiet.

After Nomara disappeared, Elaia often wished she looked less like her father. If only to remember details of her mother that may fade after time. But there was no denying she was her father's child. They had the same narrow, upturned eyes of golden brown, the same slightly crooked nose, the same pitch-black hair, and these days, the same sorrow hidden by their smiles.

The ends of Elaia's black gown swished over the floor as she approached. Despite the array of feelings swirling in her gut, a part of her was still happy to see him. Without hesitation, he wrapped her up, pulling her tight into his chest. She swore she could hear his heart trying to beat around the crack that ran through it.

"Father," Elaia murmured into his chest for no one else to hear.

His hand rested heavily on the back of her neck, and with it, she could feel the weight of the signet ring he wore on his hand. And the wedding band he'd never removed.

He pulled back, cupping her cheeks. "It's good to see you, little firefly."

The ache was instant. Elaia heard the soft cadence of her mother's voice before bed, her father's laughter, Shaye's crinkling eyes, and Rayn's giggles, all because of a name. The last time she'd heard it was from her father, the day before they disappeared. Three years ago.

She forced a smile on her face as she looked up at him. "It's good to be home. It's been too long."

Her father raised a dark bushy brow. "And whose fault is that?"

It was meant to be a joke, but the truth was, it was both of theirs. If anything, much of his own. For a while, he couldn't look at her. Couldn't speak to her. By the way pain flickered in his eyes, Elaia assumed the former was still true.

Stepping back, she put some space between them.

Desmond tapped his inked fingers on the desk by his side, raising his eyes to Rohan. "Thank you for taking care of her, as always." He let his eyes pass over Zahra. "Would you both give us some privacy?"

Elaia whipped her head back. "They stay."

"They see you more than I do. And besides, Zahra and I met this morning. I'd like to have some time with my daughter."

Elaia wanted to protest. Of course, they saw her more. Rohan had never and would never abandon her. And even when she wasn't with Zahra, she wasn't alone. Zahra didn't shut her out or look away every time she entered a room. Zahra didn't stop speaking to her for months. Zahra didn't raise her the way he did.

It was why she'd barely spent any time here since then. It was her home, yet she could barely stand to share it with him anymore.

Which was why she was going to take it.

She met his eyes with a cold stare but nodded. Eventually, he spoke again, this time as the High Shade. By some silent order from his shadows, the doors opened, the guards waiting. "Please show these two to their quarters and have a meal sent up."

Elaia dug her nails into her palm. She could practically hear both of them in her head, telling her that the argument wasn't worth it. She knew that. It still made her anger red hot. Without another word, they left, leaving her and her father in tense silence yet again.

Desmond's light brown eyes turned sharp. This was the version of her father she'd had for the past three years. And before that. More so than her mom or sisters.

"Sit," he commanded. "How was the assembly?"

Exhaustion pushed on her shoulders, tense and begging to be used to expend all the anxiety. "Did you not receive my message?"

"I did. I'd like to hear it from you." He took a sip of his tea, leaning back in the chair, somehow looking larger than he had moments ago.

"The Elders are dead. Supposedly by a Witch given the way their blood was spilled—the High Commanders confirmed it."

The High Commanders, also known as the Eminence of Three, were the elected officials from each major party in Valora. One from the Elementals, one from the Naturalists, and one from the humans. They ruled their own kingdoms respectively, but every five years, a new High Commander from each would be chosen or re-elected. Right now, it was the Vahls for the Naturalists, the Slaters for the Elementals, and Rheya Liot for the Humans.

"I don't trust the Vahls," Desmond said, leaning forward and running a hand over his stubble. Elaia said nothing since her opinion was usually ignored.

And because, these days, she wasn't even sure she trusted him. Not just with Rersa, but in general. He lied to her about everything. The drinking, the grief counseling he was supposed to be in, and his responsibilities. He also shut her out, giving her the silent treatment when she confronted him.

Beyond that, he'd been dangling the throne in her face since Shaye died. He would suggest it, then yank it away. Like a wish controlled by a teasing hand. But she'd keep wishing until she could reach out and grab it herself.

Elaia continued relaying the events of the council and the coronation for the heir of Eisera.

"So, Aydin has decided their time on the throne has ended?"

"I suppose so," Elaia mused, pushing at the food that had been placed in front of her.

Would he see the wisdom in that decision? If she asked, would he finally give her what she wanted? She wanted the power of it—power he could no longer handle.

Desmond hummed, breaking the brown grained bread to dip into the meal of sweet potato and roasted lamb. She took stock of his desk. Messy, haphazard notes that weren't at all like the handwriting she grew up with or the order he demanded from her. In fact, there was no order at all. These pieces of him that she thought remained were also fading.

She swallowed down the anxiety. "I think it's about time we do the same. Don't you think?"

The words sank into silence. Her heart pounded. "Are you insinuating that I should step down?"

"I'm asking that you consider what is best for Rersa."

Desmond's eyes had gone cold. Glacial. Just like when she disappointed him as a child. "And you think that's you?"

"I'm ready."

He scoffed but said nothing.

Frustration crawled up her spine. "I'm ready, father. I've been preparing for this my whole life. *You* have prepared me for this my whole life. It's time." More than that, she *wanted* it. She wanted the throne, the crown.

"So, you think I'm no longer fit to rule over Rersa?"

On the way here, Zahra had briefed her in detail. The country wide curfew, the placement of the Nightguard along the shores and canyons and in every major city. The higher taxes, the limitations placed on worship, and generally, his absence from his duties, all without consulting with the governors elected to rule over the seven territories of Rersa. All without consulting his council.

The council that had been with him for thirty years since he'd come to be High Shade at twenty-five. The council that had heralded times of peace and prosperity, that respected her father and guided him. They were not weak. If Nomara were alive, she'd be cursing him to Alaen—the pit of the Unforgiven.

But her fears had been real. Bit by bit, Desmond was breaking.

Like the water eroded the canyons, the loss had eroded her father.

"Answer me, Elaia. Do you think I'm unfit?"

She tipped her head. "I think your time on the throne has come to an end," Elaia said softly, trying to emulate her mother. But no one could ever be Nomara.

Fury burned in her father's eyes, and she felt the burn of it when their eyes met. "And you are?" he snarled. A leader undone. Worse, a father unraveling. "You think you are ready to protect us? To protect your people?"

She thought of the deals she'd made behind his back. The note in her pocket. She wanted to scream that she was better equipped than he was. That it was his fault they were all that was left of the family. She could handle her grief when people counted on her. She would lean on the people meant to support her.

Elaia said none of that. Instead, she quietly, confidently said, "I do. And I will do what must be done if you will not give it to me."

"You would challenge me? You'd need the council and all

seven governors to even raise it. You think you'd have their support?"

A challenge was not common. It required four of seven of the current High Shade's council support, and a unanimous approval from the seven governors. In Rersa's history, it had only been done three times. Most often, before it reached the breaking point, the High Shade would give in and name the challenger the next High Shade. What would become of Desmond and her?

Her heart pounded in her throat. "I would do what it took to win their support. If that's what it takes, I'll challenge you without hesitation." The memory of those she'd lost were heavier than her fear. Heavier than the disappointment he would drape over her.

"Get out."

Elaia stood, folding her hands behind her. "Would you hold on to the throne if it meant losing me? Would you hold onto the throne if it meant living your life alone? Or will you give it up to ensure that never happens?"

Desmond's eyes never faltered; they were cold and blank. And only silence met her as she exited. Being here often tore her in two. The girl she was, the home she loved but couldn't stand to be in, and the woman she'd become. A woman who knew grief and loss.

And now, a woman who would do what must be done.

EXHAUSTION LATCHED on to her as she traversed through the caverns. Her head ached, her body and her heart with it. What she had done, could not—would not—be undone.

I wish you were here. Elaia ran her fingers along the grooves as she wound through the narrow passageways. She hoped that they could hear her. Sometimes, when the quiet persisted, she swore she could hear the twinkle of her sisters' laughs, especially here.

Elaia traversed the high walkway, the gardens down below, a skylight allowing the moonlight, and found the hall leading toward her chambers. She strode down two twisting caverns of dark black gems and moonstones, and her doors greeted her with familiarity. Upon entry, it was a similar set up as her father's, though smaller. Incense perfumed the air of the small sitting area, and a fire burned in the hearth. All the surfaces were cleared except for two chalices and the room otherwise undisturbed.

Her stomach fluttered when she found Zahra reading on the chaise in her bedroom with only candlelight. Akiro was asleep on the bed. "You're here," Elaia said quietly.

"Where else would I be?"

She'd hoped Zahra would be here. But things had been strained, and she would've understood if she'd chosen to be elsewhere. Elaia pulled out the pastry she'd saved for her. A delicacy here, the berry compote spread on flaky butter bread, and Zahra took it with happy hands.

"For you. I'm sorry for my father." *And for everything else.*

Zahra's eyes were warm. "We are long past the point of you needing to apologize. I understand, Elaia. It's all right."

There was much to be read between the lines. Apologies Elaia didn't voice, explanations Zahra didn't care for. She knew Elaia. Even the parts she would rather hide.

"It's not." Elaia kneeled on the edge of the chaise, unsure of herself. "He's not," she whispered, knowing her words were safe here. *I'm not.*

It took Zahra only seconds to motion for her to move closer. Elaia practically crawled into the chaise, settling herself between Zahra and the cushions. For a moment, they laid in silence with only the crackling fire to join them. Elaia let her eyes fall shut and counted the rise and fall of Zahra's chest. There wasn't much to be said, and for the moment, Elaia was just happy to have her here.

Even when she was the reason they stood on unsteady ground, Zahra was a constant. One of the only ones she had left.

"It will be okay, you know." Zahra ran her fingernails up and down Elaia's spine, falling right back into the familiar.

"You've always believed that."

"I always will."

Gods, Elaia wished she could take some of that for herself. Hope. Optimism. It was a strength, regardless of what others might think—smiling in the face of darkness. Meanwhile, Elaia had bloody nails from the claw marks she left behind, trying to hold on to what was already gone.

Eventually, she looked up to find a bit of berry left on Zahra's lips. "Missed some," she murmured, swiping her thumb over Zahra's lips and taking the drop of berry for herself.

Zahra's auburn eyes darkened playfully. "I wanted that."

"We all want things we can't have."

"You can have them. You just won't let yourself," Zahra said, words no louder than a whisper. Her dark lashes fanned out over her cheeks, and Elaia couldn't help but reach up to run her fingers over her smooth skin.

"Zahra—" Elaia exhaled. "I don't want to hurt you anymore."

Her fingers played with the ends of Elaia's hair. A soft smile took over Zahra's lips, and much like the rest of her, they were soft and curved. She was all delicate features—a heart shaped face, big doe eyes, and sloping lips—though Elaia knew she was as tough as anyone underneath.

But Elaia had never erased the image of the pain in her eyes the first time she walked away. They had been engaged since they were eighteen, and still, Elaia was ready to walk away without a goodbye. She had prepared *Nomara* and was ready to sail to Aeledin, but Zahra had found out and come running to the docks, only to watch Elaia fade into the horizon.

"Then patch me up afterward," she whispered, eyes flickering between Elaia's lips and eyes. "Be selfish. Be careless. And do it with me. Always."

Elaia's heart fluttered. She could feel Zahra's heartbeat under her palm, quickening with every passing minute. No matter how hard she fought, no matter how many times she tried, they would always end up here.

"Always."

Zahra's answering smile was enough to lift the weight crushing her heart. "I've missed you. So much," Zahra whispered, leaning up to connect their lips.

Tentative at first, since it had been a few months since the last and yet, utterly familiar. They moved together in a rhythm Elaia knew like the back of her hand. Better than the castle she grew up in, better than the canyons she trained in. It was smooth, a balm to Elaia's soul that felt far away. A soft sound left Zahra's lips for her to catch, which she did with a smile. Eventually—minutes, hours, Elaia didn't care—-Zahra pulled back, her teeth tugging Elaia's lip as she went.

Her cheeks were flushed, her eyes heavy. "I have an idea. Are you up for it?"

"Does it involve leaving this room?"

Zahra pouted, their lips almost touching again. "Yes, but I promise you'll like it."

Well, Zahra had never broken a promise. Not like she had. Elaia conceded, brushing her nose against Zahra's. "Fine. Lead the way."

HIGH ABOVE, the moon shone against the night sky filled with stars. "You couldn't catch me if you tried," Zahra shouted, her words fading into the darkness. Out here, the air was a bit thinner, a bit cooler, but it was a welcome sensation over her skin.

"You know I'll find you." Elaia smiled to herself as she reached out with her shadows.

They slithered over the top of the canyon rock, following the direction of Zahra's voice. Being out here had cleared her mind in a different way than training did. In training, her mind was forced to focus and work, to be there in the moment. Here, she could shut it off and forget it all. After another moment, her shadow wrapped around Zahra's ankle, stopping her in place. Elaia glided over to her, her cheeks flushed as she came to a stop in the dark. With a quick twist, she instructed her shadow to crawl upward, tickling Zahra as she went, forcing a giggle out of her.

"Let me go. We're here."

"Where, Zahra?" Elaia groaned, unwilling to let her go.

"Would you listen to me and look," she said, rolling her eyes. Elaia had barely noticed the direction they'd traveled, trusting Zahra completely.

They were somewhere in the middle of the canyon, not far from the top but high up from the canyon floor. Here, the grooves were lighter, shimmering gray and dark blues from the sun, and there was an alcove only a few steps ahead.

"Remember this place?"

Elaia felt her lips curl into a smile. "How could I forget?"

They entered together, ducking their heads. Above, on the ceiling, there were gems inlaid in dizzying patterns by someone long forgotten in the histories or the natural world itself. When they were younger, no longer kids but not quite adults, this was their favorite place. Elaia had found it after a hard day with her father, and Zahra had followed her, despite her foul mood. And for hours, they stared at the patterns. Some similar to the constellations in the sky and others for which they made up their own stories.

Zahra intertwined their fingers and pulled them to the ground. "I thought it might help."

Resting her head on the rock behind her, Elaia turned to look at her. The returning glance was one of love. All she ever saw in Zahra's eyes was love and care and understanding, even through all the hurt. Elaia wished she was better at giving it back.

"Thank you," she said, pulling Zahra into her arms and peppering her neck with kisses until she giggled.

"Elaia," Zahra said breathlessly, a giggle escaping her lips. "Let me go."

"Nicely."

Zahra tipped her head up, her nose brushing against Elaia's skin and her fingers teasing the ends of her hair. "Please, will you please let me go?"

She leaned over as close as she could to kiss her. Until her lungs were screaming for air and the cave became warm around them. "Are you sure?" she whispered against her lips.

Zahra hummed, her hands wrapped tightly around Elaia, as if she never wanted to let her go. "No, I don't ever want you to."

Elaia smiled, kissing her again. Softer this time, but no less heated. *I don't want to—I don't ever want to.* She couldn't bring herself to say it. It was a promise she would break again.

In her arms, Zahra twisted herself to face her, cupping Elaia's face with her hands and running her thumbs over her cheeks. She kissed all her favorite parts of Elaia—she only knew that because Zahra always told her—like the bridge of her nose and the dip in her chin under her lips and the white scar beside her eye. They spent the rest of the night in that alcove, where the rest of the world couldn't touch Elaia, where the darkness of it couldn't slip in even if it tried. Not with Zahra's palms on her skin, emitting small bits of light as she went, painting them in the colors of the gems above. Not as she traced the constellations she had memorized over Zahra's skin, and not as she finally felt a sense of peace.

Everything out there seemed to be crashing down around her at various speeds. But not with her. With Zahra, the world slowed, and her heart remembered it was supposed to beat for people, that it was supposed to feel things other than pain and fear.

Elaia knew that as long as Zahra existed, she could always find something to bring her back to life.

CHAPTER 19

SHADOWS OF SECRECY

IN THE HEARTH, THE FIRE CRACKLED SOFTLY IN THE morning. Elaia sat at her desk with Akiro stretched out over the rug, rereading her own reports of the dead Scions and re-studying the drawings she'd made to memorialize the murdered animals.

Scions were never ending, it seemed. While the Gods had disappeared, their children had not. Not all of them were direct descendants; in fact, most of them weren't. As time passed, the Gods removed themselves from society further and further, disappearing into the woods or the seas or the skies as Valora expanded.

Some believed they had abandoned them for good sometime between the Massacre of the Witches and the Age of Ruin, but Elaia believed they simply created distance. For protection or for the people, it didn't matter. She still believed.

The existence of the Scions couldn't be denied, as many in the Magistrate of the Second Star dedicated their lives to studying mythology and folklore. Scions could be anything from a direct descendant or to something like Akiro, a hound that was both godlike and not. It could be the sprites that existed in the rivers and lakes or the trees or the creatures that lurked in the darkness.

The Scions that she had seen, all with slit throats and missing teeth or claws, had been hounds or the cat-like Gods of the earth, the samara. Once she'd seen a goldenwing, a small, quick winged golden bird, descendant of the gods of light. She just didn't understand why she saw them at all.

Was it a dream? A twisted reality she was stuck in? Or was it real?

A knock on the door drew her attention, and Rohan entered.

"Good morning, Princess. Zahra," he said, dipping his head to Zahra, who was moving through her stretches in front of the fire.

Most days, Zahra was with the weapons masters as she possessed a rare ability of Light Naturalists that allowed her to imbue her light into things, like weapons, making them nearly indestructible in a variety of ways. After, she would sit in on meetings Elaia was absent for when she was gone, sharing any necessary information. Even after months, her schedule hadn't changed, a shred of normalcy Elaia appreciated.

"Morning, Rohan."

He laid down a plate of food and steaming cups of tea before taking a seat across from her. "Are you still planning on calling the council today?"

It'd been a day since she'd spoken to her father. A day to sit on what she'd said. A day to decide whether it was the right choice. The note burned in her pocket again. *The shadow will continue to haunt—as long as you maintain your promises.*

"Yes. I need to know who will support me. I need time to prepare for what the governors will request." Elaia took the tea he slid her, letting the warm liquid soothe her throat.

Zahra sat up, resting her elbows on her knees, and wispy strands of her hair stuck to her skin. "You're going through with raising a challenge?"

She exhaled. It was rash. Quick. But time was not on her side. What was coming...her father could not handle. "Yes. Why? Do you think I shouldn't?"

Zahra shook her head. "No, no. It's just..." She sighed. "I wish you didn't have to. I wish we hadn't gotten here." She came over and rested her hands on Elaia's shoulders. Rings and hand chains decorated her fingers, and the anklet she always wore tinkled with her movement. "I hope he realizes the risk."

Elaia tipped her head up, meeting her eyes. "Me, too."

"Just be smart." Zahra dragged a finger down her nose before departing, the touch warm and intimate. "I'll be down in the caverns if you need me." The door shut behind her, leaving the two of them.

Inhaling, she let her head fall for a moment before meeting Rohan's eyes. "Do you think I'm making a mistake?"

"Can I speak candidly?"

She leaned back, pulling a leg under the other. "You always do; please don't stop now."

"It's not your responsibility to keep him in check. He's your father, yes, but you don't have to fix him. The High Shade is struggling, his choices unsound. But he's intelligent. I think wanting to know where you stand, in terms of a challenge, is smart. I also think you should continue to speak to him, make sure there's nothing you don't know. You're not making a mistake. You're preparing. There's nothing wrong with that."

"What if he won't listen to me?"

"Make him. As best you can." Rohan sighed. "If he doesn't, you'll know your choice is right."

And that was what she needed to do. To ensure she was putting her country first. Protecting the people she cared about as best she could. *If* that meant her father remained on the throne, then so be it. But she was ready if it meant otherwise.

ELAIA PROMPTLY CALLED a meeting of her father's council. Made up of seven members to honor the seven days the first leader of Rersa spent leading his people through the darkness.

The Commander of the Nightguard, the Treasurer, the Headmaster, The Arrow, the Citizens Advisor, the Master Healer, and the Shade's Shield.

When Elaia took the throne, Rohan would become her Shield.

Today, only her father was missing from the meeting. Elaia sat between Rohan and Zahra at the dark stone table with the council, who'd confirmed all the changes Desmond had made. The taxes on goods and imports, the increased drafting for members of the Nightguard, the restriction on worship, the required reports on any *unusual* findings, the curfew...none of it made sense.

Rersa was a free country. They had always prided themselves on their collectivism. Any major decisions were discussed with the council first, then the seven governors of the major territories, and only then were they implemented if a majority supported them.

Rersa was about community, the freedom of belief and thought, and he had slowly begun to morph into something else.

But a challenge had not been done in a long, long time. In the history of Rersa, the Obsidian Throne had only been usurped three times. Only one of those times was done without bloodshed. None of those times was the throne usurped by the only living heir.

There were rules and laws in place that kept the throne from changing hands. If a challenge was to be made, to be honored, the governors of the seven territories had to back the challenger. Unanimously.

As for the High Shade's council, out of seven, four had to support the challenge. In any event where majority was needed, it was assumed the Shield would always stand with their High Shade. Meaning only two others could deny her.

"I have asked my father to step down as High Shade." Elaia's voice rang out around the room, an instant silence following. Every eye was on her. "I have asked him to allow me to take the throne."

Instantly his Shield, Brome, was on his feet. His brows furrowed with purpose. "Respectfully, Princess, what makes you think you're in a position to lead?"

It was a fair question, she supposed. It still sent annoyance down her spine. "What makes you question me? I've experienced the same loss my father has, yet I continue to uphold my responsibilities, my duties to him and to Rersa. You've all confirmed my concerns about Desmond. I believe it is time for a change." She let her eyes fall over each council member. "If he does not concede the throne, I will challenge him for it."

Quiet shock filtered over their faces, a sense of disbelief. Though she was only twenty-five, she'd been preparing for this since she was born. The eldest child. And more, the child who always wanted it.

"We will return the taxes to what they were. The Nightguard will stand down and return to their homes, not to be wasted for a pointless watch. Under my rule, the governors will meet on a monthly basis in a forum with myself and my council. There will be no decision that is made without them present, no country-wide mandate without a conversation. My father has slowly leeched power from their hands, and I will give it back. There is no threat in Rersa; the threat comes from beyond."

"What threat, Princess?"

"A Witch killed the Elders. A Witch that is able to control blood." Unease swept through the room. The image of the woman in the snow flashed in her mind. "Beyond that, the possibility of their return and what they wrought, the consequences of the Elders' death are wholly unknown. Already, there have been quakes underfoot. Higher swells. Different patterns in the birds. Who knows what awaits us? Beyond that, I cannot share quite yet, though there is no major cause for concern thanks to the alliances we hold," she said, swallowing, fingers running over the note in her pocket. "We need to be prepared. And he is not equipped, not if he insists on tearing us apart from within."

No more questions were raised.

"I don't expect an answer this second, but I will need to know which of you would support a challenge by the next dark moon."

The dark moon was an honored time in Rersa, made to pay respect to those that had come before. How in the early days, Senka had led them through the canyons under the dark moon. It was formally celebrated six times a year as a chance to worship, to feast, and to watch and honor the countries' competitors. Each month varied, but it was a time to reset—to prepare for when the moon would rise again. The next one would arrive in three weeks.

"Understood?" She was met with an echo of *yeses.*

As they exited, she surveyed each one of them. They had helped raise her in a way, watched her go from a toddler to a girl to a woman. They helped with her teachings and supported her in her losses. She was ready, and she would prove that to them. She would make sure her plans were set and detailed, along with the failures of her father, and then, she would focus on the governors.

A sense of pride bloomed in her chest. She believed they would stand behind her. When they did, she would serve them as one was supposed to. With honor and respect.

With purpose.

Elaia turned all her efforts onto preparing her *proposal.* She needed to instill confidence in the council, to instill doubt when it came to her father. They needed to know she was prepared on all fronts—how she would solve the problems left to her and how she would position Rersa to recover. To ensure she had the trust and respect of the citizens. And of Valora.

So, she poured over texts she had studied as a child. Read the archives on the early days of her father's rule and those before. As a young girl, her father had made her study texts that discussed rises to power or falls from grace. He'd wanted her to understand what made a good leader and what would destroy them. She read them not once or twice but until she was *sure* the words were ingrained.

Zahra had spilled all the concern the council had voiced to her father and, because of Elaia's own absence, to her in their meetings. She gave Elaia the pressure points of each council member so she knew exactly where to push. Rohan collected the whisperings of those in the Nightguard and the voices that often went unheard within the walls of the palace.

Every note and letter were carefully crafted to appeal to each council member.

She believed Desmond had brushed off her comments, forgotten them. Maybe even likened them to an ignorant, ambitious young girl. Maybe he believed she was no different than the little girl who had to come in first, who bent herself backward for his praise and his approval.

But she was not that girl anymore. He'd hardened her into someone with self-confidence. Someone who believed she could have the things she wanted if she worked hard enough.

Her sense of self no longer answered to him. It only answered to her.

A GOLD EMBLEM in the shape of a Nitehound was placed on her desk, interrupting her erratic handwriting. Zahra stood in front of her, Akiro nudging his head into her thigh.

"What is this?" Elaia picked up the pendant.

There was a spark of excitement in Zahra's eyes, one she had missed seeing every day. It made her heart flutter. "I've been trying to perfect this for some time now. I've been studying light outside of the Athera. Light as a concept and what it *is*. Specifically, how it bends and how it's perceived. I wanted to translate that to things. And I think I have." Zahra picked up the emblem. "Would you pierce it?"

Standing, shadows danced at her fingertips, shaping themselves into something sharp. The dagger floated upward by her head, waiting for her instructions. Zahra threw the emblem between them, and the shadow blade shot forward, right through the center of the hound.

And the pendant, made of light and aether, turned to mist in front of their eyes. Golden shimmers fanned out, the blade of shadow disappearing, and the golden mist reforming in front of them. It landed perfectly in Zahra's palm. In perfect condition.

There was a grin on her face. Elaia couldn't help but smile in return. "That was incredible," she said, taking the emblem. Not a single scratch upon it.

"I need to develop it further, find a way to make it into armor or weapons. But if I can figure it out, the Nightguard would become unstoppable. Against...anything."

"You're brilliant."

A light flush came over Zahra's brown cheeks, pride sitting comfortably on her shoulders. She reached into the pocket of her gown, pulling out further coins.

"While I can't make weapons yet, I made these." Seven emblems clinked on the wooden surface of the desk. "I etched the acronym for each role on the council within the edge. They'll probably miss it, but you won't." Zahra motioned to her proposals. "When you deliver these, leave an emblem with each of them. All they have to do to pledge their support is return it."

Elaia rolled an indestructible emblem in her fingers, running her thumb over the ears of the Nitehound. "And we'll know who stood with me and who did not." This way, the support of her possible challenge could be done privately if they wished—in secrecy.

Zahra took a seat on the edge of her desk. "I made more. One for myself and one for you. And I can make them for whomever you like. Should things...take a turn, you can give these to those that have pledged themselves to you. As a private way to know who stands with you, no matter what."

She nodded, looking up at her. Reaching out, she curled a strand of Zahra's hair around her fingers before crawling her hand up to hold the back of her neck, their lips only inches apart. "I know it's small and probably insignificant—"

Elaia pressed her fingers into her neck, gentle but firm. "It's not. Every detail matters." A flush crawled up Zahra's cheeks, her eyes locked with Elaia's. "Everything you do matters to me." She sealed her words with a kiss, the proposals and the emblems forgotten as the warmth of her seeped into the dark room and snuck into all the places Elaia's shadows liked to hide.

The emblems could be nothing more than decoration, until they weren't. If one day, she must move in the shadows of secrecy, a flash of a gold hound could mean all the difference.

Chapter 20

Blood of the Scion

Elaia spent her days and most nights preparing her proposals.

She laid out plans of possible outcomes following the death of the Elders—war, skirmishes, political disagreements, environmental concerns—and how she would position Rersa to respond to every single one of them. Finally, after a few sleepless nights and long days, she delivered each proposal and emblem to all seven council members.

Elaia's emblem was smaller and hung on a dainty chain around her neck, and as she returned to her chambers in darkness, she found herself holding on to it as if it would chase her exhaustion away.

Before she could sink into sleep, there was a knock at her door. With a groan, she moved to answer it, not at all expecting to see her father. They hadn't spoken since her arrival. His eyes were bloodshot when he entered. The smell of liquor emitted off of him. A commonality since Nomara and her sisters. Another reason he needed to step down.

Akiro lifted his head, flicking his ears at the High Shade's arrival before returning to sleep.

"Father."

His eyes were unfocused as he entered. "I wanted to give you something." He approached her, a worn leather folder in his hands, and thrust it at her.

"What are they?"

Desmond shook his head, spinning the ring that he'd worn since becoming High Shade. "Your mother's," he said, roaming around the room. "These are the rest of her...musings. I've been trying to understand what she was looking for, what she had been warning me about—"

"Warning you?" Elaia furrowed her brows, her skin pricking. Confusion warmed her. What could Nomara have feared? Warnings of what?

This was the first she'd heard of this. They rarely spoke of Nomara, and the times they had, he'd shut down. His eyes would go dark, and the conversation would end.

"Your mother was spending most of her days in the library or with the Headmaster. I don't—I don't know what she was looking for. She tried to explain it to me once, but I ignored her."

Pain prickled over her skin at the thought, but Elaia stayed silent.

"You know she was a believer in the things we didn't understand or care to, and I always brushed it off. I never should've brushed it off," he rambled, more speaking to himself than her. After a moment of silence, he blinked as if to clear the fog, and his eyes narrowed. "Do not make the mistake I did, Elaia. Do not ignore what you do not understand."

She only looked at him, unsure of what to make of this. Would he hand over the throne as well? Or would he hold onto that, too?

Desmond approached her until they were less than an arm's length away. He reached up, cupping her cheeks like he used to when she was a little girl. But this man—this frantic, unsure man —was not her father either. The smell of alcohol was overwhelming.

"Pore over those. Her notes are written in the margins; maybe you will see something I couldn't. Or something I *wouldn't*. Can you do that?"

"Yes."

"Good." Her father gazed at her a second longer.

Elaia couldn't stop the thoughts that creeped in. Would he tell her he loved her? Like he used to? Or was this nothing more than a moment of weakness?

"Can I ask you a question?"

"Of course."

"Why can't you look at me anymore?" Her voice was smaller than normal, the question one she had held in. But she used to be his favorite daughter. And now, he never looked at her.

His eyes widened. "I—" Desmond sighed, looking a much smaller man than she once believed. As a child, her father had been as large as a God and just as imposing. But that was not who remained. "You look so much like them. Like all of them."

If that was supposed to help, it didn't. Instead, the fractures of her heart continued into her ribs.

"So, you would let your grief take me away from you, too?" Elaia stepped back, out of the cold that had grown between them. "Do you wish it had been me?"

Because sometimes...she did. Why had she survived when they were gone?

Silence was the initial response. She felt like she was bleeding out in front of him, and he couldn't even offer to staunch it.

He took a step but stopped as if trying to find the right words to say. And the idea that he had to search for them meant they were already wrong.

Pain practically reverberated off him. "There is an ache in me that has been there from the moment they left. From the moment Shaye died. An ache that is vast. An ache that devours me every day. But...I would not trade you to fill it."

Her heart throbbed once, twice, with a broken, unsteady beat.

Her voiced cracked as she said, "That is not what I asked." Maybe it was petulant and needy, but she wanted certainty. But she would not get it, not from him. He was as much a ghost as the rest of them now, a shell of himself. Even alive, all he did was haunt her.

"Elaia—"

Tears threatened to fall. She shook her head, her hair fanning around her face. Her nails left indents in her palm. She did not let go until she bled. "I'm tired, Father."

They shared a look of immense pain. Maybe his stemmed from loving her and hating her at the same time, for being the one left. Maybe it stemmed from the idea that, in a way, he was losing her, too. It didn't matter. The problem was that now, all they were to each other were ghosts of what had been lost.

SLEEP DID NOT COME EASY. Not with Akiro curled on her left or Zahra tucked into her side. She stared at the dark ceiling above, tracing the stones in the patterns of the constellations she loved.

Though the dark was her home in more ways than one, sometimes if she stared into it too long, she'd see the shape of her sister, Shaye, hanging exactly as when Elaia found her. The shape of a body no longer breathing. A soul gone because she couldn't handle the pain of loss. Another loss that Elaia carried instead.

Sighing, she pushed up, the covers falling off her body. It was hard to remember who she was. There were days when the only thing she wanted was to be the girl she used to be. But it wasn't possible, no matter how hard she tried.

Leaning over, she ran her hand over Zahra's hair, bending down to murmur against her ear, "Can't sleep. I'll be back."

"More dreams?" Zahra's voice was heavy, and her shoulders curled inward at the sound of her voice.

"Not this time," she said softly. "Just—" Elaia shook her head.

Zahra rolled over, blinking open those auburn eyes. In the

dark, they were beacons. She patted the bed. "Come here for a second."

After a moment, she obliged, laying back down so Zahra could pull her into herself. She exhaled, resting her head back. But it was no use. Even though Zahra's embrace was a slight reprieve, everything else stuck to her skin.

"What is it?"

"Everything. Being here. My dad. The Witches. The throne," she said. "And I keep seeing Shaye when I close my eyes. There are memories in every corner, along every hall of them. They used to be everywhere, and now, they are gone. And those memories do nothing but taunt me."

Zahra traced over the delicate ink on her skin and over the column of her throat. The dainty hand chains and rings she wore pressed into Elaia's skin. Zahra didn't ask if there was anything she could do, because she knew there was no true answer.

"Being home can be strange," Zahra whispered. "This is the only home I've ever really known, and there are days where it doesn't feel like mine."

Home. A word whose meaning had changed so much in the past year—a word that no longer held much meaning. Elaia felt a bit lost no matter where she was these days. In reality, it was Zahra and Rohan that provided any tangible meaning to the word. Other than that, she wasn't sure she'd ever find a true home again.

"Do you really think the Witches are back? It's been centuries."

Elaia thought again of the woman. Of how the Elders had been killed. The tears of dried blood on their cheeks. She'd expected it but not quite like that. "They are."

"Do you want me to get you anything?" Zahra readjusted them, pulling them face-to-face, their noses brushing.

Elaia traced the shape of her face with a gentle touch. "No. I'm gonna go for a walk; get out of here for a bit."

Zahra hummed, the strands of her long hair dancing over Elaia's skin. "If you need me, I'll come. Always."

"I know."

With a parting kiss in the shadows, Elaia got up, Akiro jumping down to follow her, sticking his nose into the back of her knee.

"Coming with me?"

His ears flicked in response, his tail wagging behind him. Quickly, she pulled a more casual gown of black and lace over her head and ran her fingers over his soft fur. They slunk into the dark of the private tunnel hidden in her chambers.

There were no lanterns on the cavernous walls, so she grabbed the torch that she kept near the door, striking the match and letting the fire blaze through the darkness.

Every time she entered this tunnel, memories of her father sending her deep into the canyon to find her way out resurfaced, as they did now. Her father had always been hot and cold. She was constantly at war with her memories, trying to force the puzzle pieces to work. The days when she was a little girl, her father teaching her to wield shadows in the dark and the light, and chasing her through the castle walls. And the days when her father chased her with blades made of shadow, forcing her to learn the feel of shadows in different forms.

Days when he was her biggest fan and days when she was his biggest disappointment.

She sighed, traversing through the familiar space, trying to force the memories to disperse. The tunnels were winding and curved upward until light from the moon crept in at the opening. Her eyes narrowed. A dark shape, unmoving, sat at the tunnels mouth, directly in the moonlight.

Akiro let out a snarl of unease, and she dampened the light. She dispersed her shadows along the walls like creeping hands as she approached. Blood splattered over the rocky floor and dripped down over the tunnels edge. Threads of silver were intertwined with the maroon. She swallowed thickly as she stood over the dead hound.

If Akiro wasn't behind her, she would've easily thought this was him. It was sprawled in the moonlight, its limbs splayed and unmoving, its throat cut jaggedly. Teeth and claws were missing. Her heart broke. If it was made of glass, it would've shattered.

Her hand shook as she brushed the dark fur of the Scion. It was shameful, an action committed by those with no respect or honor. Not just for religious reasons, but general compassion. These animals, their history, their bloodlines went so deep into the past, they were legends. There was little known about them other than their relation to the Gods. No one knew how long they lived or how the Aether ran through their blood. They were never studied, never prodded. They were respected.

Until now.

Rohan and Zahra might've thought her crazy, but she knew she wasn't hallucinating this. She just didn't understand why only *she* was suffering?

But someone was hunting these animals.

And they had sent her a message.

A tear fell, but she wiped it away. Elaia pulled the lips of the animal down, unfurling its deathly snarl, and shut its eyes.

Shadows surrounded the hound and curled over the cliff. Stepping up, she turned her eyes out to the canyons. While she couldn't track every inch of it, her shadows could go a fair distance, and she sent them sprawling. No odd shapes or forms came back to her as they crawled, but she kept her eyes peeled.

There! Right under the light of the moon. Another shape. A person this time, atop the canyon walls. And somehow, she knew they were looking at her.

They wanted her attention? Well, they had it.

In many sections of Varistone, central to the Canyons of Zylla, there were places where the rock had not fully eroded. Places where towering fortresses of sheer stone, bridges made of sand and black stones, connected the canyons rims. Above, the moonlight illuminated the sheer faces where the rock turned reflective and the various paths and walkways weaved into the canyons themselves.

Elaia bounded upward, Akiro following her on swift feet. The moment her pace increased, the figure moved. Her shadows crept along the walls with her, darting in and out into the darkness as she crossed over the canyon. Thin bare tree branches curled up from within the rock, and she weaved around them under the moonlight. But the figure was gone.

No, no, no! She could not lose them. But exhaustion was heavy. Her shadows were mere wisps when she needed them to be blades. Elaia crouched, resting her hand on Akiro's back. He touched his nose to her cheek as if to say all was okay. She let her head rest against him, steadying herself against the beat of his heart.

"Let's head back, Ki," she murmured, taking one last glance at the top of the canyon before retreating. But maybe *this* time the hound would still be there. She hurried back to the tunnel opening. And sighed.

Damnit.

All that remained was a singular spot of rock, darkened with blood. She scoured the ground for anything. A stray tooth or claw, even a clump of fur. But there was nothing. A twisting, heated scream built within her chest, aching to claw its way out of her throat. It was one thing after another, and she was getting tired of forcing herself through it. These days, Elaia wanted to destroy the whole thing.

When she was younger, when her mother would take them to the temples where they would honor Senka and Tasyn and other Gods in the darkness of dusk or the new sky of dawn, one of the lessons she both hated and loved was that of acceptance. Acceptance that the world was not good or bad—it just was.

But actions, choices, people, things could be one or the other. Or both, as so many things often were. Acceptance that the world didn't exist in only black and white, in darkness and light, but in shades of every color. Elaia liked to put things into boxes. She liked when things had explicit meaning. But they rarely did.

She had to accept that the same world that took Nomara and

her sisters was the same world she'd grown up in. The same world where she used to color on the stones and dance in puddles when it would rain. She had to accept that things were changing. That power or control or safety required sacrifice. That nothing came freely or easily. And that even the most powerful could be taken away. Acceptance drove her crazy. The world expected her to what? Lie down and take it? To roll over and move on because she *accepted* it?

Something wasn't right here, and she was going to find out what.

She would not accept otherwise.

PAPERS WERE STREWN around her private nook of the library, covering every surface, clinging to her desk, and decorating the floor. All of that and still nothing. Elaia collapsed in the chair, burying her fingers into her hair, scratching her scalp with her nails.

The library, ironically, was at the highest part of Varistone, extending beyond the rim of the canyons and into the sky. The walls went from gritty dark obsidian and sedimentary rock in shades of red to smooth slabs of gray and silver with streaks of icy blue, encompassing the rest of the formal colors of the Rersian empire. Grand windows were placed to capture the best light and view of the sky and canyons possible, etchings and carvings of Nitehounds were above every door, and legends and myths were painted on the ceilings.

She'd been in the library so long that she was approaching her second sunrise. Rays of light were beginning to land over parchment and pen. To no use. It was all useless. A laugh scratched its way out, twisted and dry. Gods, it was pointless. It was all—

"Elaia, you need to take a break." Zahra's voice was soft, but it cut through the fog.

She and Rohan had tried earlier, but Elaia only shooed them away. When she had a task, when something *needed* to be done—whether for the sake of her kingdom or for her own sanity—almost nothing could stop her.

"Elaia. Look at me."

She rubbed her eyes. Zahra was a blurred figure in the doorway, but she'd know her anywhere, even blind. "I told you I have to finish this."

"Finish what?" Zahra asked, entering the room and bending to say hi to Akiro, who was curled up on the only clear section of the floor. "You haven't even told me what you're looking for."

"Because you won't believe me." When Zahra only raised a brow, she continued, "It's the same as before. Another dead Scion. And no proof to show you. But it was there. A shadow hound, bled dry with missing teeth and claws. And it was right *there*." The image flashed as she blinked. The hound snarling and dead. "And this," she said, holding up her frantic sketches, "Is all I have. So I have to find something, *anything*, to back up what I saw. To prove it was real. That someone or something is out there doing this on purpose."

Akiro whined as he moved closer to her, rubbing his head against her legs.

Zahra began to sweep up the papers strewn over the floor. There was a cautious look in her eyes as she approached, but a determined one as well. "Let me help."

"I barely know what I'm looking for, Zahra. There's nothing —I've found nothing to suggest that what I'm seeing has happened before. Father ignores all my notes on it. You and Rohan think I'm overworked and seeing things." Elaia sighed, running her fingers through her hair. "And there's nothing here to prove differently. But it happened in Aeledin, now here. It cannot be a coincidence."

Zahra gave her a piercing stare. "So, maybe we're wrong. The least I can do is understand or help you find something that puts this to a stop." She sat, sweeping her thick hair out of the way.

The scent of smoke and honeysuckle—the smell of Zahra—infiltrated Elaia's space. She said nothing as Zahra's eyes began to flit over the scrawl.

This was how it always went—how it had always been. The two of them were different in many ways. Elaia retreated, preferring to lock herself away until she was needed. When her people needed her, she preferred to listen and solve. Not interpret. Because that was how she'd been taught. A problem always had a solution. Or it should.

Whereas Zahra didn't mind the messy in between. She accepted that life was chaos and one did not exist without the other. She surrounded herself with people. When they needed help, she was there; when they needed support or guidance, she was there, able to help them see things that weren't always clear.

The fact that this was because she felt the need to ensure she would never be left again was something only Elaia knew. Just like only Zahra knew that isolation was something Elaia sought out because there, she felt free from her father's eyes.

Still, for them, it worked. Because her solitude would always take a backseat to Zahra. And Zahra, though a beacon, always looked for Elaia first in a crowd.

So, they sat together and read through every archive and parchment Elaia could think to pull. They sat as the suns rose and fell again into darkness. Eventually, Zahra rested her eyes, quickly falling into sleep as Elaia unraveled the new scrolls that her father had given from her mother. Elaia expected nothing of use. She traced her fingers over the handwriting, so familiar to her, and swore in the loops of the letters she could feel her mom beside her.

She unraveled the next parchment, surprise misting over her when she saw sketches. Not that it was unusual since Nomara had taught her—all of them—how to draw, but these were...different. Darker, more hurried. And nothing she'd ever seen before. Elaia flipped through the images until she landed on a particular one. A drawing of the God of Light, the God of Lazora, the goldentail, or one of its Scions. Elaia swallowed.

In the drawing, the bird was not alive. It was sprawled, wings spread over a non-descript floor with feathers torn off and blood on its tiny chest.

"What in the Gods is this?" she whispered, struck by how hollow her chest felt. On the next page, there was another. And another. And another. Each one tore a piece of her heart and ripped it to shreds. Had her mom seen these? Dreamed these? Would she have known about the hunters if she was still alive? Or was it too good to be true?

She needed answers because right now...it was all a bunch of maybes.

And Elaia didn't have time for maybes.

CHAPTER 21

THE SKY BEGAN TO BLEED

NOVA SMELLED LIKE ANCIENT DUST.

Her fingers were covered in paper cuts, and she huffed in annoyance at the appearance of another one. With the cuts, she noticed what Asha had—how her own blood stitched back together. It was one of the strangest things she'd ever seen, the way it congealed so rapidly and came back together. One second, the tiny cuts were there, and the next, they were gone.

Under the lamp light, she watched it happen again. A tiny drop beaded from the cut, which she caught with the tissue, but that was all the blood that fell.

Bloody suns. A mewl of pain left her lips as a fractured image stole her vision. It was brief, painful. An image of her tied to that chair in Froststone. Of cuts being made over her skin at the hands of the Vahls. It blurred then. She couldn't see whether they healed or not, but she felt the pain of every single one.

It stole her breath. Thankfully, she was in the privacy of her room, a decision she'd made to avoid Cyrus as much as possible over the past week.

When she opened her eyes, the cut was gone, like all the rest. But then, why had the ones around her wrist and on her neck remained? Was it the aetherchains? Had the Vahls found a way to make her scar?

She sighed, clearing her head. *It doesn't matter.* There was too much to be done, too much information to weed through, too many archives to pull from. Every day, she asked herself what would appease the Elders. They wanted the truth...but the truth of what? So, she pulled books and anthologies on the Elders themselves, Spirit and the Gods. And for herself, a few on the Witches.

But most of it were things she already knew, nothing beyond the teachings of Valora.

There were multiple volumes on the massacre but few on the Witches beyond that. The history of the massacre was quite simple; it began all at once and lasted for almost a century. Witches, only ever women, were the only beings able to control blood. There were reports of spells and curses—other abilities that no one else had.

The massacre officially began when someone accused a Witch of torturing him by blood and killing the small town he governed. From there, it grew—stories of bloodlust and torment—until they were deemed uncontrollable. And they didn't stop until every single Witch was dead. Spirit had a vital part in the round up—infiltrating their minds to find them and to reel them in, only to destroy them.

The fault of history was that it was written by those who won, those who survived. What would the history books say if they'd been written by a Witch?

Nova practically slammed the book closed, the noise echoing through the room. *What did it matter? They were dead.* And the dead couldn't tell their truths to living.

It was deep into the night. The library was quiet. But she liked it best in the midnight hours. On the upper floor, she had found nooks high above the shelves that served as study rooms with windows that allowed her to see the moon or stars if the sky was clear. The aisles were empty at night, so she could peruse the shelves at her leisure instead of hiding from the eyes of those around her.

She headed down the dark, dimly lit aisle and returned the archive. Drawing her finger along the shelves and over the inlaid stone and the dust, she headed deeper into the dark. Nova had checked all the obvious places, checked alphabetical order, and then by age and year. Still nothing.

"Can I help?"

Nova spun, heart racing, only to find Cyrus perusing the shelves himself. Except it wasn't just him she saw; all eight Elders stared back at her from the darkness. Horror filled her. Their eyes were empty, soulless and blank, and tear streaks of red ran over their cheeks.

You are failing. You are looking for the wrong things. Their voices were deafening. *To the beginning, you must go back. The truth of the world has gone rotten—find the rot.*

She wanted to scream, to ask them to tell her what 'the rot' was. Where would the truth have become something less? The beginning of *what*? Of Valora? Of the Elders?

"Nova? Are you okay?"

His voice brought her back to the present, and when she blinked, their faces were gone. "Sorry." She swallowed. "Yes, yes. I'm fine."

"You look like you've just seen a ghost."

Eight of them, to be exact. "No, you just took me by surprise," she said, forcing a smile on her face. "It's not nice to sneak up on people." She kept her eyes on him, scared if she strayed even an inch, they'd reappear. Their words were confusing and useless.

What was the point in haunting her if they weren't going to tell her exactly what they wanted? *Find the rot*...what in the Gods was that supposed to mean? The massacre? Another war?

"I apologize. I didn't mean to. Are you sure you're all right?" he asked, moving closer. "You look—"

"I'm fine, Cyrus." She strode away from the shelves, meeting him in the middle. He didn't need to see she was investigating the massacre, not if he was privy to what happened on the Elderlands. Forcing herself to maintain calm, she tipped her head. "Are you stalking me?"

He lifted a brow, a smile on his lips. "I couldn't sleep." Nova hummed, though she was convinced he was reporting her every move to Amala. "It seems as though you can't either."

"I don't often sleep well."

"Can I help you? With whatever you're studying? I never asked before." Cyrus crossed his arms, leaning on the shelves. His green eyes were locked on her.

"In Vilies, I was studying a variety of things," she said, trying to think of something. *To the beginning.* "I hadn't yet picked one thing or another. But I'm interested in Valora's history as a whole, major events. The Gods, the Ages, the wars."

"We studied quite a lot of that—well, Amala especially. Come on," he said, eyes darting over the shelves as he went. "I always found the Gods interesting. Comparing the legends of them to what the historians have written. How they intersect and how they differ." He pulled out a large volume. "The original Anthology of the Suns are in Vilies, at least as I've been told, but they're restricted. Most of the countries have copies, as I'm sure you know, as do we. Though we've got a collection which includes different interpretations. It's interesting to see how one person might've seen something compared to another."

"Are you sure you're an architect?"

"Nothing more." Cyrus smiled, but it was off. Despite her suspicions, his blood didn't falter. "Come on." He led them to one of the private study rooms, the goldstones flickering to life and reflecting off the artwork. On the stone table, he opened the volume. "This is a version of the tenth volume. One that dissects all nine of the Gods."

She furrowed her brows. "Even the dragons?"

Stories say they abandoned the Witches before the massacre, confirming what the other Athera believed—that they were dangerous and unworthy. Some stories said the dragons died with the Witches. But all stories acknowledged they were the first ever recorded. The first Gods.

"Yeah. There are quite a few sections of them in here, and we have multiple works on them if you're interested," he said. "I'd be happy to pull some volumes I've found interesting."

"That'd be great, thank you." She started flipping through the pages, her curls falling around her face. She turned to Spirit first to find a drawing of their God—a dove. "There's not much about Spirit." Their section of the book was substantially smaller than the rest—pages instead of chapters.

"I noticed that, too." He furrowed his brow. "There's not much interpretation for Spirit either. The stories are much the same throughout the archives. Even their volume in the Anthology is much smaller, though I can't say why that is."

She made a mental note to return to that before continuing.

The first pages contained a story, or multiple stories, about the beginning of the Gods. They were noted to be fiction, but she read them anyway. She read one about Tsuna and Neráh, the first dragons, and how they came from shell and rock wrapped in Aether that had been frozen and thawed, warmed by the suns and then forgotten, until they landed on the surface to hatch. Legend, but intriguing.

She continued, turning to a page that had a rough sketch of Neráh. She traced her finger over the sketch, over the shape of the wings and the brush strokes of red and maroon and scarlet. Written underneath was the *God of Blood*. There wasn't much on the page—a few scrawls but nothing substantial.

And again, the corner of the godsdamnned page slit her finger.

A drop of blood landed on the old yellowed parchment.

"Shit." She pulled her finger away, putting pressure on it.

Cyrus looked up. "You all right?"

"Yeah," she started. "Just a cut..."

Her words trailed off as she watched the blood seep into the paper and spread out over the page. Writing appeared over every inch of parchment as her blood brought the page to life.

"Nova?"

She looked up franticly, only to find he wasn't looking at the page, just her. Did he not see it?

"I've cut myself so many damn times, I've lost track." She smiled, acting as if the page wasn't changing in front of her. "I'm going to head back to my room if you don't mind. I'd like to take notes, and I don't have my materials with me."

"Of course. I'll be making some tea in the kitchens. I'll bring you some as well."

"Thank you." She was up and out of the study room before he could blink. But the whole way she felt his eyes on her. Watching.

She locked the door behind her, reopening the book on her desk. The text that had revealed itself was still there, and she lifted the page to find that the blood hadn't soaked through. With a purposeful swipe, she cut her finger again, and watched her blood bring the next pages to life. The drop moved around and around before settling into the parchment. The pages turned scarlet, and the words appeared like magic. Sketches appeared in the margins, along with little notes.

Her blood...It wasn't logical. It didn't make sense. On the next page, under a rough sketch of blood on the leaves, a note was scrawled. Her heart pounded.

"For the Witch of the Blood...welcome back. Be careful of what you read. Trust more what you see."

A Witch of the Blood. Nova swallowed as she continued. Every page she bled on revealed more.

A dragon of the blood, a dragon of the soul. One did not exist without the other.

Their wings touched the earth and the sky and split the world in three.

Dragon of the blood? Dragon of the soul? What was the soul? Was it not the spirit?

The notes were haphazard, messy. At first, it was about the two of them, Neráh and Tsuna. How their lives intertwined. Like the moon and the suns. Neráh did not exist without Tsuna. And Tsuna without Neráh. She read story after story of how they broke from their shells together and learned to fly side by side.

It was a volume about Gods, yes. But this was so much more. Like she said, the dragons came first, that was agreed upon, but the rest was left up to interpretation. Those in Rersa believed their Nitehounds formed from the shadows themselves. Those in Lazora believed the goldentails grew wings out of the sunrays. On and on and on it went.

But this book, these stories...everything came from the dragons. A dark wing through the clouds created shadows that formed the Nitehounds. A teardrop from the dragons eye into the sea created the serpents.

What remained unknown, to Nova and the world, were the stories and the beliefs of the Witches. She believed this may be the beginning.

Her brain couldn't keep up with her eyes. Information knocked at the edges of her mind. Pain reverberated in her skull as something sank its claws into her head, into her body. She couldn't find the words to describe the pain, how it felt as though her mind was shattering like glass.

And then, her mind splintered. Her thoughts scattered, overtaken by visions that were not her own. She cupped her head with both hands, digging her fingers into her hair.

She saw dragons flying through the air, red streaked wings and black wings streaked with silver. They flew over a land shrouded in fog and clouds, like a wall keeping a secret. Shadows seeped from the clouds and into the sky, a feather of fire danced down to the ground, a golden bird shot from the sunrays, a ripple of water in the sea as their wings touched the surface. Drops of blood fell from the sky, disappearing into the clouds. All as they circled a place she could not see.

A voice that was not her own repeated: "A dragon of the blood, a dragon of the soul."

The dragons dove beneath the fog, to a place Nova could not see. A shadow covered the expanse of the sky, illuminating the suns from behind...and the sky began to bleed.

Nova opened her eyes, only she wasn't in her room. She was in a dark section of the library she'd never been before.

What in the world?

There was a book in her hand, one of the many that had been sitting on her desk that she hadn't gotten to. Confusion swarmed her head as she tried to focus. The shelves were covered in a thin layer of dust, the books, too, and the goldstone was dimmed, old. She blew air toward the books, sending the dust into a flurry. Titles revealed themselves slowly.

"Back to the beginning."

The shelves were lined with books on every war and age in Valora. She had looked for these to no avail. And now, she was just here? Directly in front of her were two books: one on the Age of Darkness, the time period after the massacre, and the following Naturalist War. She grabbed both of them, settling herself on the floor. She had no recollection of what time it was or how long she'd been here, but she wasn't likely to be disturbed, at least.

Opening the pages of the Age of Darkness, she found more drawings. Drawings of the Witches being drained of blood. Drawings of how the suns seemingly disappeared shortly after, as if in mourning—referred to as the Dark Days amongst the pages. It had happened only twice more in history, all in times of great loss. She opened the second book. The opening image was a detailed depiction of the Naturalist War. Destruction was veiled by shadow and light, hands were held to heads because of Spirit, and healers were sprinkled throughout, trying to stave off death. But the Naturalist War was violent. People hadn't expected that; the Elementals hadn't expected that. Hadn't expected darkness and light to cause so much damage, hadn't expected minds to be shattered.

She was about to slice her finger again when she felt the low, steady pulse of a heartbeat.

She reached out to be met with something slow and dark. It wasn't Cyrus. It wasn't any of the scribes she'd familiarized herself with. Who was that? Who had followed her? Closing the book, she began to track it, staying to the shelves and the shadows. But every corner she turned, they evaded her. Whatever part of the library she was in was a dark, twisting labyrinth.

The blood felt different than anything she'd ever held, heavy and thick. Not sick, not draining, just...dark.

Furrowing her brows, she continued to no avail. They were close but never in her sight. Looking back and forth, she stayed for a minute longer before finding the staircase and moving upward. Eventually, light from the high built windows streamed in, and the soft murmurs of voices greeted her ears. And that blood was never far—confirming they were, in fact, following her.

But there was no one behind or around as she entered the main floor of the library, only to run right into Amala. The touch turned her skin cold, and she quickly put space between them.

"Princess, I'm so sorry. I wasn't watching where I was going." Nova painted a demure smile on her lips, quickly sensing her blood. But it wasn't her.

"No apologies necessary. I know what it's like to be lost here. Physically and mentally," Amala said, pointing to the books in her arms. Nova adjusted them, ensuring the titles were out of view. "I assume things have been going well?"

If Cyrus was keeping an eye on her, what was the point of this visit? Did she suspect her?

"Very. I'm still learning my way around the library, but

everyone has been kind as I get back into the swing of things. Is there something I can help you with?"

The princess's eyes narrowed, but her features were schooled into softness. It didn't fit her. Amala didn't strike her as someone who made herself soft or digestible to others. "I only wanted to see how you were doing and ensure Cyrus was doing as I asked," she said.

Nova reached out, crawling around the edges of the princess's mind, and felt her blood. There was something bitter, something hidden in her head. There was an underlying sense of cunning there. Or maybe she was mistaking Amala's intelligence for calculation. Was she only being protective of her country, or was it something more?

She raised a brow. "Watching me, you mean."

"Yes."

"Do you often keep track of Cyrus's responsibilities?"

Amala's eyebrows rose. "Only when they are of importance."

Around them, others milled about. The sound of wheels rolled over the stone floor as some perused the shelves. "If it's so important, why didn't you take on the responsibility yourself? Respectfully."

The princess's eyes sharpened. Nova reached out, instantly met with the threads, which she *still* didn't understand. Mostly because she was too busy trying to read every godsdamned book in this library. But what she did know was they were twisted and angry. She didn't have time to pinpoint one and follow it and hope it led her to the answer, but it felt like...jealousy. Turning her threads into something hungry.

"Cyrus is good with people, and he likes to...avoid. To run. This way, I know exactly where he is. For the most part."

She blinked. "That wasn't an answer, Princess."

Amala huffed a laugh. The thing was, if they discovered she was lying, she would find her way out. No matter what. She wasn't going to bend to some prickly royal.

"I have other things to attend to, Nova."

"Then they probably need you there. Not here, checking in on Cyrus." She smiled, forcing herself to soften. "Besides, I can assure you, I'm nothing of importance. I don't know what's happened or what you're expecting to uncover, but you won't find it with me." Nova pressed against her mind, willing her to believe it. Just a prick. To protect the truth of what she was.

They stared at each other for a moment, a thread of tension drawn between them. Amala let her eyes fall, and she felt the moment they landed on her scar. People always tried not to stare, but they failed. Cyrus was the only one to have never lingered on it.

"If there is nothing else...I'd like to get back to my studies."

Amala raised her head but stepped back. That blood that had been following her in the background disappeared. "By all means."

With a parting glance, Nova returned to her room, though she felt the princess's gaze on her until she was out of view. Her mind spun. Did they suspect her? Had Cyrus seen more than she thought? And what was the relation between the two?

Because they were lying. They both were. As a liar herself, as someone with selfish intentions, she recognized them. Lies were a sunray hitting the center of a mirror, flashing a bright sign up to the sky.

Stop. It doesn't matter. She needed to uncover whatever it was the Elders wanted and get out of here. If she didn't, would they haunt her forever? Would her freedom—her life—forever be held in the hands of someone else? And because whenever the Vahls decided to make their play, she needed to be as far away from them as possible. Before someone looking saw something she couldn't hide.

Maybe her instincts were skewed. Maybe she was certifiably insane. Both were probably true. But she knew, deep down in her bones, that only time would tell. And she also knew, with a sureness, that her time was running out.

CHAPTER 22

CHOSEN BY NALĀDIN

Nova quickly became attuned to the habits of
the Emerald Library.

Based on heartbeats, she knew when the library was crowded
and when it was empty—she knew the patterns and the
regularities. The stray heartbeat in the hallway of her room at
midday was *not* a regular occurrence. She peered around the
corner, a heavy book in her hand, and a sliver of light from her
room was cast over the hall floor. Was there anything within that
would give her away? Her heart pounded, panic flickering over
her skin like a match.

Reaching out, she felt the familiar beat of Cyrus's blood.
What was he doing in her room? She strode forward, took a deep
breath, and stepped into the doorway, only to find Cyrus sitting
calmy at her desk.

Her eyes narrowed. "What are you doing here?"

"I was waiting for you."

She took stock of the space. Six books on the desk, one
partially open. All the pages were tan, not a sight of blood upon
them. The rest of the books she'd gathered were stacked on the
floor under the small green and silver mirror or upon her
nightstand. But nothing looked out of place. Except him.

"You could've waited in the hall," she said, keeping her voice level.

His eyes widened. "You're right; the door was open, I wasn't thinking."

Nova knew, she *knew* that wasn't true. But his heart rate was steady; he was calm. Was he lying? Or had she forgotten to shut it? The sleepless nights and whispers from the dead and endless texts were dragging her into exhaustion. While she'd only had one more vision since Amala's visit, the effects still left her reeling. They made little sense. But neither did him being here. In *her* room.

"Well, what can I do for you?"

He stood and approached, leaning against the door frame. "I thought you'd like to come see Izlena today." He gave her a gentle look, though his eyes tracked over her from head to toe.

He had crafted this look perfectly. One of ease that was no less perceptive than a searching glance.

Nova sighed, her own eyes lingering on him. When he was in front of her, she couldn't help but stare. Despite her annoyance with being watched, there was something she was drawn to. His constant steady heartbeat was comforting, and he always smelled like the forest. Pine and rain. It was addicting.

She cocked her head. "Is this your doing or Amala's?"

"Does it matter?"

She stared for a moment longer before sighing. If he had suspicions, she didn't want to add to them. "Give me a moment to get dressed."

Cyrus dipped his chin and stepped into the hall. Immediately, she shut the door behind her. Another glance let her know everything was just as she left it. Exactly. Not a page out of place. She traded the simple cotton for a deep midnight blue satin long sleeve blouse and pants. The material clung to the curve of her hips and fell off her shoulders. She added tiny silver cuffs to her braids and let the rest of her curls brush the top of her shoulders. All of it was courtesy of Cyrus, who'd brought her multiple bags of items from the city.

"Okay," she said, stepping out.

He spared a glance behind her at the books scattered about the chamber before she shut the door. Only now, his eyes lingered on her. Everywhere they landed, a small, gentle warmth remained.

They headed out in silence. A few of the scribes let their eyes linger on him. For what, she couldn't say, but she made a note of it anyway. Upon their exit, the suns were continuing their ascent in the sky.

The waterfalls from the mountains trickled into the lake, the top somewhere hidden behind Willowgrove. Lilypads floated on the surface, as did other flowers of various shades. Ripples from creatures below bubbled up every now and then.

One section of the lake seemed to touch the mountains, hidden by shrubbery. The rest was surrounded by a gravel path that led into the city. Grand stairs flanked the cave leading up to Willowgrove. There was a large bridge, separated from the castle itself, that traversed to one side of the lake to the other with archways that let the water flow freely.

She breathed in the fresh air as they walked around the pathway, heading under the bridge. Ahead, the city spread into the mountains and the valley. Smoke wafted out of chimneys, carrying the smell of bread and pastries and breakfast meats.

He led her up one of the grand staircases. From here, she could see the entire city laid out. The buildings in various shades and stones, the vines hanging with flowers from window to window, casting shadows over the people walking below. As they rose up, the smell of the forest became stronger, oak and pine and flowers mixing into one. There was a small café on the first bridge, with stone tables situated against the railing with vases of flowers.

Selecting an empty table, she took a seat as Cyrus went to the café window. He returned with two cups of steaming coffee and multiple plates. Plates filled with seasoned potatoes, a plate of pork strips and fluffy eggs, sliced fruit, and various pastries. She followed suit when he poured cream into his coffee until her own mug was a softer brown.

She looked over the small table at him. Pulling the plate with a familiar looking pastry toward her, she broke off a piece, happy to find almond cream within.

In the wind, there were flags shifting in the breeze—two different ones. One of deep forest green and another of pure silver. The forest green had the stitching of a dagger covered in vines, with the word *Ižavore* written underneath. The silver had a crown braided with flowers and a single drop of blood.

Nova twisted her head. *What in the Gods were those for?* She twisted back, finding Cyrus was already watching her.

She sighed. "Why are we here, Cyrus?"

"To eat," he said, and she gave him a deadpan look. His lips curled. "You've been locked up in that library for days now; you needed to see the suns."

She couldn't deny how good it felt to have their warmth on her skin. "That's not quite what I mean. I understand it's your job to keep an eye on me, but why are we *here*? Is it only because Amala said you should?"

"Would you think it was selfish if I said you provided an escape?"

She almost snorted. "Yes and no. Though I'm not sure how I'm serving as an escape if I'm your responsibility."

"You provide me a reason to ignore some of my other responsibilities. Or maybe I just enjoy your company."

She hummed, taking a bite of fruit, letting the berries burst on her tongue. "I highly doubt that's the case. Can't you tell? I'm horrible at conversation."

He laughed, a warm sound that danced on her skin. "You seem to be handling it fine. Though I know small talk can be extremely overwhelming. It forces you to interact with people."

"I know. It's horrible," Nova said, taking another bite, this time with chocolate.

She felt a drop land on her lip, and as she flicked her tongue to catch it, Cyrus's eyes tracked the movement. A steady heat stuck to her, budding like a rose in her stomach.

"Am I so bad? Would you rather I let you remain in the darkness of the library?"

"You're fine, I suppose."

He smiled, his brown skin coming to life under the suns. She liked making him smile. When she did, his whole face transformed. A dimple appeared in his cheek and the skin near his eyes wrinkled. "That might be my best review yet."

"That can't be true. I'm sure others would call you charming, sweet, even."

"Others. But not you?"

They locked eyes, and warmth spread through her veins. That didn't happen. When people looked at her longer than they should, she became prickly, unnerved by their gaze. It was almost like being touched...it was too intimate. Too much for her to handle. But not with him.

"Maybe in time," she said, taking a sip and watching him over the edge of the mug.

"I'm a patient man."

Her lips twitched, threatening to curl themselves. "I'm sure you are."

Those green eyes filled with something soft, kind. "I'd like to show you another place, if you're up for it."

"You mean instead of going back to the deep dark library? Yeah, I'm up for it."

He rose with a smile, his cheeks slightly flushed, and motioned for her to follow. She grabbed the pastries and stuffed them in a paper bag. They traveled over the stone bridge and up the next staircase, higher in the mountains. It curved as they rose, the trees shadowing the steps and Willowgrove growing larger with every step. On the next landing, they went toward the trees, where the path ended and the soil began.

Nova swore the drooping leaves lifted to make way. "Amala was in the library yesterday."

He tossed her a look over his shoulder. "Keep up."

She rolled her eyes.

The forest enveloped him, as if the leaves were reaching down to brush against his skin. The noise from the city, from the cascading stairways, and glittering building in the mountains became a background hum. Instead, the leaves fluttered, and the smell of water and soil filled her nostrils. She loved it. Nova loved how alive this place was. Through the branches, she could see the peaks of the mountains rise high into the sky. Birds scattered the leaves in various colors. To her right, the forest floor sloped, and on the left, it rose.

Eventually, they came to a stop. Rocks jutted out from the mountain side, a maze of shallow caves, and Cyrus climbed up to sit, letting his legs hang over the edge. After a moment, she joined, leaning back against the stone. A tiny bird of blue hopped up on the rock ledge beside her. She dropped a crumb of pastry beside it.

"What are the flags for?" she asked, turning to look at him.

His gaze remained on the forest. "Eisera is preparing for the coronation."

Panic spread like a virus through her veins. Would the Vahls have known? Does this have something to do with them? "The coronation? When? Who's attending?"

"In three weeks' time, when the next red sun appears. As far as I'm aware, those from Syris, Azis, Rersa, Aeledin, Vydara, Lazora, and the Waterlands have been invited. Though Amala mentioned it was possible others would be invited, too."

She remained calm on the surface, but underneath, her anxiety threatened to implode. Her heart skipped multiple beats. By Gods, three weeks? This was something the Vahls would've wanted, something they would've foreseen. This had their influence written all over it.

He let out a humorless laugh. "King Aydin is stepping down. I still can't believe it."

"So, Amala is taking the throne?"

He gave her a twisted smile. "Possibly. What do you know

about the way the crown works here? About Eisera in general regarding leadership?"

She glanced at him before watching the bird hop closer to the crumb. "No more than any others."

In Eisera, the royal family was kept quite private. What was known about the transition of the throne, was this—there was a challenge that took place to decide the contenders for the throne. No one outside of Eisera knew exactly what that entailed, only that it put forth said contenders.

If there was an heir or heirs from the royal family, blood or adopted, they had to be sixteen to participate. Even so, they often did not take the throne for many years after. Meaning, the throne was not given based on gender or age or bloodline, but solely on the challenge and the decision of those before them. No names or confirming factors were shared, only the number of contenders. To announce the transition of the throne to Valora, the reigning king or queen would set a coronation. There, it would be decided who would take the throne.

It had been the practice of Eisera as far back as Eisera went, at least according to the books. Currently, the Slater bloodline was the longest in history. A first.

"There are two contenders for the throne."

"Two heirs?" Nova tracked her eyes over him.

He shook his head. "No. Do you remember the Aether point? The forest?"

She nodded. "Nalādin." *This whole place must be alive.* She looked around. Various trees had flowers growing from their trunks and extending to the leaves. There were clusters blooming from the soil and between the rocks.

"Nalādin is much more than that to us. It's on the other side of the mountains, tucked between this range and the next. It—"

"Are you sure you should be telling me this?" Though she said so, at the very corners of his mind, she nudged him—just enough, to keep him comfortable. Her strength was returning, and it was about time she'd started to use it.

He sighed, resting back until he was flat against the rock. "The secrets of Eisera have a way of revealing themselves to those they choose." Cyrus motioned above her, and she was surprised to find a heavy branch bending down to her, a flower extended on the leaf, close enough for her to grab. "May as well save you some of the in between."

Holding up her hands, she felt the flower drop into her palm. Did that mean the forest—this place—was choosing her?

"Nalādin is an Aether point, yes, but it's far more than that. It's sentient, an embodiment of the Aether itself, more than a place where it simply flows beneath the surface or a place to access it. It's pure magic." Cyrus reached up and let a flower fall into his palm. "Nalādin is the challenge."

Her brows furrowed, but he continued, "In history, at sixteen, any blood heir of the throne is sent into Nalādin. The name itself means honor, and that's what had to be earned. The heirs had to prove themselves and gain the approval of the forest. Over time, the stakes heightened. One of the earlier ruling families, far before the Slaters took the throne, had multiple children. None of them gained the approval. They instated a contest open to the public of Eisera, that anyone sixteen and older could enter the forest—the challenge. While the reigning king or queen has the final say, not once in Eisera's history have they chosen different from what Nalādin has."

"But..."

"But," he said, "the Slater bloodline has existed for over a century now. They have ruled Eisera for over a hundred years. It's a legacy at this point."

Nova shook her head. "Yes, but if what you said is true...blood shouldn't matter. Not here."

"You're right. It *shouldn't*. But it does. At least to them." He turned to gaze at her. "The other contender isn't a Slater, but he is the one Nalādin chose."

"Is that what that word on the flag was referring to? The Ižavore? What does that mean?"

He leaned back. "It means chosen of the trees."

Suspicion slithered like a snake. *Was it him? Dray? Someone else?* Why did it matter? Why couldn't he just say?

"So, whoever *they* are," she said, tracking his heartbeat, "the Ižavore, should be the true heir?"

Cyrus exhaled. "Correct. And for the first time, the people of Eisera don't know who will be crowned. That's why the flags have been placed." Cyrus gave her a cynical smile. "Because they haven't committed to honoring the tradition. They're considering naming Amala at the coronation."

What did any of this mean? If it was a tradition, why wouldn't they honor it? And why keep it a secret? "I don't really understand..."

"Do you remember what I told you before? How I grew up with the Slaters?" he asked, and she nodded. "We grew up together, the three of us."

"You, Amala, and the Ižavore?" She raised a brow.

"Yes. King Aydin and Queen Gena were like second families to us. Amala is practically my sister."

"Then why did he enter the contest?"

Cyrus struck her with a heavy gaze. "King Aydin and Queen Gena entered *both* of us without telling Amala."

Nova's eyes widened. "And Amala wanted the throne."

"Amala has always wanted the throne," he said, setting the flower down on the rock. "And to the people, to the forest, it's not hers. It's been taken from her. Amala was—is—our family. But things changed after that challenge, and they've never quite been the same."

Silence fell, though Nova realized it was never *that* quiet under the leaves, and she studied the man next to her. For the first time, she saw a glimpse of sadness on his face. It didn't fit, and it bothered her. The man that had been so steadfast seemed the opposite now. And she knew pain, personally and by extension, when she watched it overtake the people she was ordered to kill.

Pain was a viper, a poison that spread sure and fast. She watched it spread over him, the pain a visible entity.

Pain she could understand. Even in its various degrees, pain was universal.

"Why would she be mad at you?"

Cyrus rested his head against the rock. "When the challenge ended, when they stepped out, I hadn't even considered that Amala hadn't—that it wasn't her. I was so thrilled. Nalādin is an honor, to be chosen is the privilege of a lifetime. But then, she appeared. And all she saw were the celebrations. The celebrations of her loss."

Nova looked out at the forest around them. It was so twisted, so...convoluted. How could there be anything but pain? She pushed deeper onto the threads of Cyrus. They pulsed with a feeling akin to grief. It was suffocating.

"So, by all means, by tradition, the throne is theirs. But the Slaters, who are like family to you both, don't want to honor that?" she asked, studying him. "Is that why she was there when we arrived? Is that why you let her give you the order? She maintains control, and you can hold on to the family you used to have? So you can be absolved of any guilt?"

"Partly. I'm caught in-between. They rarely speak to each other. Are rarely in the same room. But I do what I can." Cyrus rested his elbows on his knees, the vines winding up and down his arms. She watched, entranced with how attached they were to him. "If that means taking orders, supporting her and the Slaters how I can, then I will."

"Does that bother you?"

"In ways. But if it means avoiding a fight, I'll do it. Eisera is already fighting. I'd rather not see any more."

Hm. A loyal country in theory, in history. But in this case, what was more important? Loyalty to the bloodline or loyalty to the forest? Tradition may mean the world to some, but to others... nothing. What did he believe?

"Why are you telling me this now?"

A humorous look entered his eyes. "You were bound to become suspicious. With Amala's surprise visits or being constantly watched."

That explained him sneaking around her room. If he was trying to find information to pass along or to collect for himself. Gods, now she needed to know just who was watching her.

"Am I thought to be a threat?" she asked quietly. If so, she needed to quell that. They could not know. They could *not* suspect her. Not before she found out the truth.

They locked eyes. "If you are, I don't think you're one to us. But Amala feels a pressure to remind her parents that she's capable, that she is still the daughter they raised. One worthy of ruling."

A breeze wound around them, and she shifted in his direction. He looked tired, weighed down by it. She felt it both in his blood and the threads. He was stuck between two people he loved. She didn't understand it, but she could imagine it was exhausting.

"Who do you think is meant to rule?"

Cyrus tipped his head back, letting it roll until he was looking at her. In that moment, he was a part of the earth. The ground, the trees, the rocks—it was him.

"No one has ever asked me that." His eyes fluttered closed, his lashes casting shadows on his cheeks. "Honestly, I don't know. It's Amala's whole life. It's all she's ever wanted. And the cost of her *not* taking the throne is a heavy burden. But...Naladin spoke, and the forest has never been wrong. Not in my experience."

"I know it's unrealistic, but it would be nice if life could just *be*...and not everything come with a price."

He looked at her again in a way that made her heart stutter. "Yeah. It would be."

She rubbed a finger over the soft petal in her hand. "What will become of you?"

"I have no idea. Amala is angry at me for celebrating. I doubt she'd have me on the council. But I'd do anything they asked. Either way, it feels as though I'll lose one of them."

"I'm sorry that your friendships will change with this. That a time of joy also causes you pain," she said softly. She wasn't sure where it came from.

Cyrus met her gaze. His greens eyes swirled with an array of emotions. She could see that and sense them pounding at the edges of the forest in his mind.

Her head was reeling. It was as though she was teetering on the edge of a cliff trying to find her footing. She had three weeks to uncover the truth and get out of here. To leave without a trace before the Vahls arrived. Her head threatened to explode. She hadn't expected to like this place. Or to like him, despite him being assigned to watch her.

Because none of this would be happening if it weren't for the Elders haunting her in every mirror, forcing her to read until her eyes dried out and she was too tired for nightmares to haunt her.

What she hated, in this moment, was the idea that sadness was leeching warmth out of him. It was stealing the light from his green eyes, forcing his blood to flow a tiny bit slower, dimming him from the inside out. And she hated it almost more than anything else.

"I have a request now." She stood, looking down at him. "Would you teach me how to ride? On Rouge or Ghost?"

He smiled. Not a smirk or calculated grin but a wide, clear smile. Within her chest, throughout her body, she felt the strangest twinge of her heart. A flutter.

And she certainly didn't hate that.

CHAPTER 23

LACKING AND LESS AND MONSTROUS

"TRY AGAIN."

Nova stared at the strawberry roan horse, who flicked an ear at her. Failing was something she did in private, not in front of Cyrus. After the fifth time of failing to lift herself onto the horse, shame flooded her blood, a heavy weight under her skin. She couldn't stand failing—at anything. She needed to conquer this simply to say she had.

Even now, she heard the taunts of the Vahls in the dark corners of her mind. *Weak, weak, weak.*

She followed the instructions *again* and stretched her leg upward until her foot was in the stirrup. With a deep breath she rocked forward on her toes and pulled, kicking her leg over swiftly. *I need to train.* Nova shook her head. The push-ups in the small room of hers could only do so much. Her strength was dwindling. But at least she was finally seated on the horse.

"Good," Cyrus said, smiling as he approached. "You know the basics; go ahead and move her to a walk. After you're comfortable, try a trot."

With a gentle tap of her foot, Rouge began to move. They were in the valley, beyond Willowgrove and Lake Emora, in a pasture near one of the stables. Ghost watched from his post, lazily flicking his tail.

"Have you been sleeping?

"Worried about my well-being? I'm merely an assignment."

He huffed a small laugh. "Am I not allowed to wonder?"

She turned her focus back to the horse. Rouge moved smoothly underneath her, muscles bunching as she went. The horse's blood was strong, ready to run.

"Fine, I'll try a different question—how's studying going?"

"Good."

She'd made sure to read up on her knowledge of the Magistrate in case of questions like this. Joining the Magistrate of the Second Star, in any capacity, was lengthy. The first three years were comprised of general studies, including all of Valora's history, its legends, myths, countries, and laws.

After, they would propose a final topic to the headmasters and decide whether to continue their studies to become a historian or a Mythic. The next three years was dedicated to their selection. Historians were those who were more interested in the tangible things of the world, learning how the world worked without magic. Mythic's were those interested in understanding the Aether and how it intertwined with the world.

"Though the pages are starting to bleed together these days, I can only hope the words are actually being absorbed." Literally and figuratively. There was not a book or interest she hadn't bled on.

What was revealed disappeared after a short time, but it didn't matter because no one else could see what was shown. She gave Rouge another tap, moving up to a steady trot at Cyrus's instruction. The air was warm on her skin, the suns dipping into the afternoon sky.

"I'm sure you are. Any new things in particular of interest?"

Ah. She had to remember that he was still a servant to the heirs. Or one of them himself. Placed here to determine whether she was a threat or not.

"Nothing changed from what I said before. Your recommendations about the Gods have been great. I've started to look into the wars, the rise of Spirit. I figure I won't decide to focus on that when my training's done, so I'd like to learn more about it. And Syris."

"That's where you were born?"

"Yeah, right along the border of Vilies." *And also because I crawled out of the ground there.* All of which would've been true if she was actually a scribe. "It's a very complex place. And the histories are shallow, similar to their God...I want to know why."

The rise of Spirit was a large section in the book. Before that, they were rarely mentioned, but after their work with the massacre, they were an enigma. But every time she let her blood fall on those pages, pain spread through her, and the Elders demanded more.

"Fair enough. What's it like?"

Nova exhaled as Rouge moved below her. "You would hate it. Green is hard to come by, and life is scarce, spread throughout the cold and the mountains," she said, giving away little. "Though it is beautiful in its own way. The mountains are almost always covered in snow, and there's a quiet to the world when it's like that. But control is vital to survival—in hunting, in living, in everything."

"Is that why you're always...so stiff?"

Her eyebrows raised, pulling Rouge to a halt. "Are you watching me, Cyrus?" Despite herself, her heart stuttered at the idea of it, of him letting his eyes linger on her a bit longer than necessary.

A sheepish smile came over his face, his curls bouncing in the breeze that came through the valley. "It's hard not to notice. Sometimes it's as if you aren't moving."

Jonah had pointed it out once. It was a habit, keeping her heart rate practically immeasurable, forcing herself to be unseen. "Force of habit."

"Not breathing?"

Nova leaned forward on the horse, more and more comfortable by the second. Under her palm, she felt Rouge's heartbeat. "If I sat still enough, I would be left alone."

His voice hardened when he said, "What does that mean?"

In the distance, she stared at the mountains. "My parents weren't kind people. They weren't caring," she said so softly, she wondered if she even spoke. But Cyrus stepped closer, so she knew she was. "If I was still enough, quiet enough, sometimes they would walk right past me. Sometimes they wouldn't. But stillness...it became a defense. A habit." Nova met his eyes.

There was no logical reason the truth spilled out, but it did. Out here in the valley, only the horses and Cyrus could hear.

He was quiet. As always, his Gods-gifted green eyes were on her with a gentle gaze. "Thank you for sharing."

She sat up. Rouge flicked an ear, her tail whipping around to snap against her thigh. *Relax.* Nova rolled her eyes. She swore the horse flicked her ear in response.

With a sigh, she faced him again. "I've never told anyone that before."

She swallowed the nausea that came with the vulnerability and urged Rouge back into a trot. But those eyes of his were on her with every step. It was more than she'd ever shared before. Because no one had ever asked why. Not even Jonah.

As she circled, her eyes fell back to Cyrus in the center. The sleeves of his linen shirt were rolled up, and the vines on his hand moved slowly, as always. At some point, he'd created a seat from the earth below him, and his eyes tracked her as he went. Those forest-green eyes she'd come to...like were a constant pressure over her skin, forcing an awareness she'd never felt. Not an awareness of blood or someone's emotions, which made it easy to compartmentalize people, but an awareness of him as a whole and of herself.

As she moved Rouge into a canter, a bit wobbly at first, she felt the air on her skin, the smell of flowers in the breeze, and kind eyes watching her every move. And Nova smiled.

"You're a natural." Cyrus's voice carried on the breeze. "Good job."

No one had ever told her that. Not once.

She would not forget it.

THEY WALKED BACK underneath the cover of stars. The moon was a curved sliver in the sky. As they entered the library, she let the threads come to her—in a way, at least.

They were so different from the mind. They pulsed. They existed whether she was looking for them or not. Emotions felt different on them, but they were there. It was like she'd noticed earlier—she was convinced she could follow a single thread to the very center and find out how they all intertwined. For now, she sort of *danced* on them. It felt a bit like floating—aware of what was around her but not doing anything to affect the surroundings.

They approached her room in silence, though his was only a few steps away.

She spun to look at him and tipped her head up. "Thank you for today, Cyrus. For telling me what you did." There was a small kernel of guilt that she didn't do the same, but it was miniscule.

"You would've figured it out shortly anyway." He tucked his hands into his pockets, eyes tracking over her face. "Earlier, you asked why, and what I said was true."

"That I make a good distraction?"

He smiled. "That you make good company."

There was a heat in her stomach she'd never felt before. It wasn't hot and pulsing, like lust was. She'd felt lust. Tried on a few *excursions* to experience pleasure, sex, but the first time, the touching, it became far too much. The memory she had of it was almost killing them. From there on out, it was up to her to take care of herself. This wasn't that. This warmth was burrowing into her skin, latching on to her blood cells and lighting every nerve.

"There are very few that would agree with you, Cyrus."

Sometimes, it was hard not to burrow into that little hole within herself that found her pathetic. That found her lacking and less and monstrous.

"Other opinions don't generally impact my own beliefs," he said softly. "You should get some sleep. I'll see you tomorrow."

"Goodnight." She finally let her lips curl up into a smile—a small one but a smile still. And it remained that way until he disappeared into the darkness.

It wasn't until later, in the middle of the night, with tired eyes and a tired mind, that she noticed things were out of place. The book she'd left open was on a different page. The order of the stack was changed. Books that had been on her desk were now on the floor.

Nova sighed, frustration walking along her spine. It had all been a distraction to get her out of the room, to find out if she was hiding anything worth finding.

Leaning back in the chair, she tipped her head, staring at the ceiling. There was nothing to find. There was nothing worthy about her. She was a vessel for those she'd killed. She was a threat to those she did not know.

She was *still* just a Witch. Only now, she was in hiding.

CHAPTER 24

THE ORDER OF THE ASHES

IN THREE DAYS, THERE HAD BEEN NO NEW SCIONS. No blood spilled.

Still, as soon as the suns set, after her evening prayers, Elaia would settle atop the canyon rim to wait—exactly what she was doing tonight. Akiro sat beside her as he did every evening with his head on her thighs.

When Zahra had awoken that night in the library, she saw the drawings and promised Elaia that she would talk to the Magistrate privately to see if they knew anything. From her mother, in history, anything about Scions being hunted—so far, nothing.

Elaia was sick of it. Of the lack of answers, the lack of control. So, she would wait.

The night went on, stars blinking in and out, her eyes heavy with exhaustion. Beside her, Akiro was fast asleep, his ears twitching every few seconds. Elaia kept her eyes peeled on the canyon rim. Every shape caught her eye—a tiny bug, the shadow of a bird's wing. Everything. And still, nothing she needed.

Sighing, she rested her head on her knee. *Please don't let this be another wasted night.* Movement caught her eye, and she focused immediately, sweeping her gaze left to right. *Come on.*

She stood, causing Akiro to wake, his ears perking. She walked along the rim, eyes peeled until she saw it, saw *them*, standing right across from her.

Elaia knew they were watching her. And she was sick of being watched. Springing into action, she crossed a stone bridge and plunged into darkness. Her shadows leapt, scouring the ground and crevices and coming back empty.

"No," she said. "Not again. Not tonight."

Elaia let her shadows fall and closed her eyes. Darkness, whether it was natural or made of Aether, had similarities. For her, shadows often felt like an extension of the person they came from. They allowed her to see clues, hints about who they might be. Natural darkness was its own being—always there, always waiting to encompass the world. And she'd studied it just the same. Overtime, she'd learned how to blend her shadows into it, to hide herself away.

Sweat beaded on her nose as her shadows bent into the dark until she and Akiro were successfully hidden. Moving slowly and in a strange, off-beat pattern, she traversed the flat top. Her shadows, briefly a part of the world, sent tiny sparks over her skin when anything in the darkness moved. The canyon mouse. A tree leaf. A person.

The darkness was deadly for those who didn't understand it. And so was she.

On quiet feet, she moved closer, waiting to strike. They were right there, and they weren't getting away. Instinctually, her shadows erupted from her, the light coming back as they wound tight around the figure, a grunt the only sound confirming they had them.

A writhing shadow covered the mouth of the hunter, but his eyes were hot with anger. Elaia bent down, her shadows safely encasing them for now. The tendrils of darkness wound around and around until every part of him was tied together.

"Who are you?"

The shadow slithered away from his mouth. Hazel brown eyes shone in the moonlight, and a crooked smile came over his face.

"We've been trying to capture your attention, Princess. Do we have it?"

We? Who was this? *What* was this? Akiro growled, circling the hunter. "You have it. Now answer my question." She cursed herself as she realized she didn't have her blades. Instead, she held a blade of shadow to his throat.

"We have a mutual goal."

"We?"

His eyes narrowed, almost predatory. "The Order."

Confusion crawled down her spine. "The Order?" She'd never heard of this. Not in passing, not in a story. Never. "Explain."

"We want the same thing," he spoke, attempting to shake her hold, but she tightened her shadows.

His brown leathers were dusted in dirt, as was the skin of his arms and cheeks. Loose brown curls fell over his forehead, hiding thick brows and sharp cheekbones. Stubble dusted his jawline, and freckles dotted his tawny skin from his cheeks to his neck to his chest, where they continued under the pendants around his throat and the neckline of his shirt. Even now, Elaia knew the man was corded in muscle.

"We want to remove your father from the throne."

Who in Senka's fangs were these people? What power did they hold to remove someone from leadership? And how did they know that?

Elaia straddled him, ensuring he was pressed to the ground. Two blades of shadows floated by his throat. "Why would you think that's something I want?"

"The Order is everywhere, even where you'd least expect them," he said. "We've been watching you for some time now, waiting until our goals would align."

"So, it was you leaving those dead Scions for me in Aeledin?"

"Yes and no. The Order is vast, stretching between your wildest dreams."

"You sound like a bunch of losers with nothing else to do,"

she snarled, hair sticking to her cheeks. He snorted, his eyes narrowing. Heat floated over her skin. "And how could you help me anyway? All you've done is make me seem crazy. Killing those Scions and removing them. And you think I'd agree to what—work with you?"

"The Order only reveals itself in time to certain people. That's how it remains a secret."

Heat ran hot over her skin, and she jumped up to find sparks falling from his fingertips. A Fire Elemental. Great. Flames ran up his arms like a snake, her shadows dissipating the moment the heat touched them.

He moved slowly, calmly. "You need all seven governors to stand with you, correct? You need us. If you want the throne, we can ensure you get it. Or we can ensure you do not."

Someone on the council had sold her out. Someone who would've been privy to the conversation. Who knew she wanted the throne. Who knew she would need to work for the governor's blood signatures.

She was going to rip them apart.

"And what would you and your *order* get out of it?"

He smirked, the corners of his eyes curling up. "That's for you to find out later."

Elaia had enough. "Akiro, now."

In seconds, Akiro was kicking up dust as he began to circle the hunter. She spun, whipping out blades of darkness toward the hunter. They floated around him, sharp and thin. Two pointed at his temple, one at his jugular. People often forgot shadows were deadly. They forgot they stole secrets. They forgot they struck when you least expected them.

The blades, while wispy and blurred, were deadly.

He smiled without laughter. "So, the little shadow bites?"

With a twitch, both blades of shadow touched his skin. Two droplets of blood beaded in response, one sliding down from his temple.

"She does."

She moved fast, but he avoided her blades and swept a wave of fire in her direction. Elaia rolled, recalling her shadows and spreading them out over the canyon floor. They became a whirl of dust and moonlight and fire and darkness, bursts of flames trying to capture her and walls of heat shielding against her blades. Even outside, the heat quickly became heavy. It rippled through the air and sparked her skin, but she evaded each blast.

Fighting was always a dance, trying to learn the other's steps and rhythms and still ensuring a strike. To keep fighting, even when exhaustion became a part of the battle.

Her blades never let up. Even quick and hurried, coming from a sweep of her arm or a kick of her leg, they went right for him every time. Behind him, Akiro nipped at his heels, careful to avoid the flames but tripping him up, making sure to interrupt the hunter's dance.

And interrupt it, they did. He defended much of her blades, but it was an onslaught. This stupid Order. The death of the Scions. It fueled every strike. She watched with pride as her shadow yanked his ankle, pulling him to the ground, and Akiro pounced. They had him. This time, her shadows bound his hands and ankles and choked his throat.

The heat had become a simmer. But the darkness was everywhere.

ELAIA SAT on the opposite side of the fyrestone bars, a Creator-made invention for practically indestructible containment. The hunter stared at her from the other side. There was a ring of darkness around his throat from her shadows, but otherwise, he looked the same.

"What's your name?" she asked, pulling her hair away from her face. Despite her instincts, she sat here alone. No Zahra. No

Rohan. No guard. Because unfortunately, working with the Order had piqued her interest.

He sat against the wall, legs pulled up in front of him with his elbows on his knees. Aetherchains circled his hands and ankles. "Xerxes Otar."

"And why, exactly, should I agree to work with you?" Elaia leaned forward, shadows weaving between her fingers. "How many have you killed? How many Scions have you deemed deserving of death at your hand?" She cocked her head. "Does it bring you pleasure? Fulfill some sick need? Why kill them? For what purpose?" He only stared, and her lip curled. "Scared to answer a question, Xerxes?"

"You're so brave from the other side of the bars, Princess. Why don't you step inside?"

Elaia could feel the heat emitting off him. She raised a brow. "I'm the one that put you there, aren't I?" They locked eyes for a moment. He looked amused. She hated it.

Xerxes exhaled. "I don't kill them. It's not my job."

"Oh, great. So, you just instruct others to do so?" She huffed. "Why? Why them? Why couldn't your Order find some other way to draw my attention?"

"Tradition."

"How long have you been watching me?"

His stare felt bone deep. "Years."

Elaia ignored the anxiety walking up her spine. "What would working together entail? Why do you want my father removed?"

"The Order wants him removed for reasons that are above me. From what I understand, they are similar to yours. They are unhappy with the increased presence of the Nightguard and the curfew. I believe it's probably because they have no control, no power, over him."

"You will not have power over me."

He shook his head, running a hand through his hair. "That's not necessarily what I mean. They don't want control the way you're thinking of it. They want..." Xerxes trailed off, turning his eyes to the ceiling. "They want the ability to sway. The peaceful opportunity to make a difference. To suggest change. With him, they don't have it."

"And they think they'll have it with me?"

"A better chance at it, yes."

Akiro sat dutifully by her side, ears perked. The cells, placed strategically in shallow caverns, and the halls that led to them, were dimly lit with no more than two lanterns to a space. Even in the faint light, she felt him studying her. Every pause, every word, every movement.

"And they think I would agree to that? Giving away power?" The thought made her skin crawl.

"That's not what they're asking. I've provided only a miniscule amount of information. You've been promised that the governors will back your challenge; how would the Order do that without influence? You'd be gaining an intricate network. All they want for now is a seat on your council when the time comes. A member of your choosing."

She gave him a deadpan look. "If they're so powerful, why do they need me?"

Xerxes cocked his head. "Your influence. Your protection. The Order is longstanding, but this still is only the beginning."

Protection? For what? Crime? If the Order was willing to kill Scions, animals and creatures often worshiped—those *she* worshiped—what would they stop at?

"What do they want, Xerxes? A real answer."

"What does anyone want? What do you want?" His eyes were heated. "They want control."

If they could sway the governors, infiltrate her council..."They seem to have it already."

"No," he said. "They have the ability to *make* it. There is a difference."

She studied him for a moment. "And if I decline?"

Xerxes shrugged. "I suppose that's a risk you'll have to take." There was a level of indifference about him, something she didn't quite understand. Like he was just doing his duties. And she was only doing hers.

But if this network was as large as he insinuated, that could be vital. If she didn't work with them, they would find another way. And if she did, wouldn't she gain a bit of control herself? Over this entity that seemingly existed underneath everyone's noses? And if they promised her the throne, wasn't it all worth the risk?

Still, it felt crazy that she was even entertaining it.

He seemed to sense that she was caught. "Don't take too long to decide, Princess."

Elaia struck with him a glare as she stood. The lanterns flickered, leaving Xerxes in darkness as she shut the secondary door between them, effectively locking him into the room. Out of sight, she rested against the wall, bending down to pet Akiro.

"What am I doing, Ki? Is the throne worth it?"

There was so much uncertainty—with the Elders dead and with the darkness she couldn't speak of. Every time she tried, her brain spun as if to make her forget it. But she could not forget the note she carried. *The shadow will continue to haunt—as long as you maintain your promises.*

In order to ensure the shadows remained, that Rersa stood, that those she loved were safe, she needed to have the throne. Not her father.

ELAIA PACED past empty cells and the cavern halls. The Order. If they'd been leaving the Scions, that meant they had been watching her and probably for far longer than the hunter revealed.

The smart thing to do would've been to find Zahra or Rohan. And to tell them.

But she couldn't. They would only talk her out of it. They didn't get it, how badly she needed the throne. They couldn't see how badly she needed to ensure everything she'd done and endured and lost was worth something.

The shadow will continue to haunt—as long as you maintain your promises.

But what else would they want from her? There was no way into this without giving up a piece of power...but could she stand that? Was the loss worth the gain?

She took a deep breath and rolled her shoulders, pacing down the hall. A scuffle of rock echoed. Furrowing her brows in confusion, she followed the sound down a long twisting cavern until she came to a cell. A scratchy voice crawled from under the cell doors.

"Please, let me out."

Confused, Elaia opened the first door to come face to face with an old prophet, one who taught the ways and history of Senka and of shadow. What in the Gods were they doing here? Upon closer look, it was one she recognized.

"Master Dayne? What is going on? Who put you here?"

Dayne looked bemused and frantic, as if they were unable to pinpoint where she was. When they finally turned, their eyes were black. *What in the world?*

"Master Dayne, it's me, Elaia Zūne. Can you see me?"

"No, no—I can't see anything. What is happening?"

"Okay, calm down. I'm right here, I'm coming in." Behind her, Akiro whined, his tail nervously wagging behind him. She waved a hand, instructing him to sit, and opened the cell doors.

Dayne had been her mother's favorite prophet. Varistone had royal prophets, but Dayne lived in the Zylla Canyons, and it was one of the clearer memories Elaia had of all of them. Nomara and the girls going to hear the teachings of Master Dayne.

"I'm right here," she said, holding out her hand.

"I can...I feel you." Their breathing calmed, and Elaia helped them to sit.

"Can you tell me what happened?"

"I was teaching yesterday evening, the story of Senka meeting

Tasyn—I remember when you were girls, you all loved that one," they said, swallowing. "It was late, not yet past the curfew when the guard stormed in. They ordered everyone to disperse and brought me here. The High Shade was waiting when I arrived. I don't—he didn't give me any reason. He just stared, and all of a sudden, I couldn't see. And he left me here."

Her skin heated. He had blinded them? How could he do this? Why? Elaia cleared her throat, trying to dispel the anger.

"I'm so sorry, Master Dayne. I'm going to get you out of here. The blindness is temporary and should fade by tomorrow. I'm going to have you brought to a room where I can ensure that before taking you home, all right?" Dayne nodded. "You will be fed and taken care of. I can't say how sorry I am. I don't know why he'd do this, but I will find out."

Dayne gripped her wrist. "He is not the same as he once was. Ever since your mother left, he has been darkened by grief and pain. The crown is made of spikes and will bleed him dry."

Though they couldn't see, they seemed to look right at her. Dayne often spoke in a melody of myth and tales and warnings. When she was younger, she was sure they were a Scion themself. She knew better now, but sometimes, the feeling remained.

"He is not the same," she said, grasping Dayne's hand. "But he will be free of the crown soon. I promise."

ROHAN MET her somewhere in the middle of the canyon, flanked by Sacha.

She relayed who'd she found and the others she found shortly after. A total of five prophets and sybils were locked and blinded. A small number given the amount within Rersa but a number that should not exist. Those without cause should not be in the cells at all. Certainly not at their High Shade's hand.

"There are riots in Darkbay, Ztar, and Lyian. Reports are coming in from the remaining cities of unrest."

Her father was unraveling before their very eyes, and it seemed he was determined to take Rersa with him.

"Send the Nightguard and the *Izion* if needed—on my behalf, not my father's—as aid," she said, calling in the silent guard of the *Izion*, a faction of the Nightguard. "They are not to draw weapons. They are there only to help those in need. You let them know I sent them, that *I* will be fixing this."

They dipped their heads. Rohan halted, hand on the hilt of his sword. "You've done well, Elaia. I'm proud of you."

"It's only the beginning, Rohan. Let's ensure there is a country left to rule."

"Your Highness," he said, disappearing into the dark.

She took a deep breath before turning to Sacha. "Wake the council and have them meet me in the cells. Immediately."

Tomorrow night, the dark moon would enter the sky, and Elaia would know whether or not they stood with her or against her. Before they made that decision, they deserved to know just what her father had done. The lines he had crossed.

All seven members of the council were draped in loose robes, eyes heavy with sleep.

"What is the meaning of this, Elaia?"

She didn't bother to see who was talking as she paced in front of the entrance to the canyon cells. "Tomorrow, you'll decide whether you would support me should the need for a challenge arise. You should know that tonight, I found five prophets locked in the cells and blinded. At the hands of my father."

Murmurs of concern rose behind her. She told them of the reports, of the riots coming from each territory. Rumors of more missing Prophets and complaints of the increased Nightguard presence.

When she turned, she was met with the heavy stares of all seven council members. "I know that you have concerns about what a challenge would mean for Rersa. Whether or not I am ready to take the throne. But I assure you, I am. I may have been gone, but I never *left* Rersa. It never left me. My heart is here, and it is my home. And I do not wish to see it descend into madness."

Elaia paused, folding her hands in front of her as Akiro sat steady by her side. "My father has left Rersa behind. He is here, but he has forgotten. I have not. I don't wish to watch the country I know and love fade away. It is my hope that you share the same wish, and that tomorrow, you give me your answer accordingly."

From behind, Sacha watched, her eyes filled with pride and respect. A sense of calm floated over her skin. Despite their choices tomorrow, Elaia would not let her father stay on the throne. Not after this. Not anymore.

She would take it—by all means necessary.

CHAPTER 25

BURNING FLAME

AKIRO BOUNDED ONTO THE BED, WAKING ELAIA FROM A dead sleep.

High above from the handmade slits, rays of the sunlight cut through the room.

The hound settled beside her, nestling his muzzle into her chest with a whine. "All right, all right," she murmured. Beside her, Zahra lay undisturbed. She was convinced the girl would sleep through world's end.

Turning over, Elaia burrowed into the warmth of the heavy blankets before pushing up and placing her feet on the carpet. Akiro crawled toward the edge, black ears perked and eyes bright. She ran her nails over his forehead and his soft fur.

In the muted light, Elaia dressed in her training leathers and pulled her hair back. Akiro followed her with hushed footsteps into the dark cavernous hall until they reached the opening. They climbed to the rim, where the dawn sky was a mirage of muted colors and headed away from the edge toward the grassy planes of Zylla, where it smelled of soil and Earth.

Inhaling, she felt her muscles wake and her senses sharpen. She fell into the familiar rhythm as her feet pounded against the ground and the cool wind blew through her hair. Despite having an obvious adoration for darkness, sunrise was her favorite time of the day. It made her feel strong when often she felt weak—it made her feel that no matter how downtrodden she felt or how off kilter the world was...the suns would still rise.

Sometimes, the weight of the world from the previous night lingered into the next day. The shadows that were parted from her were significantly heavier today, given that she'd sent one to attach to Xerxes. The further one's shadows went, the heavier they became. It wasn't a common practice among the Shadow Naturalists. For some, it was deadly. But her mother had perfected it.

They felt similar to her grief. Even on days when the past was a mere reminder, she was always aware of their weight sitting on top of her shoulders. Elaia figured if there was no way to rid herself of the emotions entirely, she could out train them. Be better than them. Swifter, sneakier, faster. As if they were people she was competing with and not haunting wraiths only she could see.

Akiro kept pace with her, stretching his long legs out beside her as she ran. She passed under gnarled tree branches and over the roots as the suns warmed her skin. Her lungs burned, thirsty for oxygen, but she pushed through. Her legs were tired, heavy, but mile after mile, she kept running. Daggers of shadow hit tree trunks and flower buds as she ran, nailing each one perfectly before the blades dissipated as she passed.

Some thought perfection was unattainable. But Elaia was never given an option.

By her father or by herself.

When they finished, the suns had risen over the canyon, and rays streaked over the colored sandstone. Elaia let her breath return and felt the ground beneath her. Akiro settled, small shadows dancing under his big paws as he stretched out.

Tipping her head back, Elaia let the warm rays dance over her cheeks.

A moment of peace before the chaos.

SHE KICKED a tray of food underneath the cell door. "Wake up."

She raked her eyes over Xerxes's disheveled appearance. His black leathers were worn but well-made, molded to his body. It was his eyes that drew her attention, piercing hazel with a bronze ring narrowed on her features.

"No need to be aggressive this early in the morning."

Elaia placed her elbows on her knees, spinning her ring of gray moonstone. "I have limited time."

She'd thought long and hard about her decision and the consequences it may bring to fruition. There were dangers in it, as there were in all things, but there was danger it not knowing, too. She hated that before yesterday, she'd never known of the Orders existence. By agreeing to work with them, she was not only positioning herself for the throne but positioning herself to understand the order and its intricacies. And how to destroy it if she needed, too.

"I need to know all I can about the Order before I officially agree. What is it? Who runs it? How do I know you aren't making this up?" She leaned back, running her hand over Akiro, who sat beside her.

Xerxes broke a piece of bread. "I have no reason to lie."

"And I have no reason to believe you. Either talk, or you can die here by my hand."

A flicker of amusement filled his eyes. "The Order of the Ashes has been around longer than I will ever know. The information shared is only what is necessary to a cause. We don't learn more than we need, so what I can tell you is limited," he said.

"What is the Order's purpose?"

"It has many. Control, power, sway." Xerxes set his piercing eyes on her and continued, "There are factions, each designed for a specific role. The Kytes, the Fangs, and the Shades are respectively hunters, assassins, and spies. Bottom ranking if you prefer to think of it that way. There are the Scarlets, which are members who have trained in at least two of those factions, but often all three. And the Chairs, the leaders, underneath only one —the Ashmaker."

"Which is?"

He smirked. "No clue. And if I knew, I wouldn't tell you."

"And what are you?"

"A Scarlet."

"How do I know this is true? How do I know any of this is true?"

Xerxes shrugged. "I suppose technically, you don't, though it'd be quite a lie to spin. And I don't care for that."

Question after question piled in her head. "Are you born into it? Do people seek it out?"

At that, a darkness came over him, a dead weight to his eyes. "You can be born into it with family ties. But most often the Order finds you."

"And if one wants to leave?"

"You are either granted permission by the Ashmaker, or you are killed."

Elaia cocked her head. The time for more could wait; he'd given enough information that she could take to the mythics or search the archives for, but the one question that haunted her most was about the Scions.

"What about the Scions? Why are they killed?" For a moment, he said nothing. She leaned forward. "No matter how you present it, I lose something here. A fragment of power is gone by agreeing to work with you. I need that information."

He tipped his head against the wall, but there was no confidence lost. "The Scions are killed for two reasons. One, as a notice that you—or whoever sees them—is being hunted, recruited, by the Order."

"And the other?"

He took a breath, his voice a low rumble as he said, "The other is because the Order wants to make new Gods."

What? She laughed in disbelief. He couldn't be serious. *New* Gods? There was no such thing as a *new* God. "Are you insane?"

"You wanted the truth. I gave it."

The truth. How unfathomable that these people, this Order, thought they could create something of legend. Of honor. She cocked her head. "Have they succeeded?" Her words were tilted with an unshed laugh.

Xerxes's eyes flashed like small bursts of flame. "As far as I'm aware, no."

She exhaled. The thought of more dead Scions was unnerving. Could she agree to work with a group that apparently had no honor, no respect, and believed themselves to be masters of the world? She remembered the rumbling underfoot after the Elders' deaths, the tiny quakes she'd felt since. And the black entity she didn't quite understand but knew was coming— waiting to strike.

Her heart warred. Her faith, once steadfast, felt unsure.

But if this would get her on the throne, she had to take it.

Elaia sat back, swallowing her guilt. "What are the next steps? What is required of me?"

"I will be the emissary, so to speak, for the Order. We will need to sign an agreement that I'll provide to the Chair for our records. We will ensure you have the governors signatures, and you will need to be initiated into the Order. But like I said, once you're in the Order, there is no easy way out." Xerxes's voice was unflinching, and his eyes were locked on to her with a severity she hadn't yet seen from him. "Is it worth it?"

She dug her nails into her palm. She felt death on the horizon. A darkness, sick and twisted. A decay. "Yes." Elaia took a breath. "And what's in it for you, Xerxes?"

Silence fell like winter snow. Xerxes averted his eyes, focusing them on the hound instead of her. Light from the lanterns cast shadows over Akiro, turning his black fur gray like a living shadow.

His eyes fluttered closed, and heat rose throughout the small room. It rippled through the air and sparked over her skin. There were small crimson flames flickering at the bands of the aetherchains. Powerful still, even confined. When he struck her with a gaze, his eyes were brightly flared.

"My freedom."

AFTER WORKING out a few more details—Xerxes would appear as a spy she'd hired for information, and that on her end, no mention of the Order could be made—Elaia removed the chains.

"You will remain in my section of Varistone. You will travel with me at all times unless instructed otherwise. Your access in and out will be limited in the waking hours. Your communication with the Chair will need to be shared with me. I will be informed of everything. Is that clear?"

Xerxes rubbed his hands over the marks left by the chains. "Perfectly, Your Highness." He adjusted the pendants around his neck, a myriad of different symbols.

She led him toward her private section in the canyon, Akiro flanking him, ensuring he stayed in line. They avoided any paths that would be crowded this time of day, carefully sneaking into a small room only a stone's throw away from her own.

"I have your weapons, so don't bother looking for them," Elaia said, stepping toward him, her gown swishing around her legs and sticking to her curves. "And let me be clear. We may have an agreement, but this is my home. It's my throne. And it's my country. Not yours and not the Order's." Her eyes sharpened, shadows twirling around her fingers. "If you threaten anyone or the safety of my home, I will kill you. Without hesitation. Is that understood?"

Heat emitted from him, and the gaze that landed on her was searing, like being touched by a flame.

But she cared not for his anger or hatred or whatever it was that kept him going. She cared only for herself and those around her. If he would not bend, she would make him. If he threatened her world, she would bring the whole thing down around them.

ELAIA WAS NOT A PATIENT PERSON.

It was a lesson her father had constantly hammered into her. His methods grew less than desirable as she got older. From teaching her how to do puzzles with a careful eye to waiting hours in dark, silent caverns with nothing but the constant drip of water from the rain or noise of the crickets in an attempt to teach her how to control her thoughts and her mind. Anytime she showed an ounce of anxious energy or rash decisions, she was put in the tunnels.

She could still hear it in the silence some days. The noise, buzzing in the back of her mind.

Her patience was a double-edged sword. Something she'd learned to be when the time called for it, and something that she hated being for the memories it dragged up.

But still, she waited in the tunnels. Ever since she'd left Xerxes in that room, she'd been waiting. She'd purposely left the tunnel opening unlocked because she believed he would try to exit— whether for good or to inform the Order, her gut told her so. And the shadow she'd attached to him had been writhing all night. Never calming or steadying.

Gods, she wanted to be in bed with Akiro and Zahra, but here she was. Waiting.

Could he take any longer?

Elaia could hear her father's scolding voice, telling her to find her center. Her nails pressed and released in her palm repeatedly—anything to release the adrenaline. It was as if she could sense each individual second in each minute passing by.

Then, the shadow moved.

It wound through the tunnels and toward the opening that would deposit him in the canyon where she waited. As she felt him traversing, the stars blinked above her. She found each constellation of the Gods. Each shape a beautiful collection of stars in the midnight sky. Elaia had done this so often when she was trapped in those canyons as a girl. Staring out the single window to count and trace the shapes. Honestly, she could probably do it without even seeing the sky.

She sighed. Some days, she wished she could go back. To when actions had clear purpose, a clear reason and result—to learn or to adapt or to grow. Now? Life was full of the unknown, forcing her to figure it out on her own. Youth was such a fleeting, funny thing. You wished for it gone, and then, you wished for it back.

The cracking of rock drew her back to reality as Xerxes reached the edge. After a moment, he plunged down into the dark canyons, and Elaia followed. She was silent amongst the city of rock. It was dim, the air heavy with sleep except for a few stragglers. Xerxes moved with ease and familiarity as he bounded through the city, eventually stopping at a building built into the canyon itself, a line of homes and businesses attached to it. She sent out her shadow to reattach to him as a figure opened the door.

Luckily, buildings like this often had tunnels within the canyon created as escape routes or protection measures. With her shadow attached, she could separate and follow, doing exactly that. She crawled through the small tunnels, following her shadow. She came to the second floor of the building, finding a small way to enter. There was a soft drone of voices coming from below. As though she was walking on shattered glass, she moved slow and composed. As she drew closer, she looked above for the ventilation system, long ago made by the Creators and a mirage of Athera to keep homes cool or warm. Not every home had them, but most of those in Rersa had implemented them due to the cold that could fester in the canyon.

She tracked backward until she saw it—a rift in the ceiling. She used the hilt of her blade to extend her arm and find the split, pulling it open. Thankfully, the ceiling was low, and she dug her nails in, using her feet along the walls to pull herself up.

Her skin crawled immediately. She wanted nothing more than to get into the shower and let the hot water strip it away, but she progressed. The voices grew until she was directly over top of the room. She could feel small drafts of air passing through the slits along the tunnel. She just had to find one she could see out of.

Careful not to disturb too much dust, Elaia found what she needed. Pressing herself to the bottom, she was able to just make out those below. Xerxes was seated in the center, calm and stoic. Almost bored.

The others, only two, were positioned around him. Their faces were masked.

"She's agreed."

One of them exhaled. "Good. If all goes to plan, the initiation will be within three weeks' time. Was there any indication that she knew of the Order?"

Xerxes shook his head. "None."

Why would that matter to them? Elaia shook her head. It didn't matter. It didn't matter that she couldn't see their faces. It didn't matter if he returned or not.

All she needed was to confirm their existence. The Order of the Ashes.

And she had.

For a second, she swore Xerxes's eyes glanced up, searing her like a burning flame. Lucky for Elaia, she wasn't afraid to get burned.

CHAPTER 26

An Official Challenge

Xerxes was back in his room by dawn.

She'd waited for him to return before retreating to her own bed. Then, she'd sketched everything, from Xerxes to the masks, until her fingers were stained black, and they were shoved in with the rest of her drawings. After maybe an hour or two of sleep by the hearth in her office, Elaia stood under an ice-cold spray of water, hoping it would wake her up.

She rested her head, damp black hair sticking to her cheeks.

The past few days had felt relentless. They allowed her no time to rest or recover; it was all endlessly constant. The Elders. Her father. The crown. The Witch. The Order.

Too many things were out of place—too many things slipping from her grasp.

Her mother would've told her to be patient. But that was Shaye. Her mother would've told her to stop trying to force the world into order, to let it be. But that was Rayn.

I am my mother's child. I am my mother's child. The mantra had been a constant, especially on the days where she felt nothing like her mother and only like her father.

I am my mother's child, she repeated both with love and disdain. She was her mother's child, and yet, she wasn't. For those that she loved, she'd run herself into the ground with the heaviness that love required of her. But for those that threatened them, she would ground the world into dust.

Her mother would've said it was rash, irresponsible. The reward not worth the risk.

But her mother wasn't here anymore. She was dead.

"What's going on, Elaia?" Zahra walked into the room, standing outside the glass doors. "You've been in there for twenty minutes," she said, reaching her hand in, only to draw it back at the frigid temperature. "What are you doing? Get out of there."

Zahra gave her no choice, shutting the water off and pulling her out, forcing a towel around her. "I'm fine, Zahra. Stop."

She rolled her eyes. "Gods, you're so willing to forgo yourself in all the chaos. That can't happen."

Elaia sighed, taking a seat on the floor. "I need to tell you something." Zahra gave her a look but crouched. Elaia trailed her eyes over her warm brown skin. "I was right about the Scions. They weren't my exhaustion, they weren't illusions, they were real. And I caught the hunter." Elaia swept her shadows through the room, ensuring they were alone. "They are a part of something called the Order of the Ashes. They've promised they will be able to help me ensure my challenge is accepted. You cannot speak of this to anyone, Zahra. No one but me and only when we are alone."

Zahra pressed her fingers into her head. "The Order? I don't —have you agreed? Have you even confirmed they are real?"

"That's where I was last night. I followed him." They locked eyes. "I agreed."

Zahra's head fell, dark waves almost touching the floor. "Elaia, why? What you're doing—is the throne worth this? They've haunted you with dead Scions. What else are they willing to do?"

Elaia shook her head. What else they did was not her concern right now. "The throne is worth it. It's worth it," she whispered.

"And what about me? Do I get a say? Or am I nothing more

than a pawn to stand beside you?" Zahra's nose flared as it always did when she was angry.

"You know that isn't true. You're invaluable to Rersa," Elaia said, their lives flashing before her eyes. "You're invaluable to me. That's why I'm doing this. No one else—I will not lose anyone else. Certainly not you."

She softened. "You don't need to protect me."

Elaia knew that Zahra's optimism did not equate to weakness. "I know that, but it's not about that. You can't protect yourself from what you can't see. You don't understand what's coming—"

"Then tell me!"

"I can't. Not yet." Elaia closed her eyes and saw the bodies of the Elders with tears of blood on their faces. Saw the Witch covered in blood. Saw the dark entity crawling around the room.

Heard the words, *the shadow will continue to haunt—as long as you maintain your promises,* ring in her head. "But I have to do this. And you have to trust me."

Zahra sighed as their eyes met, waiting to see who would fold first.

Their fears were similar yet contradictory. Her own had come later in life when most of her family was taken from her. The fear of loss dug its claws into her heart, forcing her to ensure that going forward, she would not lose anyone again. But Zahra's stemmed from being left. She'd ended up in Rersa because her parents, transporters of the Ambersands, had not realized she'd fallen out of the caravan and left her behind. Zahra survived days in the Evha Canyon until she was brought to Varistone.

Her fear of being abandoned wasn't something others may have known, but Elaia did. She knew how often Zahra gave in or worked to appease people in order to keep them around. And right now?

Elaia wasn't ashamed to say she would use it. Because she would not bend.

Eventually, Zahra's resolve faded away. "What can I do?"

The pressure lifted. "Keep doing what you always do. As long as you stand by my side, with the help of the Order, I won't be denied." She wrapped her hands around Zahra's wrists. Fear crawled through her blood. "More importantly, I need you to find a way to turn your light into weapons. Like the emblems. If we can outfit the guard with weapons like that, there is nothing we cannot prepare for. Witches. The Order. Anything. And we need to find out anything we can of the Order, if it even exists in history."

Zahra helped her stand, tucking a strand of hair behind her ear. "Understood."

She leaned forward, bringing their lips together in a gentle embrace. Guilt swam in Elaia's stomach, but it wasn't enough to undo what she had done. She would never abandon her, not in this life or the next, but that meant she had to *live*.

ELAIA KNOCKED and entered without waiting. Xerxes sat in the chair by the window, staring at her with heat in his eyes. "You followed me." His voice was coarse and heavy with frustration, as sharp as a knife on her skin.

"Did I?"

"Don't play dumb, Your Highness. It doesn't suit you."

Elaia shrugged, pacing back and forth slowly in front of him, her tangerine gown swishing on the polished stone floor. "I had to confirm I wasn't being lied to. For all I know, I still might be. Those could've been nothing more than people from the street. Though I don't think that's the case, Xerxes." His name rolled off her tongue, smooth and bitter. "But I needed assurance. I know now that the Order is real. Should this go left, I'll make sure the Order is destroyed. But as long as you uphold your end of this agreement, there will be no need."

He held her stare. "You think you'd be able to do such a thing?"

"You don't know me very well, but you underestimate me."

Xerxes said nothing, so Elaia studied him. His loose brown curls brushed his chin, and the lighting seemed to dance over his tawny skin. His strength was palpable, the aura of it.

On another day, in another life, she might have found him appealing. Or more so, taken the time to pay attention to him. Given his beauty—a soft, shimmering speck of light in a room of shadow—the attention it deserved.

Xerxes let out a small laugh. "You underestimate the Order."

She clicked her tongue. "No. I don't *know* the Order. There's a difference."

His hazel eyes turned molten, heated through and through. "You should be careful, Princess; you will find yourself in affairs that are beyond you, that are beyond this. Affairs that will only threaten you."

Ha. If he only knew she already was. Thanks to her own obsession with things that disrupted her, she was always in affairs that were dangerous. Elaia let her mask settle, her guard come up. She wasn't scared. Let them come for her. Elaia would meet them in the dark with her blades sharpened.

"From this point on, you are a spy. You've been working under my jurisdiction. You've provided information, and you've provided support. Nothing more. Nothing less. You will go nowhere without Rohan or Sacha by your side. You do nothing without my knowing." She ran her eyes over him. "Welcome to Varistone, Xerxes."

A KNOCK on the door drew Elaia's attention. The last time she looked up, the grand meeting hall had been bathed in sunlight.

Now, through the skylights above, streaks of orange and red from the setting suns fanned out over the floor and the large stone table.

"Come in," Elaia called, setting down the missive, ignoring the ache in her hand from the reports she'd been writing.

The door opened, and instantly, the smell of coffee, imported from Eisera, calmed her nerves. Sacha appeared, her dark brown skin draped in the black clothes of the Nightguard, her light curls freshly cropped. With her was Rohan and Xerxes.

"For you." Sacha placed the steaming mug by her side, cream swirling within the dark liquid.

"Thank you." She gave her guard a smile and fought back her nerves. "Have they all arrived?"

"They have," Rohan said, glancing at Xerxes.

He had been less than thrilled when she told him she had a *spy* gathering information from each of the seven cities. More, he'd been skeptical, forcing her to spin a lie about Xerxes and his upbringing. She suspected, more than anything, it was hurt that she had not consulted him.

"Please bring them in. And then get my father." Elaia exhaled as they dipped their heads, leaving only Sacha behind.

All seven governors, or their chosen officer, had arrived. She'd requested their presence shortly after she'd found the prophets and sybils in the cells, along with the council members. The only one unaware of the meeting was Desmond.

"Who is that from?" Sacha asked, pointing to the letter to her left.

The scrawl sent a thrum of annoyance down her spine, and she folded up the envelope to hide the seal that had a dove on it. "Only Vittoria," she lied. "Sending an official date for the coronation."

Sacha raised a brow. "How are you doing?"

She wanted to laugh. Instead, she took a slow sip. "With?"

With a sigh, the guard continued, "Everything. The riots. Your father. The throne. Is all of this worth the risk, Princess?"

"The risk of doing nothing is worse. Don't you think?" If she didn't grasp power, what would Rersa become? Within its borders and beyond?

If her father continued, there would be riots, of that, she was sure. And if she didn't grasp power and uphold her allegiances, Rersa would fall with the rest of Valora when the hunt began.

Sacha tipped her chin, resilient eyes meeting Elaia's. Her strength was visible even seated, as was everyone in the Nightguard. Trained in the darkness of the Evha Canyon, or the canyon of the lost, they were extensions of shadows themselves. Even more impressive was that Sacha was human, and yet, she was as good—if not better—than any others.

"I think trying to weigh the risk ahead of time is often useless. It'll never tell you exactly what's at stake or what may come. But you're smart enough to know the difference between risk and senselessness."

"Thank you, Sacha. Will you send Zahra in?"

The guard rose, and Zahra entered upon her exit. She was draped in fabric the color of sand and orange like the canyon, and her dark hair was braided away from her face. Lowering herself beside her, Zahra turned. "Do you think they'll stand with you?"

"I can only hope this is, at least, the beginning of convincing them to." Elaia took a deep breath.

"Have you found anything?"

The door opened, and Zahra turned to smile. "We'll talk later," Elaia whispered before they stood to greet them.

Everyone was ushered in. The council, the governors, and those wrongfully imprisoned. Elaia locked eyes with each one, confirming their eyesight had, indeed, returned.

Her crown, a twisting combination of obsidian and silver, sat firmly atop her head, and the seven drops of gemstones, alternating between onyx and moonstone, were situated perfectly, one centered on her forehead.

"Welcome, and thank you for joining on such short notice."

The governor of Lyian, Adrine, stood, dipping her head as she said, "Your Highness. Please accept the apologies of Ira and Sené. They couldn't make it. Myself and Viana will serve as their representatives."

A hum of annoyance settled over her skin. They couldn't be bothered to attend? They would dismiss her so easily? Elaia bit her cheek. "Understood. Please inform them another meeting will be called for them to attend." Adrine dipped her chin, though her eyes were cold. "I've asked you here today to officially put forth a challenge."

To them, she was steady. She was the shadows she was born in. Within? She felt nothing but pressure. The pressure to succeed. The pressure of failure. The consequences of either choice.

Quiet murmurs of shock went through the room.

At the end of the hall, the door swung open, the noise echoing around them. Desmond appeared, furious. The anger was so palpable, Elaia was sure she could scrape the air and hold it. The ink on her fingers moved as she ran her hands over the desk.

"What is the meaning of this?" his voice boomed.

"Will you concede the throne, Father?"

His eyes were black with rage, only for it to diminish when he saw the faces of the religious leaders. He had been caught. Still, he answered, "No."

"Then I am officially putting forth a challenge. You've wasted my time and exhausted my patience. You will lead Rersa down a dark path if given the chance, and I will no longer let you," Elaia said, her words ringing out.

She had Senka to thank for the fact that her voice didn't shake. That her hands didn't tremble. This was the way.

"What is the reason, Princess Elaia?" Iyman, the governor of Ymos, asked. "Officially."

"Officially, I am declaring Desmond Zūne unfit to rule. He wrongfully imprisoned the five prophets and sybils that sit with you today, and the riots that ensued were his doing. The curfew, the diminishing trade, and the increasing presence of the Nightguard, all done without his councils consultation, stand as only a few official reasons. Our Healers have also documented the increasing use of sleep medications and use of alcohol. The scribes will also confirm his absence for required meetings and court. He is no longer serving Rersa as High Shade but merely a placeholder. And it is time that comes to an end."

Across the room, her father's eyes felt like blades digging into her skin.

The pressure felt like the sharp tip of a knife dragging against a fresh scar, with the only goal to re-open the wound. Gone was the look of her childhood, when he used to look at her as though the entire world could one day dance at her fingertips. In its place was a look of disbelief and betrayal.

"I, Elaia Zūne, will be challenging for the Obsidian Throne."

CHAPTER 27

THE CARDINAL

THE WORDS LOOKED LIKE NOTHING MORE THAN BLACK ink on paper.

Nova leaned back and took a sip of the tea that had long cooled, tea Cyrus had dropped off an hour ago. There were books stacked over every inch of her room.

Still, the voices from the Elders did not stop. The pain they pushed onto her did not end. She had not found what they wanted.

Air from the vent system flowed in, cool against her skin, carrying the smell of Earth and water from above. There was a fresh cut on her finger not yet healed over, and her curls were tied back away from her face. She let her eyes fall closed for a second. Sleep came in spurts, and most often, it was interrupted by nightmares or haunting voices of the dead. Sometimes so bad, she'd rather force herself to stay awake.

With a sigh, she did just that, pulling the books under the lamp. She re-opened the cut over a new page of the book. As soon as the drop of blood fell, words appeared, and her head began to pound. The pain spread like fog as she was pulled in.

The dragons flew over the same shrouded land covered in fog, their wings touching the wispy edges as they flew. The dragon, streaked with silver, banked upward toward the sky and the suns and disappeared into the clouds. Red streaked wings dove down—down past the fog and the clouds and into shadows covering the land and sea.

Pain struck at the base of her neck. Memories pushed at the edges of her brain, memories she refused to set free but got louder every day, demanding freedom. But what was the cost of uncovering what her brain had made her forget? What else would she learn about herself?

All that came to mind was that it would be nothing good. Nothing but more pain.

The red-streaked wings unfurled in a world of darkness, another land with a starless sky. It flew over the ground, uprooting dirt and debris after powerful flaps of its wings. A river of red ran through the land, stones of white poked up from the soil, and echoing screeches seemed to fall from the sky. Voices grew in loud cacophony, battering her eardrums.

Remember. Remember. Remember.

The wings tore upward, out of the darkness and into the sky. It banked away from the fog-covered land and went north. Over the icy mountains of an isolated place. A place cold and white and barren. A low growl from the dragon's throat, and heat filled the air.

She fought through the haze, but she could barely breathe. Her throat closed. It became hard to swallow, and her eyes stung. Clawing at her throat, she coughed and tasted dirt. No. *No.* Nova cried out, twisting her own blood until her eyes blinked open and she felt oxygen in her lungs. The vision faded with every passing second.

"Bleeding suns," she murmured, resting her head on the desk. That place...that was Syris.

Those mountains were where Froststone stood. All she could think of was Asha. The nightmares she couldn't remember, the part of her that *supposedly* called out for help when Asha healed her. *Gods, maybe she was right.*

But that was the first time Syris had appeared, and that had to mean something. Nova flipped through all the books she had collected in her room, lined up on every surface and every corner. She opened every book she had. The Gods, volume eight specifically, the one of the Dove and of Spirit. The book on the Naturalist War, the anthologies written on the Rise of Spirit. Every single one.

She saw her reflection in the mirror, the reflection of Elders flashing in and out. Though no matter how many times she'd seen them, no matter how deeply she knew they weren't there behind her, it always felt like it. The air was tighter, the room smaller.

It was bloody suffocating, and she wanted them gone. She couldn't live much longer with their haunts clasped around her throat like a rope. She just...wanted to breathe. To be free. Of all of it.

She swallowed the nausea and sliced her fingers again and again, letting her blood fall over the pages. Images and words unfurled one by one, and every mention of spirit, of their existence, on every page before the massacre was crossed out, stricken with red or black ink.

*This doesn't make any sense...*She turned to the Gods and their short section. And the same, all the Doves were drawn out of existence. Notes were sprawled under the word *untrue* written and re-written. Underlined and circled.

Her eyes read and re-read the words in front of her. She found accounts of sickness tearing through the Naturalist, physically and mentally—illness unable to be healed by humans or the Athera. Someone had re-written the legends of Spirit and compared them to the rest, allowing her to see just how false Spirit was. Their stories, their tales, their God...were pulled from the rest of Valora.

All the other Gods and Athera had multiple legends. Multiple myths. Because no one could ever really know—so how was their only one story to explain Spirit? To explain the Dove? When history melded with legend, there was no single truth. Historians would disagree, Mythics would've discovered other tales. But not with the Spirit.

There was only one version of their story, and it was pulled from all the rest.

And if that was true, it meant they had no real Gods. No legends. So where did they come from?

Where did their magic come from?

Who—*what*—were they?

She strode through the walls of the library, her damp curls flowing behind her as she searched for Cyrus. If he wasn't in Willowgrove or Izlena, he was here, and right now, she needed him. She needed Asha.

People were littered throughout the hall, their robes dusting the floor and climbing the ladders of the shelves. But none of them were Cyrus. Impatience got the better of her, and she reached out for the blood of everyone with a pulse. She knew what Cyrus's felt like, how it appeared to her, and it wasn't here.

"By the Gods," she mumbled to herself. The one time she needed him.

She headed through the tunnel, which always felt like moving between worlds, until she felt the suns warmth. Much of the city was still quiet, the air filled with the smell of pastries and coffee. But there, underneath all the others, amongst the trees, she felt him.

Calm and strong and steady.

"Cyrus," she said, partially breathless, "I need a favor."

"Good morning to you, too, Nova." Cyrus handed her a cup of coffee. She blinked, lost for words. "I have a surprise for you." He motioned toward the doorway of the small eatery, The Yellow Rose, and there, like magic, was Asha.

"Asha." She looked between the two of them, though she lingered on him when Cyrus met her gaze. "You brought her here?"

"I did. I mentioned getting a letter to her, but I thought this might be better." He stood as Asha took a seat at the table, leaving some coin on the stone top. "I have some things to handle in Willowgrove today, but I'll be back later this evening."

As he passed, Nova dipped her head, her curls shrouding the small smile. He was kind, thoughtful. She'd never experienced that before. Though at her feet, a tiny, minuscule flower bloomed beside her. One with twisting vines and faded pink flowers. She forced herself not to look back. She waited until he was gone, his blood out of her reach before sitting across from the old healer.

Asha raised a graying eyebrow as she brought her mug to her lips. There was a knowing smugness emitting off of her.

Wretched old woman, she sighed. Her lip practically curled. "I need your help."

"About time."

SHE IGNORED Asha's disgruntled look upon entering her room. "You should really think of cleaning up after yourself." There were books everywhere. The little clothing she did have was strewn about the room, and multiple glasses of water lined the desk.

"I've little time to be concerned when I'm being watched." She cocked her head at the old healer.

"By whom?"

"Amala, Cyrus, Dray. All of them," she said, taking a seat at the desk. She hadn't confirmed who it was—if it was one of them or someone else. But the only place she couldn't be watched was here, in this room.

They wanted to watch her? Fine. All she needed to do was ensure they had nothing to find. Nothing to suspect.

"Why would they be watching you?" Asha asked, eyes sharp.

Nova held her gaze. "I—"

"I expect our agreement still stands, Nova. Where we agreed not to lie to each other."

Unease grew like a root within her. Could she trust Asha? If she lied, would Asha see the truth within her memories anyway? Was there anything to gain in keeping it from her?

"Because they are looking for a Witch. One who controls the blood. One who leaves tears of blood behind."

"The Cardinal?" Asha's eyes widened.

Nova hated the name. It was whispered amongst Syris, whispered amongst those she was ordered to kill. It had spread like a wildfire. It was ironic, too. That a bird thought to symbolize a lost loved one had turned into a nightmare. She'd first heard it in a tavern in Pyth; some drunkard had been telling the story. A story of slit throats in the darkness and tears of blood left on the cheeks of the dead.

Once a symbol of remaining love, it became a warning of death. They said the red bird would appear moments before she did, the Cardinal, as a warning of what was to come. They said if the bird was there, it was already too late to stop the tears.

"Yes. And what do you know about the Cardinal?"

Asha pursed her lips. "That whoever it is haunts the shores of Valora, leaving death in their wake." Asha's eyes narrowed. "Why would that concern you?"

Irritation clawed up Nova's spine. "How would one leave tears of blood behind?"

Asha blanched. Her deep, dark skin seemed to turn sallow. "You're the Cardinal." Asha's blood flared with anger. It was a specific feeling, similar in everyone, though still varied person to person. Their blood became concentrated, hot. "Do you know how many people you've killed? How many deaths you've delivered?"

That was the thing. Nova was starting to think she didn't. Some of the visions she was having, some of the nightmares, were not familiar to her. But they felt as though they should've been.

She swallowed. "I know I have killed. I remember most of their faces—I don't need you to remind me. But I am starting to think that more has been hidden from me. Memories taken."

The faces—the *feelings*—of all those that had died at her hand, that she remembered, rose up like a sand snake. She could feel the Elders behind her, *existing* in the air.

Waves of anger and sadness, heavy grief, rolled off of Asha and over her skin. Had Asha lost someone because of her? Was that it? The emotions curled around Nova, tightening and choking her. But the feeling, that strangulation, was something she lived with every day. She wasn't sure of the last time she actually took a deep breath.

"Why would you think that?" Asha asked cooly.

"I was born in Syris, raised by the Vahls themselves. And Spirit can be a nasty thing in the wrong hands," Nova said, not shying away from Asha's glare. "I am not saying I haven't killed. I have. And I would do it again if it kept me alive. But it's at their hands, their instruction who receives death. The Cardinal—*I*— do their bidding. They have had their claws in my mind for as long as I can remember."

Asha scoffed. "And what? You expect me to help you? To pity that you've killed at someone else's order? Do you think I'm a fool?"

"The Cardinal is a myth, a story. But *I* am here. Standing in front of you," Nova said, digging half-moons into her skin with her nails. "Try to separate the two." Nova had tried time and time again, and she failed often. Maybe someone else could succeed.

In the midst's of the revelation, Nova had moved to the door, blocking it.

"I could escape if I wanted."

"No, you couldn't." She leaned against the heavy door. "I don't want to hurt you. That's not why I asked you here. That's not why I need your help." A dark emotion swirled under her skin, a sick self-loathing that often reared its ugly head.

But she meant what she said. She would kill her if she had to. If it meant surviving or holding on to a chance at freedom, she would do anything.

"Have you considered whether you deserve it?"

Something curled in her stomach at the look in Asha's eyes. It was anger darker than she'd ever seen. Deeper, hotter. A rage that burrowed into the skin and stayed there like a thorn.

Maybe it was because now, Asha saw what had been believed. That Witches of the blood were bringers of death and nothing more. They had made Nova into what people had feared. And maybe it was rage that Nova had killed someone that Asha once loved. It didn't matter what fanned the flames of the rage, only that it existed.

Despite it, she didn't need to make excuses for her actions. She'd killed many people—a lot of them without remorse. Some of them with. But it took her a long time to realize her blood did not belong to Mikel and Mireya. Most days, she was still unsure that it was really hers. And *that* information didn't belong to anyone else. Not even Asha.

"Do you think I don't wonder that every day of my life?" Nova asked. "I am what they made me. And I have done what was required of me to live. I'm not asking for absolution. I'm not asking for forgiveness." Nova believed, more than anything, those things would never come. "You are the one who said you didn't believe in Witch hunts. That the truth often exists underneath the stories. I am both the Cardinal and someone else, someone else I have not even had the chance to discover. Have you tried to see that? Tried to look beyond the surface of the truth you now know? Or am I only something to be condemned?"

The snarl on Asha's lips fell slowly. The threads within her warred with one another. Nova felt each and every tug and pull of the emotional spectrum. She sensed the respect the healer had shown her before and the anger she felt now, looking at the killer that appeared to be in front of her. Silence passed between the two. Tension thrummed on the air like sparks from an Athera's fingertips.

She needed her to say yes. She didn't want to hurt Asha, but the truth of the matter was that she would. There was a part of her hoping that Asha would see *her*. To see the person under the surface. But she'd avoided herself long enough to know it was easier that way.

The healer's heartbeat turned steady. When Asha looked up, her brown eyes glimmered in the flickering orb light—a crack in her guard. "What do you need?"

"I need you to make me remember."

Chapter 28

Path of Violence

"Remember?"

Nova let herself fall to the floor, sitting against the wooden door. "The memories you felt when you healed me. Of the blockage keeping them at bay." She met Asha's eyes. "I need it gone."

Images replayed in her mind of visions that appeared when her blood spilled, of the dreams that would not let her rest.

Since being here, the dreams and blurred memories had become constant—a friend to the Elders that haunted her. But she couldn't see them, she couldn't *remember* them.

She needed to. She needed to the know the truth of her own life, her own past, before she could break through anything else. And she needed to do it before the coronation, before the Vahls came and found her again. Before they dug their claws in deeper.

She cleared her throat. "Can you help me or not?"

"You seemed to want nothing to do with that before," Asha said, tapping her foot.

"Things change."

For a split second, Asha's lips turned up. But the smile didn't last. "I told you the truth had a way of making itself known."

Painfully so. Between the dreams and the Elders shouting at her to discover it, the truth was not to be ignored.

Rolling her eyes, she tied her curls behind her head, a few pieces falling forward. "He'll be back in a few hours. How do we do this?"

NOVA STARED at the ceiling above her. Her wrists were tied down as best Asha could manage.

"This can only last as long as you can handle it." Asha stirred something in a cup she'd found from the kitchens. "And you'll need to drink this."

"How do I know you haven't made some poisonous mess to try to kill me instead?"

A glint shimmered in Asha's eyes, an unreadable one. "We agreed not to lie to each other. For me, that remains true."

She sighed, rolling her head. "What is it?"

"Blackclover. A mixture at least," Asha said. "Only enough to keep you settled."

"Okay." As best she could, she swallowed down the tea from Asha's steady hands.

She knew it wouldn't kill her. She'd tried. Multiple times.

The taste of the clover—and whatever it was mixed with— struck a familiar chord. Tugged on a painful memory of despair.

"This is going to hurt. Memories are...sensitive and often unwilling participants. Made worse when their host is the same."

"Get on with it," she said, her throat scratchy, her fear hot. Asha leaned over her, gray curls braided back to keep them at bay. "Wait. Will you be able to see them? To see my memories?"

Though slight, the softening of Asha's brown eyes was unmissable. "Some may come through. Only pieces, fragments. I won't be able to see the whole picture. Mostly, I will feel what you feel. For a moment, we will be connected. But your memories are your own. Only you can choose to share them. You should know that though the seal keeping them away may be broken, it may not be as simple as remembering. You may only have pieces of the full memory until you work to uncover them completely."

Nova exhaled. Her body felt heavy, her magic becoming distant as the blackclover set in. It was different from the chains, more muted, yet it felt deeply rooted within her, sinking and swirling through her blood. If she wanted, she was pretty sure she could separate each particle of the ground-up plant. But now wasn't the time.

The press of Asha's hand was soft at firs, then firm. Her skin shuddered, but the pain came like a lightning bolt—quick, pointed, and blinding. It spread over her like a wildflower, and the depths of it dug into her like talons. Asha shushed her gently from above, murmuring softly, but the talons broke the fortress around her brain and ripped it apart.

Bleeding suns, it was as though she was being torn apart at the seams.

Everything happened so quickly. One second, the scar on her throat burned with the heat of the summer suns, and her neck was scorching as though rivulets of blood were dripping down her throat. The next, she couldn't breathe, the scar aching as she fought for air against some invisible choking force.

It flickered between the two, the pain switching off and on. Blackness clouded her mind, a brief respite before the talons returned, pulling away the fog.

Parts of the memory were out of focus. She saw herself on her knees, younger, with no scar on her throat and wild curls around her head. Though it was her, she barely recognized herself. There were tear streaks on her cheeks, and her eyes were alight with rage, something she never allowed to come to the surface now.

A dagger appeared in the memory, held right in front of her— a pure obsidian hilt and shimmering snow-white blade.

And she watched an invisible hand drag it across her throat.

The blood fell onto the ground in front of her—*drip, drip, drip.*

A tight sensation wrapped around her throat, stealing her air.

"Stop...stop!" she said, but her voice felt miles away. Pain fractured over her skin, and she couldn't move, she couldn't—"Please."

Again and again and again, the memory repeated.

She lost count of how many times her blood was spilled.

But the pain would not stop; the talons wouldn't let go. The memory was living and breathing with claws buried in it. A pitiful sound crawled up her throat as she watched the blood poor out of her own neck. Hot tears streaked out of her eyes that she couldn't open.

"Nova, can you hear me?"

There were glimpses of other scenes. Two faces she did not recognize leaving her at Froststone. The room she had been locked in time and time again. Bodies with tears of blood and faces she did not remember killing. Dirt pouring over her and into her, choking out her air. One second, she was suffocating, and the next, she was falling through the blackness, caught by invisible hands and hearing whispers in her ears.

And then, it repeated.

Her neck being slit, the blood being spilled, and the suffocating darkness.

Asha spoke, but her voice was muted and lost, despite Nova reaching for it. Over and over again, she tried to fight her way back to reality. Whether it was the blackclover or the pain or the shock, she wasn't sure. But she couldn't escape. She could hear her own voice calling out—

Let me out.

The heaving breaths and the shattering pain dancing over her skin like wraiths in the night.

Let me out.

The silence became a deafening roar in her ears. There *was* no way out. *There would never be a way out,* she heaved. *I am nothing more than what I have always been. I will never be more than what they made me.* The scar pulsed and pounded, the memories replayed, and tears cascaded down her cheeks.

Let me out.

But there was no escape from the memories.

Not when they needed to be heard.

The pain was gone.

That was the first thing Nova became aware of. Second, was the dampness on her cheeks, stemming from her eyes in falling tears. Her eyes opened, and the room returned in spurts. Instead of rope around her wrist, there were vines—living, moving vines keeping her tied down. Panic returned. Beside her, Asha sat with her eyes closed and lips moving in quiet whispers.

And in the corner—where all the books had been placed into neat piles—sat Cyrus. His eyes were narrowed and focused, his elbows on his knees as he stared at her. Nova swallowed.

"What—" Her voice was abrasive, but it caught the healer's attention.

"By the Gods," Asha said, visibly exhaling. "Here." She thrust a glass of water in Nova's direction.

It stung as she gulped it down, as if the memories had re-opened every wound. On her throat, the scar throbbed. Asha's brown eyes dipped, focusing on the pulsing tissue for a moment before meeting Nova's eyes.

"What happened? What is he doing here?"

She felt his blood pulse angrily. A first. "What am I doing here? What are you doing?"

"Both of you, quiet," Asha snarked, a look passing between the two of them—one of reassurance. "You were shouting and thrashing, and he was returning. You broke through the ropes and...your nails...."

Her skin was marked red and angry. She must've tried to claw herself awake.

Nova looked down at the vines; though they were tight, they were gentle, barely a brush on her skin. When she looked at Cyrus, she saw the same vines on his hand, the ones that were always there—his living jewelry. They looked out of place on her skin.

"What were you doing?" He rose, stalking over to them. His demeanor was different, more predatory, more formal.

Despite herself, defensive anger flared. "That's none of your business."

Asha clicked her tongue. "Hush. You were a danger to yourself. He put a stop to it." She refilled her water. "Drink."

Cyrus's gaze was a heavy weight on her skin. The silence between the three of them was unbearable. She broke it. "What happened?"

The healer glanced between the two of them before landing on Nova. "I've never felt anything like that before. Your memories..." She started but took a breath. Cyrus watched, listening intently. "All memories, hidden or not, have a feel to them, whether that's happy or angry or broken, but yours seemed to have a mind of their own. Alive in their own right. Begging to be heard."

There was a heaviness to herself that hadn't been there before. As if she had stones tied around her wrists threatening to pull her under. A phantom pain snapped across her throat, her hand quickly cupping her neck, but no blood fell. No new wound existed. Asha leaned forward, pushing her hand out of the way and running her thumb over the scar.

Discomfort wound around her skin, and she pulled her neck away.

"Can you undo the vines please?" Her heart pounded, but within seconds, the vines retracted, not a single mark left behind.

There was something building within her—a heavy, twirling storm threatened to crash over her. "Can you—can you give me a minute?" The words were breathless, and her eyes burned.

What was happening? What is this? This panic...

"I'm going to go get more water." Asha departed quickly, but Cyrus remained by her beside.

"Please go," Nova pleaded. She didn't feel like herself.

She couldn't gulp down enough air, and her nails were dragging over her skin. She felt dirty, marred with death and blood and—

"You're panicking. Look at me."

He was blurry. *Why was he blurry?* She shook her head but froze when she felt his hands on her skin. He pulled her nails away from her arms and placed them flat on the bed, removing himself from her as quickly as possible.

"I want you to leave."

"Look at me," Cyrus said, gentle and firm.

With heaving breaths, she shook her head. "I can't—I can't." Panic was attacking her in towering waves, battering at her head and her skin and her body to get in, to overtake her. "Make it stop."

And if she opened her eyes, she didn't stand a chance. It was too much....*it was all* too much.

She couldn't breathe, she couldn't—

All she had become—all she was—was rage and desolation and despair. Sadness so dense and heavy, she didn't recognize it. She couldn't stop it from taking over the rest of her like a hungry wolf in a barren forest.

Despite Cyrus's efforts, Nova dug her nails into her skin, feeling the release of blood and the sharp stinging pain that distracted her from the rapid beat of her heart.

Weeding through her emotions was not something she was good at, mostly because she didn't feel them, didn't acknowledge them. It was easier that way, to do what her parents had expected of her. But now, there was a storm of them, whirling around and around at breakneck speeds with her at the center. Emotions from the past and the present battered her until she was nothing but skin and bones and blood with no way out.

The storm would not stop. Someone had dragged a knife across her throat. She had killed more people than she remembered, she could've drowned in the blood. She was a monster, as they believed her to be. The pressure would not lessen. The pain—

"Nova, I need you to look at me. Now." The strength in his voice broke through the swirling winds and pulses of pain. She blinked her eyes open, immediately coming face-to-face with his green ones. "Good. Now listen to me. Focus on my voice."

But her breathing was rapid, and her pulse had taken its own course; how could she focus? How could she even try?

"I know. I know it's hard. You're going to have to trust me," Cyrus said softly. She furrowed her brows. Trust...that was not something she gave. And how could he help her? "I'm going to touch your hand again, just for a second, okay?"

He waited.

And waited.

And waited.

Eventually, she found enough air to say, "Okay."

With a featherlight touch, he lifted her hand and unclenched her fingers. Moments later, there was a movement on her palm as something wound around her fingers and down her wrist. Tears still fell from her eyes, but she blinked them away to see the vine.

Once meant to constrict her, the vine was now moving in time with her pulse. Little flowers bloomed on the tendrils, their petals fluttering with the pace of her heart. Did he do that for her?

"Good. Is that okay?"

"Yes."

"If you focus, you can feel the vine itself. How it breathes. How it moves. Can you try that?"

Nova glanced between him and the plant before taking a

shallow breath. Eventually, her heart rate began to slow and her eyes began to clear, the dampness on her cheeks drying in the air.

The constricting feeling around her throat began to loosen. Unease still lurched in the background, panic dancing around the edges of her mind, but they were not overtaking her. She wasn't sure how long they sat like that. Only that eventually, the silence returned, replacing the rushing in her ears, and her blood slowed.

"Good. How do you feel?" Cyrus asked, his patient eyes tracking over her face.

Embarrassment and frustration settled heavy in her gut. "I asked you to leave."

"I know." He leaned back, giving her space, but left the vine on her palm.

"Why didn't you?" There was a bite to her words, but he didn't seem to care.

"I was worried you'd hurt yourself further. Or get lost in the panic. I've dealt with them myself, and it didn't seem right to leave you to figure it out alone," he said softly, barely louder than the beat of his blood. His forest-green eyes were locked on hers, shining with sincerity. "I apologize for not honoring your request, but I don't apologize for ensuring that you were safe."

Nova furrowed her brows. She could feel the truth and gentleness behind his words, as if they were emitting from his being in shades of golden and green. But did she believe them? All the lies she'd been told, all the memories that she constantly had to remind herself were fake... It wasn't easy to believe the truth, even if it felt like she could hold it in her hands.

So, she pivoted. "Is that how you knew what to do? Because that's happened to you?"

"Yes and no." Cyrus twirled a silver ring, the ghost of a smile on his lips. "You cannot speak of this, certainly not to him, but Dray used to get panic attacks, too, when he was younger. Mine started after Nalādin," he said, his eyes taking a faraway look.

The skinny vine on his hand moved slowly in its usual

rhythm, and Nova looked at the one moving on her own skin, touching her with only the faintest pressure.

"I can make that stop."

"No." She shook her head. "Please, leave it." Her heartbeat was steady, yet quicker than normal. Not for fear or panic, but for something else—the weight of his eyes and his unwavering gaze.

"Can I ask you something?"

She nodded.

"The restriction...does that help you? Ground you?" They locked eyes. "You don't have to answer that. I'm only curious."

Gods, her instinct told her to retreat. Yet, she *wanted* to tell him—about how familiar restriction—chains—felt to her. The person he appeared to be, at least to her, deserved that much. But what would she tell him? That the Vahls used to chain her in a room? That while she hated it, they made her *feel*...less.

"I'm not really sure I know myself," she started, her thumb stroking one of the small flowers. A memory of the chains being placed around her flashed, and then, it was gone. "I think it's a crutch. Something that was forced on me has now become a saving grace. And a way to keep me from hurting myself."

Cyrus watched her without pity or sorrow. Only patience. She felt his eyes track over her, differently than before. This time, her scars seemed to be screaming for attention.

She wasn't ashamed. Her scars were who she was. What she'd survived, whether she had wanted to or not. Cyrus didn't look at them with disgust as some others did. Instead, he looked upon them with care.

And a flame of anger that she believed, wholeheartedly, was not directed at her.

"That's the first time you've truly looked at the scar on my throat."

Cyrus leaned forward, resting his elbows on his knees, bringing them only breaths apart. He cocked his head as he gazed upon the scar that had been reopened in her memories more times than she could count.

"I've always looked at it. It is a part of you, and therefore, I have seen it." His eyes swept upward to meet hers. "But today, it appears to be a living breathing thing of its own. One of anger, vengeance. I imagine it has something to do with the memories you were searching for. And I can only hope that whoever did this to you will come face to face with it—with you—again one day. Because they deserve to pay for it. For all of it."

Nova swore her blood heated at his words. The idea of revenge fueled the only fantasies she let herself have.

"How did you get it?" he asked softly.

Her heart pounded. Could she tell him? Could she share that part of herself? "Someone dragged a knife across my throat," she whispered.

His eyes cooled. Once bright as the summer forest, now cold as an emerald blade. "Why would anyone do that?"

The memory flashed, but still, no faces appeared. All she saw was her blood. Nova shook her head, unable to find more words.

"I know that sorry does not fix anything," Cyrus said, his vines moving over her wrists. "But I am sorry that happened to you. I'm sorry."

Nova swallowed. No one had ever said sorry to her. No one had ever felt empathy for her. Maybe if he knew the truth of her, it would go away, but for now, she would bask in it.

She wasn't sure what to make of this version of him. Until now, he'd been calm and levelheaded. Peaceful. But as she revealed parts of herself, he had done the same. Between them, the air seemed to spark. She was enchanted by him, his kindness, his beauty. How grounded he was. Maybe it was stupidity or weakness—it didn't matter—because the truth was, she'd begun to care for him.

She liked that he was kind, even when he didn't need to be. She liked that he constantly needed to be amongst the forest or the flowers and the mountains. And even if she hated to admit it, she liked the way he looked at her. Gentle, patient, kind. It was foreign but left a lingering warmth on her skin every single time.

But caring about him meant that he would be caught in the wreckage of her selfishness.

Nova dragged her eyes away.

Cyrus leaned back, the coldness turning into something softer. This was not the priority. Not when the feel of her memories tumbled within her alive and writhing, no longer trapped but not quite ready to reveal themselves. Not when the histories and the truths were on pages she only needed to bleed on. Not when she could feel the Elders within her head.

He was not her responsibility.

And yet, long after the removing of the vine and his departure, she felt the weight of his gaze on her skin. Tracking over her face and her scars and seeing nothing more and nothing less than the person in front of him.

The thought of letting him suffer for her choice to leave, of letting him deal with the act of her disappearance, of leaving him in the path of violence...well, that felt heaviest of all.

CHAPTER 29

MOONFLOWERS IN THE SOIL

"Come on," Cyrus said from ahead.

"I'm not sure I'm up for it."

"You need it. You've been cooped up in that room too long."

Nova sighed. Above, the sky was midnight blue and dusted with stars. The suns had dwindled hours ago, making space for the moon. She followed as they rounded Lake Emora. For the past two days, she'd relived what happened time and time again. The blurred faces. The slice of her neck. She could feel her memories fighting to fully reveal themselves. And the Elders, whispering to her over and over again.

She was sure rest would never come again.

The thing was, she *knew* she should be back in the library, trying to appease the dead Elders. Trying to find whatever it was they wanted before the coronation. Before the Vahls arrived. But he was right, she needed a godsdamned break.

The fresh air felt good on her skin, and the smell of the forest forced her senses to life. Around them, Izlena seemed to sleep. Only the taverns remained open, but they, too, were quiet. All the lights that lined the stairs and bridges of the towering castle had been dimmed, barely infiltrating the night sky. Right now, the forest seemed to loom over them. No matter where they stood, the mountains became towering shadows—a fortress to protect their city.

As soon as they touched the first valley beyond the town, Nova slipped her boots off, grateful to feel the grass underfoot. She could've sworn the strands of grass greeted her, curving around her skin. Lights were strewn amongst the valley ahead, indicating the other districts that were a part of Izlena. Many were burrowed into the side of the mountain where the valley began, and others were more sporadic. She imagined they went all the way to the sea.

"I thought you might like to come out; I packed some food for us. I couldn't have you spend another day and night in that room alone," Cyrus said as they stopped at the stables, his eyes focused on her.

She gave him a once over. "I'm used to being alone."

"I know that. It doesn't mean you always should be."

She didn't quite know what to say, though she felt a strange heat on her cheeks.

A smile spread over his face when she simply dipped her head, and he led them to a pasture, where Rouge and Ghost were standing side by side. Ghost lifted his large head, ears perking at Cyrus's arrival. Nova tipped her head to the side, a fluttery feeling in her gut when Rouge took a few long strides toward her, greeting her with a gentle nudge of her head. Her big brown eyes met Nova's with an unexpected warmth.

In response, she reached out her hand, running it over the horse's neck and under her mane. And she couldn't help the ease that she felt in response, as if a tiny light sparked within her, pushing back the darkness she'd been feeling for days. Instinctually, she rested her head against the horse, falling into the steady lull of her breathing and the blood within her.

"Seems like someone's taken a liking to you," he mused quietly from beside her.

Nova turned her head, not lifting it from Rouge. "I think the feeling is mutual."

"I'd say so. Come on." He led them through the large pasture, the horses following with steady gaits.

There were other pastures attached to the stables, so she pushed her touch outward, feeling each and every heartbeat of the animals within her reach. At the edge of the pasture, trees were bent over the fence, their leaves hanging down and their roots providing nature-made seats.

Cyrus unpacked the small leather satchel, revealing slices of fruit and bread, dried meats and cheeses, and another more carefully wrapped package. "This is for you."

She unwrapped it to find the pastry she'd liked the day they'd gone into the forest. "You didn't have to do this," she said motioning to it all. Her heart felt warm. No one had done anything like this for her before. "Any of this."

"I noticed you liked it; it's no trouble to get it."

All she could think of was Jonah and the almond pastries he would bring her after a hard night. Nights when she was more of the enigma she'd become than herself. "A—" *friend.* That was the word she couldn't say because she wasn't sure if it was true. "Someone I knew back home used to bring me almond pastries all the time. So...thank you."

"We have something similar here. I'll make sure you get some."

"You don't—"

He interrupted her. "I want to."

She blinked but broke a piece of the pastry off. "Can I ask you a stupid question?"

"Ask whatever you like."

Her heart beat inside her chest. It was dumb, Gods, it was *stupid.* A pointless question given the guilt she had felt when he was there after the memory recovery. Pointless given that it wouldn't last but...she couldn't help herself.

"Are we friends?"

As soon as the words left her mouth, she wanted them back. *I am a godsdamned idiot.* She kept her eyes off him, instead watching the two horses graze beside one another. Gods, she'd put all her inner thoughts out there in the open for him to hear. But she'd never had a real friend, and she couldn't help but wonder how much—if any—of his kindness was solely to give her a reason to stay in line?

"I think so," Cyrus said softly. "Or at least, the start of a friendship."

The words slipped out before she could stop them, "I'm not sure I've ever had one of those." When she met his eyes, she couldn't stop herself from thinking that maybe she didn't deserve one.

"Well, that's no good. We have to rectify that immediately."

She smiled at the lightness in his tone. "And how does one do that?"

"I have to know something embarrassing about you."

"Embarrassing?" she asked, popping another piece of pastry into her mouth. "You first."

Cyrus raised a brow, those green eyes sparkling with only the moonlight. "Asking me to spill my secrets. Interesting choice."

Ghost nickered lowly a few feet away. "He wants to hear it, too."

Cyrus rested his head against the tree bark, cutting an apple with a small knife. "After Nalādin, after the contenders were named, including Amala, I attended more meetings. It was the expectation at the time that I would serve on either of their councils. For some reason, I was a nervous wreck, despite having spent my life around Amala and her parents. I couldn't help but wonder what the council would think, and she was barely speaking to me at the time." A brief glimmer of sadness flickered over his face before disappearing. "But when I entered and all their eyes landed on me, I had no idea how they expected me to treat Amala or Aydin or Gena, so I took a knee and bowed my head in greeting. That's not done here. That's *never* been done here."

She was unprepared for the laugh that burst out of her.

Instantly, her hands shot up to cover her mouth, and Cyrus's lips twitched. "You didn't," she tried to say, unable to stop the laughter from spilling out.

"I did. Worse was Aydin trying not to laugh themselves. The king trying to hold in their laughter because someone bent their knee to them. And it wasn't as if I could leave. So, I sat there, for upward of two hours, avoiding looking at anyone in the room," he said, taking a slice of apple and handing her some as well. "And they never let me forget it."

"I can't imagine they do." She couldn't keep the smile off her lips, and she couldn't stop another laugh from slipping out, a light, airy sound that didn't feel like her at all.

But it relieved some of the pressure that had been sitting on her chest, and that feeling—*that*, was addicting.

"I'm glad you find it amusing," he said, his eyes locked on to her.

Between hiccups of laughter, she dipped her head. "Thank you for sharing."

"Oh, you're welcome, but I expect a story in return. Whenever you're ready."

She thought of all the times she'd felt embarrassed and realized none of them were like Cyrus's. There was no friend to lighten the moment after, no one to talk to. No one but Jonah, and if he were here, he would've agreed that the moments she was thinking of weren't embarrassing but cruel. All caused by the Vahls.

How pathetic was she? That there was not a single moment not impacted by them?

She swallowed. "Can I tell you something else instead?"

"Whatever you'd like."

"It's going to sound stupid," she said, looking up at the star-covered sky.

"I doubt it."

He was so sure of himself. Of everything. Even the littlest things. "I know so many people are, but I'm scared of the dark. Actually, no—not scared. I hate it. Not for the reasons others might. I'm not worried about what might be hiding within the shadows, but...I can't control it. I can't make it do what I wish. I can't—" She took a breath. It wasn't just the dark, but things without a heartbeat, without a mind. She was lost there.

"Control is a funny thing. It won't bring you peace, but it makes you feel safe," Cyrus said, eyes softening when he looked at her. "Can I show you something?'

"Sure."

He crouched over the ground and motioned for her to join him. Cyrus reached out, his fingers only a small distance away from her skin. "May I? Only for a moment."

After a brief hesitation, she nodded. Cyrus's fingers wrapped around her wrist, her heart picking up speed before settling when he placed her palms flat on the ground, right where the roots of the tree dug into the earth below. She pressed her fingers into the soil and reached out, wondering what she would find.

Maybe it was an illusion or a phantom feeling, but Nova felt it —a sedated, measured beat deep within, further than she or anyone could ever reach. As if Valora had its own heartbeat, pumping blood into the world they knew. Into the trees and the oceans and the rivers and even the tiniest flowers.

Beside her, she felt the gaze of Cyrus's eyes on hers. Looking over, there was a tiny smile on his lips. "You feel it, too." He took a deep breath, the vines moving slowly over his skin, while in front of her, moonflowers poked through the soil at the base of the tree, and the grass seemed to say *hello.* "I can direct it. I can encourage it to grow or diminish, but I can't truly control it."

He sat back, their arms brushing again, though it wasn't like before. Or others. The touch lingered, though not unpleasantly. She didn't know what to do with that or how to make it disappear.

"I'm not sure if that makes me feel better or worse," she mused, running her fingers over the grass.

He laughed, a deep melodic sound. "My intention was to make you feel less alone. There are some people that might think they control it, but I don't think that's true. It's a part of me, but I don't own it. I think it goes both ways. You hate that you can't control it, but it can't control you either."

She looked at him, unable to look away. "No, I guess it can't."

Without a word, Nova stood and wiped her hands off before striding directly toward Rouge and Ghost. In her palm were the slices of apple Cyrus had given to her. Flattening her hand, she held it out. Rouge nuzzled her palm with that soft nose and ate them right up. Ghost watched her with careful eyes, but his ears were perked forward, one twitching when Rouge nudged her chest.

Cyrus followed, resting his arms over Ghost's back, watching her again.

"Would you like to go back?"

"I'd like to stay."

Cyrus smiled, and for a second—a brief flash of time—Nova felt like she was worthy of being smiled at.

CHAPTER 30

CAREFUL WHAT YOU WISH FOR

THOUGH IT HAD BEEN DAYS, THE WORDS OF THE governors had not stopped haunting Elaia.

Maybe it is time that a Zūne no longer sat the Obsidian Throne. Maybe the reign has come to an end. The whispered agreements. The coldness in their eyes. They were going to deny her.

A challenge will not bring us together, Princess. We are unsure we can pledge our support.

The Zūne's have ruled long enough. Maybe it is time we raise someone else to the throne. We let the people decide.

How could they? Was it because of her father? The riots? They could not deny her, not like this.

She ran her nails over the scabs on her arm that she'd picked after the meeting. Every day she woke, she picked them, they bled, and she'd done it again and again and again—

"Elaia, stop," Zahra murmured, plucking Elaia's hand from her skin. "What do you need?"

"I need the governors to back me. That's what I need. Can you get that?" Elaia asked, her words sharp, pointed.

Zahra's eyes sharpened. "Your *hunter* should take care of that, shouldn't he? Isn't that why you agreed to work with them in the first place? It doesn't matter what they said, then. Not if you have the Order."

Elaia inhaled, her skin tight. "Right. Right." Akiro pushed his head into her lap, her fingers scratching his favorite spots. She'd been so obsessed with their denial, so hyper-focused, she'd almost forgotten. "Have you found anything?"

"Nothing. It's like they don't exist, unless we just don't know what we're looking for," Zahra said, taking a step back, creating more space. Still, Elaia did not apologize. "Except this." Zahra held an old, slightly familiar discolored pendant in her palm.

Zahra plucked the pendant and rolled it between her fingers, using a shimmer of light to illuminate it. Once gold, the material had tarnished, but the image was clear.

A fyrebird with its beak tipped up to the sky, wings extended, and flames falling down. It was not the sigil of any Fire Elemental country—not Vydara and not Pyth. Elaia had never seen it before.

"You found this here?"

"I remember it. It was one of my first days in Varistone after leaving the healers. They had given me a room near the three of you, and your mother helped me get settled. But I was free to explore, and I was so entranced. The way the light seeped into even the darkest corners," Zahra mused, fighting a smile. "I loved it immediately. I found myself in the central cavern, in the gardens, and it was there, hidden in the edges of the soil. I'd never seen the symbol before, and it was pretty, so I kept it..." She trailed off, and Elaia knew the rest.

Because only seconds later, Elaia had found her. And from that moment on, they were inseparable.

She'd seen it too many times to count—tucked in Zahra's pockets or spinning on her fingers out of habit. But it'd never struck her as anything important. Just a piece of metal.

"It might be nothing, but for that to be here in Varistone, it had to be someone invited in. Someone close."

"Or it could be nothing. A coincidence."

Elaia choked down a remark. Coincidences weren't real. At least not the way other people believed.

There was a story her mother used to tell her about all the threads in the universe. How they shimmered from sapphire to the blue of the sky, to the pinks of the gems inlaid in canyons and lit by the suns, to the gold of the specks of dust in desert lands. They were everything and everywhere all at once. The threads were always in play, whether you believed or not. Whether you could feel or see them, they were there. Always tugging and pulling people into place. Everything was a tiny piece in a very large puzzle.

Or at least, that was what she believed.

She pressed the onyx cuff in her ear in a pattern for Rohan. Seconds later, the door to her chambers opened, and Xerxes entered, Rohan closing the doors behind him. In the few days since she'd followed him, he'd sent letters across Rersa, detailing in a coded way where he was and what he was doing. Plainly, he'd told her those within the factions of Rersa would be aware and preparing for her initiation to the Order. She'd been trying to figure out which of them was on her father's council, but they gave no hint. And Xerxes would not tell her.

He eyed the both of them as he sat opposite her, his eyes lingering on Zahra. Elaia had tried to keep them separate—if only to protect Zahra from his sharp eyes and the eyes of the Order—but Zahra made it clear she didn't need, nor want, the protection. And that she could take care of herself.

"Would you give us a minute, Zahra?" Elaia asked.

Something flickered in Zahra's auburn eyes. Elaia was unsure of what exactly. Sadness? Disappointment? Either way, pain knocked on the shell of her heart. But Elaia couldn't have her here, under his eyes. She couldn't push her away completely, but she wanted her as far away from it all as she could keep her. Out of harm's reach.

"Of course," Zahra said with a smile, one that wasn't much of a smile at all. "Let me know if you should need anything. Be careful."

"I always am."

Elaia watched her walk away and wished she had the power to really truly let her.

Silence filled the room. Elaia waited until her shadows no longer felt Zahra near, and she turned to face Xerxes. "Here. The governors are hesitant. These are some of their demands." She slid him the papers. "Will these cause any problems?"

Xerxes rose a brow. "You could deny every one, and I could still ensure you receive their signatures."

"How?"

He leaned back into the chair. "There is a member of the Order on every one of the governor's committees. Have been for years. We have information. And we have fear. We'll use them how we see fit."

She exhaled. Gods, what was she doing? Maybe it wasn't too late to stop. *No.* She needed this. Rersa needed this.

Xerxes spun a ring on his finger. "You should begin preparing for the initiation. It is different every time, molded to the initiate. Though, I imagine yours may differ given your title. Just know it's coming."

She narrowed her eyes on Xerxes. "Is that all?"

"It is the same as I've already said. They are everywhere, in places you can't fathom. The sway they have is unimaginable. What's important, is that the Order believes in helping those who cannot help themselves."

Elaia rolled her eyes. "I'm sure that is exactly their goal."

"And yet you still agreed to work with me, Princess." Xerxes danced a tiny spark over his fingertips, the same spark dancing in his eyes.

Deep breaths. This isn't going to get us anywhere.

Exhaling, she let her indignation dissipate. "Does this mean anything to you?" She held the pendant up and watched his eyes widen. With a careful hand, he plucked it from her grasp, turning it over.

"Yes," he whispered, clearing his throat. "Yes, it does."

He almost looked haunted, tortured by something she didn't understand. Elaia asked, "What is it?"

"It's the sigil of the Order. But these are given sparingly to select members of the Order. Whoever this came from had to be at least a Scarlet."

From what she remembered, it was the Kytes, the Fangs, the Shades, and then, the Scarlets. Lower than only the Chairs and the Ashmaker themselves.

"If they don't give out the coins, how are you expected to know?"

Behind him, light streamed in from the windows, molding around his shoulders like flame. "The Order ensures you can never truly leave them behind. If you try to escape, they'll know, and they'll find you." His words should've been heavy or light, but they were empty.

Xerxes stood and rolled up his thick top to reveal the tawny skin of his muscled abdomen. Healed scars were dotted over his ribs and stomach, interrupting the dusting of hair in haphazard patterns. Elaia watched the rise and fall of his chest as he breathed, tracked the planes of his firm stomach and the freckles, before forcing herself to look away.

She hated that she didn't want to.

On the bottom of his rib cage was a mark—wings of feather with flames scorching the edges. At first glance, she thought it was white ink—like the black ink on her skin—based on the fine, clean lines and the details. But it was raised, a little jagged at points, and under the light, held that faint pink color of healed scars. It was a fyrebird with its beak tipped up to the sky and its wings extended, just like the coin. Some parts of the mark, namely the flames, were darker and redder. Scars of repetition. He turned, and on his other side were three more in a line on his ribcage. A blade with scars made to look like flames. A spider. And a wing lined in pink scars.

When she looked up, Xerxes was already staring. His hazel eyes had hardened, as if to hide the past and all the emotions that came with it.

"If I tried to run, they would know exactly who I was. Even if they let me go, they would never stop watching me." His eyes looked almost dead as he pulled one of the pendants from around his neck. He pressed his nail against the edge to flip it open and reveal the same symbol. "Is that sufficient?"

Who were these people? They scarred their members? Fear crawled over her skin, reminiscent of the spider burned into his. But the fear that lived in only her mind, put there by someone else, was stronger still. *The shadow will continue to haunt—as long as you maintain your promises.* She was stuck between two choices of violence, of rage, of their own goals—so what was worth sacrificing?

"For the time being, yes," she spoke, before clearing her throat. "Thank you."

Xerxes said nothing, simply dipping his head in return.

Elaia couldn't drag her eyes away, as if she was looking into a mirror, except he was the reflection. Part of it was anger. Whether that was at the Order or something else, she didn't know or care. It sparked the air, invisible and charged, sitting there under the surface. And the rest...well, it seemed like pain. She couldn't be sure, she wouldn't bet on it, but somehow, she knew. Concealed underneath all the heat was something that looked a lot like her pain. Sharp and buried underneath the skin, rearing its ugly head at the worst times.

Elaia cleared those thoughts. They were not alike. Not in any way that mattered. "Zahra said she found it in Rersa years ago when she was a child," she said running her fingers through the black strands of her hair.

The round pendant looked tiny in his palm. Scars littered his skin, disrupted by only the freckles he had. Under the light, his hair shone golden, and his hazel eyes were bright. He worried his lip as he took in the coin, the ghost of a dimple appearing in his cheek.

"Only a select few receive them. Having a tangible sign of the mark is an indication of importance, of leadership within the Order," he began, pausing to fix her with a firm look. "If you look closely, there are slight differences in the coins and the burns. If you didn't know to look for it, it wouldn't register. But on the coin, what falls from the sky aren't flames. It's ash."

Xerxes turned his attention back to the pendant. A tiny flame sparked from his fingertips and wrapped around the coin.

Elaia shot up. "What are you—"

"Wait."

With a glare, she kept her eyes locked on the pendant and watched the flames lick away the faded old bits. When they stopped, it was a glimmering coin of iridescent orange and red, molded after the flames themselves. The mark was bright and clear now, the wings in painstaking detail that every feather was visible, and the ash falling from above. Xerxes handed her the pendant, dispensing it in her palm, where its warmth sank into her skin.

"You said no one really escapes the Order. How is this—working with me—going to get you your freedom?"

Xerxes took a long look at her, his eyes tracking over every inch. The focus was unnerving. "I've been with the Order a long time. Long before I ever should've been. I received my first mark when I was only thirteen years. I have done everything they have ever asked of me. Climbed the ranks, trained new members, killed who they have asked, spilled secrets others would die to keep. I've given them my time. Once I complete my task here, they will let me go." He shrugged. "Sure, they may keep an eye on me for the rest of my waking life, but I don't care. As long as I'm not in it."

Her heart pounded. Everything she learned painted the Order in darker, more violent light. And yet the unknown, the Witch, the threat she kept in her pocket and that pounded at her head, was there at every turn. "But you would lead me to it? To free yourself?"

Something sharp flickered. "I owe you nothing. You wished for the throne, you want the challenge, the Order is merely ensuring you get it. Is it not what you wanted?"

It was. "What do you wish for, Xerxes?"

His freedom felt more like a need, something he needed to survive. She wanted to know what made him tick. What kept him going.

For a moment, the whole world fell silent. It didn't matter really, she supposed. What he said, what he wished for. They were a means to an end to each other. Nothing more. And yet, Elaia hung on the quiet air, waiting to hear it.

Xerxes's voice was barely louder than a breeze brushing flower petals as he said, "I stopped wishing long ago, Princess."

CHAPTER 31

SHARP, POISONOUS GRIEF

EVERYTHING SHE'D DONE HAD BEEN FOR MORE control.

Yet, Elaia never felt further from it. Because it all hinged on someone else's promise.

If she did not get the throne, she would not be able to uphold the promises she'd made to her alliances. About studying the Canyon of Evha, the Aether point. About supplying the Nightguard. She would not be able to ensure that Rersa was not a threat if someone else was in charge. And if Rersa became a threat, that darkness—that damn darkness—that she couldn't understand, would destroy them.

If she did, if the Order delivered what they promised, she could make Rersa look compliant. She could *aid* in the Witch hunt. She could *aid* in the research. She could protect Rersa and her loved ones, if they only appeared as willing accomplices.

She paced back and forth in a section of the canyon long ago eroded in a way that allowed the sunlight to stream directly in.

It was a garden, not their main area of crops within the walls, but a garden for nothing more than enjoyment. Flowers of Iris, shadow violet, and silver lilies dotted the space, some growing from the canyon walls itself. She sat alone in a patch of grass, studying the drawings from before. There were more of her own, ones of every mark on Xerxes's skin, and the sigil of the Order. There was a new one of Zahra, too, and the look in her eyes that Elaia couldn't erase.

But she'd determined the ones in front of her were not her mother's. Nomara's style was lighter, more abstract. Shaye had given up as a child, only ever playfully drawing stick figures with them. The ones to take Nomara's lessons seriously were her and Rayn.

These drawings were Rayn's.

Her youngest sister's initials were scrawled in the corner. The realization hit her hard, taking the air from her lungs. Had her little sister been the one to see the dead Scions? Was she being hunted by the Order? Pain crept in through every crevice, and pressure built behind her eyes and around her heart. She didn't understand why. Was this why they left? Why they ran?

Frantic, she collected everything and darted through the halls to her father, where she entered unannounced. He sat at his desk, staring into a glass of amber liquid.

"Did you know about these?" She slammed the drawings down. It took a moment for him to register them or her.

"What?"

"Did you know?" Elaia gritted her teeth, fighting back the urge to scream.

"These are your sister's. These are Rayn's." He looked at her, his eyes cloudy. "They're just drawings."

She felt every inch of her heart weaken. "Just drawings?" Was he a fool? Was he playing stupid? "You can't be that blind, Father. You can't. You knew about these. Did you do anything?"

"Your mother was worried, paranoid even, but it was nothing, Shaye." Desmond's eyes widened. "Elaia, I—" Pain shimmered in his eyes, clear as night.

She laughed, irreverent. "Shaye isn't here anymore. She's dead. They're all dead. And I'm starting to think it's all your fault." The room was dark, lit with only candles, and they painted shadows on his face. She was partial to take hold and turn them onto him. Make him feel what she felt. "Why didn't you listen to Mom? She was worried and what? You just brushed it off?"

"Don't you dare insinuate—"

"That it's your fault everyone in our family is dead but us? That Mom and Rayn left for no reason? That Shaye strangled—" Her voice cracked, and she closed her eyes. But all she could see was her sister with a black mark around her throat.

"This is all your fault. You failed to protect them. All of them. And still, you fail them. You fail me. You're so blind to it, saddled with grief and guilt, you won't accept that you can't see anything but yourself. Everything you do is for you. Not for me. Not for them. You."

Desmond stood. His eyes were bloodshot, and weak wisps of shadows emitted from his hands. "You don't know that Nomara and Rayn are dead."

"Holy shadows, you're a fool. I feel the loss of them every day! Every day, their absence is a knife in my gut, and you think they're alive? They are *dead*."

Shadows swam around her ankles and crawled up her wrist, circling her throat. She was living, breathing darkness.

The truth was, they would never know. Unless her mother and Rayn walked through the canyons to come home or unless they were given bodies, they would never, ever know. Whether they had disappeared or been taken. Whether they were alive or long dead. She knew that at least a part of him believed that they were still out there.

But Elaia did not.

Rersa was one of the more religious countries, the Shadow Naturalist more devout than others. Nomara believed steadfastly in the Gods. In the divine above and in those Scions that walked among them on the same soil. She was spiritual, and she was faithful. Nomara trusted in them, even when she felt alone. She prayed to them, even when they did not answer. Because that was faith—believing even if it was not logical. She taught the girls the same. She told them stories of how Senka and Tasyn made the canyons and the shores, how shadows crawled out from under their footsteps, and how they would always be there to protect them, even when they couldn't feel them.

The story that stuck with Elaia was the one of the Daemon Realm. Of the afterlife. How anyone ready to pass over had to pass through Senka and Tasyn first. When she was younger, she hated it—the story never shied away from the pain their two Gods would feel at the loss. At the brief beat of emptiness the world would feel in result. Elaia used to cry imagining the hounds she worshiped whimpering in pain. But eventually, she found solace in it. How the two would follow the souls to the afterlife to guide them.

Deep down, she knew that if anyone she cared for ever died, she would know, even if she didn't see it. It was her intuition, her own faith that led her to believe that she would feel the emptiness they left behind.

And there was a hole in her world, a pain in her chest that had been there for months, that was different than before. For much of the three years, she'd believed as Desmond did. But not anymore.

Somehow, Elaia knew they were gone. There was no world in which she would not know they had left.

Her voice lowered, sharpened as she said, "They will all see you for who you are soon. When the throne is carved with my name, they will know you as nothing more than a fool. And a failure."

"You have no right to speak to me like this."

"You have no right to parent me anymore." Her voice was ragged. "I'm not the eager little girl looking for your approval now. I'm just a girl who's lost her entire family, and you, the only one that remains, left me to pick up those pieces on my own. And you expected me to sweep up yours, too. For three years, I have been half of myself, and you never noticed. So, I'm done," she said, shadows swirling between them, incensed and despaired.

"You can stand in the wreckage of your failures. I will not. Enjoy the throne while it's still yours, Father. Your time has come to an end."

She didn't wait because there was nothing that he could say. Not a single word.

Everything she'd done all made sense again. He had failed to do anything to protect her sister, and because of it, both her sisters were gone. For a moment, guilt had begun to eat her alive. He was hurting. He'd lost them as she had. For a moment, she thought maybe she was being too rash.

Not anymore. She hadn't stopped hurting for three long years. Every breath was filled with pain and grief. Yet, she kept going, even when her lungs and heart were being sliced open. No, she didn't feel guilty anymore.

All Elaia felt was rage.

ELAIA SPENT an hour on the edge of the inner fields, staring out at the farmers. Above, the stars filled the sky, and she only felt... empty. She'd tried to pray in the small cavern dedicated to Senka, but that had proven useless. The Gods weren't going to bring them back. Forcing herself to stand, she began trekking back to her room when laughter from the hall grabbed her attention, the sound light and fleeting and joyful. She traced her fingers along the canyon walls, trying to calm the storm brewing in her head. But the truth was, anger had burned through her, leaving her fragile and exhausted, a weight that hadn't left her shoulders in days, weeks.

And more than anything, she missed them. She missed Nomara and Rayn and Shaye.

The laughter made her think of them. She remembered her mother's voice, the soft lilt to it from her time on Pyth and the lightness in her laugh. She remembered Shaye's laugh—a loud, booming thing that demanded the rooms attention. But...

When was the last time she heard Rayn's laugh?

What was the moment exactly? Her heart faltered, aching behind her ribs, as she searched her memories for something, *anything*. Was it a moment that happened so often that she'd deemed it insignificant, unaware of what was to come? Or had so much time passed she just lost it? Tears burned her eyes, embarrassment cloaking her thick and heavy. Akiro whined behind her, his footsteps hurried and loud over the floor, high-pitched barks echoing through the room. Panic clawed at her shoulders as she brought her knees to her chest, curling into herself. Her chest wouldn't calm. Her heart wouldn't quit racing. *Why can't I remember her laugh? When was the last time?*

Oh, Gods, this was awful. This was—

"Elaia? Are you all right?" Zahra's voice was a gentle caress on her skin. She was nothing more than a blurred figure in the doorway, clearing as she approached. "Hey, what happened?" Zahra's thumb brushed over her cheek, a tear running over it.

Reaching up, she wrapped her hands around Zahra's forearms and attempted to push her away. "I'm fine. I'm fine," she repeated though it was useless, and Zahra didn't budge.

"You're not fine," she scolded. "What happened?"

"Please, Zahra, let me go," Elaia said, though it was more of a sob. Zahra would too easily see how broken she was if she let her close.

She scoffed. "One day, you will let me care for you like I wish to. Hopefully before I'm in the grave."

The grave. She said it so casually. Elaia broke, her eyes blinking open in anger. "Don't say that. *Don't*." A sob cracked out of Elaia's chest. "I can't remember the last time I heard Rayn laugh. I heard laughter from the hallway, and I-I can't—I don't know what we were doing or when it was—I don't remember *anything*."

Remorse filled Zahra's eyes. "Oh, Elaia, I'm sorry." She took a breath, pressing her lips against Elaia's for a moment, only causing more tears to fall from her eyes, turning their soft kiss salty. When Zahra pulled away, she let their foreheads touch. "I'm not going anywhere. I'm right here."

Grief was the worst thing Elaia had ever known. It was a thief —hiding in crevices and tucking itself away until something struck it. It caused her pain *every day*. It threatened to skin her alive until she was blood and bone *every day*.

Grief had sharp, poisonous teeth and venom for which there was no cure. And it would not let her go. She could not be free. It had sunk its teeth into her, wound around her like a snake its prey, and it *suffocated* her.

"I remember," Zahra whispered, her voice knocking at the edges. "I don't know why I do, but I remember. You told me about it." The weight of Akiro started to sink in. The comfort of Zahra's touch began to soften the shards around her. "Maybe some part of me knew that it was important. Maybe some part of you did, too. You were both in Rersa, and you'd gone out to catch fireflies on top of the canyon. For some reason, Rayn thought she could do it backward."

A memory started to come back, blurred and unclear, but there.

Zahra laughed. "And she tried, but there was a lip she didn't see, and you described it as her flailing backward into the air, hands looking for something to grab, but all she got was a mouth full of dirt."

A wet sound left Elaia's throat. "She looked so dumb," she said, words interrupted by the sobs, hiccupping as she tried to laugh instead.

That was one of the last times she ever saw her sister. Rayn was six years younger than her, but she was free and calm and patient. Such the opposite of herself and the perfect match to Shaye, but they were sisters. More so, they were friends.

"She'd be proud of you."

"Yeah," Elaia murmured, her hand sinking into Akiro's fur. "I know." *I hope.*

She hoped that they were together, wherever that was. In Thāna, in the Fields of Liion, or wherever Senka led them, she hoped the three of them were together. And happy, if that was possible. She hoped they were proud of her. Maybe it was crazy, an illusion made of grief, but Elaia swore there was a phantom brush of her hair, exactly how her mother used to do it.

"You need to sleep. Really sleep, Elaia."

She nodded, though she made no movements. Her eyes stared straight above at the vaulted stony ceiling. Zahra bent in front of her, hands cupping her cheeks, her auburn eyes wet with their own unshed tears. "Come on. I've got you. Let me help. Let me take care of you."

She swallowed her tears and swallowed down the pain, even though it felt like glass in her throat.

And still, Elaia stood, even if the world wanted her to sink.

Nothing could've woken Elaia from heavy sleep.

Except being abruptly dragged from her bed by her ankles. Shock rippled through her as she fought to regain consciousness. Her eyes were covered, and her mouth was bound. A cloth was pressed against her nose, a sickly scent seeping in. Sound was muffled, and her senses felt far away. Elaia couldn't hear anything. She was drifting, unable to feel her body or her bones or her skin. Her blood was heavy.

Trying to flail was useless. Everything was so heavy. It was too much. And Elaia was tired. A sickly sweet sleepiness blanketed her, a whimper crawling out of her throat before it went black.

CHAPTER 32

DAUGHTER OF THE DEAD

NOVA AWOKE ATOP FRIGID GROUND.

Somewhere dark and musty. It smelled like soil. Like the soil that had once choked her, buried her. Her breath quickened. Every inch of her body ached, and her mind was hidden in a haze she couldn't fight through. Even with her eyes open, she could barely see the ground in front of her.

Crawling forward, she felt for anything that might tell her where she was. But the ground was cold and cracked and nothing more. Aside from the brief reprieve with Cyrus...the days felt the same. Every day since Asha had been here, her mind had pierced her like a freshly sharpened blade. Dragging through her memories, dancing like a phantom over her skin.

Her scar had not stopped aching in four days; her body had not stopped—none of it had stopped. Everywhere she looked, she saw the Elders and blood, tears, and bodies on the floor flashing in her head.

She was fighting it. She was still *bloody* fighting it.

Angry sobs crawled out of her throat. *What am I supposed to find? What am I supposed to learn?* All she wanted was to go, and they wouldn't let her. They wouldn't *let* her! No one answered, not that she expected them to. Nova had killed for her freedom, but she wasn't free. Not from the Vahls, what they'd done to her, and not from herself, who she wasn't even sure she knew. And not from the dead.

A gut-wrenching scream escaped her, blood bursting under her skin and flowing hot through her veins. It all rang in her head, but all she could hear was the same: *Witch of the Blood. Trust what you see. Witch of the Blood. Trust what you see.*

She dug her sharp nails into her head, curling over on the floor, begging it to become clear as she forced herself to relive the memories. The sharp pain of the blade on her throat by blurred faces. *No. Let me in.* Her mind fractured under her own power, splintering and opening before her.

Slowly, the fog faded, and the memories came into view.

At first, it was only a door of gray stone and black swirls. From a high view, an outsider's view, Nova saw herself as a child for the first time. She was there, standing between two people, whose faces would not clear. Her parents? Her *true* parents? A blink, and the memory shifted. A slightly older girl inside of Froststone, walking between the Vahls.

Alone.

A child left to the snake pit.

She flashed back to the memory she wanted to uncover. The scar on her throat. Who did it? Why? She couldn't explain why it haunted her more than anything, but it did.

A younger version of her was there, kneeling on a rocky shore, cliffs towering over her as the cold ocean water pierced her legs. In the background, a familiar stone fortress. Behind her was none other than Mikel and Mireya.

She watched with perfect recollection as Mireya dragged the blade haphazardly across her throat. And she felt them, even in the memory, controlling her mind. Her hands could not move to stop the bleeding; she couldn't have fought back if she wanted to.

Mireya kept cutting over and over, slicing the same spot. A blade of white stained with red.

Nova realized with a cry they must've seen what Asha did.

Her blood finding a way to heal her. But they didn't even give her a chance. They made sure her blood would spill out on that rocky shore. Every last drop of it.

Why had they done this to her? That was all she wanted to know. Why? Why her?

Below, the stone floor did nothing to cool the heat of unbridled emotions burrowing through her. There was no love lost, no grief she hadn't already felt—but there was pain. *This* was what she remembered when she pushed through the dirt. Them. That bleeding castle of gray. Her mind had done this to her. It had forgotten the pain, blacked and blurred out the years and the truth, and led her straight back to them. They were the ones that put her in the ground, and all she could remember was that stupid, godforsaken castle. She'd practically crawled to their doorstep, covered in dirt and lost both inside and out.

All alone.

She was always alone.

What had she done to earn this life? This life that brought nothing but an endless ache? Her entire being, her entire *soul*, was tired. Battered and barely pulsing. Her blood was begging for release, her body holding it captive in the depths of its blazing despair. She'd never...This wasn't...The sobs wreaked havoc on her, lashing and clawing their way out as the smoke cleared. The bracelet on her wrist welded over her fingers to take its shape, and before she thought better of it, she pierced her skin with the sharp talon, watching the blood bead.

Relief was instant and fleeting. It wasn't enough. *It wasn't enough!*

She was so stupid. How could she not have known? How could she have been so blind? *Why, why, why did I go back?* Only to let them wrap their control around her again and hold it tight around her throat.

And now, here she was...bombarded with vague words from dying Elders and books and relentless visions that made no sense.

Freedom. That was what she had wanted—*that* was the deal

she'd made. She didn't know what it looked like to her because she never had it. But it was *all* she wanted.

Not this crap shoot of the unknown.

More images flashed underneath the memory of her throat. Blood in her hands, circling her and others. Horrified faces. Being poked and prodded with needles. The Vahls were everywhere.

"Let me give them back," she pleaded, her whispers unheard in the dark room. The memories. She didn't want them. They were *torture*.

Her blood dripped on the floor below her, as it felt like inside, her soul was ripping itself to shreds. Everything felt muted and not.

"You can't give it back. You had to see."

Nova whipped her head around, her eyes wide and wild. The room she was in must've been deep, deep underground. There was no natural light, no window to the outside, just a thick door and the smell of ancient parchment paper. There were rolled up archives and records and anthologies overflowing from the Elemental-made shelves.

But there was no one here.

"Who—"

"It doesn't matter. It is your time. You had to see. You had *to see."*

She fell to her knees. Her blood droplets were scattered over the floor and the cracks within the stone. "Who are you?" All her emotions had become volatile, kindling set on fire.

"Who we are—"

"We?" Her mind was shattering. The threads of who she was, what she'd known, were unraveling. Around her, the world felt unsteady, the air thick, and the ground felt like it was going to fall out from underneath her.

"It is your time."

Those words...she'd heard them before. Reaching into the mess of her conscious, she pulled and tugged on the threads. Various colors and feelings danced along each one, an intricate network of her person. They were all there now, waiting for her to discover them when she was ready. Nova took a deep breath, calmed her blood, and closed her eyes, trying to *feel* her way through the network, to hear those words again.

As soon as she felt the familiar sensation around her throat, she knew—when she was choking on the dirt, fighting to escape, she heard those words. She had heard them all the way to Froststone, back into the arms of the people who put her there.

Nova's voice cracked when she said, "You let me return to them. You—whoever you are. You let me go back." The voice was silent. She studied the room, looking for anything. A strange shadow, a crinkle in the air. But there was nothing. No one.

"*You must keep looking.*"

"For what?!" She stood and walked along the shelves, trying to follow the voice that seemingly didn't exists.

"*A dragon of the blood, a dragon of the soul.*"

This again. There was no order to her now, no formality, only anger. Only wildness. With a hasty eye and unsteady hand, she looked for anything of note, ripping out rolled up parchments and tossing them to the floor.

Frantic, she kneeled, unraveling the papers and anthologies, her blood spilling on the pages as she tore new wounds. The visions repeated from before, of wings breaking the sky. Of a land shrouded in fog. Of a sky bleeding.

"I don't know what you want from me," she said, unsure if she was going completely crazy. "I don't know what it means."

"*Trust not what's been told, instead, what you see. The spirit is dead, unlike the soul. The Daughter of the Dead will make the world whole.*"

Nova paced, frustrated and lost. Was this the Elders? Was the truth the key to rid herself of them? Was it hidden in these words? In these riddles with no answer? It was all shit. And she was tired.

"*Threads of truth tied, falsities spun. The Daughter of the Dead will make them undone.*"

She tugged at the ends of her curls, squeezing her eyes. She didn't trust anything. Anyone. That was the problem. "I am not what you need me to be. I am not who think I am. I..." She tipped her head back. "I am nothing."

"*You are anything but nothing.*"

This was the second time now that phrase had been uttered. Daughter of the Dead. For a moment, she was back in the ground, choked by soil and suffering a lack of oxygen. But that would not result in a title whispered only by the Elders.

"*You are what we have been waiting for. It is your time.*"

There was a beat, and then utter silence in the room. It was an unexplainable sensation. Whoever spoke, whoever that was, whoever *they* were, was gone. Only emptiness remained, both around her and within her. Whoever she was—the Cardinal. A Witch of the Blood. This...*Daughter of the Dead.*

It didn't matter.

It would never matter.

WATER DROPLETS LANDED on Nova's skin, shocking her awake. She sat up with a vengeance in the same room as before, except she was not alone.

"Cyrus." She swallowed, moving to stand, except there was a ring of flames around her. Flames? From who? In the shadows behind him stood Dray. Beyond the room, heartbeats—slow and steady. Vines crept along the floor and the shelves, taking up the whole room. "What happened?"

Why was he here? Where exactly was *here*?

For the first time, Cyrus's eyes were almost cold. "I was hoping you could give us the answer. This vault is locked. No one is allowed down here. No one but the family is given entry. And yet, here you are."

Around her, the flames flared just as her annoyance did. As soon as her focus narrowed, Dray's blood beat in her palm.

She took a breath. "I don't know how I got here. I woke up, and this is where I was." Dray snorted. "I have no reason to lie, despite what he might think," she said, eyeing him. "Why are you questioning me?" she asked, eyes flickering between the two.

A pit of dread began to unfurl within her. There was an emblem pinned on Cyrus's collar—the symbol that was on the flags all over the city was pinned to him. To Cyrus.

"Stand down, Dray."

The flames lowered, barely. "Who are you?" She stared at him. At Cyrus.

"You haven't figured it out yet?" Dray snarked from behind, darkness emitting from his threads.

"Quiet!" Cyrus demanded. He swallowed, letting his gaze land on her. His heartbeat was steady, where hers was not. "I am the other contender for the throne. I'm the one Nalādin chose."

She was so bloody stupid. *How did she miss this? How?* Her nails clawed at her head from where she kneeled. She was blinded to it, distracted. Lazy.

He was an heir to the throne. And she had bloody missed it.

"My real name is Killian Cyrus Zroñ."

She knew that everyone lied to get what they wanted. Information. Truth. Power. She wished it made her angry. But it didn't. Everyone lied. She was a liar. What made her angry was that she hadn't seen it coming. That she'd believed Cyrus—*Killian*—that she had let herself be fooled.

She repeated herself, "I don't know how I got here."

"And the explanation for those?"

Around her, texts were opened and spread about the room. She had a vague memory of spilling her blood on the pages, though it was gone now.

"How did you even know I was here?"

"The world talks. You should know that." Killian crouched

down to rest his elbows on his quads. She'd never seen him look like a predator until now. All the muscle was poised, ready to protect his world if he needed. 'Tell me the truth, Nova. Why are you here?"

Heat tickled her skin from the flames dancing around her, but all it did was fuel the anger. At all the truths that were hidden behind a fog she was expected to clear. Ever since that first step on the Elderlands, everything had been different. Her body, her mind...her blood. Constantly, it was changing, twisting her into shapes she'd never felt, twisting her into someone she was having trouble recognizing.

As if that wasn't hard enough, she'd never even had a chance to know herself. All she had ever been was twisted into something at the hands of someone else.

The Cardinal. The Witch. There was no *Nova*. All she was, was something else.

All she wanted was to be free.

And still, she was not.

She pushed to her knees, her eyes narrow and cold. She said nothing.

A spark flickered in Killian's gaze. "Tell me the truth of why you're here," he repeated, lowering his voice. "Of what you are."

Nova cocked her head, her heart pounding. What had he figured out? Which truth of hers was he starting to suspect? "I don't owe you that."

Vines crept in under the fire, twisting and curling like tree roots. "I never said you did. But I'm asking you to tell me."

She reached out, and even tired, her power was there at the tip of her fingers. Wisps of it crept out, toying with the edge of his mind, but it was sealed. She could hurt him, make him suffer. But she didn't want that.

All she wanted was to be free.

"Why? Because I should trust you? What happens if I tell you the truth?" She stood, her blood burning hot. Around her, the flames burned higher. "You throw me in a different type of vault with chains around my wrist? Go ahead. Give me another scar. Another memory to forget. I don't care."

Killian approached the circle of flames. If it weren't for them, they'd be close enough to touch. Over the tops of the flames, his eyes met hers, as steady and unyielding as the ground he stood on. "I am not them."

She felt more than saw his eyes flicker to her scar. *Them.* The ones who did this.

And he wasn't. Or he hadn't been.

But it wasn't just *them.* It was that Nova didn't want him to see her the way they did.

The way *everyone* else did. She didn't quite understand that, what that feeling was, but...it wasn't just them. It was everyone. The Elders, calling her what they had—insinuating there was more to her than there was. It was the voices, whispering in her ear in the dirt and now, expecting her to be someone. It was Asha, looking at her with abhorrence.

And it was Killian, too. For so many days, he'd treated her like she was a person. Whether she felt like one or not, he'd given her kindness. But wouldn't that fade, too? Once the truth was out— whichever one of them she shared—wouldn't he look at her like all the rest?

What happened when she lowered the veil and he saw what everyone else did? It wasn't that she didn't understand; she did. Every time she saw her reflection, she saw the culmination of things she'd done to get there. The blood she'd left behind pooling on the floor all because they told her to. She saw all the memories of families she'd destroyed, lives she'd taken, truths she had made others believe. All for a freedom she'd yet to have.

Killian would see all that. And she would have to live with someone else knowing the truth and hating her for it. Nova didn't want to be free to avoid the gaze of others. She wanted to be free of herself. To be someone else that she didn't hate just as much.

That was the truth she really didn't want him to see. No

matter how much others detested her, no one did more than herself.

"And what happens when you become them?"

There, behind the fire, his eyes softened just so. Just enough. If she could make him trust her long enough, she could go before he saw what everyone else did. "Dray, go."

"Killian—"

"Go."

The flames flickered, and she didn't move until Dray's blood became distant, blending into the rest, though not far enough to be out of her reach. They stood alone in the vault, staring at one another. Killian was dressed in black leathers from head to toe. His arms were bare, vines snaked around them, and a silver and gold band tight around his bicep. There were weapons hidden somewhere. She just couldn't see them.

"You came dressed to fight."

"I wasn't quite sure what I would find here," he said, standing tall.

"But you knew, somehow, it would be me, right?"

"I did."

Her throat tightened. It was naïve of her to *want* to share anything with him. She barely knew him, and still...she wanted to know him. Maybe there was something she could tell him while still protecting herself until she could leave. Maybe he deserved that.

Killian took a step forward. "I need something, Nova. Otherwise, you'll have to stand before Amala, before Aydin and Gena, and answer to them. I don't believe you're here to hurt anyone, but I won't risk it any further. They are my family."

Silence answered him.

"I saw the way you healed. I watched your injuries stitch themselves up when I first found you on the shores before Asha was ever around. And this time confirmed it. She never touched you." His eyes flickered to her arms where fresh scars should be. "No healer can do that. To themselves or otherwise."

Her weakness was her downfall. Another truth revealed because she was too weak to withstand it.

"I've only read about it once. In this very room and there is only one type of person who can do that." Killian crouched, his fingers running over the books sprawled out on the floor. "I thought it was a story they made up, a lie from the decimation. But it's true. And I assume it's only a peek of what you can do."

"I won't hurt you. I don't wish to hurt anyone," she said, swallowing. Though she would if she had to. "But you cannot tell."

At least...not before she could make him forget. He was too well guarded, his mind too fortified now. But maybe later, it wouldn't be.

The prince—because that was what he was—took a deep breath and dipped his head. "You won't be crucified here. We—I don't believe in that."

"Does your family share those feelings?" Whether or not he did, he was not on the throne yet. "Or am I only safe if you sit on the throne?"

"You have my word, you will be safe."

Crouching, she began to collect the books, unable to look him in the eyes anymore. Every book she touched, she remembered spilling her blood on the pages, the things that were spoken to her.

"Asha said the truth has a way of making itself known," she said, glancing over to him. "I wish she had been wrong."

"Asha and I agree on many things, including our beliefs."

The implication was clear. Nothing more was said as they put the books away, though she memorized the letter and number indicating the volume. She had no idea how she got in here, but she would need to return before she left this place for good. The truth seemed to have too high a cost and far too little reward.

Together, they cleared the floor, all the texts and anthologies back on the stone shelving. "How deep underground is this place?"

Killian finished placing the texts on the highest shelves, using vines where even he couldn't reach. "Far. It was built long before the rest of this place. Some say it was built by Emaris," he said, speaking the name of their god. "From what I know, no one but the family has ever been down here. At least, not for centuries."

Except for you. Those were the words he left unspoken.

Killian paused, staring at her. "I—"

Beneath them, the ground began to shake, a low rumble. Dust expelled from the walls, and the texts rattled around them. Below her, the earth shook, and it showed no signs of stopping.

CHAPTER 33

WITCH OF THE SOUL

THE HEAVY VAULTED DOOR OPENED, DRAY STANDING IN the entrance. "We must go. Now."

"What is happening?"

Killian spared her a glance but crouched, placing his hands against the cracks in the stone. "A quake. In the Crosslands. How bad?"

Dray was dressed in similar leathers to Killian, two weapons strapped to his back. "Mal sent word. They need help." The prince rose and stood to leave, only stopping when he remembered she was there. "You should leave her here," Dray snarked, his untrusting eyes like thorns in her skin.

Fear crawled over her. She tasted dirt, smelled it. She was *not* staying here. "I will claw my way out. You will not leave me here."

Behind her back, where her fingers were intertwined, her hand shook slightly. This room reminded her of another place all too well.

She looked at the prince, reaching out once more, gently prodding at the fortress of his mind and working the tiniest opening. Or he let her in.

Either way, she only needed a brief moment as she whispered in his head, *"Please do not leave me in here."*

She took in all the threads that made him up, finding the one that was hesitant, untrusting. And she watched it flicker under the weight of her words. The threads were still new to her, but they were so different than what she knew.

"She comes with us," Killian said, his words firm enough they left no room for argument. She saw his threads as well, clear as day. Angry, yes. But worried. Cautious. Killian approached, a piece of fabric in his hands. "I haven't decided whether I believe you or not on how you got here. But for now, you need to wear this until we are out."

Without protest, Nova let the fabric send her into darkness, and Killian's hand gently wrapped around her arm, only to be replaced by a vine. "Hold on to that. Let's go."

The Crosslands was a small town on the edge of the mountain range that separated Nalādin and Izlena, built into the mountains and the hills, made of wood and stone, and it was in tatters. Wooden slabs were cracked, the foundations of their homes unsteady and angled, destroyed by the break in the ground below. She followed behind Killian and Dray, taking in everything she could.

No one seemed gravely injured, at least not on first glance, but many had cuts and scrapes. Around the break, multiple people stood on each side. Some crouched, collecting the soil from between, and the others dug in their hands and their feet, positioning themselves, she assumed, to reconnect the ground. She'd never seen anything like that.

Among the broken homes, there were depictions of Emaris. The Samara—a large jungle cat—that was the Earth Elemental's God. There were both, depictions of her in her human and animal form. There were some in Izlena, but far more here at the edge of the sentient forest. All around her, she could feel every single one of these people. Their minds were unprotected and mostly unguarded —the threads, that orb-like figure where they twisted and turned— and she recognized each emotion, each feeling, with no hesitation.

As they headed deeper into the town and toward the mountains, more guards appeared, dressed in leathers with the sigil of Eisera stamped onto their uniforms and colors of deep green and silver on the hardware and hilts. Hesitant to be around them, she slowed, moving in the shadows of the trees high above her, watching Killian stop and speak to the citizens, calling for help when needed or comforting them when able.

The chatter of voices, some distressed and some calming, surrounded her as she walked.

But it was the ear-splitting scream that drew her attention. Without hesitation, she ran deeper into the forest, past the houses and fallen trees and into the shadows of the mountains. The scream came again, jumbled and unclear, but the distress—it felt so familiar. She knew that feeling.

Within the earth, the crevice was far reaching, curving through the forest and the base of the mountains, and Nova followed it in search of the voice. Birds flew above her before turning their wings to the sky and flying high into the peaks. The large leaves began to block the sun, only tiny rays striking through, and then, it all stopped.

Around her, the crack left by the quake began to move. It was in front of her, and then beside her, and then all around her, encasing her on a single spot of Earth.

What in the Gods was this?

Voices rang out again and again, circling all around her. Nova couldn't focus on anything as she was spun and pushed into the woods. Everything was alive. The leaves on the trees swaying in the windless sky, the trunks twisting and bending as the ground stopped and the forest closed around her, entrapping her in darkness. Only a glimmer of light remained, casting her shadow on the ground.

"Nalādin." Her whisper was swallowed by the heavy soil, and yet, it echoed around her.

There was no godforsaken scream. There was no one in need. There was nothing and no one but her. Before she could even breathe, the forest fell out from underneath her, and the ground swallowed her whole.

NOVA WAS LOOKING at the ground from underneath it. Trees hung upside down without leaves, their empty branches curling like fingers might to reach her.

From above, something dripped between the tears on her sleeves and onto her arm.

Drip.

Drip.

Drip.

The dream from Asha's came back, of blood dripping onto the leaves, but it was only water dripping from above.

"Hello?" Nova shouted. No echo. Nothing but pure, encompassing emptiness.

She heard the scream again, so loud it made her ears sting. Her eyes fell closed until the pain subsided, and when she opened them...she saw herself again. It was her all along. A scream from her past leading her here.

The image was blurred, but she was older, and she was tied to a chair that was so familiar. A chair she'd been tied to more times than she could count. But she didn't remember the scream that came from her lips. Invisible hands that she knew in reality had belonged to Mikel or Mireya, cut her skin and placed black leaves overtop. She didn't remember that—that they figured out how to keep her bleeding.

But she remembered the things they'd made her believe, the things they'd tricked her into believing. That she was drowning. That she was being buried alive. That she was being pulled under with decaying hands. And Nova watched herself scream over and over and over again.

And above, the godsdamnned dripping wouldn't stop, so much that the water felt like a knife.

No, enough. She ran through the world underneath the world and watched the image fade as soon as she approached. She spun around and around. She couldn't reach the branches. She couldn't climb out of here. Behind her, a puddle had formed.

Nova bent, her reflection appearing. Dirt was smeared on her face, her curls were wild and untamed, and the scar on her throat was pulsing, the veins under her skin bright and angry.

"What is happening to me?" Water pooled in her eyes, tears of frustration, but she didn't let them fall. Instead, she swiped her hand out, disrupting the surface of the water, only to be pulled under it.

Or really, pulled through it.

A scream left her lips that was swallowed up as she was spun off balance. Nausea bloomed as she took in her new surroundings —a graveyard. *No. No, no, no.*

She was in the ground again, covered in dirt, and there were hands all around her. Her skin crawled as their fingers found her, wrapping around her skin and bones. Above, the suns were burning red, and orange dripped into the gray sky as she was pulled back under the earth—choking all the way down.

Air became thin and heavy at once, and her sight was gone. Around her, she felt the presence of others. Of their *being.* But there were no threads, no minds. No blood. Nothing she could control or pull apart.

"Where am I?"

"An in-between." Multiple voices melded together as one

when they spoke. "Nalādin and yet not. Somewhere else. We've met before."

"Gods, I am so *sick* of this," she exclaimed, resentment leaking out of her mouth. "What do you want? Why am I here?" She dared not move. Fear had struck deep, keeping her in place.

"You must know what is coming. What will be," they said. "What they did to you was only the beginning. *The spirit is dead, unlike the soul.*"

"Repeating your insipid riddles is not useful." She felt them move around her, wispy touches of whatever they were on her skin, leaving goosebumps in their wake.

"We're tired of repeating them. Listen."

Nova was pushed and pulled until she was flat on her back, invisible hands holding her down. "You are not just one. You are so much more. They don't see what you see. They can't change what you can change. They are sick. They are false."

"Who?"

"You know who. They are not what you think. They are not what the world has been *made* to think."

The pressure grew, her skin buzzing uncomfortably in the dark. When they spoke again, the voices were louder, ominous, and in perfect harmony. "*Look above and look below, a dragon of the blood, a dragon of the soul. Buried in a land long forgotten, truths go unknown. The spirit is dead, unlike the soul. Blood drips over the soil and bones, a sacrifice given, deeds now atoned. They rest in silence, a place unseen. Trust not what's been told, instead what you see. The spirit is dead, unlike the soul. The Daughter of the Dead will make the world whole.*"

"No..." Nova whispered, the words sinking into her.

She thought about everything.

The way they had infiltrated her mind, there was no thread pulled or tugged, only thoughts and visions so powerful, she was convinced they had been real. A special type of torture, but never her emotions. And Isla, the way she was always a bit...off. The nosebleeds, the twitching of her head like a gnat was caught in her ear, the faraway look in her eyes.

And she thought about the text, only uncovered by her blood.

Their God...They had no origin. No history.

"Oh, Gods. They aren't—they aren't real. They're false. They made themselves." The truth was like a punch to the chest. What about her? "But then, what am I?"

"You were never like them."

Though she remained held, a vision swam, one she had no tangible memory of. Of her as a little girl in the frosted woods, one hand with a line of blood through the palm and another with a mist of white hovering above her palm. Within it, she could see a million tiny threads.

"You are so much more than them." Around her, the air stilled, and the truth landed on her skin like snow on cold ground. "A Witch of the blood. And a Witch of the soul," they spoke quietly this time. Yet, the weight of the words was heavier than all the others.

"Can I see you? Is there a way?"

The darkness cleared, and misty shapes appeared before her eyes. Details were not quite there, a blur to their shape and their features, but she saw enough. Shapes of women old and young stood before her, barely touching the ground but not quite floating.

All of a sudden, whether by her own volition or theirs, their threads appeared. Some faded, maybe long lost to history and some brighter, closer to reality than death.

"Go on," one said, the voice familiar.

Nova came face to face with the voice that had spoken to her through the Elder. She remembered every second of it. "I—"

"No need to apologize. Though you shouldn't have given them the vials, I understand why you did. We all do."

"You are watching me?"

"In a sense. Reach for the threads. You'll understand."

They seemed to call to her, begging her to uncover them, to

learn what lay within. She'd never *seen* them like this before, out in the open. She was unsure of herself—she still didn't understand the threads, not quite. And the times she'd seen them, she hadn't been able to see them like she was now.

They came to her, vague and blurred, little more than mist itself. Instead of emotions, she got memories. Nova felt them expand and open, welcoming her into them. And she saw everything they had. Not of their lives, but of their part in *her* life. All of these women had pushed her from the grave. They were the voices as she dug her way out by her fingernails.

And she'd been one of them.

It was strange, watching her life play out in pieces through their eyes. Not all the images were clear or put together—that was still work she had to do after the healing with Asha—but it was enough. Put in a nondescript grave by some guard employed by the Vahls and left to rot under the soil. Except she didn't. She, her *soul*, was greeted by them.

"Where was this? Where did I go?"

"Thāna—the Daemon Realm. Your soul was never measured, so you remained with us, in Iysus, the in-between."

She watched as they guided her soul through the realm. All of it unclear, but she understood. They took care of her. They molded her, held her. And pushed her up when it was time.

"We have always been watching you." They stepped up, circling her and blurring as the group grew. "You have *never* been alone."

Anger bubbled up unexpectedly. "That isn't true." A sardonic laugh crept out. "That isn't true! I was left at their doorstep, under their thumb for years, only for them to slit my throat. And then to end up back there," Nova said, the words disrupted by her laughs. "To end up back there with them. To be made—made into *this.*"

"We were always there."

She shook her head, backing away from them. She couldn't separate it all. She was furious and distraught. Alone and yet not alone? What was she supposed to believe? Who in the world was she supposed to trust?

"Not when it mattered. You saved me and left me to return to those that slaughtered me." There was no blood to control but her own. She wanted it. Wanted the power and the control, and she didn't have it. She never had it. "You watched them turn me into...into an executioner, into a pawn. And you did nothing!"

"It wasn't you."

"No!" she shouted, surrounded. "It was. It *is*. They molded me, and I let them. My mind believed them, succumbed to the weight of their punishments. I couldn't fight them because I didn't know how. I was weak, and you let me be weak. They took it—my autonomy, my body, my mind—and they used it. They turned me against myself."

She couldn't clear the memories. The touching, the streaks of pain when they cut her, the false memories of being grabbed and pulled underground, the pain they made her suffer through. That was all in her head. "And my body failed me. I failed me." A sob cracked her chest. "And you let them."

"We couldn't interfere—"

"Then what was the point of it? You didn't stop the Vahls from making me into this; you didn't stop the things they did to me. You left me. I have *always* been alone."

They seemed to grow around her, their voices becoming louder. "You will understand. Until then, you must find the others."

"I want out of here. Let me out."

Nova's ears rang as their voices spoke as one and yet as many. "You must find the others. You must uncover the truth." The next voice that spoke was the Elders, kinder and gentler than the rest. "You will understand one day. And when you do, we will be here."

She was done. One day was not today.

Nova grabbed each thread and wound them around until she had control. She could feel the magic in her palms, the way even here, they felt like living things. Mist emitted from Nova, silver in the darkness around her.

Immediately, she realized she couldn't change them or influence them, not since they were dead, but she could scatter them. Give herself enough time to get out of here. With a broken yell, she twisted them, unyielding to the pressure in her ears and her head, and ripped them away from the ghostly figures.

Yet, their voices grew.

Nova moved away from them, running or floating over the ground, the red suns above her shining on her skin. She was lost in the darkness as their echoes chased her, no way to get to the surface.

"Let me out!" she shouted, falling to her knees. It was useless. If they'd ever listened, the Gods never answered.

Nova had only herself. Below, the ground was pliable, damp. And she dug. Her skin itched, uncomfortable, as the dirt never seemed to end. So, she crawled over the ground, searching until she heard it. Until she felt it. The drip and the echo of a drop into a puddle.

Again, the women appeared in front of her and all around her. They were in her space, encroaching. "You must find the others. Ones like you. You must stop them."

Nova's sight was taken from her as her mind fell to their powerful, wispy hands. She saw blood curling around her fingers like water. She saw the Vahls walking through a room, people—so many people—following behind them. They were faceless— nothing more than apparitions.

Blood dripped on the floor, more black than red. Their steps were unsteady, unsure. Some of them crawled. She saw destruction. Cracks in the floor and the walls. Shattered glass. Cries of loss piercing her ears. She saw a man fall to his knees, the earth coming up to cradle him.

"You must stop the Vahls," the women repeated. "And you will."

She crawled through them, the mist of their shapes

dampening her skin. "I don't want to. I want to be free." Her voice cracked, echoing through the empty world.

"You will be. But not yet."

On her knees, her forehead touched the ground, tears leaking from her eyes and onto the soil. Her words a shaky sob, she said, "I have given enough."

"Not yet."

Under her tears, a puddle formed. "Please, please let me out." Maybe Nalādin would take mercy on her. If not them, if not the Gods, the forest. "Please, let me out."

Her tears rippled the tiny puddle as the shapeless forms closed in on her. With a shaky hand, she brushed the surface of the water and was pulled through. A breath of relief left her lips before getting swept away. Around her, the water tossed her, leaving her floating in what felt like the center of the universe. Still, they did not leave her.

"You cannot run from it."

Closing her eyes, the darkness surrounded her as she surrendered herself to this *world*. She hated being helpless, but she couldn't fight it. A rough tug pulled her through another body of water, landing her on her knees in heavy, constricting soil.

She cried out, digging her nails and pulling. Pulling and pulling until she was breathless. Underneath, something cool and sharp brushed against her legs and her ribs and her arms. *Please do not let that be what I think it is.* Nova shook her head, clearing the thoughts., ignoring the possibilities.

The misty shapes of the women appeared in front of her, doing nothing to help. Somewhere in the distance, there was a sound that seemed to reverberate from the ground itself. A rumble that grew with the air it breathed until a roar echoed through the atmosphere. An angular thing wrapped around her ankles as she tried to save herself.

For the first time in a long time, Nova wanted to live.

Even if it was to see a starless sky, she wanted to *live*.

If only because she wanted her death, whenever it came, to belong to her. Not anyone else.

An incandescent cry escaped, echoing into the world between worlds and dispersing the misted shapes. *There*! Something to grab. Her hands wrapped around the gnarled thing, a root, and she heaved, forcing the soil to release her.

In front of her eyes, the root grew, a large black tree with leaves of shimmering red into the sky above, and she climbed. Nova dug her nails, bleeding and raw, into every crevice and flung herself up branch by branch.

Still, they followed, their voices coming from all around, attacking her from every angle. And their voices became haunting and intoxicating as they found harmony, words spilling into the world like an incantation, and falling like raindrops on her skin as they said:

> *"Under the cloaking shadows, under the red-streaked suns,*
> *let the soul bleed, let the blood run.*
> *Oaths of false honesty will start to unravel,*
> *and bones of the dead will begin to rattle.*
> *Veins of blood curved over stone,*
> *voices echo between the unknown.*
> *Threads of truth tied, falsities spun.*
> *The Daughter of the Dead will make them undone."*

Yet, Nova climbed. Despite the way her blood hummed to the words as they sank into her skin. As they sank into every scratch and scrape and mixed with her blood, Nova kept climbing, hoping the sky was in reach.

She dared not look down. She knew they were there, floating around her, the words now a chant and a whisper. That rumbling roar sounded again from somewhere she would never find, and the whispers crawled into her ears and embedded in her memory.

As she broke through the surface, chasing the air, they spoke again with a note of finality:

*"Look above and look below,
a dragon of the blood, a dragon of the soul.
Buried in a land long forgotten, truths go unknown.
The spirit is dead, unlike the soul.
Blood drips over the soil and bones,
a sacrifice given, deeds now atoned.
They rest in silence, a place unseen.
Trust not what's been told, instead what you see.
The spirit is dead, unlike the soul.
The Daughter of the Dead will make the world whole."*

CHAPTER 34

SOMETHING UNKNOWN

SYRENA STOOD OVER THE MAP MADE OF WHITE STONE and sea glass.

On the table beside her were notes written by Commander Ikina, listing the exact coordinates of the sounds coming from beneath the sea, a collection of what was known, which wasn't much. And with that was the official invitation to the coronation in Eisera, also serving as a makeshift assembly to raise or send along any concerns that didn't get answered previously.

Now that the Elders were dead.

She couldn't help the *giggle* that left her lips, thankful she was alone. The news wasn't new. Farah, the Reyna of Mykor, had sent her a missive the moment she'd returned home. But every time she thought of it, uncomfortable laughter bubbled in her chest. Because she couldn't fathom it.

The Elders...*dead*! The Elders were supposed to be infallible —they were beyond what was known. Not Gods, but not human or Athera, either. Something more. A guide of the Aether. Voices of those before them. Gone.

There had been quakes weekly. Animal patterns had changed, birds flying north when they should've been flying south. Tides had shifted. The world was changing—suffering—and it was only the beginning.

Outside the window, the sea enveloped her. Fish swam by in schools of bright color, some creatures scurried on the fortress that was the underwater city of Nvene, and others were shadows in the dark sea. A steady, quiet blinking drew her attention back to the map. It was a similar map to the one she'd stared at on her coronation—a day that now felt years from her—that blinked with every possible underwater disturbance. Except this one was larger and more detailed. Not only was it the entire seafloor of Iyvia, but of Valora, mapped long before anyone today had lived, updated over the centuries, and it was alight with color when it should've been white.

Lights of opal, sea green, and blue were spread about, each color meaning something different. Strange animal activity, an unknown substance, acts of aggression. A deep, bright orange indicated the Aetherpoints amongst Valora. And one more, a single light of red blinked below the Isles of Iyvia. The rift.

Today, a second appeared. A steady pulse of red coming from the East, off the coast of Lazora, lost in the Syros Ocean. It was close enough to Mykor that Farah most likely knew, but it was strange. These changes...these rifts.

What could this be? Was anyone else aware? Sighing, she copied her own thoughts, comparing them to the scientists. The rift hadn't grown. It hadn't moved or changed. It was just there, leaking those strange tiny bubbles. Again and again, she traced the colors and how they spread throughout Iyvia. Were they patterns? Was she missing them? Was there something right in front of her that she just wasn't grasping?

"Your Majesty."

Syrena startled, turning to find Torin in the doorway with a severe look on her face. "Yes, Torin?"

"Come with me."

A prickling sensation dripped over her skin like rain drops, leaving a chill behind. Syrena grabbed the crown she'd removed and placed it back on her head, scooping up her notebooks as well. The room, made of all windows except for the ceiling and doors, dimmed as they exited—a sensor system put newly in place to track when a room was occupied or not. Sconces of light were placed carefully along the walls, and the floor was made of a light but almost indestructible stone found on the seafloor that extended into the hall.

This wing was dedicated to learning, to knowledge. It held a small, very controlled library managed by a select group of Athera, along with schools dedicated to various professions, including and a majority, dedicated to science and integrity of the world's oceans and seas. Whether that was working alongside healers, both Athera and not, to study diseases and the health of Athera, and humans, studying the ocean floor to become an oceanographer, the biology of life undersea, or becoming an educator for Iyvia. This wing was always experimenting with new architecture, new weapons, new breathable suits for non-water Elementals and beyond. Other schools of thought were mostly taught above the sea, though there were always exceptions.

The pathways alternated clear windows and sections of dark marble inlaid with sea glass. Time was easily lost down here. Only certain times of the year, at certain hours, did the rays of the suns penetrate the deep parts of the city. Most days, like today, it was dimly lit. Syrena liked those days. She could see the lights from the glowfish deep within the water.

It was an eerie, beautiful thing. Blinks of luminous light, reflecting briefly on the panes of the city. Something that many people would never experience.

"What's going on, Torin?"

There was a newly placed crest on Torin's clothing. The sigil of Iyvia, the serpent God, Zaphine, depicted as they believed, with two translucent wings and sharp horns, placed there by Syrena only two days after her coronation, officially making Torin the Reyna's Spear. Her guard. Her personal advisor.

"Commander Ikina and Professor Caro have found something."

"No need to sound so grave, Torin," she said, side eyeing her. "If the world is ending, I'd like to know about it sooner rather than later."

Silence. Syrena stopped.

"Is the world ending, Torin?"

Her dark brown eyes were unreadable. "Not yet," Torin said, continuing to move down the hall.

Sighing, she followed, spinning the ring on her finger. The chill had not left her, and she figured at this point, it wouldn't. Eventually, they came upon another room, the door sliding open and revealing Ikina and Caro. The two were bent over the metal table filled with microscopes and vials, staring at a small dish between them.

Torin cleared her throat, and the two frantically rose, dipping their heads to her. She hated this part especially. She hated the bows. No decision of hers could be decided without the approval of others and vice versa. Yet, because she held the title, she received the bow. She knew for them, it held meaning, but to her, it was a useless, empty show of respect if the respect was not earned.

"Please," Syrena said, waving her hand. "Torin said you have found..." She trailed off, the grave look taking over their faces as well. "What is it?"

Ikina's curls were braided away from her face, and the lights above highlighted the blue specks in her brown eyes. "Come see for yourself."

She handed off her books to Torin and approached the table. On it was a re-creation of the rift, and in the center, were those bubbles, floating in contained water. They drifted up and then sank back down before repeating the process.

"You were able to transport them—good." Syrena bent over, watching them move.

In the light they appeared clear, silver maybe, like the Aether, but otherwise, they were completely normal-looking.

"Ikina, would you do the honors?" Caro asked, their hand shaking as they pushed up their glasses.

Carefully, Ikina used a ladle to transport a bubble to a flat dish, and that crawling sensation returned when she watched the bubble roll like a marble over the dish. Ikina took a scalpel and dragged it, opening it to reveal a dark inside. The thing wasn't clear. It was reflective, able to camouflage itself.

Silver and black dripped out onto the dish, writhing around, searching for something that wasn't there. Then, Ikina grabbed a dropper. "Blood," she explained before squeezing a single drop into the dish below.

It sank like a stone in the water as the blood mixed with the threads and started to pill. The blood separated from itself and then fell to the threads. A quiet hiss rose from the dish as the threads pulled it apart bit by bit, surrounding it, enveloping it, until the blood was a strange, warped version of itself. As if it had fingers, it reached out and crawled. It was stronger, harder, and pulsing with silver.

Another hiss, until there was nothing left at all.

Dread filled every crevice of her body. *What in the world?*

Syrena was frozen in place, staring at something that no longer existed. Blood, destroyed by something unknown.

"What in the demons was that?"

There was no answer because they didn't know. She let her eyes fall closed, counting the heaves of her chest as she tried to breathe. When they opened, she found Torin staring at her. She felt the weight of the world in that stare.

"What do you want to do, Syrena?"

Her heart pounded. What did *she* want to do? Beneath, her knees buckled. She was the Reyna now. She was in charge. Questions swarmed her. Could this be contained? Could they stop it? Was this a result of the Elders? Or just a weird coincidence?

Her head spun, and she felt out of body. Still, she found her voice and said, "Draft an emergent missive. Ikina and Captain

Ravai can send it along as they see fit. Prepare to send it to Valora. But not yet." Syrena took a breath. "Run more tests immediately."

At that, she departed with a confident nod, though she felt anything but. The moment she was out of view, she fell back against the wall, heart pounding in her chest.

Whatever this was...maybe it was the end of the world after all.

And who was she to save the world?

PART THREE

CHAPTER 35

IŽAVORE

Nalādin did not let go of Nova without leaving claw marks in her skin.

She'd been spit out under the cover of giant trees. Large trunks spread wide, their roots deep in the ground. Water sloshed around her ankles as she stood, dizziness attacking her like bees to a flower. Above, the suns barely filtered through the thick leaves, shrouding her mostly in darkness. Scrapes and cuts were specked over her skin, arms, and legs, one still bleeding on her cheek.

Though she knew they would heal shortly.

There were a million memories swirling in her head that she'd never seen before. One of the Vahls convincing her that instead of healing when injured, her body attacked her, widening the wound and infecting it, ensuring that she never allowed herself to be hurt, to be touched by a weapon.

So, she would never know the truth.

Nova keeled over, dry heaving onto the grass below her. Was anything about her real? Would this ever stop? Her fingers dug into the earth below her, feeling that distant, steady beat of the heart of the world that Killian had shown her. *In and out. In and out.*

She was so tired of the tears leaking out of her eyes, of the tangible weakness her body couldn't help but expel. They dripped off her cheeks, landing on the damp soil and disappearing below. Wind rustled through the thick leaves and chilled her skin.

Time to go, she took another deep breath and tipped her head up, *please. Let me go.* Forcing herself up, she put one foot after another, heading deeper into the forest.

She wasn't sure what was real and what wasn't. Exhaustion was a prickly stem she couldn't avoid. It kept prodding her and poking her. There was a rustling from her left within the shade of the large trees. A giggle of laughter bounced off the flower petals and echoed through the woods. There, on a large, thick frond sat a forest sprite staring directly at her. Nova wiped her cheeks with the back of her hand.

The sprite was small, maybe two hands high, but her eyes were big and bright. Her wings were pale, translucent with lilac and rose running through them, and her hair seemed to be made of flower petals. Fearlessly, the sprite flew to her, floating in front of Nova's eyes.

It was wondrous and beautiful and familiar, the same sprite from before that gave her the medicine. She tried to speak, but her words were lost somewhere in the forest.

The sprite smiled. Nova had no idea how aging worked for them, what their lifespan was, but the way the petals were still in bloom and the blush on her tiny cheeks, she assumed the sprite was young.

The sprites voice was melodic when she spoke. "My name is Marri."

She cleared her throat. "My name is—"

"We know who you are." Marri reached out before she could recoil, touching her small fingers to Nova's cheeks, making the tears disappear. In response, her petals seem to grow. "Nova. The Witch." She giggled.

Nova's heart fell, her eyes lowering to the ground. That was all she ever was. Not a person, not a woman. Just a Witch.

"A Witch!" Marri practically sang, repeating the words and

spinning with her fluttering wings. The light reflected off of them like a chandelier. "We've been waiting for you."

A strange kernel of something warm grew in Nova's chest. "Who?"

The sprite's excitement, her warmth, was refreshing. "All of us." She motioned behind her to the forest.

Above, the sky darkened, the leaves closing in to block out the suns, and around her, Nova saw so much more: translucent, fluttering wings, sharp feline eyes gleaming in the dark, creatures leaping from tree to tree, the distant sounds of the forest. She could feel the heartbeat of it all—of all of them—in her palm. There was so much and yet nothing at all.

Marri flew closer, handing her a tiny multicolored petal. "You must go. Your journey must begin."

Begin? What exactly did the world want from her? "But—"

"We will meet again, Nova. But you have to go. Nalādin will show you the way."

Darkness enveloped her again, but not the heavy kind. It was only the absence of light, not the darkness that stole her life. The heavy heartbeat grew louder, beating slower than her own and thrumming through the forest. "And remember, trust the one of the woods. The Ižavore." Her ears rang as wind whistled past her. Killian. What did he have to do with this? With her? "We will not leave you. We are with you. We have been waiting for you."

Nova felt the brush of fingers over her cheeks and nose. A gentle touch—so gentle, she did not flinch.

"Let the forest guide you. Let your path be true. You will soon be free." The sprite's whispered words embedded themselves in her chest.

Around her, the forest shifted. It grew silent, but she knew it would all be different. Fronds brushed against her skin only to disappear. Droplets of water rolled down her arms before evaporating, and the air swirled around her. When she opened her eyes, she was alone. Truly alone this time. There were no waiting eyes, no heartbeats but her own.

It was only Nalādin.

Darkness fell, though she knew that was the forest, the sky eaten by the leaves. In front of her was a path weaving under and through the thick trunks. Flowers and vines grew up from the soil and onto the large trunks. Petals hung off the leaves, some red, like blood dripping to the forest floor. Vines had weaved themselves into copycat trees. And the path called to her.

What choice did she have?

Nova stepped forward, turning to watch the trees close her in as she expected, and let the unsettling silence fall. She had no idea what version of herself she was anymore, but she would not let the world win. Whatever waited for her, she would face it.

And then, she would find her freedom.

By the time Nova saw the break in the trees, she was practically crawling.

"Please do not close. Please do not close," she whispered to herself and to the trees her palms touched. If another path cut her off, she would find a way to destroy this Gods-cursed forest.

Willow fronds danced over her dirt-covered skin, the wind pushing her forward. Everything was weak. But she needed *out*. She couldn't be trapped in one more place. Nova gulped down air like it was fleeting as the sun rays touched the forest floor. Finally, she broke out of the woods and felt the suns on her skin. The chirping of the creatures returned. The rustling of the wind and all the sounds that disappeared returned, ringing in her ears.

Her eyes pricked at seeing the sky and the mountain peaks. At hearing the world around her. The air smelled of damp soil and flowers. And she was so, *so* tired. Nova crouched, running her palms over the grass, the life teeming deep below. It was welcoming, and she sat, resting on the ground, trying to catch her breath and failing. The ground was soft, and she felt so godsdamned weak.

After all the riddles and the prophecies and the paths...Nova wanted to rest.

Around her, the world faded in and out. Noises became shrill and raucous before silence left her ears ringing. The world cleared and then blurred.

"Nova? Can you hear me?"

Killian's voice had become familiar to her now, the gentle cadence, the low timber of it. She wasn't sure when that happened, but it had. His blood was level. An unfamiliar sensation fell over her like warmth from a hearth, a sensation that allowed her muscles to loosen, her mind to stop fighting.

Trust the one of the woods. Killian. The Ižavore. That was the title on the flags that flew in his honor. Still the only one worthy of receiving what fragile shards of her trust she could give.

Even if she was always going to leave him to clean of up the fragments of what was left behind.

THERE WAS a warm sensation on her forehead, a steady singular pulse not far from her that spiked as she blinked her eyes open.

"Thank the Gods," Killian breathed, removing the washcloth and replacing it with a hotter one. "Are you okay?"

"I—" She swallowed. She wasn't sure the last time anyone asked her that question. If ever. "Yes."

He raised a brow, his threads ringing with disbelief. And he was right, she wasn't, but she wasn't going to admit it. Nova sat up, realizing she was not in her room. The walls were made of intricate stones, decorated with emerald and silver gemstones. It had a domed ceiling, sparkling sconces, and chandeliers. The large windows were open, and fresh cool air circulated in.

"Where are we?"

"Willowgrove."

Panic filled her chest. She ran her hands over the crown of her curls, which she'd haphazardly braided before all this started. "I can't be here. Why did you bring me here?"

"Stop. Breathe." He looked at her like he saw everything she'd rather hide. "It was safer."

"How? I can't be here. I can't—"

Killian stared. "Listen to me," he commanded, stopping her words. "I know you do not want to, but right now, you have to trust me."

Trust the one of the woods. But he'd lied, kept who he was a secret. "Why should I?"

He scoffed. "If not me, you'd be at the hands of Amala right now. And she would sooner have you in a cell than first listen to what you might have to say."

She swallowed, and the air around her turned sharp and cold as her memories of being chained up assaulted her.

"By my bringing you here, the Slaters will listen. They know I've been watching you for her, and they will believe what I tell him. They will respect my choice. If I tell them you aren't a threat, they will *listen.* Do you understand?"

She simply nodded. Whether she wanted to or not, this was the choice.

Killian rose, something akin to frustration tugging on the threads of his soul. Even though the room was large, grand, Killian looked ever the prince that he was. Tall, strong, and regal.

He'd changed from his leathers to a finely made draping shirt of green silk. The silver rings on his hands looked freshly polished, and his short curls were barely brushed away from his face. For the first time, there was a small, opalescent pin on his collar—the insignia of Eisera. A ferocious depiction of the Samara, roaring into the air, revealing sharp canines.

Behind him was a wall of books and scrolls, tucked into wooden shelves that looked centuries old. Artwork was painstakingly hung on the walls, and plants bloomed in clay and stone pots situated on every surface, wild and alive. Hand-carved woodwork of the creatures native to Eisera were placed all over the room. It was luxurious, yet Nova knew it was all him.

"I need to know, Nova, why did you come here? Are you a threat?"

"Well, if you remember, I washed up on this stupid place."

Killian gave her a deadpan look. "Don't play dumb; we both know you aren't." He exhaled, tipping his head back to the ceiling. She watched him breathe, watched his pulse beat in the crook of his throat. Unfortunately, her heart decided to flutter when he turned his eyes back to her. "I'm asking you to trust me. To tell me what it is you are really here for. To tell me what happened with Asha and in Nalādin." Killian took his seat beside her again, leaning back in the chair.

Nova pulled her knees up to her chest, curling her arms around them. Her curls danced over her legs, brushing her skin. "Why do you care? Why have you been so willing to help me?"

He scoffed. "I wish I knew."

"All you had to do was leave me alone." She stared at him. He could've watched her from the shadows or in silence.

"I know."

"So, then why?" she asked.

Why did he care when no one else did? Her life was insignificant; that was what she believed, though it seemed the world had other ideas. She was nothing more than a Witch. A killer. A girl who wanted freedom. Freedom that had been granted, and still, she was not free.

And Killian was looking at her in ways she didn't understand. How was she supposed to think with those green eyes on her? How was she supposed to disappear when he was dead set on seeing her?

"Emotions have a funny way of not explaining themselves. We can't control them. We don't always know why they tell us to do the things we do. The more time I spent watching you, the more I wanted to spend time with you. You seemed like you needed a friend."

"And you decided to take that on?"

He looked to the window, and something despondent flickered over his face. "I needed one, too. Someone who didn't know me. Someone who wouldn't deign themselves because of my title. Eisera is a vast country, but it's hard to get lost in it when you're not allowed." He sighed. "My problems are barely that, but sometimes, it gets difficult when I imagine the life I could've had and am thrust back into the life I must live. And sometimes, I think those close to me forget that I was a person before this. That I was a friend, a brother. All they see now is a prince." Finally, his eyes found hers again, and they almost crinkled at the sides. "You did not."

They were so different. Nova knew that. He was a prince, potentially a king, and she didn't really know who she was. All the titles she'd been given were just that. They weren't said with respect but with fear and admonishment. A catalyst for something else. But...she recognized the ache in him. The ache of not knowing, the ache of loss, the ache of life.

"I know I lied about who I was, but I have lied about nothing else," he said, looking directly at her. The words were soft, quiet, but they demanded an answer. "You can trust me, Nova."

But you can't trust me! She wanted to shout, to scream at him until he understood. She would go without a second thought. She was using this place for her own freedom. She had not earned his trust.

The image flickered in her head of a man fallen to his knees and the earth meeting him. Of the bodies crawling through destruction. He already knew what she was, even if he hadn't said it. And the least, the very least, she could do was warn him of what might be coming.

She could be different. Killian had earned it.

The Ižavore.

"I will tell you what I can, what I know. But you must agree to my terms," she said, her fingers tracing the scar on her throat.

"What are they?"

"You must not tell anyone what I am. You must not share who I am. You will not imprison me. And on the day of the coronation, you must let me leave." Risking the Vahls knowing she was here was not a possibility she could stand.

"Those are quite the terms."

She straightened her spine. "Take them or leave them."

He gave her a heavy stare. It was a drowning wave, an encompassing darkness. "I'll take them."

CHAPTER 36

THE BLOOD REMEMBERS

Nova told Killian the truth.

Or...a twisted, warped thing that, in some ways, resembled the truth and, in most, did not.

"My parents, upon discovering that I was a Witch, took me to the Vahls as per the order in Syris. And they left me there," Nova said. "The Vahls became my parents, or at least, my guardians. Maybe at first, they believed my parents were wrong, that I didn't show signs of being a Witch. But when they saw for themselves, I became...one of their many pawns."

Killian's eyes darkened. "Go on."

She weaved the lies into her story like a tight braid. A story of how the Vahls used many powerful Athera as weapons to do their bidding, not just her. A story of how they were hungry for power. They wanted full authority of the Eminence, authority of every Aether point in Valora. Even for her, the details became fuzzy. Nova knew now, thanks to the dead, this was their doing. They had not only created false memories but warped the true ones.

"I...I don't know who is working for them. I don't know who is aligned with them or against them. I can't—" Her throat became thick. "Before I left, I overheard them talking about the Elders," she continued, tracking Killian's threads for any signs of disbelief. "About how they wanted them dead. That's when I left, but they had known. They knew I was listening. They opened my mind and saw that I knew what they were planning. And no one who ever knew their secrets, secrets that weren't shared, survived. So I ran," she said, keeping her voice level.

She told as it as though she believed it, as though she hadn't made the deal herself. "I left. Stowed myself on cargo and passenger ships until Lazora, where I could find another. And then, I ended up here. So, I lied about coming here for the library. It just so happened to work in my favor. There were things I didn't understand about them, things that I was sure they erased."

From my own mind. From history.

"Okay." Killian sighed. She could practically see the wheels turning.

Since the vault, since Nalādin, the threads began calling to her. His mind was guarded, his thoughts encased, but the threads —they reached for her. There was a thrumming of distrust that she calmed, as if she was running her fingers over a fragile petal. The act was new still. She could only hope it stuck.

"They don't know where you are?"

"To the best of my knowledge, no. But I don't plan on finding out."

He fixed her with a steady gaze—a man ready to take on the problem. To protect his people. "What do you need?"

"All the books in my room from the library. And a map of Valora."

His brows furrowed. "A map?"

"When I was in Nalādin, they showed me—"

"They?" he interrupted, leaning forward with a steely gaze.

She looked on blankly at him. "*They* were Witches, young and old and dead. I think." She couldn't bring herself to tell him of the riddles or her lovely new title. "I don't—Nalādin was strange, and I'll share when it's necessary. But they showed me a land covered. Hidden. It's on no map I've ever seen. West of Eisera and north of Iyvia."

Something dawned on the prince. He swallowed, and she watched the knot on his throat bob with rapt attention. "I might know. It's in the vault." Though his blood was calm, she felt the thrum of anxiety on his threads, like a thorn in his side. "What else happened there? Anything that may help?"

She swallowed down the urge to tell all. "If I think of anything, I'll share it."

He met her with an unwavering stare. His eyes tracked over her face, and her skin prickled at it, but she remained motionless, silent. "Let's go," he said.

For now, that was that.

NOTHING about this place was as it seemed. She followed Killian down a series of tunnels, burrowing deeper and deeper into the earth, but they remained unshakable. They departed from his chambers, a door hidden within stone in his office that was only movable by Earth Elementals. From there, it spread out into an intricate system that would take someone months, if not years, to learn.

After a gradual slope downward, they stopped on a curved platform, where the smooth stone turned into gritty dirt. Nova followed the curve around the hollow chamber. There were multiple platforms all directly beside hollow tunnels of darkness.

She wanted to speak, though she had been privy to the array of emotions emitting from the prince and thought it best she kept her mouth shut. He took a deep breath, the vines tightening around his hand and wrist as he steadied his feet and raised his palms. With it came a platform of Earth.

"Come." Killian turned, holding out a hand.

She blinked. "You want me to get on that *thing*?" Her gaze flickered between the platform and the prince. His outstretched hand...it scared her because she wanted to put her hand in his. That'd never happened before, the desire to feel another person. Her other option was a floating rock that she couldn't control.

She swore his lip twitched, almost curving. "I promise you'll be safe." The words felt heavier now.

With all—or some—of her dishonesty out in the open, with the threat of the Vahls arising, a promise of safety felt fleeting.

Ignoring his outstretched hand, as apparently that was still the more terrifying option, she strode right onto the floating piece of rock. Killian stepped up beside her, and the dirt rustled, a gnarled root growing from bottom.

"Hold on to that," he instructed, doing the same, and as soon as she gripped the root, they descended.

Slow and fast and winding all at once, her curls danced by her cheeks and her stomach flipped, but they were on the ground in seconds. The moment her legs were steady, she was on the *unmoving* ground again. A dark, dingy tunnel greeted her, along with a door made of heavy stone carved with intricacies there wasn't time study.

Killian held his hand to the door, and she watched his vines unwind and slither into the locking system, a series of clicks echoing. And they were in the room once again.

How in the world did I get in here?

Sconces lit as they entered, the shelves flicking in the shadow's light. "Look on the shelves and see if you can recall the books you had. I'm going to call the map."

Nova had already begun eyeing the shelves. "Call the—"

A rumbling sound had her spinning to see a table of stone rising from the center of the room. Killian rolled the sleeves of the green satin shirt, his rings glinting in the dim lighting of the room.

Though she remembered the volume numbers on the texts, she closed her eyes, wondering if there was something to be said for the words the women had whispered: *the blood remembers.* Was that true? How else would she have known what texts were important the first time? She let herself feel the room, the ground underneath her feet, and the books on the shelves. Maybe they were right or maybe she was as stupid as a fly. *Come on, where are you?*

All at once, the sound of pages fluttering filled the room, and around her, the texts pulled themselves off the shelves, landing at her feet.

"What was that?"

She stared at the books before her. "The blood remembers," she whispered. Not just her own, but the blood of those before her.

Killian suddenly crouched across from her. "What do you mean?"

"How much do you know about blood Witches?"

"I know what's been taught about Witches in general. The blood lust, the urge to kill. But I've seen the truth, too. The ones I've met had affinities for the elements much like an Athera. Asha has helped a few of them—those who were turned in or suspected—and I've helped Asha," he murmured, not meeting her eyes.

She knew he hadn't believed the lies, but she hadn't known he'd met other Witches. Elements? Was anything they knew true? Or was everything a lie?

"There is so much I don't know about them," she said, dejection dripping off her words.

"You can learn. We can learn." A vine crawled across the floor and touched her hand, twining around her finger before returning to Killian. He gazed upon her, firm and confident.

Clearing her throat, she continued, "It was something they said to me. The blood remembers. Maybe my blood recognizes those before me, remembers them. But that would mean someone would've been here. To have spilled their blood before me."

Silence fell as Nova gathered the books, placing the heavier ones in a pile, and holding the scrolls of text in her arms. Killian stayed by her side as she approached the stone map painstakingly carved by someone long ago. Black stone made up the base. The oceans had been painted white and inlaid with blue gems, leaving the continents in the same black stone. Gems were inlaid throughout to show mountain ranges and volcanoes and canyons spread across Valora and the main cities and ports. It was old, but it was updated.

There, on the left, were three land masses she'd never seen before. They were carved close together with all the same gemstone colors, indicating that they were one country.

A whispering echo filled her head: *the Witchlands, the Witchlands, the Witchlands.* Her visions flashed. Of the wings cutting through the foggy sky and diving toward an unseen land and the blood dripping from the sky. A ringing ricocheted between her ears.

"You all right?" His hand hovered over her but never touched.

She panted, fighting for her breath, and she swallowed. Lifting her head, she nodded, though it felt forced. But when she met his eyes, they were wide with unease.

"You're bleeding," he murmured, reaching his thumb up to her cheek and swiping.

A drop of blood beaded on the tip of his finger. Her eyes were wet, but she had thought nothing of it. When she pulled her own fingers away, blood beaded there, too.

"I don't—that's never happened before."

"You're exhausted. I shouldn't have demanded answers from you."

She snorted, wiping her cheeks. "You wanted honesty, Killian. And you deserved it. This is not your doing." She rested her palms on the edge of the map. "I'm not in pain. I'm fine." Truthfully, she felt ill, and her legs were weak underneath her.

"May I?" he asked, holding out his arm. Gods, she couldn't deny that he looked strong and sure. But that nagging voice tapped at the weak spot. "It doesn't make you weak, Nova. And I won't hurt you."

She hated that he saw all the ugly, damaged parts of her that she would rather peel off like a scab. How did he do it? How did he *see* her when she could not see herself?

Yet, she wanted to feel the touch of his skin. Maybe it was weakness, maybe it was the lifelong loneliness, or maybe it was just Killian. Nova twined her arm with his and leaned against him as much as her skin and her mind would allow as they looked over the map. There was a tingling sensation, an uncomfortable buzz, but for the most part she felt safe.

"Have you seen that before?"

He sighed. "Maybe once, after Nalādin. I've been in this room no more than four times, though. I don't really remember. But that's not on any map in Willowgrove."

"The Witchlands," she said, and he gave her a sidelong glance. "They whispered to me."

"In the forest?"

"Just now, but I've seen it before. Sort of. In visions that started recently, of a land covered in fog. Hidden from the world." Frustration snaked in as she said, "I don't understand anything that's happening to me."

His heartbeat was slower than her own, and she found herself trying to breathe in time with it. "Maybe there is something in this room to explain it. All of it. Or at least"—he sighed, motioning to it all—"something to begin to explain it."

She traced the continent of the Witchlands with her finger, round and round. Two large continents, separated from Eisera by a channel of water. Stones indicated mountain ranges and cliffs along the shores. A rigid edge marked rough seas between the two continents and underwater formations. Beside them sat a third continent, though more of a small island. Mountain ranges made up the entire shore, and rivers flowed within. Nova couldn't explain the feeling, but seeing these clouded lands settled a part of her soul she hadn't known was empty. Maybe she was alone now. Left to find the pieces of the hidden truth and the shards of the past.

But she had not always been.

Even what has died is not gone—*the blood remembers.*

"They said something else, something I think you should

know," Nova began quietly, and then, she repeated the words that were already impressed upon her brain. "*Look above and look below, a dragon of the blood, a dragon of the soul. Buried in a land long forgotten, truths go unknown. The spirit is dead, unlike the soul. Blood drips over the soil and bones, a sacrifice given, deeds now atoned. They rest in silence, a place unseen. Trust not what's been told, instead what you see. The spirit is dead, unlike the soul.*"

She couldn't bear to add the last part, *the Daughter of the Dead.* Something told her not to.

"A land forgotten," he repeated, looking directly at the Witchlands.

She worried her lip. "Spirit is false. They have no Gods. No history shortly before the massacre. They didn't exist. They are not true. I think they're the ones who have altered history, because in doing so, they erase themselves or the lack thereof."

Killian's grip tightened ever so. Her heart raced, but she remained steady. "And the soul?"

"The dragons are the Gods of the Witches. If there was one of the blood and the soul, it's likely that's true for the Witches."

There was still so much unknown. What if she was being fed lies?

"What if this is all a lie?" He turned his eyes to her.

She held them for a moment, tracing the swirls of green. "What if it's all true?"

Their heartbeats moved as one as the weight of their words sank in. If it was true, what could they do? If Spirit had been operating for centuries, who were they to do anything? Nova wanted no parts of that. She just wanted to *go.*

But was this...would this be enough? Had she uncovered enough truth to appease the Elders? Nova wasn't sure she had anything else to give.

CHAPTER 37

SHARDS OF WHAT ONCE WAS

"If I'm understanding the riddle correctly, that means you..."

Nova walked beside the prince as they re-entered his chambers, their footsteps in time with one another. She could lie, or spin the truth and make him believe her. But despite all she kept from him, she wanted to tell him.

"They said I was not like them. The Vahls." Phantom pain rippled over her skin. "They can change your memories, make you believe false ones, and hide the truth beneath those—control your decisions. I can't do that."

Thinking back on all the times she'd entered someone's mind, she wondered if she was different at all. She'd been able to enter people's minds, to read some thoughts or interpret them, to push them to believe something, to twist a memory—but she couldn't alter it. Eventually, the fog would clear and the truth would reveal itself. She could speak to them, like the Vahls, but it had been easy for her. The biggest difference was she never felt like she had to fight for it like they did. So often, even when they tried to fight, memories, emotions—they came to her.

It hadn't changed tangibly until she'd stepped foot on the Elderlands. And that was still beyond her understanding.

"I see—" The sound of multiple heartbeats drew her attention. There were many. Some strong and steady, others slower and quieter. But they were all coming this way. "Do you hear that?" And there was one, at the head, hot and indignant. "Dray," she said, her skin warming.

The footsteps echoed beyond the walls of Killian's chambers, heavy, rhythmic footfalls that grew louder with every second. Nova retreated toward the window, feeling the rays of the setting suns on her skin. Something quiet but wrathful befell his face.

"Amala."

Nova glanced at him but was quickly drawn back to the noise as the doors to his chambers were pulled open by two guards. Dray and Amala stood at the head, no fewer than five guards behind them. Nova's temper raged, unfurling like flower petals.

Dray's heated gaze landed on her. A scornful smile took over his lips. Nova reached out, and his threads met her in the middle. Dark and writhing, heavier than they should be, and muddled.

The feel of them, of Dray, had her pulling back as if struck. Gods, it felt like poison. Was that hatred? Was that anger? Something else?

The guards made to enter behind the princess and Dray, but Killian's voice was like ice. "Do not take a single step into this room."

They halted, anxious energy practically floating off them for her to read.

"What are you doing here?" This time, Killian's words were directed toward his family.

"You brought her into our home?" Amala's eyes were sharp and lethal. The deep-green leathers on her body were skintight, weapons were sheathed at her thigh and her bicep, and jewels decorated her fingers and ears.

Nova's eyes flickered between them, but she knew, she just *knew*, this was Dray's doing.

"I haven't done anything to endanger us," Killian said, and

though no crown sat on his curls yet, Nova could practically envision it.

The princess laughed, an empty sound that lingered in the air. "You cannot be serious, Killian. I gave you an order. I told you to watch her. Given what has happened, knowing what we've been looking for, you brought her here?"

"She's not responsible for that. She's shared the truth. She isn't who you are looking for." Unease circled Nova's throat, her lies strangling her. He continued, "She has information that is vital to us. That is important. More so than *who* killed the Elders."

Amala cocked her head, her umber hair dancing with the movement. "And you've decided this on your own, have you? You didn't think this was important to discuss with me? With Aydin or Gena? You brought her to our *home*."

"I was unaware you were interested in a Witch hunt, Amala," he said, his words sharper than a blade. "Next time, I'll make sure you know."

The tension between the two was palpable, poisoning the air. Nova felt a strange sadness at it. This was the *sister* he grew up with. To him, she was still his family. But she could see the shards of what once was on the floor, discarded by Amala.

"You expect us to believe that?"

He turned his angry gaze to his guard. "I expect you to trust me. You do not wear the crown yet, Amala. That decision has not been made. I still hold importance, and you should know that my judgment is not in vain."

That did not stop Dray, who strode toward her. Though Killian maintained his place between them, Nova wouldn't hesitate. "You have walked around this place without consequence, without guard. You've been given freedom and freewill."

With a gnarled smile, Nova approached, stopping only feet away from him. "Oh, I'm sorry. I was unaware that I had to plead for those. Would you like me to get on my knees and beg? Bleed for it?" It was right there. His blood was right there, heavy and thick in the palm of her hand. "You'll find between the two of us, your blood will spill first," she snarled.

Red-orange flames sparked within Dray's honey eyes. "It doesn't matter now. You'll be confined below, in the cells of Sylos, before nightfall."

A stab of fear shot through her. She would *never* be imprisoned again. Not by them. Not by anyone.

"I dare—"

"Enough!" The words should've echoed, but instead, they prowled through the room, stopping everyone in their tracks. "Nova will not be going anywhere near those cells." He steeled his gaze on Amala. "That's why you came here? To take her and imprison her?"

"If you don't have the strength to keep us safe, I will."

"You think you have that jurisdiction?" Something darkened within him, and his threads became cold and hardened. "Your parents may still choose you come coronation day, but do not forget that the forest, that Nalādin, chose me."

The air stilled. Every heart rate dropped; everyone's breath held. Nova couldn't help but let her eyes rest on Killian, who was still as stone.

There was an ache within the princess, a pain so loud, the thread practically latched on to Nova, begging to be helped. Amala gritted her teeth. "Apologies, Prince," she spat the words. "But you must put the safety of your people, your family, above an unknown Witch. Who knows what she may be planning."

Nova rolled her eyes. "*She* is right here," she murmured, though it was loud amongst the silence.

Amala spared her a glance, locking her fingers tightly in front of her. "You must choose."

The worst part was that he had no reason to choose her. Sure, she'd shared some, but she'd kept the rest close to her chest. What good were half-truths if they weren't selfish ways to keep herself protected? They were useless to him. Insulting even. And before she could stop herself, she was scratching at the edge of his mind. The guarded forest opened a small path for her.

Do not choose me, Killian. There are still things I haven't shared, and I can take care of myself.

It hurt her, whispering that in his head. Not the act, but the choice to let him in a little bit more. It made no sense, the strange appreciation, the strange urge crawling out of the ground, telling her to trust him. All to make sure he did not suffer because of her.

He turned to her. "Is anything you've told me untrue?"

Every eye was on her. "No." The word tasted venomous in her mouth.

But she couldn't risk it, not even for him. For now, they were safe, and she had no desire to hurt them, but if they knew who she was, what she had done, she would have to leave this place with blood dripping behind her.

"I'll take her to Aydin and Gena, to share with them what I've learned. But I will not imprison her. We are not at risk." Killian was firm, his words final. "You may go," he said, directing his words to the guards. At his order, they dispersed.

Before she realized it, Dray was flying through the air, a spark landing on kindling. With a blade in one hand, he wrapped his arm around Nova's throat, the dagger pressed against her skin.

"Release me."

"Dray, let her go!"

Killian and Nova spoke in time with one another. Apprehension filled the prince's eyes as he watched Dray turn them, his back to the window.

The guard's entire body was emitting heat. Amala and Killian stood still. "No."

"I told your prince I could take care of myself. I suggest you heed that warning."

It was wrong, all wrong. There was a twisting of his mind, a darkness curling around the edges. The closer she was, the more she could feel it, like it was trying to leech onto her as well.

"I will not." He pressed the blade further into her skin, barely enough to break the skin, but a drop of blood rolled down her throat.

Nova met the prince's eyes for a second before becoming a whirling creature. With Dray's blood in her control, she twisted and attacked. An elbow had him gasping for air, but his grip tightened as he tried to kick her to her knees. Her blood sprang to life, adrenaline sparking on her skin.

It was a fight she could see and feel, and she breathed the air in like rain after a long drought. Like stars in a dark sky. Her hand twisted his blood, though she was careful not to leave any bruises. She spun, secretly controlling his blood, and feigning a fight until she stood behind him with his own blade pressed against his throat.

She bent, her lips a breath from his ear, and whispered, "Some guard you are, Dray. Leaving your prince and princess vulnerable. To me, of all people."

She laughed and wiped the blood dripping down her cheek from her eye. Seconds later, she smacked the hilt against his temple, rendering him unconscious.

There was a glimmer of something devious in the green of Killian's eyes. His lips fought to remain still, but she tracked the way they wanted to curl at the edges as he took her in. It appeared there was still much to discover about the prince.

"We must speak to your parents," Nova said, crouching to tuck the blade back into the guards sheath. "Sooner rather than later, if you don't mind."

Amala looked upon her with a deadly fury. Though Killian remained regal on the outside, she felt his threads flare when he looked at her. A spark of life in his eyes. One she probably didn't deserve but cherished anyway.

"Killian, we cannot—"

He steeled his gaze. "We can."

Amala laughed, her eyes wide. "She just rendered your guard, Dray, unconscious."

"He had no right to attack her. But trust that will be

discussed." He stalked forward, looking more like a descendant of the Samara than a man. A deadly predator. "If you would like to challenge me, Amala, please, go right ahead."

Only silence answered him.

For he was the chosen one of the trees. An heir, just as she was.

CHAPTER 38

YOU'RE NOT ALONE

KILLIAN STOOD UNWAVERING IN THE CENTER OF THE room with Nova.

The king and queen, Amala, and Dray, all stood opposite him, as did what Nova assumed was their council. Another stood off to the side—a woman with white-blonde hair streaked with silver and ivory and hooded doe eyes of orange and brown. There was a thin crown atop her head of ice-blue stone and streaks of snow and cherry. The colors of Azias, the kingdom of the Air Naturalists.

The woman was Vittoria, Killian's betrothed. At first, she hadn't understood. If they were unsure who would be crowned, why waste time with an engagement? But it was originally an idea offered by the Farrs, in search of extending their alliances and trade with the western countries of Eisera. They gained more than the Slaters, and Killian, in a push to earn Amala's affection, had agree to the arranged marriage so she didn't have to.

Personally, Nova thought that was shit, but what did she know.

"Explain." King Aydin's voice was resonant and rich. They had deep, golden brown skin and sharp brown eyes. Rings of gold sat upon their fingers and pendants hung from their neck.

"Amala has told you I have unsafely brought a Witch into Izlena. Is that correct?" Killian stood with his hands loosely in front of him. Her heart pounded. Would he reveal her truth? Or keep it secret? "Nova is *not* a Witch. Not the kind you are searching for. Not the one that killed the Elders. If anything, she is a descendant of them, distant. She does not deserve to be hunted or studied as Amala would wish," he said calmly and surely. All eyes were on him as relief spread through her. "I was not careless. She means us no harm and has information about the Vahls."

Amala scoffed, stepping forward. "You kept this from us. You knew, despite my orders, and you failed to share. That's the issue, Killian. You may trust her, but that doesn't mean we will or should."

Nova rolled her eyes. Maybe she should show them that if she wanted to be a risk, they could do little to stop her. Though she knew that was probably rash.

"Despite what you think," he said, his voice low and sharp, as sharp as she'd ever heard it, "I don't take orders from you, Amala."

The princess scoffed but was interrupted by Aydin. "She makes a good point, son. You could've brought this to us immediately. But you hid it. Why?"

"I didn't hide it. Amala instructed me to keep an eye on her, and I did. There was no reason to share anything because she is not who you're looking for. She does not possess the abilities you were warned about at the assembly. No reason to share because she is not a threat."

But his sister would not let up. "She attacked Dray."

"With good reason," Nova said, unable to stay silent.

Royals. Always concerned with tradition and order and rules. None of it would matter if they did not prepare for the Vahls.

All eyes landed on her, except Killian, who maintained his strong gaze forward. The council was made up of eight, their eyes unreadable but their threads were composed. Even the king's and queen's were steady. Amala's was only buzzing. It was Dray's that continued to alarm her. They felt like poison to her, reaching out and trying to leech her life away.

"Enough." Killian raised a hand, the light from the windows glinting off his rings. "We found her in the vault of Eisera. We still know not how she entered the room, something to do with the past, but she gained access to the vault. The information she learned about the Vahls, about Valora—it was all right under our noses. But we have been left blind. Nova could have left. But she has stayed."

Vittoria cocked her head, her eyes innocent yet sharp on her betrothed, and Amala grew more furious with every second. When no one spoke, not Aydin or Gena or Amala, he took a deep breath. Right now, Nova was more of a ghost against the wall than a living, breathing person. But this was not her fight.

She made a promise to herself she would help Killian. That only extended to them through him. If they were unwilling, then she would go.

"After the quake, she was taken into Nalādin. The forest called, and she answered without knowing. She came out alive. She earned the forests approval and respect, though I know some of us have complex feelings about the choices Nalādin makes, about the people it chooses," Killian said, cutting a glance toward Amala.

In a second, the air thrummed with tension. There may as well have been sparks on the floor between them, a chasm of the cracked earth separating them. Within Amala, Nova felt her threads go red hot, writhing with frustration and pain. Intrigued, Nova pushed, as if she was walking on the thread like a path. Memories of Amala's appeared.

Only in flashes, but she saw the moment she exited the forest, only to find Killian already there, being touted and awarded. Felt the pain that had snapped Amala's heart. Felt the hatred— warranted or not—strike up like a freshly forged blade. Even without searching for them, the pain of Killian's threads came to her, as if looking for benevolence. Pain was latched on to them like a choking vine. All the threads emitting from those memories were heavy, a constant ache bursting off of them—a bruise that never healed. It was obvious to her, and to seemingly everyone in the room, that things had not been the same since that day.

Since the day the forest chose Killian and not her.

Killian's voice drew her back to the room. "The forest speaks true. It always has." He motioned to Nova. "It chose me, whether that is honored or not in ceremony. And now, it has chosen her. I suggest you honor that."

Silence fell. Light from the suns streamed in through the windows that made up the meeting room. Compact but tall and grand all the same. Vines and flowers and Samaras were etched into the windows with white stone, and some of their shadows danced on the floor. The distrust was a low hum along their threads, too many for her to manipulate.

But maybe she could show them flashes, make them see what she wanted them to? Like the Vahls had done. All they needed to see were bits and pieces that would make her story believable.

Just as she was to step forward, the king dipped their head, something like respect in their eyes when they looked at Killian.

Then, they turned them to her. "You will come with us. You will share with us what you have with the prince, and you are welcome to remain under his protection. Understood?"

She shared a look with the prince. His eyes were calm. Comforting. Imperceptibly, she stepped a bit closer to him. "Understood."

"YOU'LL HAVE to stay in my wing. I'd like to keep you close by."

She raised a brow, unable to hide her grin. "You want to keep me close?" Her smile grew when a pink flush spread on the prince's cheeks. "Is that all it takes? A little show of honesty?"

His heart beat increased before slowing as his eyes swept over her. He studied every inch of her, from the frizz of her curls, to the smile on her face, to the tips of her flats peeking out from under her pants.

A slow, heated gaze. A look Nova had never been given before. No one had ever looked at her like *that*.

"Perhaps." His lips began to curve upward. "And what would it take for you?"

"More than that, Prince." She stepped up, brushing her shoulder against his arm briefly. When *she* touched him, there was less...anxiety, fewer reminders. She didn't fear the touch when she was in control. "Are you going to show me to my room?"

After a lingering glance, he dipped his head, moving his hand to the small of her back before quickly pulling it away as if he'd been burned. "I apologize, I didn't mean to—"

"It's all right." She swallowed, trying to force away the anxiety. She hated it. Hated that she wanted him to touch her and hated that she wasn't sure she could even stand it. "Really. Thank you."

They continued silently. The formal meeting room they had previously been in was a deeper point of Willowgrove within the mountains. Killian's wing was located within one of the towers, built partway into the mountains itself. Most halls had large, sprawling windows—either stain-glassed or etched with details of Eisera. He led her around the curving hallway, which she recognized from earlier and a few feet past his own door. A vine extended from where it rested on his skin and slid into the lock, revealing a room similar and only slightly smaller than his own. She could see the mountains from the windows, and cool air from the altitude snuck in.

"Thank you, Killian."

"Of course. There's a bathing chamber attached, along with a small reading room. The air turns cool this high up; you'll find a fireplace in there as well. And I'm right across the hall if you need anything." He approached the small shelves of books and texts beneath the wardrobe. "I had your clothes from the library brought up and others added in case you needed them. I know you won't be staying long, but please let me know if there is anything you need."

She sat on the bench at the end of the bed, her hands gripping the carved wood. "You've done enough."

His green eyes brightened in the setting light of the suns. "I'll leave you until dinner."

"Wait," she called. He turned to face her, pocketing his hands. A sliver of warm brown skin was visible between the buttons of his white shirt, and his eyes were earnest. Nova swallowed. "I— thank you for what you did today. For keeping my secret. For using your position that way. Especially against Amala." His eyes lowered to the floor. "Do you think you two will ever be what you once were?"

A deep sadness emitted from the prince immediately, latching onto Nova so much, they threatened to choke her. "No, I don't. I would still do anything for her if the world required that of me. But the moment she walked out of Nalādin to find me already there, I think that changed for her. I can't say it would be malicious, but I can't say that it wouldn't be. I think she would hesitate. If there was a choice to make between me and an opportunity to ensure the throne, she would hesitate, where she once would not have."

She had never felt so strongly on behalf of someone else. She knew empathy was not her strong suit. Mainly because she barely had it for herself. Right now? Right now, she was furious. For Killian.

"I know I've asked before, if you want it or not. Does that change?"

"All the time." He smiled, but it was sad. "Power is a peculiar thing. Those that desire it are often the ones who shouldn't have it. And whether I want it or not is beyond me. Nalādin chose. And I respect that. If they honor that, I'll accept. Over the years, I've come to believe I could lead Eisera positively, cautiously, and with care. Some days, it's all I want." Killian leaned against the stone wall behind him and took a deep breath. "But some days, I think that Amala being crowned would be better. Easier. It would mean I could go back to how things were. But that's the thing about the past. We can't go back. I could fight and claw my nails into the ground until I bled, but I can't go back. I can only go forward."

She frowned, feeling his sadness wrapping around her. "Our past is so often a product of choices we don't understand, decisions we don't make, and the consequences we bear. And there is always loss. It's not fair."

He strode forward, crouching down in front of her. His vines unwound and extended themselves to her outstretched palm, wrapping around it. They were touching—kind of.

"With every step forward, something gets left behind. It is inevitable. Loss is the price we pay to become who we need to be. And if you never feel grief, what was lost was never that important anyway. I'd rather have something to lose than to care about nothing at all."

She did not understand this man. This prince. Too smart, too kind. For so long, she believed—and mostly, still did—that the world, that the people in it, were only in it for themselves. To grasp on to power or strength, no matter the cost.

It seemed that most were. But not Killian. She understood why the forest chose him—why he had earned such a name among his people. The Ižavore.

Nova tracked her eyes over him. The green of his eyes, the swell of his nose that was slightly crooked on the bridge, and the gentleness that was etched into every line.

"If it's any consolation, I think you would make a good king."

For a moment, the sorrow on his threads calmed, as if satiated by her words. "Thank you, Nova."

The vines tightened on her palm, like he was squeezing her hand, and she liked the feel of it. Liked that her heart raced at it. Hated the pathetic sadness that came when they retreated.

"I'll leave you until later."

Nova only dipped her head and watched him exit. The sense of safety went with him, and she was left alone. Again.

BLACKNESS CREPT in at the edges. Underfoot was something sharp and long, cracking when she stepped. Something dripped in the dark, sliding over her skin, leaving a singeing and painful path behind. The Vahls appeared like wraiths, the shadows moving for them, because the shadows were just shapes of people. People with writhing veins of black.

"Look what you have done," their voices echoed. Nova looked below to see the ground littered with bones and pools of blood. "You were a fool to listen; you are no better than us. No different." Above, wings breached the dark, bleeding sky, but spiraled downward with a screeching cry. Her chest seemed to crack, and tears leaked from her eyes. "You will never be anything other than what we have made you. And we are the only ones who can destroy you."

Horror ran through her veins as figures approached, their threads heavy and dark and crushing. Black blood leaked from them, pooling under their feet and rolling to the ground where she kneeled. The threads wrapped around her, suffocating every limb, and the black blood burned. Her skin seemed to crack, and her own blood became violent and hot—poisonous. She tried to stop them, to reach for what she could control, but they attacked her instead.

The sky bled, and so did she.

She opened her mouth to scream, but nothing came out. Nothing came out. And nothing would save—

"Nova," a voice, clear and resonant struck, and she shot upward, her cheeks damp and her skin cold. "Woah. Open your eyes." Killian crouched over her, his hands on her skin and vines wrapped around her wrists, his own eyes wide. "Look at me. I'm right here." She couldn't—she swallowed, but she had no air. "Nova."

The world snapped into view, clearly this time. "I can't—"

"You are okay. You're in Eisera. In the mountains. You're safe."

She wasn't safe. She was *never* safe. Nova shook her head, attempting to move, but he stopped her. "I need you to focus on me."

It was too much. His skin on hers, the dampness on her cheeks, the image replaying in her mind, and the feeling of her skin, of her blood failing her. As if he knew, Killian went to remove his hands, but the emptiness left behind was worse.

"No, no—please don't let go." She squeezed her eyes shut but the images came right back. The hair of her arms stood on edge, a chill rushing over her.

"Okay, okay. I'm right here." He removed one hand, only to drape the blanket over her shoulders. "It was only a dream. A nightmare. It's over now."

Slowly, her breathing returned, and her heart rate settled. The touch from Killian was warm and gentle, so different from the cracking pain in the nightmare.

"How did you know?" she whispered.

His thumb moved ever so softly over her arm, his eyes meeting hers. "I heard you scream." A tear trailed down her cheek, and Killian did not hesitate to reach out and stop it. "You are safe here, my *ravn*. No one can hurt you."

Gods, she wanted to believe him. She wanted that to be true. Beyond just this moment, she wanted that to be true. The space between them was small, the air warm against her skin. Through the windows, streaks of moonlight splayed over the bed and the prince. Shadows from the etched windows were like stars on his skin.

"I don't know what to do, I—when I close my eyes," she said, holding her shaking hands in her lap, "it starts all over again."

He nodded, moving his thumb back and forth. "You're not alone. It was only a dream."

A dream. She knew that, but it did not *feel* like that. It was though the Vahls were in the room with her, their scratchy, droning voices in her ear, and their callus hands ready to rip her open.

"By the suns," she cursed, her voice shaky as she wiped away another tear. Nova tipped her head back, letting the tears run, staring at the blank stone ceiling.

"Come with me, just for a moment." Killian stood, holding out his hand for her. And for the first time, she took it.

His skin was warm against hers, and he held her hand carefully, barely squeezing it, just letting her exist. He padded through the darkness and to the tall, imposing window, carefully pulling it open, revealing a small balcony. Vines and flowers wove around the railing and along the stone walls. Clouds shrouded the night, but hovering over the mountain range was the moon in the center of a star-filled sky. They sat on the tiny balcony, barely enough room for both of them, and she stared up at the stars.

"Whenever you want to go inside, I'll stay until you fall asleep," he said, her hand still wrapped around his, resting between where they sat. She felt the warmth of his gaze on her face.

"You don't have to do that."

He shrugged, turning his head up to the sky. "I don't want you to be alone."

And Killian stayed.

WHEN NOVA WOKE the next morning, Killian was asleep in the chaise beside her bed.

For a whole night, she had not been alone.

CHAPTER 39

MAY THE ASH FALL GENTLY

ELAIA WOKE ABRUPTLY, CHOKING ON HEAT AND ASH. Something scratched her mind, dragging sharp claws around the edges. Sharp stabs of pain whirled over her skin, and blood seeped into her mouth.

Panic overtook her in the darkness, and heavy shadows rested upon her shoulders. She sat up, trying to quell the growing fear in her belly. *Where am I? Who—*

Her head began to clear. The Order. She remembered the sickly sweet scent, the hands around her ankles, dragging her in the middle of the night.

What have I agreed to? She forced herself to take a breath and then another. What else awaited her? The fear grew like a thorn on a vine, sharp and quick, tearing at her lungs when she breathed. She spit out blood, a sharp, stinging taste in her mouth. Desmond had her ingesting most poisons in small doses as soon as she was old enough, and she knew the taste of blackclover like second nature. With it, her shadows would be weak.

Was there really no better way? She wasn't even *joining* them, merely forming a partnership.

But she'd agreed to this. And that was that.

She sighed and crouched. The air smelled of sunbaked soil,

meaning she was outside, but it was cloaked, too. Restrained. Below, the ground was dusty, her fingers catching on small pebbles. She was somewhere in the canyon. Smoke snaked its way into her airways and lungs with every passing second.

She ripped a piece of the dark fabric of her shirt, thankful it was old and nothing she cherished, and pressed it against her mouth and nose. No light creeped through the dark, meaning whoever wielded the shadows was powerful. She dragged her fingers over the ground, hoping she would meet a wall of some sort to orient herself.

But when she did, flames crackled over her fingers in blistering pain.

Elaia bit her tongue to keep from crying out, blood spilling into her mouth. *Pain is inescapable. You can either face it, or you can fall to it.* Her father's words were like a hymn to her. *Do not feel it. Become it. Beat it.*

With a shaky hand, she reached back out just far enough for the flames to light and to see the dark obsidian walls of the canyon. Using the cloth as a shield, she took a deep breath, and began moving swiftly in one direction. Heat encroached her, a wall of flame hidden by the dark blocking her path.

"Wrong way, Princess," Xerxes's voice sounded from behind her, but when she spun, the heat was gone.

A growl crawled out of her throat, her shadows fighting to emerge in something more than wispy creations. Turning, she pressed her back to where she believed the wall was, taking small careful steps in reverse, but she grew too close, and yet again, her skin burned.

She had to pass. She needed them to keep their promise. She would succeed, no matter what.

"I hope Senka returns and eats every one of you." Her words were swallowed by the dark, an echoing laugh the only response.

She closed her eyes and felt for her shadows. They were there, heavy under the weight of the poison, but she pushed through it. Like a wolf running through a forest for its prey, she battled through, heaving for air after seconds. But if she could just grasp them, push them against these shadows, she could see. She could fight.

Do not feel it. Become it. Beat it.

Tears of exhaustion dripped from her eyes, but she tugged. And like a loose thread on clothing, it all unraveled. Every shadow was a heaving effort under the poison, as if she was trying to move a rock wall. Slowly, painfully, they curled around her ankles and her palms. She forced them against the others, destroying the cloaking shadows like the parasites they were.

It took everything in her not to collapse.

The world came into view; the stars above the canyons were clear, and the wall of flames around her was visible. They molded to the canyon walls, copying the shapes and swells of the rock, but kept her locked in a particular section. Xerxes stood across from her, his flames eating up the sky, flickering high above him but low enough to be unseen by those passing. The flames warmed his face, his eyes bright and sharp.

Flanking him stood four others. Their faces were hidden by veils of orange and red, shielding their eyes. They were ornate, made to imitate the wings of a fyrebird, with feathers crawling around their faces like a ribcage.

Elaia stood when her shadows returned. Blood dripped from her nose, and she wiped it away with the back of her hand. "Is this," she said, motioning to them, "necessary?"

Some of their lips curled in amusement, but they remained quiet.

"You agreed to the terms." Xerxes raised a brow.

"Unfortunately."

One of them snarled at her, lips curling at the edges. They stalked forward. "This is an important ritual to join us."

Elaia rolled her eyes. "Well, it seems a little over the top."

"You still must past the initiation, Princess," the Order member spat, their own shadows curling at their fingers. They shared a look with Xerxes before taking a deep breath. "What is learned here cannot be repeated. We must know you will keep the secrets of the Order under any circumstances that arise. That you will not falter."

A test for pain, then? For resilience? Whatever it was, she would pass it.

She needed their help. This was a price she would pay.

"The choice is yours. Earn our trust, and you will stand under the protection of the ash. Fail, and you will burn."

Gods, they were so dramatic. "Yeah, I get it—"

Her breath was stolen before she could finish speaking as if a rope was wound tightly around her throat, and with every movement, threatening to choke her completely. Her knees hit the rocky ground. Shadows, not her own, swarmed in as clouds of dark fog as the members of the Order disappeared from view.

Composure is key to survival. And you must always survive.

Her hands moved swiftly over her legs, as quick and poised as possible, while she took small swallows of hair. But they had taken her blades. Because why wouldn't they?

But not her ring. All her jewelry remained. Idiots. She found the moonstone band on her right hand and twisted it accordingly. In response, the metal expanded, forming rings over her fingers with sharp spikes shooting out of each one. A hand of daggers.

The invisible rope around her throat loosened, and Elaia sprung while she could. She needed to find them, incapacitate them. They couldn't steal her air if they were parrying her blows. She moved through the darkness, unperturbed by the foreign shadows. Just because they weren't hers meant nothing. She'd spent hours fielding others' shadows and hiding in them, thanks to Desmond. She moved against the wall, hoping the Air Naturalist had lost her. The flames grew hotter, and she turned inward, looking for distortions within the shadows.

Elaia's eyes flickered, tracking the space. Power and strength were hard to determine in all Athera. Some could darken the sky but not make a blade of shadow. Some could send flames to the sky but their flames unable to burn. To her left, the cloud of shadows glimmered, faltered, before reforming. A weakness. She beelined, her eyes sharp and feline-like in the darkness as she approached. A face appeared through the fog, masked and violent.

"Took you long enough," they spoke, striking fast. Elaia pivoted, crouching low and swiping.

The spikes of her ring slashed through their leathers but spilled no blood. Blows, heavy and light, were exchanged. Not once did they strike with shadows. Elaia took another swipe of their legs, and blood spilled, their knee buckling. Sweat dripped down Elaia's forehead as she danced out of the woman's grasp and made quick slashes of visible skin. Disappearing into her own shadows, Elaia approached from behind, cracking her elbow against their temple, watching as they fell to the ground. With it, their shadows fell.

Xerxes and the remaining three stood waiting.

The Air Naturalist stood in the middle, a cyclone of air in his palms and a sardonic smile on his face. Stealing the dagger from the fallen member, Elaia tucked it and ran. Air slammed into her in a whirling mass, exactly what she wanted. He twisted, whirls forming from his hand and feet that Elaia avoided. In the mess of it all, she flung the dagger through the eye of the air storm and watched it connect with the center of his palm. A sense of pride bloomed within her.

Composure is the key to survival.

She repeated the mantra as she moved around the clearing like a shadow herself. Even without them, she was dangerous. Deadly. Elaia let her mind quiet, let the violence become a rhythm. She was darkness personified. The clearing became a battlefield, one where she stepped out victorious. So far. She immobilized the Air Naturalist quickly.

This was for the throne. For protection. For Rersa. To keep that darkness that clawed at her head at bay. *The shadow will continue to haunt—as long as you maintain your promises.*

Xerxes and the other two were all that remained. The masked members leaned against the canyon wall.

"Finally, Princess."

There was blood caked under her nose and sweat all over her skin that smelled faintly of the blackclover. Her shadows were still diminished.

"Sorry to keep you waiting," she snarked, running her finger over the dagger. Sparks fell on the ground by her feet, blazing flames appearing in beams around her.

Flipping the dagger once, Elaia struck, just missing his waist. He pivoted, wrapping a hot hand around her wrist with a smirk. *Composure is key.* Her skin was hot with anger, so the heat was nothing but a spark. The flames cast shadows on them from above.

With honed perfection, he pulled her inward, holding the dagger he now held against her throat. "I thought you'd be better than this."

Elaia smiled. He wanted a fight? She would give him one.

A bead of blood spilled out as she struck with her ringed hand and then with her knee, forcing him to release her. She became a whirl, strike after strike amongst the flames, the dagger lost somewhere on the canyon floor as he defended each one. Around her, the fire grew hotter, and sweat now dripped off her skin, her hair sticking to her forehead, but she never let up.

Anger got the better of some, but not her.

She had long ago learned to hone her rage into a weapon.

Elaia never let up. Exhaustion was heavy on every limb, but she barely felt it. The burning rage ate it all away. If this was what it took to protect Rohan and Zahra and Rersa and even her father, she would do it. She would go down screaming with fire burning her skin before she gave up. Her hits were bruising, her kicks swift, but Xerxes was just as strong.

Maybe he was just as angry as she was. But sweat beaded on his forehead, and she couldn't help but smile, despite the heat licking her skin.

Still, they grew hotter. Xerxes captured her wrists, blood seeping from his palm over her spiked hand, and he pressed closer. "Oh, little shadow. I'm not the one you need to worry about," he said and disappeared into the flames.

And then, the flames died, and blinding pain battered her skull. A wretched Spirit Naturalist. Because, of course. Elaia gritted her teeth, her feet carrying her backward until her back hit the canyon wall. Through her tears, she saw the woman striding toward her. Slow and controlled, like they had all the time in the world to scramble Elaia's brain.

It was like a million hands dragging her down, trying to drown her. Scratching their nails along her skull and her spine, every nerve ending alight. Panting, Elaia did not let her in. Her guard would not fail her now. Pushing herself up, every step was weighted, every breath a chore. The woman faltered a step but pressed harder.

Pain is inescapable.

Pain is inescapable.

Pain is—

A spine-chilling scream escaped her lips as Elaia pushed forward, her nails ripping into the woman's clothes and pulling her down. Elaia was blind through the pain, but her hands latched on and did not let go. Dust landed on her skin as she twisted them until Elaia remained above, the Spirit Naturalist unconscious below her.

Only then did she open her eyes.

Elaia stood, and more blood dripped out of her nose as she crossed the clearing. Xerxes stood with his hands behind his back, the sweat cleared and his hazel eyes bright with humor. *Arrogant prick.*

Beside him was the man from earlier, his masked face still and disturbing as he eyed her.

She curled her lip as she stopped in front of him. "Sufficient enough for you?"

Xerxes smiled. "Go on, Lezi. When all is finished, meet us in the cell." Stepping closer, Xerxes cocked his head, picking up a strand of her damp hair and drying it with the heat from his fingers.

Elaia wanted to bite him. Wanted to make him bleed again.

"For now. Come with me."

THEY WALKED DEEP into the canyon, sections even she had never been to before. They could be south or east or anywhere in the Zylla canyons, but these tunnels were unfamiliar to her, something she'd have to rectify.

"The least you could've done is let me clean up."

Xerxes looked over his shoulder, raising a brow. "Why? Don't want the others to see you as anything but a princess?"

"You need to expand your vocabulary. There are so many more things you could call me other than princess." Elaia ran her fingers over the rock wall, her heart settling when she felt the familiar grooves that had been put there long before she existed and would remain long after her.

"Oh, don't worry. I call you plenty of things." Xerxes pointed to a small tunnel under a low hanging wall of rock. "After you."

With a roll of her eyes, Elaia crouched, and after a few steps, she was able to stand in a large cavern. Behind her, Xerxes followed, his tall body folded to fit. What was previously a quiet journey through the canyon was no longer. The familiar hum of voices bounced off the walls. The cell. Nothing more than a cave tucked deep within the canyon with walls of midnight black and sand.

Torches painted shadows on the canyon walls, and tables made of rock sat around the clearing. People were scattered amongst the cavern, all of them with masks similar to what she'd faced in her...initiation. But in the light, she saw the detail carved onto them. The mark that existed on Xerxes's ribs, wings made to look as though they were flaming, blades wreathed in fire and vines and shadows. Amongst them sat the four members she'd fought, and Lezi, the healer.

Low and high on the walls were other tunnel openings, as was much of the Zylla Canyons. Elaia had read about how the tunnels were used in previous wars as a means of escape, protection, and communication. She'd never seen this cavern before.

She scrunched her nose and took a breath, trying to quell the frustration that this *Order* existed under all of their noses.

"Welcome to the Order," Xerxes said, glancing at her. Something flickered in his eyes that she hadn't seen before. Not pride or the usual smolder of confidence. No. It was something different. Something darker. "This is only a fraction of what the Order really is."

She dug her nails into her palm to keep from scratching angrily at the blood caked around her nose. "How is this possible?"

His eyes were cold. "The Order is seen only when it wants to be."

"Do they always wear the masks?"

"No. If there is an initiation, they are required. Members maintain their privacy until they deem the new initiate trustworthy. In the case of our *partnership,* they know it's you," Xerxes drawled out the word before continuing, "But they've kept the masks on as protection. From you."

"Perfect." As soon as the words left her mouth, it seemed as though every eye landed on her.

Even though she could not see their faces, she lifted her head, despite the blood and dirt over her skin. Their suspicion was palpable. How many of these people had she seen before? Would any of them be familiar without their masks?

Her eyes were sharp as she took in as many details as she could. Of their eyes, of their masks, their builds. Just because she was desperate enough to need their help did not mean she was stupid enough to trust them.

"What's next, Xerxes?"

"You'll be greeted, and then myself and the four that you've already met will discuss in more detail how we can help you." His eyes sliced to her. "Then, you'll be officially introduced to the Chair." Xerxes raised his hand, and those she'd not already faced stood and approached.

Though she stood there alone, she could feel the image of her that others held flicker. Often, she let her mind get the best of her.

She burdened herself with the weight of perceived disappointment of those close to her. Every decision she made, she weeded through what they would think of her. What Rohan and Zahra and her father would think. Of what her mother and sisters would think.

Would her mother approve of this? Would she understand the decision was being made in order to protect them? To protect all of them? Would Rayn think less of her? Would Shaye?

You are your father's child. I love you still. Elaia could hear the words her mother often whispered to her when she was being rash or impatient, often times as a joke.

But it had stopped being funny to Elaia a long time ago. She loved Desmond, but she didn't want to *be* him.

She wanted nothing more than to be like her mother. But the more she fought, the further she fell.

The combined weight of all of their opinions, the ones Elaia had conceived, threatened to push her to the floor.

In single file, the members of the Order dipped their heads to her, some greeting her with cautious eyes and others hungry.

As they went, they repeated the words, "May the Ash fall gently upon your shoulders."

CHAPTER 40

TO VENGEANCE, TO HATRED

"Let me be sure I'm understanding you correctly." Elaia glared across the stone table. "Not only do you receive a seat on my council, you want me to support you in running for Governor of Revohr? And you want to control a division of the Nightguard?"

Zoran, a Shadow Naturalist and the Chair of Rersa of the Order, sat with his legs kicked up and his fingers intertwined. He had not been a part of the initiation, but he had watched it from above.

"Myself preferably, but any nominated member will be acceptable. As for the guard, you'd be completely aware of what takes place."

"Why? If you have all of this," she said, raising a brow, "this power that you've claimed to have, why do you need a measly governing position? Why do you need the Nightguard?"

Zoran gave her as steely gaze. "There is power in secrecy, in the shadows, as I'm sure you know. We have influence, but not control. Not how we'd like it. These positions prevent stagnation. There is always more power to grab, more control to wield. Why should we stop reaching for it?"

"Is there a limit?"

Zoran smiled—cunning, like a canyon fox. "If there is, we have not reached it yet."

After a moment, she exhaled. They only wanted power, as she did. "Fine." Given the circumstances, the asks weren't outrageous. Maybe it would give her a way to learn more about the Order without looking suspicious.

The six of them stared at her—Zoran, Xerxes, Lezi, Saija, Akori, and Veren. Each of them had an emblem embossed on the leather band around their wrists. They hadn't been wearing them previously, but they were now to represent the subgroups of the Order she'd learned about earlier.

The emblems were only worn in the safety of other members. There was much they wouldn't share, but it was only a matter of time. Elaia would rip the knowledge from them in time.

Zoran uncrossed his legs, resting his elbows on the table. His brown skin rippled under the shadows from the torches, the tattoos of Rersa painted on his skin. Only he and Veren, the other Shadow Naturalist, had the customary ink.

"Then we have a deal. We will ensure you sit the Obsidian Throne. You will have access to our knowledge, our network. And you will foster the growth of our control. This is only the beginning, Princess."

Dryly, Elaia said, "The beginning." She wiped the cloth they had given her against her face again, resisting the urge to scrape off the dried blood until she bled more. "Anything else?"

Zoran sat back. "That will come in time."

From what she understood, the Order was, in fact, everywhere. Those she'd seen today were only a piece of the members on Rersa alone. There were Chairs on every continent, factions smaller and larger than this one all over Valora. The extent of what they'd done, what they'd influenced, could be beyond what anyone knew. They could break a throne's rule or make it.

And she would do anything to ensure they broke nothing of hers.

"Then, I suppose we shall begin."

Across the table, Xerxes met her eyes. A heated glance shared between them. "Welcome to the Order, Princess."

"THEY TOOK YOU?" Zahra paced around her room with relentless abandon.

"It was part of the deal—"

"Are you insane? Has Azotz poisoned you?" The demon of hatred and vengeance. Well, Elaia couldn't deny it was fitting. "You were taken in the middle of the night by the wretched Order, and you agreed to give them seats of power? To support them in their reach for it?"

"You knew I was working with them."

"Not to this extent! I had no idea you would agree to demands such as this. For what? Signatures?" Zahra laughed, but Elaia swore she saw tears streak her cheeks. On the other side of the room sat Rohan and Sacha, silently watching the exchange. "Elaia, what are you doing?"

It had been two days since her official meeting with the Order. The night had been long and endless. But it instilled her with the confidence she needed. She held Rohan's eyes. Sometimes, she wished he would just tell her what to do, what to say. But he wouldn't.

"I'm doing what I have to. I need their signatures. I need the throne. No matter what."

"Oh Gods," Zahra muttered, taking a seat on the stone floor. "Maybe we made a mistake; maybe we shouldn't have done this." Zahra's voice was sharper than any blade, anchored with hurt and discontent. "Your father is a good leader."

"Was." Elaia stalked over to her, crouching before Zahra and pulling her hands away from her face. "Was, Zahra." And he had been. Once, he'd been involved, holding forums for every governed territory, inviting the citizens for celebrations or visiting during sacred times. He'd listened, he'd cared. He trusted his people.

Elaia swiped away a tear from Zahra's cheek. Her long brown hair shrouded her shoulders, strands sticking to her face, but it was her eyes, the auburn eyes that Elaia knew better than anyone's, filled with a desperation that cracked Elaia.

She sighed and said, "I can't trust him, not anymore. He knew something about Rayn and my mother before they left, and he never told me. He knew they were in danger and did nothing. Everything he has done since...is a poor attempt to maintain some type of control. But he is no longer capable of protecting us."

Elaia wanted to scream that *he* was responsible for Nomara and Rayn. And in that way, he was also responsible for Shaye. He had failed them all. But no more.

"Do you trust me?" Elaia asked, for once unsure of the answer. She was right to be scared. The briefest glimmer of doubt flickered in those auburn eyes. She would've preferred a blade to the heart.

"I do," Zahra said eventually.

It wasn't enough. The way she looked at her...was different. It was changing. Elaia hated it. "I will make it so, Zahra. I will prove to you that I am the same girl. I just can't lose you. I cannot lose anyone else."

Zahra looked at Rohan and Sacha over her shoulder. They were steadfast. "You believe this is the way?"

"We believe in Elaia. We trust the princess."

Elaia dipped her head in thanks to them. Whether or not they agreed, for now, they stood with her. She allowed her thumb to swipe over the soft skin of Zahra's cheeks until she returned her gaze.

"Do not keep things from me anymore, Elaia. I won't stand for it." Zahra reached out her hand, cupping her cheek. "I know you feel you must protect us, but I cannot lose you either. I will not let you lose yourself to vengeance, to hatred."

"I have no hate toward my dad." She wasn't sure if that was true or not, but the words came out regardless. "I have no vengeance." Questionable. "I only want to see my country safe. I only want to protect those I have left."

Zahra ran her fingers down Elaia's arm, intertwining their fingers and meeting her stare with a firmness. "I stand with you, Elaia. I always will."

Relief fell over her in waves. She would soon be seated on the Obsidian Throne. No matter the cost.

No cost was too great for those she loved. And Elaia was willing to pay them all.

Chapter 41

Almost Free

In the following days, the suns moved closer to overlap, the red-sun—the bleeding sun—approaching, as it did almost every four or so weeks. For a day, sometimes more, the sky would exist in shades of orange and red and pink.

This time, Nova felt it was more of a warning. *Something is coming,* she sighed, *something I need to run from.*

Every day since her nightmare, she'd spent with Killian, the king and queen, and silently, Amala. Dray was nowhere to be seen, though every once in a while, she'd sense his heartbeat lurking in the dark. The time between now and the coronation was dwindling.

Together, they poured over the map, recreated from the one located in the Vault, as Nova repeated what she knew. About her *upbringing*, the Elders, and the Vahls general use of other people. Which was true. Everyone in Froststone was a pawn of some sort, either willing or not.

They stood in a room full of windows that spanned from floor to ceiling, the mountains of Zimos all around them. Above, the ceiling was made of glass, though tempered, so the sun's rays were muted.

"What would they want with the blood of the Elders?" Queen

Gena repeated, a question that had left her lips more than once in the two days. "Do you think they have a Witch capable of killing them? Is that the Vahls doing or a way to keep us blind from their motives? To use the possible existence of a blood Witch to hide their tracks?"

Her skin crawled with the burden of bearing the lies. The burden of upholding them. But she swallowed it down, and like bile, it burned.

"I have no idea. I ran before I could discover anything further. I doubt they killed them. The Vahls don't like to get their own hands dirty." Nova kept her voice steady. "Beyond that...I'm not sure."

Nova heard the voices of the Elders in her mind as clear as day. *"Take the blood and get rid of it. The blood spilled will be of no use, too long dead, too long exposed. But the blood in those vials...they* must *never touch it."*

Whatever was to come...she was to blame.

"Maybe they believe the blood will heal them? The sickness," Nova said, standing to the side near a window. "I didn't see signs often, but maybe others did. The bloody nose, the ticks. The frazzled mind."

"What about their guard? An army? Anything of that sort that you saw?"

Outside, the peaks of the mountains disappeared into the clouds. "The Royal Guard is smaller than most, similar to the size of Ceron's. Not like yours or the Nightguard. But they're well trained."

The Spirit Guard trained high in the northern-most mountains of Syris, amongst the cold and the barren. Much of their training focused on the mind. If they weren't Naturalist— or, whatever they *were*—they learned just how to break people. To no surprise, she'd been one to practice on. More than once.

"But an army on top of that...I never saw or heard anything of the sort." Nova padded over to the map, looking over Syris and Valora as a whole. There were markers for the Aether points, places like Nalādin. She let her eyes skate over the tiny carved thrones of each kingdom. "They want power. Many do. But they...feel disrespected. After assemblies, you could tell they felt as though others did not respect them. Did not fear them." She looked around the room. "I can't say what they want exactly. But you should be ready, be prepared...for anything."

Their eyes were glued to her. Their threads thrummed with unease, a bit of distrust, but mostly, resilience. They would be fine. The people of Eisera, the Slaters, they would be fine. Even so, it did not stop her from preparing to leave.

BETWEEN THE TOWERS of Willowgrove was a space of open air that smelled like soil and flowers. Tall towers of green and white stone seemed to touch the sky, as if part of the mountains themselves, while other shorter towers were made up of stained or etched windows, casting a rainbow of colors onto the stone ground. Toward the edge, toward the city of Izlena, was a training ring made of soil and stone.

Behind her, a garden was built between the towers with benches of carved wood, arches of vines and flowers of yellow and greens and violets, and tables of marbled stone.

It was completely empty except for the two of them—herself and the prince.

Scrolls were laid out on the floor in front of her, texts and books opened to various pages. She was sure the tea of lemon and berry that Killian called for had gone cold.

"This is useless. You can't see any of these?"

His curls were brighter under the suns, streaks of gold in the deep brown. "No."

Tipping her head up, she took in the view again, more focused this time. It felt as though she was looking at the whole world. Killian looked at peace, though that was no surprise. He belonged amongst the trees, amongst the mountains. In any capacity.

Tearing her eyes away, she grabbed the small dagger she'd found in her room, slicing it against her finger again to drip her blood on the pages. She made sure it landed on as many of them as she could, hoping to reveal things she'd missed before or things that had yet to be revealed.

He watched her with narrowed eyes. "I wish you didn't have to spill your blood."

"Blood loss is the least of my concerns," she responded, watching as curved scrawl and sketched images appeared in front of her. "Anything?"

"No."

She frowned. There was one—one scrawl on which her blood revealed the contents to him. But that was it. The blood of the past was picky, which allowed him to see and which didn't. "It must be a spell. Can I try something?"

"Of course."

"I'll need to cut you," Nova said, holding out her hand. A smile danced on his lips. "I realize that sounds more violent than it should."

He only shook his head, his green eyes shining like damp moss in the sun, and held out his hand. Gently, she pricked his finger and waited for the blood to bead. She cut herself again, and with a swipe of her finger drew his blood into the air before mixing it with hers and watched it drop on the pages.

"By the Gods." Killian dropped down beside her, leaving his chair behind, and took in the pages. The original contents were faded, light. What was revealed was the color of blood.

"Can you see it?"

He ran his finger over the scrawl and the drawing of dragon wings. "Yes."

Nova explained the pages she'd seen before, Killian listening intently beside her as his eyes tracked over every inch of the pages before flipping to pages she'd not yet seen. But nothing new. There was *nothing* new. More half-written prophecies that she'd already read. More about the Spirit Naturalist she already knew.

Nova dug her fingers into the edges of her curls. It was all so godsdamned annoying. These Witches of the past, these—

"Okay, that's enough." He rolled the scrolls and closed the books. "Let's take a break."

"Killian." She shook her head, reaching for them, only for him to swipe them away.

"Enough. You've bled on those pages enough. We'll try again later." He stood and tipped his head. "Besides, I'd like to see exactly how you took down Dray."

Her eyebrows rose. "You want to spar?"

He only smiled and padded toward the clearing. She followed, thankful for the clothing they had offered her, and pulled her curls back into a loose bun with the leather tie.

"You're going to fight in your satin—" Nova was interrupted by the prince unbuttoning his shirt, revealing the strong planes of his stomach. Her heart beat rapidly in her chest as the suns danced over his skin. "Well this is just showing off."

She saw the ink on his back as he turned. There were wings that encompassed almost the entirety of his skin. Spreading from shoulder to waist were the dark wings of what looked like a raven. Staring at his skin, at *him*, she heard the whispered name in the midst of her nightmare. *You are safe here, my ravn.* Her heart stuttered in her chest.

She fought to drag her eyes away, but before she could, he turned, grinning when he saw her. "My eyes are up here, Nova."

She rolled her eyes, blushing.

His smile grew, and he slipped off his boots and steadied himself in the soil. She felt the slow and steady pace of his heartbeat, as it always was, and settled herself. Something predatory came over the prince. To her, he'd been kind, protective. Here? This was a warrior. *This* was the man that walked out of Nalādin.

"Are you sure about this, Prince?"

His lips quirked. Instead of responding, a wave of Earth shot toward her. Nova side-stepped, only to be met with another. In quick succession, the prince shot stone after stone. It had been a while since she'd done anything but run or find ways to push herself in a tiny room, but her instincts returned with a snap.

She ducked and weaved, moving closer with every step. In the soil, beneath, she found that steadying pulse of the world and felt it shimmer every time he moved. Under a haze of dust, Nova swiped a cut over her palm, and drew her blood, creating tiny shards, and spun, throwing them at the prince.

They clinked as they sank into the stone, blood leaking down the sides. But she fired one after another, pushing him back, all without even touching his blood. The ground seemed to sink, the soil threatening to swallow her. Vines and stems of green wound around her ankles.

She smiled. How many times could the world hurt her anymore? Like it or not, she had been forged by pain. The Vahls had picked her apart and reforged her time and time again. Made her shattered pieces and spilled blood into something for themselves. And since, the world had tried to do the same. Told her what to do, who to be, who she *would* be—pulling her in different directions until the threads snapped.

Yet, underneath it all, was still her. Bits and pieces she'd swept up to piece together however she could.

And those bits of shattered glass made a woman, who made herself a weapon.

Reaching down, she tore the vines, only for them to wrap around her wrists. A wall of rock shot toward her, and with her hand tied, she twisted, finding his blood and stopping the rock in place. She pressed again, twisted further, until the rock fell and shattered and the vines loosened. Heaving a breath, she shot toward him, avoiding smaller shots until she was able to get close. Sweat dripped down her forehead, and her limbs burned, but it was a feeling she'd missed.

They traded blows, hard and quick, soft and lethal, as they danced among the soil. Every step or so, she'd twist his blood and stop him up until the earth itself seemed to power him through. With a swipe, she stole his legs out from underneath him and held his blood, freezing him in place as she straddled him, pressing the blade to his throat.

His green eyes were brighter than the suns. Sweat beaded on his rich skin but still, he smiled up at her, his heart racing in his chest.

"You are a vision," he said, a spark in his eye. "But..."

Suddenly, vines looped around her, disarming the blade from her hand and holding her wrists back, breaking her hold. Underneath, Killian regained control, flipping them, and now, the blade was against her throat.

"Impressive, Prince." She pressed her throat against the blade. "Careful not to let me bleed."

He only smirked before pulling the blade back. She realized then how much of their bodies were touching. She'd never been this close to someone in a fight—never realized all the ways she might touch someone. Only to find that, with him, she didn't hate it. Her body didn't immediately start to revolt. Instead, it was warm, heavy. A strange comfort.

Above, his smile fell into something softer. His eyes tracked over her face at a leisured pace. What did he see? She wanted that knowledge like she wanted to breathe. What did the prince see when he looked at her? Under his skin, his heartbeat had quickened—only by a beat or two, but enough for her to notice.

The vines were gentle on her skin, barely a brush, similar to how it felt to have him look at her like that. Then, his smile fell, and he reached up with his thumb.

"You're bleeding again—"

A calm but tilting voice breached the space. "My prince, I thought I may find you here. Are we interrupting?" Two heartbeats joined them.

With a sigh, he pushed upward. Vittoria and Dray

approached side by side, and Nova stood, quickly swiping under her eyes to clear the blood.

He dipped his head. "Your Highness." The Princess of Azias approached with a sugary smile, pressing her hands to Killian's chest and allowing her lips to brush his cheek, though her eyes, those strange orange-brown eyes, slanted to Nova.

"None of that; you know better." Vittoria smiled up at him.

A thrum of annoyance bloomed, but Nova choked it down. She'd only met the princess once, mostly from the shadows. It was a meeting of trade between her and the Vahls. Nothing more and nothing less. But she had been prepared to strike if the Vahls had ordered her to.

"What brings you here?"

"You're needed for a fitting," she said, her shoulders back and high, like a royal. Nova couldn't deny she looked regal, proud as she stood next to her betrothed. His coronation, the make-shift council, was in only four days.

Soon, he would be King. And soon, she would be gone.

A pit grew in her stomach and crawled its way up to her heart, where a tiny prick of pain landed. She rubbed her fingers over the spot as if to press it away.

Gods, was she *sad*? What a wasted emotion, like the others. The only one that had ever done her good was indifference. Besides, he wouldn't miss her.

She was nothing more than a wrinkle in the thread of what his life would be. And she would not give up her freedom again because she was *sad*.

Killian turned to look at her, but Vittoria spoke first. "I can take her—"

"Nova," he said.

Vittoria met her eyes with a cock of her head, her lips playing at a smile. "I can take Nova back to her chambers." She motioned to Dray beside her. "But Dray would like to speak with her first."

She furrowed her brows but squared her shoulders. Dray approached, his eyes flickering to Killian before landing on her.

He cleared his throat, heat emitting off of him. "I would like to apologize."

She snorted. "Go on."

"I was wrong to attack you." The bruise on his temple had turned yellow. "I am sorry. It was disrespectful to you and to Killian." His heartbeat was steady, but when she touched his threads, they burned her, too hot for her to read. But that dark feeling surrounded her once more.

Killian patted the back of his friend and his guard with an accepting face.

Without speaking, she dipped her head, but once again reached toward the prince. *Something is not right with Dray. I don't know what, but be careful.* Killian turned, looking between his betrothed and herself, though his eyes were unreadable and his threads quiet, carefully contained.

"You'll be all right?"

She glanced at the princess, wiping sweat from her brow.

"Don't worry yourself. She is in good hands," Vittoria spoke first with a wave of her hand, sounding a lot like the Vahls.

Killian met her eyes once more. For a second, she imagined it was only the two of them again. But before she could capture it, the moment faded. "I'll find you later."

They both watched Killian and the guard disperse, only the two of them left amongst the mountains.

Beside her, the princess stood directly under the rays of the suns in a dress of sky-blue and jewels of white. "Shall we, Nova?"

Begrudgingly, she gathered her things. They exited through the arched tunnel of vines and took the curved staircase, trading the open air and mountains of gray for stone of marble. Some of the stone was cracked and crawling with vines.

Vittoria was taller, yet petite. Clothes draped over her like water, whereas they clung to Nova. Jewels of ice-blue and white decorated the princess, while white kohl lined her eyes. Her heartbeat was slow, slower than others, but strong, quiet almost. Every few steps, she felt the princess looking at her.

"Will you be joining us for the coronation?" Vittoria asked, her lilting voice echoing against the stone.

"I haven't been invited, nor do I expect such, Your Highness." Nova eyed the princess's dress and shrugged, a demure movement that felt foreign to her. "I don't have anything to wear, either."

"I can solve that for you. I am certain Killian would love to have you there." They moved slowly through the winding, open air stairwells.

"There is really no need for that. I'm not much of a socialite." The joke fell flat, but the princess's sugary smile remained. It was unnerving.

Something she'd learned since discovering these *threads* was how different and similar they were to the spirit. They were similar in the sense that they were rooted in who the individual was, their emotions, their memories, their lives.

The mind and body were connected, obviously, but the mind was more of a manipulation. Making them believe they had done something, dreamed something, lived something. Slinking past their guard and planting a seed—of doubt, of joy, of fear—and then watering it. Setting it alight and fanning the flames. The mind was conscious. A well-trained mind might be aware of the intrusion, and a powerful Spirit Naturalist could use it against them.

The mind was easily manipulated but more easily guarded.

The mind could twist, but Nova felt if she was stronger, she could *alter* the threads. Change the very being of who someone was.

The threads were their entire being. If what the dead Witches had said was true, that she was of the *soul*, it made sense. Within, the threads were a moving, ever-changing energy form. A person's aura, so to speak, but so much more. She'd felt them pulse and anger. They had writhed and floated. They were gentle and quiet. Like a living, breathing entity within someone. And they changed colors. At least, in her head or when she felt them, they changed, adjusted to what the person was feeling. She didn't think they could be guarded, but maybe with practice, one could learn? They called to her—some welcomed her, and some didn't—but they didn't fight back like the mind.

Except Dray's. Though it was still unclear what exactly they were trying to do—to warn her or hurt her. But she didn't think he was conscious of it. Just like Vittoria wasn't now. The princess's threads were wound tightly but pulsed quietly. With her, too, they were *off*—twisted of sorts. Dray's were dark but wrong, like a poison. Vittoria's were just...dark. Incomprehensible.

"I still think you should attend." They began down the hall of Killian's quarters, or as she liked to call it, the tower of vines. "He's never used his position against Amala before. Nor the king and queen. Not even to escape our betrothal."

Her breath caught, but she coughed quickly to cover it. The prince had never petitioned the crown before? Against *any* of them?

"I don't know why he'd do such a thing."

They stopped before the door to Nova's room. "He must trust you. Must believe what you have told him."

"I'm glad."

The princess nodded, taking a step back, tilting her head like a bird of prey. Her orange-brown eyes sharpened, exactingly. "I do hope you join us. If not, thank you for all you have done for us, Nova. Sincerely." Vittoria smiled once more before turning away.

A precipitous, jagged sensation crawled down her spine as Vittoria practically floated away like a ghost searching for a place to haunt. Nova did not move until her heartbeat was out of reach. As she slammed her door shut, nausea bloomed in her stomach.

Only four days.

I am almost free. I am almost free.

CHAPTER 42

BLOOD, SIGNED AND SEALED

ELAIA STOOD FACING THE SEVEN MASKED FIGURES IN front of her. Zoran and Xerxes stood beside them.

Only a single flame lit the cavern, casting shadows on all of them. "Who are they?"

Zoran swirled the glass of dark amber liquid around, taking a long sip before meeting her eyes. "Who they are is not important. It's what they will do. Each of them are from one of the seven territories of Rersa. They will be the ones to ensure the governors provide their support. In your...usurping of the throne."

"The throne is rightfully mine." Elaia stood alone. Though even in the dark, she felt Xerxes hazel eyes on her. A hunter through and through—never losing sight of his prey.

"Well, if it was truly yours, you wouldn't need us, Princess." Zoran's eyes were alight with a twisted humor.

She bit her lip, drawing blood. "How will they do it? I need all seven signatures. In blood. And fast." Elaia could not wait. Rersa could not wait. Before the coronation in Eisera, she would—she *needed*—to be on the throne. *The shadow will continue to haunt— as long as you maintain your promises.*

Zoran smiled, sinister in the shadows. "You will have the signatures in two days' time." With that, the seven faded into the darkness, and only the slightest crack of rock gave away their movement. "Have you chosen who will sit on your council?"

Akiro stood beside her, his tail curled around her ankles. Elaia ran her nails through the fur of his neck. "I have," she said. "Xerxes will sit my council." She didn't trust him, but she trusted the rest of them less.

"What?" Xerxes exclaimed, stepping forward.

Zoran's eyes brightened. "The spider. A smart choice. He will serve you and the Order well."

The spider? An image of a scar burned into his skin flashed behind her eyes. Each leg had been scarred differently, and she remembered every single detail of it.

Heat sparked in the dark cavern from Xerxes himself, she was sure. He stepped up. "Zoran, you can't—"

"Enough, Xerxes. She has chosen." Zoran cut him a steely glare. "We'll be in touch, Princess. We have a throne to win."

When he was gone, Xerxes's voice cracked the room with anger. "What do you think you're doing?"

"Oh, enough." She waved her hand and put out the flame.

Weaving through the darkness, she stopped only inches away from the hunter. She both despised his presence and had come to accept it. But if she could get closer to him, get him to trust her, she would have an insider's look at the Order.

She didn't care if that pissed him off. This was the deal. She'd made her choice. "You're half the reason I'm in this mess. You'll be there to see it through."

Heat blistered between them. They so often teetered on the line from hatred to understanding and back again. But now? He was stuck with her—she would make sure of that. Xerxes brought the Order to her, and she would ensure they saw it through.

"You did this to yourself. You wanted power. You gave in."

"I don't deny that. I *want* power. I want safety," she said. "But your freedom is not my concern nor is it my responsibility. You made a deal, and he broke it. Not me. I've simply done what I think is best for me and for those around me."

He stepped in, crowding her. From behind, Akiro let a low rumbling growl. With a quick cut of her hand, he stood down.

"And what happens when the flames grow too hot, Princess? What will you do?"

She laughed coldly. "Are you going to spread the fire, Xerxes? You should know, I'm not afraid to get burned." Through the dark, she saw sparks in his hazel eyes. She liked it. When he looked at her, she knew he was seeing the full spectrum. Zahra's gaze had turned cautious, nervous almost. But not his. As though he couldn't decide whether he wanted to burn her or burn with her.

She stepped closer, their chests a hairsbreadth away. "And what of you, Xerxes? Where will you be when the fire catches?"

Cocking his head, their noses almost brushed. "I hope to be far from it. Far enough that all I see is ash."

"Well, then it's a good thing you gave up wishing and hoping long ago, isn't it?" She smiled, tipping her head up. Heat bloomed at the briefest touch of their noses, and she was glad for it. "Now, come. We have a council to position."

Another breath, their lips so close she could almost taste him. "And a throne to claim."

SHE COULD DO nothing but sit around and wait.

Elaia paced every chamber and corridor in Varistone from sunup to sundown. What if the letters didn't come? What if the governors did not back her? She tried not to think too hard about what the Order might do to ensure they signed, but she hoped it was not with only violence.

Shaye's soft voice had been loud in her head recently. *Your only responsibility right now, is to sit with me. Can you do that?* Even as the middle child, Shaye was calm, level-headed, and yet, free. Free in ways Elaia was not. Shaye never over-thought. She never worried about things she couldn't change. She excelled in acceptance. And she never stopped trying to get Elaia to breathe.

She missed that. These days, some days, she wasn't sure she knew how.

And nothing was calming her nerves—not pacing, not drawing, not training.

Not when this was the last confirmation she needed before proceeding with the challenge. And she *couldn't* control it more than she had. It didn't help that Zahra had been burying herself in work, trying to mold the light and mostly, trying to avoid Elaia.

That meant spending the past two days with Xerxes, her new council member.

"How did you find the Order?" she asked, her legs dangling over the tunnel's edge. She couldn't stand to be inside at this point; the air grew more suffocating with every breath.

"I didn't. They found me." A flame danced in his palm, flickering off the cavern walls. "As far as I can remember, Kisyn was home to me. That city raised me, whether it should've or not."

Kisyn was the capitol of Pyth, the Fire Elemental's secondary land. From what she knew from the legends she'd read, Pyth and Vydara may have shared abilities but were as different as could be. Pyth itself was a hub for all people, Athera or not. Though the island was small, the amount of people that lived there filled it from shore to shore. With a vast school system and various opportunities for trade or specialized work in science or art, Pyth was often sought after, especially by the younger generations.

That also led to an array of issues. There wasn't enough housing for everyone that came to the island. There were never enough jobs, and because of its distance, trade was rare and expensive.

She'd once heard someone say that Pyth either chose you or it didn't.

"Have you ever been?" he asked, and she shook her head, meeting his eyes. "I'm sure from the outside in, Kisyn might seem like a great city. And it is, in many ways. But the Order is all over that place. Crawling in the alleys and searching for the weak to recruit." A cold smile curled his lips, the tiny flame flashing blue. "I was the weak. The city raised me. Not parents or family or friends—I had none, at least none I remember. The Order found me when I was ten because I was alone and vulnerable. A person —a kid—with no ties. No one to worry what might become of them."

Sadness emitted from him, a suffocating warmth, so different from his usual heat. Maybe it had been a mask—a mask of fire— to keep the other emotions at bay.

She crossed her ankles, leaning into Akiro. "What use did they find for a ten year old?"

He tensed. "Plenty. At first, it was easy. They gave me a place to sleep, food to eat. They brought me along throughout Pyth to low-level meetings, greeted me and the other kids they recruited. Then, they put us in a room and told us whoever was left alive in the morning would remain under the Order's protection. Every year, they repeated that task in various ways. Always the same outcome."

Her heart stuttered, taken aback. To become something besides yourself. And to be that for almost twenty years...how could he not be sad?

Xerxes slanted her a glance, his eyes a deep brown in the moonlight. "I accepted. I made sure I was alive come morning. Then, I started training officially. First as a Kyte, then a Fang, then a Shade," he said. "The Order was about efficiency, about success. There was no warmth under the ashes. I caught on and worked my way up. From spilling secrets that had no stakes to stealing lives that meant nothing to me—because I was safe. And I had only ever known the opposite."

"That's why you want to leave?"

He shrugged. "One of them. I'm tired of existing only for them. I've existed for the Order for so long now, sometimes it's hard to remember there's a whole world out there without them."

Xerxes raised a brow. "Though it's clear I won't be going anywhere for a while."

And that's my fault. Guilt and reassurance warred in her head. She didn't trust any of them, but of all, he was the only choice. But now, she would be the reason he belonged to the Order for even longer.

"Why do you ask?"

It was her turn to shrug. "I'm still trying to figure out the Order. How it works. What makes it run."

He exhaled, the flame dancing over his skin as though it had legs. "No matter how hard you try, they'll always be one step ahead. You'll never *quite* understand them as much as you want. I've tried."

That wasn't an acceptable answer to her. She would not remain at peace with the little knowledge she had. Knowing Rayn had been hunted, knowing that she had chosen this, she would not settle for not knowing.

Elaia bit her lip, picking at it with her teeth until she tasted blood. "I'll catch up. I have to."

"You're worried they won't provide you the signatures?" He turned to face her, leaning his back against the walls. Akiro watched him from her left, his ears perking at every movement.

"Can you blame me?"

Their eyes were locked. Just like they were—tied together now because of the Order. Because they both wanted things the Order had promised. But if they were willing to take it away from him, what could they do to her?

"No. But the Order will have them, that I am sure of." He pointed to the moon. "By the time the moon reaches its peak, all seven letters will be delivered."

"Do you know what they had to do to obtain such a thing?"

"Some had easier jobs than others. Based on your information, Lyian, Ztar, and Irisdenn will be easier signatures. Darkbay, too. The others...I can't say exactly how they'll get them, only that they will." He cocked his head. "Isn't that enough?"

The vague answer did nothing to quell the anxiety, but she expected she wouldn't get anything more. And even so, it wouldn't change her mind.

"I suppose I don't have a choice anymore."

Xerxes cocked his head, watching her with sharp hazel eyes. "No, you don't. Not as far as the Order is concerned."

Elaia sighed, turning her eyes to the moon. All she could do now was follow the current of the plan she had agreed to over the cliff and hope it didn't end in a deadly pool of jagged rocks.

Upon entering her chamber a little past midnight, she found two folders awaiting her. One was heavy, and when she turned it upside down, she counted five golden emblems. In the light, she saw each signature, and she knew *exactly* who would stand with her.

The other folder was filled with seven pieces of parchment. There were drops of blood on the material, right along the edges.

In the soft firelight of the hearth, she counted all seven blood signatures. Some were perfect, not a single drop out of place—an intentional cut. While others were a bit unkempt. What the Order did was not her business. How or why, it didn't matter. Not now.

Because the blood was hers, signed and sealed.

Now, it was time to use it.

CHAPTER 43

FILAMENTS OF FEAR

ELAIA DRESSED IN THE SILENT DARK.

Not a sound could be heard in her bedroom. Black silk draped over her skin, crawled up her neck, and left her arms bare. It cut in at her waist, leaving the skin exposed, as gems of moonstone and onyx decorated the seams.

Within, an array of emotions fought for purchase. Guilt for what she had done—was doing—to her father, was a double-edged blade, threatening to strike. Pride pulled on her shoulders, ensuring they were held high. But there were ghosts in the room. The memory of her mother and sisters slunk in the corner, lurking over her shoulder.

Was this what they would've wanted? Would they look at her with shame? With pride? Or with something else? She closed her eyes. They were no longer here. They no longer had wants or needs. Grief pierced her heart, another cut for it to bleed from.

Her blood would not bring them back.

Her wishes and her wants would not bring them back.

But ensuring that no one else left her was as close as she would get. After a deep breath, she opened her eyes. Everything she had done, everything she was about to do, was for Rersa. For her people. For her loved ones.

Maybe someday, her father would thank her for it.

If not, it would only be another cut that never healed. A cut that always bled. And that was not enough for her to wish away the righteousness that stood beside her like a wraith.

She was the heir to the Obsidian Throne. Her father had ruled it for her entire life—more. For thirty years, he had ruled. But that rule was over.

It was time that Elaia took her rightful place on the black stone.

It is time.

"ARE YOU READY, PRINCESS?" Rohan spoke so only she could hear. Behind her, Zahra stood on her left, Xerxes on her right. Sacha and what would be the rest of her council stood behind them.

Elaia only nodded.

Ahead, the towering heavy doors to the Obsidian Quarters began to creak open. The carvings in the stone held all of Rersa's history. Everything was carved on those doors, even the past usurpations of the throne. Maybe one day, hers would be there as well. As the doors opened, the light from the goldstones flickered at the entrance, and Elaia made her way in, Akiro by her side.

Eight, including her father, sat at the great table. Even from afar, her father's cutting glance was cold. His council went silent.

"Elaia, what is the meaning of this?"

In a split second, she realized that everything was about to change. It was easy to manipulate the undercurrents, to manipulate those shadows that slunk by the walls—but face-to-face with him, with the man who raised her, the weight of these decisions threatened to sink her. But she would bear the burden.

"Father." Elaia let her hands rest on the table, keeping them still. "I come to offer one last time."

His gaze went glacial.

"Step down from the throne and name me in your place. Or I will take it from you."

A beat of silence. Her father, the High Shade, stood. "You are foolish, Elaia. A foolish child."

Foolish. Childish. Young. Frivolous. Gods, she hated those words. He flung them at her whenever he could. Whenever he wanted to kick a leg out from under her, he struck the bruise he'd given her.

"Your rule is over, Father. The challenge was raised. Your time is up."

Brome, her father's Shield, stood, his face incredulous and his hand on the hilt of his sword. Elaia whipped out her shadows, sending them across the floor. "Remove your hand, Brome, lest you want to lose it."

"You come here and you threaten the High Shade? You threaten me? On what standing?"

"The standing that I'm the only heir left." She met her father's gaze and watched pain bloom in his eyes. "I am the only heir to the Obsidian Throne—a throne that should've long ago been mine."

"You insinuate I'm the reason for your mother's disappearance? For your sisters?"

She choked down a laugh. "They are dead."

"You don't know that—"

"There is no world in which I do not feel the loss of them. You failed them. You failed to protect them. You are failing to protect Rersa. I won't have it anymore."

Under the light, he looked ever the High Shade. Draped in black and gray and silver, there was jewelry decorating his fingers and hanging from this neck. The tattoos of Rersa covered most of his skin, and his eyes became calculating. "What choice, then, are you offering me, Elaia?"

She placed her hands behind her back, tapping them together, but let a haughty smile form. "You can step down peacefully, or you can accept my challenge and lead us to bloodshed."

Desmond huffed, a scornful sound. "Your mother would be disgraced."

You are your father's daughter. I love you still. She raised a brow. "With you? I agree."

"You don't have the numbers. You'd need four people sitting at *my* table. You'd need a unanimous vote from the governors to raise a challenge. What makes you think you have that?"

Glancing around the room, she made eye contact with five of his seven council members. One by one, they rose. One by one, they moved to stand behind her—the Commander of the Nightguard, the Headmaster, the Treasurer, the Master Healer, and the Arrow. All stood with her.

Anger trickled down her father's face like a veil sliding. Only two stood with him. Two she would easily replace. "What have you done?"

"If you were the High Shade you were supposed to be, you would've seen this. You would've noticed. The father that raised me would have known," Elaia said, her lip curling. She slid the folder over the table. "All seven governors have given their signature to support my challenge." She watched with a twisted satisfaction as his eyes widened upon each document. "Are you going to risk it?"

"You should have waited. I have told you—"

"I am ready. You have failed to see it." She tipped her chin. After a second of holding his gaze, she strode forward, the lights flickering over her shoulders. "You'll risk dividing your country, you'll risk bloodshed over my claim, and yet you think *I* am not ready? You are delaying the truth that your time has come to an end."

All eyes were on her. It was a heady type of power having every eye on her.

She also felt the suffocating pressure of it.

"Call a forum. Name me heir. Or accept my challenge and deal with the repercussions," she said. Her heart pounded. Her shadows threatened to erupt. Still, she would not falter.

Her father remained silent. Fine.

With that, she spun, her gown swishing over the floor, and left, leaving her father and hopefully, eventually, the past behind.

He would see that she was making a smart choice, a lethal play—he would respect it. He had to. Right?

As the doors began to close, she spared one final glance in his direction. Those eyes that had once viewed her as something precious, eyes that had once seemed larger than life when he looked at her, had gone vacant and cold.

Didn't he know he made her this way?

Elaia raised her head, returning his gaze with resolution.

Let him deny her challenge. Let him be responsible for the unrest that would ensue. Let him falter when his support weaned. Let the filaments of fear creep into his bloodstream. Let him suffer, as she had. Because she would rise.

"Stop," he called, halting the doors in their place. Desmond narrowed his eyes. The crown he rarely wore sat heavy atop his head. "I accept your challenge. In two days' time, I will meet you atop the canyon, and we will see who the shadows favor."

A slow smile spread across her lips. "I'll meet you in the shadows, Father."

Chapter 44

In Life or In Death

Elaia laid on the canyons rim, staring at the night sky. Stars blinked in and out. Clouds passed across the sky and shadowed the moon. Akiro was steady underneath her, his slow inhales forcing their bodies to rise and fall in sync.

Out here, she felt like a little girl again, holding Nomara's hand with her left and Rayn and Shaye beside her. Most altars to Senka were built in the open air with access to the sky, and often, her mother brought them out here to tell stories, to teach them to make their own altars.

In the quiet, for a moment, it was like they were beside her again. Under the light of the moon, she felt the presence of their ghosts by her side. Closing her eyes, she let herself believe it. Believe that Rayn was resting her head on her shoulders, that Shaye was trying to stay awake, and her mother was whispering tales into the darkness.

A rumble from Akiro forced her back to reality. Up here, the canyons looked like nothing more than a scratch across the world, the depths of them unseen. Up here, it felt like she was on another world, in a different plane of existence.

At the crack of a pebble, she spun, going quickly for the blade on her thigh. Instead, Zahra appeared in the dark.

"I thought you might be up here," she said, approaching Elaia and taking a seat beside her. Akiro grumbled happily, stretching his large body out to encompass both of them. Elaia turned her eyes to the horizon, scared of what she might see in Zahra's eyes up close. "How are you feeling?"

"I'm fine, Zahra."

"That isn't what I asked."

She sighed. "I feel like you're all waiting for me to realize I'm being rash. Waiting for me to realize I'm being foolish. When I'm not." Finally, she turned to look at Zahra. "There have been quakes almost every week since the Elders were killed. Large swells upon the shores. Calls in the night from shadow hounds. And a Witch hunt is poised to begin," she said, the note, as always, sitting in her pocket—a deal she could not let them see. "My father will not lead us through it. He would let us fall to it. He is weakened by his grief, given into it. He has grown smaller in front of my eyes. I know grief is heavy, but I've been running his country. I've been bearing the burden of decisions. Not him. And yet, he is who they listen to when he makes careless orders. We will not survive with him on the throne. And he won't give it up," Elaia said, breathless. "So, I'm taking it. Of that, I am sure."

Zahra stayed quiet, cupping Elaia's chin, brushing over her jawline with a gentle touch. Warmth from the light emitted from her fingertips.

"I'm not worried for that, Elaia. You're a smart woman. I'm only worried that you're forgetting yourself. I'm worried that anger fuels you." Zahra sighed. "I'm worried that you are going to lose yourself in the process."

Did no one understand? Did no one get that she was *always* angry? She had been angry every single day for three years. For three years, her sadness and her rage fought for dominance within her. And still, she came out on top.

As for losing herself...well, sometimes she wondered if she had ever *truly* known herself. Because it wasn't possible to lose something you never had.

"You should stop worrying. It doesn't do you any good," she murmured, staring up at the moon.

"I'm allowed," Zahra said, grabbing her attention. "I'm allowed to worry about you, Elaia. You don't get to tell me that I can't."

"That's not what—"

She continued, her long brown hair fanning behind her as her cheeks flushed with anger. "Well, *this* is what I meant. You are so quick to assume the role you think you need to take on. The protector. The one responsible. You aren't responsible for me."

Elaia shook her head, the heavy feeling tightening in her chest. "It's my job to protect you."

"No. It isn't. That's what you've been made to think. By your father, by the loss of your mother and sisters. By the role you were born into. But that is *not* your job when it comes to me." Zahra tucked a short strand of hair behind Elaia's ear. "It is your job as my friend, as my love, as *my* Elaia, to listen to me. To care for me. I don't need you to protect me. No one can ever be fully safe; that's not how life works," Zahra said, tone softening. "I need you to love me, even with the fear that you might lose me."

A tiny speck of light bloomed in Zahra's palms, her eyes wet with unshed tears. There was something heavy stuck in her throat, something sharp digging a hole in her chest until she felt hollow.

"Can you do that?"

The question hung between them, a line drawn, and Elaia didn't know where she stood. She felt more that she was hanging off the edge of the cliff, and either answer would send her crashing to the bottom.

"I think...I'm going to give you space to figure that out," Zahra said, her words wet with the tears Elaia knew she was holding back. When she looked at her, there were streak marks on her cheeks.

Her heart tore, and her hands shook. "Zahra, don't."

She only shook her head and leaned forward, pressing a salty kiss against Elaia's lips. No more than a gentle touch, a soft pressure. A million things unsaid within. In the dark, she intertwined their fingers.

"I will stand beside you always, Elaia. I will be by your side at the challenge, anywhere you go, if you wish me to be there. But I need you to ask yourself if you can love me that way."

"What about what I need? Love means protecting. The people I love will always, *always* receive my protection."

"Of course." Zahra squeezed her hand. "But do your needs eclipse mine? Do your needs eclipse what I want?" Moonlight danced on her cheekbones. "Would you lock me away if it meant you could keep me safe, Elaia?"

A brief hesitation was all it took.

"I love you. I have loved you every day since I met you. When we used to come out here, the light of sunset or sunrise would catch your eyes, and they would shine. You would let yourself smile freely. I think about that often, the girls we were. How free you used to be." Zahra ran her thumb over Elaia's cheekbones and down her nose, resting on her lips. "I wish you could let yourself be free again."

The silence was cutting. Zahra pressed another kiss to her lips before standing and disappearing back into the darkness of the city.

Elaia did nothing but watch as she took the light with her.

"I know you're there, Xerxes. What do you want?" Her voice ricocheted in the empty stables—only the horses, and now the Fire Elemental, to join her.

"Can't sleep, Princess?"

"I haven't tried." She tossed him a look. "Haven't you heard? I'm overbearing and too protective."

He gave her a sly smile. "Actually, I have. I overheard earlier."

Of course, he did. She breathed out her annoyance. Varistone used to belong to her, and now, there were lurkers in every corner.

She rolled her eyes, running her hand over the mare's neck. "And you're sharing that with me? Most people keep that to themselves."

Xerxes moved closer, resting his arms on the barn door, the horse within stretching out his nose.

He struck her with a steady gaze. "Love is a funny thing. Everybody wants it, though many claim they don't. And we all have different meanings of it. We all want different versions of it," he said, swallowing. Something she hadn't seen before flickered over his features as he let his eyes fall closed. Resignation? Loneliness? Or nothing more than sadness? "And none of them are ever good enough."

A sharp pain struck her chest. Recently, looking at him was akin to looking in a mirror. "What kind of love do you want, Xerxes?"

His eyes met hers, and it felt like the world stopped. Heat flushed her skin. Why did she like it? When he looked at her like that? He wasn't Zahra, and yet, she couldn't deny the spark that so often came to life between them.

"I would take any kind."

For all that was not perfect about her life, for all that she had suffered, she had known love. Love in varying degrees, good and bad. But she'd known it. She had it. From her mother. From Zahra. From Rohan. Even in his twisted ways, her father. A life without any? She could not...imagine.

"I hope you find it someday."

Xerxes smiled softly. "Me, too, Princess."

Turning away, she grabbed a flat brush and began running it over the mare's coat in repetitive motions. He didn't leave, but he didn't say anything further. They simply existed in the same space.

"What do you think? Do you think what Zahra said was

true?" Her voice had become shaky. Gods, what was she doing asking him? "Never mind."

"You both spoke what's true. What's true for her isn't necessarily what's true for you." The curls on his head bounced as he adjusted, his brown leathers molded to his skin. "You love her, but you're fearful—"

"I'm not afraid," she said, narrowing her eyes.

Xerxes scoffed. "Yes, you are. You're afraid of losing her, of losing people. Of losing control." He moved closer, holding out his hand to the mare now opposite her. "Fear is inevitable. You can't escape it, and believing you're above it is ignorant. You aren't ignorant, Princess. I think...fear is the smoke after a fire. No less dangerous than the flames. It steals your life away quietly, poisoning you until there is nothing left."

She studied the ground, unable to look him in the eye.

"Fear is always there, no matter how much you wish it weren't. You can learn to befriend it. You can learn to face it, but it will always find you. You love her, and there is fear in that. But I imagine she feels the same. You're both scared to lose each other but in different ways. Besides, fear isn't all bad. It only means you have something to lose."

"I didn't know you were a scholar," she said, unable to stop the bite. Her skin felt freshly burned, like any touch would become a searing pain.

A small laugh escaped him. "When you go without something, you tend to obsess over it."

She hated this version of him. He was too smart, too good at reading her. "What do you fear?"

His smile fell in an instant, and he took a step back. The world began to spin again, the air pulling tight. "I don't fear, for I have nothing to lose."

AS THE NIGHT threatened to turn to morning, Elaia shook off the covers since sleep was avoiding her. Akiro had curled his body around her, a soft snore coming from his snout, but the bed was empty without Zahra. Letting her head fall forward, she pressed her palms against her eyes. *What am I doing?* Crawling out of bed, she wrapped her black robe around her shoulders and padded through the dark.

The halls of Varistone were often cold, especially in the late days of summer before the heating flames were lit, and goosebumps danced on her skin. She entered the chambers quietly, stalking past the low burning fire in the hearth and straight to the bedroom. Every time she looked at Zahra, that choking sensation of fear snuck in. It was up to her to decide if it was enough, but that was not a decision she needed to make tonight.

Crawling in, she burrowed into the warmth that seemed to emit from Zahra at all times. Instantly, her arms wrapped around Elaia, her hand burrowing into her hair.

Neither of them spoke. Elaia fit herself into her spot as she always did, and Zahra curled around her back with the weight of her arm a steady comfort. She swallowed, finding Zahra's hand and twining their fingers together in front of her chest, holding it tight to where her heart beat behind her ribs.

For now, it would be enough. She had no answer for Zahra. Whether that was good or bad...it was the truth. Lying would get her nowhere, but she wasn't going to lie to herself either.

Fingers traced up her arm in the dark, leaving the warmest sensation that Elaia had ever known behind until they pressed beneath her ear, only to be replaced by Zahra's lips. In sync, they both exhaled, as if the touch was all either of them needed. She loved these kisses—the ones done in the shadows, in the haze of sleep, because the need was too strong.

Elaia loved her. She needed her. But fear was a powerful thing —a sword made of the strongest metal. There was a choice to be made. One path of fear with two different outcomes.

She just didn't know which was worse.

The fear of loving someone in life. A version of them she could not have.

Or the fear of loving someone in death.

CHAPTER 45

MAYBE ONE DAY

ONE BY ONE, THE MESSENGER BIRDS BEGAN TO ARRIVE. Only those traveling from the furthest parts of the country had left. A feathery ice-blue bird from Ceron. A slick cream and golden bird from Azias. The strange spotted bird from Syris. Nova had watched the masters greet them atop Willowgrove amongst the clouds, a chill imbedded in her spine when she saw the off-putting bird of her homeland.

And yet, she stared at the dress hanging off her wooden door —a dress of deep dark red in layers of silk and lace. There was a note attached in perfect handwriting that read, *In case you decide to stay.* The aching in her chest was different, both sorrowful and joyous. He wanted her to stay.

A part of her that she had quieted, forced into submission, wanted to stay.

But the time had come. Other messenger birds were predicted to arrive today. The earliest guests to arrive tomorrow, as the coronation, subsequent celebrations, and official council were scheduled for the following days. Tomorrow, she would be leaving under the cover of darkness. Outside her window, the suns had risen, the early light creeping into the sky, and within, her room was tidy. The books from the Emerald Library were stacked neatly, her notes tucked away in a small bag hidden under her bed. It was stuffed with food that would last her and a small collection of sharp objects she'd found within Willowgrove.

The birds had her on edge. Her skin felt tight, her mind ragged. Gods, she wanted to plant her feet and stake her claim. Something about this place and...Killian had made her feel welcome. Like a person, not a pawn. But like other places, she did not belong here.

You are still here now.

The casual gown billowed in green around her legs as she exited her chambers and strode down the hall toward the prince's room. She knocked, and his voice rang out, instructing her to enter.

Oh. *Oh.* Killian was shirtless—*more* than shirtless. Only tight shorts covered his body, stopping mid-thigh. Practically every inch of him was visible—the cut of the muscles in his arms and legs and the side of his torso, every place the ink of his tattoos were melded into his skin. A piece of measuring fabric was placed in various places over him, an attendant marking what they saw.

"I can come back," she said, making *sure* to meet his eyes.

But they were alight, his smile tugging at the sides and drawing wrinkles into his cheeks. Inwardly, her blood warmed, her skin growing hot. She swore the air warmed, her soul settling.

"No need. We're finishing up here. Thank you," Killian said to the attendant, who quickly dipped his head and made his exit. Sunlight danced over his skin as he stalked toward her. Nova stood her ground despite the incessant pounding of her heart. "Good morning, Nova."

They were inches apart. She wanted so badly to reach out and touch him. The only person she'd ever *wanted* to touch. Dark hair was dusted over his arms and torso, barely there but visible in the light. Tiny scars of white over his skin and lean muscle rippling with every movement. She wanted to run her fingers over every inch. To memorize it. To feel it. Just to say she had.

"It's my last one," she said, a breathless note to her words. His smile faltered for just a second. "Would you have breakfast with me?"

The gentle teasing smile grew into something more, taking up his whole face. "Of course. I have something in mind if you're up for it? I thought you may want to go for a ride."

She couldn't stop the smile from tugging at her own lips. "I would like that."

"Good." He stepped back, putting some space between them, and suddenly, she could breathe again. His arms stretched high as he slipped a loose shirt on, the muscles under his skin stretching as he did. The collar dipped low, leaving some of his skin exposed. It was work to drag her eyes away. "See something of interest, Nova?"

She rolled her eyes despite the heat on her cheeks. "Nothing exceptional."

"What a shame. I can't say the same," Killian said, his eyes never leaving her.

The feeling that bloomed was hazy and warm, heat dancing over her skin. "Let's go, Prince."

HOURS LATER, after letting Rouge and Ghost lead them from the stable tunnels built long ago with Willowgrove to the mountains, they sat in a small cove high above the lake. From this altitude, it was minuscule. While Nalādin had the title of the sentient forest, even here, high in the tall trees on the mountains, away from most of the kingdoms inhabitants, the world felt alive.

Under the swaying of the trees and wind curving along the peaks, there was the light tinkling laughter of the sprites, low growls of mountain cats, most likely descended from the Samara, and the cawing of various birds as they flew through the sky.

He had packed pastries and cuts of cheese and meats, placing them on a small plate between them. "When you said something about Dray, what did you mean?"

She rested her arms on her knees, watching the clouds move slowly. "Something feels dark. When I reach out to someone's mind, I'm usually met with a wall, a guard of some sort. But since the *soul* has come into play, I've been seeing these threads. It's complicated, and I don't quite understand it fully myself, but Dray's are heavy. And they strike out." Nova turned to look at the prince. "I don't know him, but you do. And what I feel does not feel like the person you've described to me," she said quietly. But she knew he would listen.

"Thank you for telling me. I'll keep an eye on him, maybe take him to Asha to ensure nothing is wrong." He gave her a smile. "He's not so bad."

She snorted. "To you. To his friends and his people. All I was to him was a threat." After a moment of silence, she asked, "Have you told them of our deal? Will they let me leave?"

"Would you let that stop you?"

"No." She shrugged, her teeth tugging at her lip. "It wouldn't."

Killian let out a soft laugh. "I didn't think so. But no. They don't know. There are tunnels that are unprotected, old and mostly useless. I'll give you a small map." His eyes raked over her, warming her as they went. "Where will you go?"

"The Witchlands."

He nodded, the heat from his eyes that of the suns. "I figured as much."

"I don't know what I'll find—if I'll find anything," she said, the prophecies and riddles repeating in her head even now. "But maybe something about..." *Who I am.*

"About you." He had a knack for reading her mind, even when she didn't share. "You should. You deserve it—the chance to discover who you want to be." Within, a sadness settled on his threads.

Instead of speaking, she asked, *Will you miss me, Prince?* The words sank into the forest of his mind.

His lips tugged, and his eyes sparked. A gentle tension made the air come alive. "I will." She let her curls fall over her face, shielding her warm cheeks. Killian's vines, only barely covering his finger, brushed against her skin. With a steady hand, he tipped her chin up. "It looks like I won't be the only one."

Around them, the creatures of the woods appeared. Though they barely stepped past the forest line, she saw forest sprites dancing along the branches and the leaves, birds with colorful wings, a set of feline green eyes, all peering out at the two of them. And in the dark of the forest behind them, she swore the blurred shapes of the women below appeared, watching her as nothing more than shadows under the suns, only hours away from eclipse.

"Thank you for sharing what you did with me. Because of you, we can at least prepare for what might come, whatever the Vahls may have planned," he said, drawing her attention again.

"It was the very least I could do." She was torn. She wanted to spill everything, to tell him *everything*, but what good would it do? More riddles would not reveal the Vahls intentions. The truth about herself would only shatter what lay between them, and none of it would make her stay. "Thank you for everything, Killian. For your kindness and your friendship."

"You say friendship like it might sting you." He laughed, his blood pumping.

In some ways, what he said was true. Would opening up, even a little, come back to hurt her like everything else did? "It's still foreign to me."

His eyes softened. "I know. For that, I'm sorry. I wish it wasn't."

"Don't be sorry, you showed me it doesn't always bite," she said, resting her head in her palm, eyes focused on him. More words hung off the tip of her tongue, and she forced away the hesitation. "Thank you for seeing me as more than a Witch."

The vines he controlled wrapped loosely around her wrist and his, holding them at the same time. "You are much more than that."

"You're the first to see me as anything else."

She couldn't help but wonder if he would still feel the same if the rest had come to light. If she told him about the blood she'd spilled, would he still look beyond? Or would he see a monster like everyone else? Like she did.

The tightening of the vine calmed the thoughts. "I hope you find what you're looking for out there. I hope one day you return."

Nova let her eyes trace his face, committing it to memory. "Maybe one day."

THE SMALL BAG was packed tightly, full of everything she could think of. Scrawling notes, a poorly copied map from the prince, and as many clothes as she could manage. Everything else would be left behind. Taking one last look at the dress, she tucked the note in her pocket, thumbing the prince's handwriting before shutting it behind closet doors she would never open again.

Outside, the moon was sharp and curved, illuminating only the peaks of the mountains. It was time to go. Nova forced herself to move, once again knocking at Killian's door. His heartbeat was steady in her palms as she recounted its beat until he appeared in the doorway.

Sleep was heavy on his face, but his eyes were red. He had not slept at all. In the dark, his eyes were endless. "You're leaving?" he asked, and she only nodded. "Not that you need my advice, but be careful. Follow the map, and stay the path. The forest will guide you."

A coy yet sad smile formed on her lips. "Thank you, Killian. You'll make a good king, deserving of the crown." The look he gave was weighted. "The other night, you called me something. A—"

"A *ravn*." His eyes were locked on her. "An old language word for raven. There's a myth here in Eisera of the raven. No one knows whether it's true or not, but there was once a young prince who had lost everyone, and Eisera was at war within itself. He had no one. No family, no council. Nothing. But there was the raven, who would appear every night without fail on his window sill. They said in the dark, the raven would tell him the plans of the war, what battles were still to come. And the raven kept his secrets, became his friend. The prince became a king, and the raven never left him."

She hated that the story made her heart tug and pulse behind her ribs, practically begging her to stay. The similarities were painful. He was a prince about to become king. The difference was, she was leaving, when the raven would not.

"Thank you," she said, her voice thick. "Thank you for telling me that."

"One second." He stepped back into the dark of his room, reappearing with two flowers in his hand—a moonflower and one of violet and white with many leaves. "A dahlia."

She took them in her palm, his fingers brushing against her skin. No one had ever given her flowers before. The petals were soft against her skin but not as soft as Killian's touch. "Will you think of me?"

His eyes widened. His heart picked up pace. "Often, I think."

Nova looked down at the petals, her stomach alight with butterflies. *And I, of you, Prince.*

He smiled at her voice in his head. Before thinking better of it, she rose to her tip toes, one hand landing on his chest to steady herself, and placed a soft kiss on Killian's cheek. She lingered long enough to feel the warmth spread in response and then pulled away.

Goodbye, Killian.

And into the dark she went.

CHAPTER 46

BATTLE OF SHADOWS

MUCH LIKE EVERYTHING IN RERSA, THE CHALLENGE was rooted in ritualist history.

It took part in a section of the Canyons of Zylla, only accessible by tunnels within or directly above. A formidable place, where the first High Shade of Rersa settled, until they eventually moved. One of the many stories about the formation of Rersa was that the group, led by the first High Shade, followed only the light of the moon or the glowworms of the canyons. Here, in this clearing, the moon shone directly down and glowworms lined the walls, blinking like touchable stars.

Elaia had studied and re-studied the rituals, committed them to memory along with the stories of the previous eight challenges. But nothing could've prepared her for it. Instead of her council, seven members of the *Izion* guard, a special faction of the Nightguard that took a vow of silence, surrounded her. Everyone else would be seated upon the groves of the canyon, as low as the ground and as high as the canyon's rim. The tunnels were dark, and Akiro's fur against her skin was the only thing that felt real, reminding her that she was, too.

She would've given anything to have Zahra or Rohan here.

Gods, even Xerxes would've been a distraction. *No. I chose this. I am ready for this.*

Outside in the clearing, her people were silent, as was custom. To other kingdoms, the silence might be deafening, but here in the darkness, the silence was their friend. Ahead, the light of the moon crept into the tunnel. The guards peeled off one by one to either side, leaving Elaia to stand front and center. Her skin prickled as every eye lining the canyon seats struck her skin.

She only looked ahead. Her father stood across from her, only the pebbly canyon floor separating them, and stared at her with cold, empty eyes. Her choices were the reason they were here, but it was a thorn in her skin to have him look at her like that. In his hand, there was a double-edged spear of obsidian, though she knew under the light, it would shimmer green. She knew that weapon almost as well as he did. Desmond spun the spear as if it was merely an extension of him, and against her thigh was one stiletto blade.

The challenge allowed one weapon and the magic you had or didn't. Today, it would be a battle of shadows.

Colt, the Commander of the Nightguard, stood from the edge of the clearing, draped in robes of black. "You both understand the rules? No speaking. This ends in concession or in death."

They nodded. Desmond's eyes lingered on her, and she sneered. But the challenge demanded silence of her, too, so a measly nod it was. "Today, under the light of the moon, you all witness the ninth challenge of the Obsidian Throne. May Senka guide you. May the shadows reveal the master."

As the Commander settled back into his seat, heavy darkness filled the air—Desmond's shadows. Typical. They always thought they could choke her out, make her drown in the dark. Big and brute. She preferred precision.

Here we go, Elaia sighed, crouching. *Things will never be the same.* She let the dark envelop her, hoping it would chase away the mourning that flowed through her blood like a virus. She'd done this. She hadn't expected to feel so damn sad about it.

Inhaling, she stood, curling her fingers and calling the shadows to her until the clearing came into view and daggers of black levitated in the air. But her father had moved quickly, only a few feet away. Elaia commanded each one. Shot after shot. At his footsteps. At his arms. At his throat. She curled them around his neck, moving her body like a branch in the breeze. But Desmond, as strong as he was, was swift. A blast of compact shadow came flying at her, crawling over the ground as it dissipated, threatening to grab her.

They blinded her. Oh, she wanted to laugh. He'd trained her in the darkness—forced her to *become* darkness—and yet, maybe he did not know her at all. She felt the quiet whoosh of his spear on her left and then right. She rolled and spun, landing on her feet. And her shadows spoke to her.

Behind. Right. Center. Right.

Elaia avoided each strike, dancing over the ground like she was made to.

He was fighting angry, letting his rage get the best of him. Elaia began to defend, striking with lithe, thin shadows to disrupt him, one after the other in quick succession.

She was close enough to feel the air move with his spear, but as she reached out for it, the shadows cleared from her eyes and snuck around her throat. Desmond's eyes gleamed in a way she'd never seen before as he commanded them to tighten. Air became scarce, her skin prickling as panic threatened to creep in, pain sparking as he pushed her back with his spear across her chest. *In and out. In and out.*

Far easier said than done, but Elaia did it. Swallowed little gulps of air with every step until her back hit the wall. Desmond pushed the spear into her chest, and she curled her hands around it until her nails dug into her palm. In seconds, it replaced the shadows at her throat and pressed down heavily. He snarled, and she let her hands fall to the side, let her breathing turn shallow.

When instead of giving in, she found her blade and unsheathed it, striking at his side without remorse.

The little girl is all grown up, Father.

Pain flashed in his eyes as she cut his side. He pulled back, winding up, but it was enough. Elaia slipped down just as the spear crashed against the canyon and fired multiple shadow blades in his direction. Desmond spun the spear swiftly, defending almost every one.

But she did not let up.

She became a shadow herself. An extension of the darkness. She let her rage out in punches, small but sharp shadows waiting to strike. She let it leak into the air until she was rage. Not overpowered, not weakening under its pull—no. Elaia *was* rage.

It did not master her. She was *its* master.

She flew through the air in sweeping arcs, avoiding her father's hits and heavy punches of darkness. Some landed their intended shots, and she was sure bruises would decorate her skin tomorrow, but she did not stop. It could've been seconds or minutes or hours. Sweat dripped off both of them. Their shadows weaned and replenished. They traded blows with his spear and a strike of her blade when the shadows retreated. And danced in the dark when they returned.

He had taught her everything. Forced her to avoid his blows in long halls of canyon rock and sit in rooms with water dripping to learn patience. Forced her to withstand the heavy pressure of controlled darkness and expectations and how to wield shadows to her every whim.

He'd taught her everything, and she had learned. Time and grief sharpened the weapon he made her become. Elaia had been his pride and joy and also his misery. She had been the recipient of his love and the carrier of his anger. She was everything and nothing. A blade now, sharper than the one who forged it. And he not been prepared to defend against it. Against her.

With every shot of darkness, she moved closer, shadows answering her call and spinning to strike.

Desmond had nowhere to go. His back was against the wall as hers had been. Fighting past the exhaustion and the weight of the consequences and the eyes on her from above, the shadows were hers, as would be the throne. They came from the canyon crevices and from the rocky floor until he was pinned to the wall, his spear useless.

But even so, she was precise. Only five cuts lanced his skin. Only drips of blood landed on the ground. Her shadows shimmered in the air as she approached with her blade in her hand. Blood seeped from a cut on her forearm, and her knee was throbbing from a heavy hit. But she stood tall.

Elaia pressed her blade against his throat, a blade of shadow dancing at his temple. The challenge did not require death, though some gave it. But he was still her father. And part of this was to protect him. *If* he conceded.

Desmond met her eyes, and the pressing darkness around them fell. A concession. And all around, the people of Rersa saw her.

They saw *her*.

The new High Shade of Rersa.

CHAPTER 47

STATUES DON'T SMILE

ELAIA LET THE BLACK, SILVER-TIPPED WING BIRD GO, its wings spreading into the sky with a message curled in its talons. The *Nomara* awaited her on the shores only feet away.

The last time Elaia had been to Eisera, she was only a daughter. A princess. Now, she was High Shade.

Varistone had been silent since the Challenge, as was custom —a mourning of sorts. Only whispered words shared in her chambers or the council room. Her father would present her to the other Kingdoms in Eisera. Or he was supposed to. Elaia couldn't decide whether he would or not. In the day since, she'd replaced two members of his council that would not stand with her. And now, they belonged to her. They answered to *her*.

She needed that. After the coronation, she needed to know that those on her council were loyal to her and to Rersa. That they would not falter under the weight of change. Things, of her making or of others, were going to change soon. A darkness was swirling under the surface, waiting for its chance to strike.

The clearing of a throat drew her attention, and Elaia turned to find Zahra. Her arms were held in front of her, an awkward tension on her shoulders.

She approached, her fingers finding the material of Zahra's dress. "Are you ready?"

"Are you sure we should be going? That it's smart to leave?"

"The danger was here, not there. This is only an interruption, but we need to show them we're united. That we, that Rersa, stands strong."

Frustration filled Zahra's eyes. "What danger, Elaia? What danger do you speak of that you haven't told me?"

So much. There was so much she had not shared, secrets she had kept close to her chest.

A darkness hiding on the wings of a dove, waiting to strike. A silent threat held to her throat at the hands of those she'd made promises to. Maybe it was superstitious, but speaking them out loud would give them power. There was still a small chance none of it would come to fruition.

"I can tell you later," Elaia murmured, pushing closer, desperate to feel Zahra's warm skin and gentle touch. She needed to confirm that she still cared for her. "But we need to go."

But Zahra stepped back, the distance fracturing Elaia's heart. "If you can't share what you're keeping from me, then I can't do this anymore."

"Can't do what exactly?" Elaia swallowed, her words cold. "We're betrothed, Zahra."

Tears lined Zahra's eyes. "I don't know how to hold on to this version of you, this person who keeps secrets from me. Who keeps me at arm's length." Sorrow may as well have been a rain cloud between them. It was bleeding out of both of them. "When we return, who will we return as? Will I be someone you confide in? Someone you treat with respect? Will you be coming back as my Elaia or the High Shade?"

"Why can't I be both?" Was she so different from one version to another? Did Zahra see something she couldn't? Or did Zahra refuse to see what she didn't want to?

"That's not a question I can answer." She sighed, her fingers clutching her dress. "But if you can't treat me as an equal, as your love and as the person who's supposed to stand by your side, not be pushed to it, than I can't do this."

Everything I've done has been for her, for them. And this is what she thinks? Her stomach turned.

Why couldn't Zahra comprehend that Elaia could not lose anyone else? If that meant keeping her in the dark, to keep her from seeing what Elaia feared, then that was what she had to do. Zahra should've known, should've trusted her.

This time, Elaia stepped back, putting more space between them. "I guess we'll find out." The waves crashed angrily against the shore, similar to what her heart was doing in her chest. "I'll have a separate quarter made for you on the ship."

She moved to the side, giving room for Zahra. The scent of smoke and honey infiltrated her senses as Zahra walked by. They were going together but they felt miles apart.

There was a chasm between them, as if they were standing on two separate cliffs with only jagged rocks to meet them should they fail. She wanted to chase after her, to run up and grab her hand and board the ship together. But her pride would not let her.

As she boarded the deck, Zahra looked back. Even from a distance, Elaia could see the tear streaks on her cheeks. No one moved, no one shouted an apology. There was only a look.

Elaia waited until Zahra was out of view before she boarded herself.

At the dock, Xerxes and Rohan waited for her, Akiro sitting on his haunches beside them. She counted her steps by seven, keeping a certain rhythm. And then, they were gone, the *Nomara* departing Rersa. In seconds, the shore was distant on the horizon. Above, the suns were lowering in the sky, the eclipse growing closer by the day, the rays becoming red and orange and lighting up the sky.

Xerxes approached the railing, his gaze heavy. "Stop looking at me like that, Xerxes."

"Like what?"

She slanted her eyes toward him, nails tapping the railing. "Like I'm going to shatter or toss myself overboard."

He snorted, resting his forearms over the edge. "You wouldn't do that. If anything, you look like you're trying to make yourself impenetrable. A statue. Not glass."

Her nails found Akiro's head, scratching the spot between his ears he liked. Every time Xerxes revealed something about her that she didn't want uncovered, she felt weak. Vulnerable.

And she hated it. "And what if I push you over instead?"

Xerxes laughed, *really* laughed, and the sound threatened to make her smile. "Now that sounds more like it."

Even Akiro gave a playful bark from her side, brushing himself against Xerxes's leg.

"You're a pain."

"You chose me for your council. This is what you get."

"Great," she said, sarcasm dripping off her tongue, her lips curling at the sides. "I see we have a long, lovely future ahead of us."

He held a hand to his chest. "Is that—is that a *smile*, Princess? Statues don't smile."

"Enough." Elaia sent her shadows to cover his eyes. Dumb. All that was left was his smile and the dimple in his cheek.

"The dark doesn't scare me, Elaia," Xerxes said, voice low, curling around her name like early flames from a fire. She was thankful his eyes were covered. So he couldn't see the heat on her cheeks.

For now, the reprieve that he gave her was nice. The relief of pressure on her chest was welcome—she could breathe for a moment. What waited ahead would be a darkness she'd never walked through. Navigating a throne without her father backing her. Navigating a world that was ever changing and only looked to change more. She had made her alliances. Staked her claim.

She only hoped it would be enough.

It had to be.

CHAPTER 48

EASTERN ALLIANCE

THE GUEST QUARTERS IN EISERA WERE AS BEAUTIFUL AS the rest of the country, as to be expected. But the wood and stone detail were not what had Elaia's attention. Instead, the note resting on the chest at the foot of her bed was.

Scrawled in dark, leeching ink was a note signed by the Vahls. *The shadows remain—we will meet soon.*

Gods, she *hated* them. They were like parasites—existing quietly until they needed to feed. But Elaia had done what she had to do. Rersa and her people and her family would not be their food, even if it meant aiding them on their path for destruction.

The Vahls reached out shortly after the disappearance of Rayn and Nomara to offer their condolences, ensuring that should any information cross their paths, they would share it with her. Everyone knew the Vahls had networks the rest of Valora could never fully understand. Those with the power to infiltrate minds were hard to sniff out, and besides, it often came in handy—to know what was being done behind closed doors throughout the world.

They had sprung on Elaia when she was weak without her father's knowing, telling her that others were disappearing at random. That they had reason to believe those killed with tears of blood and these disappearances were connected. That the Witches had returned. And that those who agreed to help them would be under their protection should violence strike.

So, Elaia agreed to work with them, officially calling to order the Eastern Alliance, an alliance formed long ago after the War of the Athera. As peace fell over Valora, the alliance became more of an ideal—something that existed but was not sealed into oath. It mostly ensured trade and information was shared between Azias, Rersa, and Syris. Once, Lazora had been a part of it, but the Light Naturalists turned inward and withdrew, keeping to themselves. By signing into the agreement, Elaia had ensured Rersa's safety— as long as they cooperated with the Vahls and the Farrs.

Because the Vahls believed they could stop it—stop the Witches—if they had access to all the Aether points of Valora, including the Canyon of Evha.

The issue was that the countries home to the other Aether points had denied the Vahls' request. And the Elders, who could issue orders ahead of those leaders, denied the Vahls, too—the Elders, who were now conveniently dead.

So, Elaia had done as they asked—arrived on the shores of the Elderlands early to lead the Witch to the shores and ensure she was delivered to the coast of Eisera. She'd sent members of the Nightguard to both Syris and Azias in return for promises of safety.

All without anyone knowing.

Until now.

She would be meeting with them shortly, alongside Rohan and Xerxes. Whatever they had planned, Rersa would be safe. No matter what. No matter the cost.

Rohan and Xerxes stood outside her door. The latter now bore the emblem of Rersa with a small seal pinned to the linen he wore. Next to Rohan, who stood at attention at all times, the Fire Elemental looked bored. Though that was to be expected, she supposed. They had not asked for each other in their lives, but now, the deals had been signed, and this was what life would be.

Zahra remained locked in the study of their room that she had turned into her own sanctuary. She'd tried to talk to Zahra before leaving, but she'd been met with hostile silence.

It stung, but her pain could wait. Akiro remained asleep on her bed, tired after the quick and tumultuous travel over the seas. The mechanisms that allowed them faster travel were time saving, but they could be rough on the body.

"You know the coronation isn't until tomorrow, right?" Xerxes broke the silence first, and Elaia only rolled her eyes.

"Do you have somewhere else to be?" She began walking toward the Vahls' quarters, down the intricate stone corridor and past the windows, where the moon shone from above the mountains.

"I could be sleeping, as you should be."

Elaia looked back, only to see Rohan scrunch his nose, the only sign of his annoyance. "You'll have time to sleep. But secrets don't share themselves; you have to be awake to hear them." The two men shared a brief look before she spun, facing forward again.

They entered a bridge of sorts that curved outward over the lower levels of the castle and the city below, decorated with open arches and flowers that grew off the vine. There was a muted sound of the waterfall that led into the lake on the ground far below and the wind that curved and decorated her skin with goosebumps. Guards stood only at the entrances of the bridge and at various tunnels within the castle, though Elaia was sure that the Slaters had other methods of ensuring safety. The earth was a funny thing. Much like the shadows or the sea, it had a way of talking to those that listened.

After a short walk, they appeared at a door similar to Elaia's, where she knocked and was promptly greeted by Vittoria, Killian's betrothed, the prince who, tomorrow, would become King.

"How nice to see you again, Elaia." Vittoria smiled that strange, off-putting smile Elaia hated and stepped back. "Please, come in."

Elaia forced her lips into a smile and dipped her head. "And you, Vittoria."

Behind her stood the Vahls. Instantly, she could feel the light pattering on her mind of their intrusion, and she ensured her defenses were well-fortified. They may be working together but she, by no means, wanted her mind prodded by the likes of them.

"Princess Elaia, welcome," Mireya Vahl said, her voice deep and languid with the accent of Syris. Mikel stood quietly behind her, along with their daughter, Isla.

She squared her shoulders. She'd fought for her title, and she would demand its use. "High Shade now. Thank you."

A look of sharp humor entered Mireya's eyes. "How wonderful."

Behind her, Rohan leaned forward, his voice low as he said, "Elaia, what are we—"

"You must trust me, Rohan," Elaia returned, moving forward into the room and taking a seat beside Vittoria at the table. Along the edges of the room, beside Rohan and Xerxes, stood guards for both the Vahls and Vittoria.

"No need to prod, Mireya. If there is something you need from me, just ask," Elaia said as the sensation pricked against her skull once more.

Despite what she said, she was well aware of the fact that Mireya could likely disregard her barriers if she wanted. Isla let out an off-pitched laugh that echoed in the silence.

"Of course. Habit. Is your father here?"

"He will announce me as the new High Shade tomorrow during the meeting."

Mireya smiled. "Lovely. Shall we discuss?"

"Please. I need to rest before tomorrow," Vittoria said. "Big day and all."

"Indeed," Mikel spoke for the first time as he rose and unveiled a map they'd all seen before—one with every Aether point in Valora marked in red.

There were five known Aether points. The Elderlands, the northern land mass known as the Godlands, the Canyons of Evha in Rersa, the Ambersands in Lazora, and Nalādin. Though it was believed there were others, these were the five whose existence were confirmed.

After this council, the Vahls would have access to all but two.

"During the meeting tomorrow, we will show the others our *discovery*. We will give them a final chance to join us, to allow us access to the Aether points," Mireya said. The discovery was the darkness that had been haunting Elaia. A disease, so to speak, that the Witches controlled and that only the Witches could stop, when in truth, it belonged to the Vahls. "Still, there will be those that deny us."

"You're sure of that?" Elaia asked, running her fingers along the edge of the armchair.

She hated the glimmer in Mireya's eye. "They have denied our wish for access to the Aether thus far. Ignored our further warnings. They are too preoccupied with the Elders, too careless in their hunt for the Witches. And they find us disposable, of that, I'm sure."

With a nod, she leaned back. Even if they did...would the Vahls simply make it so they didn't? That's what they wanted, right? Power and respect. Elaia was confident they would start a war to get it.

The queen paced the room, her steps uneven and off beat, though her movements still appeared fluid. "We will show them, to convince them they need us, to join with us to protect themselves. And then, the Aether point will be ours."

Ours. It was a partnership, sure. They wanted the Nightguard, and Elaia gave it to them. But she wanted nothing to do with the rest. She only wanted a promise that her people would not suffer what the Vahls planned to spread if she cooperated—and she got it. Behind her, the quiet wrath of both Rohan and Xerxes prickled her skin. Another consequence she would bear.

For another hour or so, they continued to drone on about setting up guards at every Aether point, ensuring the safety of the alliance, and plans for the future to reach the Godlands and Lazora, though Elaia mostly droned them out, letting the information filter in. Eventually, the night seemed to come to a natural close, the signs of exhaustion starting to creep in on her shoulders.

"Elaia, wait," Mireya called, forcing her to turn in her tracks. Everyone else departed, including Rohan and Xerxes after a short stare off, leaving her alone with the Vahls.

"Yes, Mireya?"

"You will need to send more members of the guard after the council."

Elaia folded her hands in front of her. "A ship of mine waits off the coast with a unit of soldiers. They will move when we tell them to."

Mireya stepped forward, an off-kilter smile on her face, and her strange ice-blue eyes were sharp. Slowly, she reached out a hand, delicately running her fingers over a strand of Elaia's hair. She wanted to flinch, but she held steady. "I have some news for you," the queen said, a forced sadness to her words.

"What?" Elaia asked, brows furrowing. "What is it?"

Mikel stepped up to stand with them. "We believe we have found your mother and your sister," he said. "Or...at least their bodies."

What? It couldn't be—Elaia knew within herself they were dead. But their bodies? The world spun, nausea heavy in her stomach. Their bodies. Oh, Gods. She covered her mouth, willing the sob not to crack from her chest.

It was a miracle there was anything left of her heart. It had been tattered and torn—thrown across the floor like a shard of glass and shattered into a million pieces. And somehow it still found a way to break again.

Her legs shook, and Mireya guided her into a chair, running her hand up and down her arm. Elaia wanted it to stop, but she couldn't find the words. "Where? When?"

Mikel crouched in front of her. The movement was stilted. "Not long ago. A few weeks? They had washed up on the shore in an old boat. We've taken to preserving them, in case you would like a burial. But we brought you these."

In her hand, he dropped the pendant her mother always wore —a skeletal hand curved around a stone of black, forged to look like shadows cased within. Elaia curled her fingers around it, only to find it cold. And in his other was the plush toy her sister had carried with her since she was a girl—a small canyon creature native to Rersa with big ears and a tiny body. Even as a teenager, Rayn went nowhere without it.

A wail threatened to crawl out, but Elaia clamped her lips. She had known they were dead...but *knowing* they were dead was different.

Mireya wrapped her arm around her, and she hated it. She wanted her mom, not this woman who wanted war. "We think we can find a way for you to talk to them again."

Elaia's head whipped around. "What?"

The queen rubbed her thumb over her cheekbone. "Not for sure. But with the Aether points, we have been studying ways to communicate with those we've lost. You will be the first to know."

She hated that hope bloomed like a flower in the dark, slow and sharp. But it wasn't strong enough to break through the truth. The gentle coos of the Vahls were quiet and grating, but she couldn't stand. She couldn't feel the ground beneath her feet. Elaia covered her mouth, choking back sobs as it reverberated like a bell in her head.

Nomara and Rayn were gone, and she would never see them again.

They were dead. Really, truly dead.

CHAPTER 49

YOU COULD NEVER BE FREE

THE DARKNESS GREETED NOVA LIKE AN OLD FRIEND.

Her path was winding. Tunnels of old were cracked and less ornate the more distance she placed between herself and the castle, and the moon was her only light when she crossed into the forest.

With every step, she knew the Vahls were growing closer.

With every step, her heart ached. Guilt clawed at her gut at leaving Killian to the mercy of the Vahls. *Take your freedom, you fool. You almost lost it once. Do not lose it again.*

Within, her heart was steady, only increasing with effort, but the world was loud. As she passed under willow trees and the watchful eyes of the forest creatures, every heartbeat, every soul, met her skin. It was not her responsibility. The world was not her responsibility. But every beat latched on to her, weighing her down. They pounded in her ears and scratched against her skin.

In the darkness between the tree trunks, dark misty figures swam at the edges of her sight.

Will you save us now, Daughter of the Dead? Daughter of the Dead, will you save us?

They expected everything from her when they had given her nothing? Sent her to a life that gave her nothing but pain? She scoffed. One step after another. One at a time. Just keep moving.

The spirit is dead, unlike the soul. The Daughter of the Dead will make the world whole.

Do not *give them the vials.*

Threads of truth tied, falsities spun.

They will damage the world irrevocably.

It all became deafening. The echoing words of Elders dead and Witches trapped in a world she didn't understand. The guilt eating at her. The fear walking beside her.

A low cry left her lips as the beats became faster and louder. She let her head fall back, tipping her chin to the sky. *Let me go.*

Frustration overflowed as she sliced her palm, letting her blood pool and her power reach out until she could no longer count all the pulses in her palm. The power was thick and heavy and too much for her, but she called for it to stop, nonetheless.

Nova willed them to slow, to steady, to stop *screaming* at her like she was a savior. And they did. Within the forest, beyond what she could see, heartbeats steadied and grew quieter, melding to that slow, rhythmic pulse that came from deep within Valora.

"Thank you," she sighed, letting her blood drip on the ground below. "Thank you."

But the silence allowed her brain to turn sharp, and memories, real or not, started to replay. Experiences, real and not, repeated. Not only what they did to her but what they did to others. Drilling into their minds and twisting their emotions and their thoughts. Making them scratch their skin until they bled, or shred their own eyes, or rip their own nails out one by one. The list went on and on, spinning the nausea in her gut. The limit to the things they could convince others to do...was endless. She absentmindedly traced the scar on her throat, shutting out the memory she'd forced herself to remember. What if they did that to Killian?

Or made him watch as they did it to his family? To Amala? To Dray? To his people?

Something strange burrowed into her chest, digging until she felt hollow. *Shit.* Guilt and worry and *fear* weren't things she often felt for other people. Sympathy, sure. But empathy...she had a hard time extending it when she suffered so much at the same hands.

But Killian—the kind, gentle prince who'd treated her with patience. Who had believed her and trusted her, even if he shouldn't have.

Could she leave him?

The forest went still and silent, waiting for her to decide. She couldn't—she couldn't leave him. Not with them. The world had been unkind, but he deserved better from her, even if her better was someone else's worst.

Nova would not leave him with them.

Turning, the beating hearts of the world came back, but steadier, less heavy, as if they exhaled with her. Within, every step was a war with herself.

Giving up your freedom again, Witch? The Vahls' voices were mocking. *We told you—you could never be free of us.*

Nova shut it out. She retraced her steps and kept moving. She counted the heartbeats of the forest, saw sprites dance along the branches above her. Sharp eyes watched her from the dark. But beneath it all, there was another, faster. Like it was exhausted, pushing blood through the owner's skin with effort.

Someone had followed her. What a godsdamn idiot.

Quickly, Nova found a tree with low hanging branches and hauled herself upward, placing herself in a position to see. A dark, twisting sensation shot out of them, threatening to choke her. She'd recognize that darkness. It tasted like burning ash and heavy smoke and something rancid.

Dray.

Rolling her eyes, Nova pushed through the off-putting feel of him and tried to follow the threads. But it was poison in her mouth. It made her blood curdle. Was this Killian's doing? Doubt crept in, but she shoved it down. He would not take her freedom away from her.

The Fire Elemental had slowed, tracking through the woods

slower now. Sparks danced between his fingertips, and his other hand readied his weapon. His head twitched, and his movements were *off*. Nova furrowed her brows.

Dray had never moved like that before.

She watched for a second longer before slicing her palm and letting her blood circle her hand. On her left, the bracelet transformed into its claw, and she shot her blood out, wrapping it around his ankles and wrists, a grunt leaving his lips as he fell to the forest floor. Nova jumped down, landing in a crouch as she twisted her hand, forcing his own to spasm and release the weapon.

Able to get control of his other, he shot out sparks and bursts of flame in her direction that she easily dodged. Heat only brushed her skin until the darkness swallowed them. With a twist, she rendered that hand defenseless.

"What are you doing here?"

"Follow the Witch. No matter what, follow the Witch. Ensure she does not leave," Dray said, but it was a twisted version of his voice. His eyes went in and out of focus.

"Dray?" She kicked his ribs, but his eyes only continued to flutter.

"Follow the Witch. No matter what, follow the Witch—"

Nova sent a mask of blood to cover his mouth, but it only muffled the words he kept repeating.

She had no idea how or when or why, but she knew that this was the Vahls' doing. The forest had gone quiet, but she felt the watchful eyes of its creatures. She took a few deep breaths, trying to quell the resentment to no avail. In this world, she was nothing more than a tool. For the dead. For the Vahls.

Her nails curled into her palm, drawing blood as they did to relieve the ache. Guilt thrummed. It had been days since she last caused herself pain. Nova quickly slowed the guard's blood until his eyes fluttered shut, and with a hold on his slow pulsing blood, began to drag him through the woods.

It was clear that maybe there was no saving herself. Maybe she just wasn't worthy of it.

But Killian was.

CHAPTER 50

HEAVY IS THE CROWN

SYRENA FELT THE SEAS CHANGE ON THE SHORES OF Iyvia.

Of course, it was more mental than physical. She wasn't so blind to think she could feel changes in the entirety of Valora's water, but she just knew that the other Kingdoms had departed for the council in Eisera. There was a larger ripple amongst the deep sea, an undulation that did not match the paths of the trade ships. She removed her hands from the ocean, the water rolling off her dark skin.

"Release the bird, Torin." Syrena watched the dark blue bird with spots of opal take flight, blending into the sky in an instant.

"The ship is ready for you, Your Majesty."

She nodded, her hair twinkling with the movement. "And the results of the contaminate?"

"Within your chambers on board."

Syrena exhaled, the crown heavy on her head. "Thank you, Torin. You know to send messages should anything urgent arise here. Send a bird, send a storm, I don't care. Do not leave me in the dark."

Torin dipped her head. "Your Majesty." Her eyes rose to

somewhere behind Syrena, the ship presumably. "It is time. *Aiva* is ready to sail."

With a final lingering glance, she strode across the sand and toward the ship. Her lightweight gown brushed against the wood as she boarded. Made of dark oak, details of teal and opal were etched through the planks, jewels inlaid and carvings done by the artists of the islands. Guards stood on the deck, their light clothing loose for the summer heat. Though she knew underneath, they wore armor made from scales, like a second skin.

"Your Majesty." Milana, her secondary guard, greeted her.

The others fell into their positions on the ship as soon as she passed. Instead of heading straight to her quarters, she approached the deck overlooking the ocean seas. Her brother would've known what to do. With the contamination, about the rift—about all of it. He would've known exactly what to say, exactly how to remain calm.

But the thing was, she always had him to lean on. She'd never known her parents; they died before she could remember them. But Zvon had been her entire life. Her protector, her best friend, her parent—whether that was fair or not—he never complained. Never let it infect their relationships. She was alone, left to rule over the islands and protect her people and the water that gave them life.

As they headed into deeper waters, the loneliness stuck to her skin like the briny salt water.

She wished she could mold the loneliness into a puzzle that could be solved or a problem that had an easy solution, but she couldn't. It was a persistent, venomous thing that crept in through the cracks, no matter how hard she tried to patch them up.

Right now, she felt as though it always would.

SYRENA SPENT most of the journey in her quarters, pouring over the findings of the contaminant. There were multiple descriptions of its appearance, how it became reflective, and its movements. A creeping thing. It had seemingly no effects on water or the air, but blood, it did. Time and time again, test after test, it destroyed any blood it came in contact with. According to the findings, there was nothing like it in existence. At least, nothing that those upon Iyvia's shores had seen. How would she broach this topic? How was she going to tell people there was some destructive liquid seeping up from the ocean floor?

And even so, would they believe her? A new Reyna? Would they think her naïve? Stupid? Brush her off because she didn't know how to rule?

There were only two people in the world that could've quelled her fears. Her brother, who was dead. And...the one that she hadn't seen in almost seven years. Both of them had left her. It was up to her to quell her own fears, to conquer her own misgivings. Alone.

With a sigh, she let her head fall forward, burying her fingers in her hair. *What am I doing? I can't do this.* Her breath grew shallow. *I'm not meant to be Reyna. I was never meant to lead.*

Bitterness was thick and choking, threatening to drown her from the inside out. Death was a strange thing—it wrenched everything out from hiding. Grief, sorrow, love. And anger. Death forced all those things front and center until they could no longer be ignored.

She loved her brother—she missed him every day. And she was also furious with him. He had left her here, left her to wear a crown she never wanted, left her to live in a world without him, on a path that had shattered when he died. Every step was like walking on shards of glass, but no matter how much her feet bled, she couldn't stop. He'd trusted her with this, and she would not fail him, not even in death.

A knock on the door was a welcome distraction. "Enter."

Milana appeared. "There is something you need to see."

Furrowing her brows, Syrena stood and followed her guard over the wooden deck and down below to the ship's hold. Two sailors and two more of the guard stood in front of her in a semicircle. Something unmoving laid in the center.

"What is that?" she asked.

Every eye landed on her, and she was quickly met with bows.

"No closer!" One of the ship's sailors shouted, panic clear on their features. "One of my men felt something in the water, disturbing the fishing nets. This is what they found."

A creaking light crackled to life above the thing, illuminating its body. It was a fish—at least of some sort. Carefully, she moved closer, only enough to see. She was alone here, though. No Ikina, no Professor Caro, no Torin. It was only her. The guard instantly had their swords out in front of her, forming an X to stop her from moving closer.

"He pulled it up, found it tangled in the net, but noticed this..."

They bent down slowly with a small dagger and poked the fish. It flopped aggressively on the floor and immediately began to bleed—except the blood wasn't red. It was black and streaked with silver. The blood made a plopping sound on the floor, and seconds later, red blood leaked out behind it. But instead of congealing or stopping, the black and silver mass began to writhe.

No...it couldn't be.

Horror clamored under her skin, rattled against her bones. The mass continued until it found its way back to the fish, re-entering its skin, and once again, the fish flopped aggressively, angrily. Water splashed from its tail and its fins, and a strange low sound escaped its jaws—a sound never made by any creature she knew under the sea.

Beside her Miliana whispered, "Serpent, save us."

The fish grew more and more aggressive, demanding a wider berth. Under the light, she saw its veins, its fins, its eyes become inflamed, threaded with black and silver. It burrowed and reappeared, the fish growing angrier with every second. Suddenly it flipped, the sound echoing below the deck.

"Gods, what is that thing?" The sailor's voice trembled.

"Did it bring that fish...back to life?" The fish continued to flop around, though it wasn't heaving for air. Its gills were still. It was *alive*. But it had been dead.

Syrene swallowed and ignored the fear growing deep in her belly. She called to the water, and the water answered, droplets rising from the grooves in the ship and pearls of her earrings. With a step forward, ignoring her guards, she swept, watching as the water wound around the fish and squeezed.

The mass of *stuff* plopped out at every orifice, once again writhing on the deck. With her other hand she circled them with water until they were encased. She could feel them now, all the way to her bones, moving and writhing and fighting the water, imitating it. One of them jumped, threads of its strange body reaching out. Shouts of concern surrounded her. From the corner of her eye, she saw her guards settle into position, water floating around their hands, too.

"Surround it. It needs to be completely submerged," she commanded, willing her voice not to quiver. Her hands circled, working with the water that joined her to keep their bubbles solid and large enough. "Hold it."

With a twist, she sent a shock of cold through it, freezing them slowly. She held and held until each bubble turned to ice, rendering the *thing* still.

Though she was half-sure they were still moving within the ice.

"Get that fish out of here. I don't care what you do with it— get it out." At the command, everyone began to move, except her and Milana.

"Your Majesty—"

"Find me a chest or a box or *something*, and bring it here now. I need to..." She sighed, wanting to laugh. Though, she was scared if she laughed, she would only cry. "Gods, I don't know. Just go. Now."

Sweat beaded on her forehead and dragged down her spine. Gods, what was she supposed to do? What *was* this? Did it have something to do with the Elders? The rift had happened shortly after, based on the dates of the assembly and the notices from Ceron and Mykor. Was this a consequence? Was she only just seeing that?

Syrena's eyes pricked. Was she blind? Had she missed that? Would every rift result in something like this? Some death leaking from beneath them? Did she bring this ashore and show it to the others? Did she keep it hidden until she had even a minimal understanding of what in the world it was? Would freezing it hold?

What happened if it didn't? What happened if they didn't believe her?

She had no answers—no one would. Because it was only her. She was in charge. She was the one who had to protect her people and her country. There was no one else to lean on, no one who could tell her what to do. It was only her. It was her duty now.

And even if it killed her—if that was what duty demanded— she would exceed those demands.

Whether she wanted it or not, Syrena bore the crown.

Part Four

CHAPTER 51

DEATH OF HONOR

By the time Nova had made it back to Willowgrove, the castle was bursting with life.

Even from a distance in the woods, she could see attendants bustling back and forth, preparing for the celebration. So, she waited. With the insufferable guard knocked out at her side, she waited like a bird in the trees until the suns began to lower.

Dragging Dray was no easy feat, but she'd done it and then tied him up and stuffed him in the closet of her room, which, thankfully, was untouched. She had kept his blood at a low enough pace so even if he woke, he'd would be unstable for a bit. The gown still hung on the door, and Nova forced herself to inhale.

She released her curls, allowing them to touch her shoulders, and began to ready. She needed to be invisible—able to watch from a distance and disappear again if need be.

This is so beyond stupid. She sighed as she slipped the dress on, only to realize she was unable to lace the back up herself. *By the Gods.* Nova placed her hands on the wardrobe in front of her, bent over with disbelief. What in the world was she doing? She should not have come back.

She needed to go. Now.

As she made to move, the doors to her chambers opened. She had their blood in her control in seconds only for Killian to appear, just as surprised as she.

"Nova?" he asked, closing the door swiftly behind him.

The prince looked far more like a king, wearing fine clothing draped over his build, a vested top of the deepest black with accents of silver and green in the stitching and carefully made slacks. Silver cuffs sat upon his bicep and his forearms with carved flowers of black and gemstones inlaid. All as his vines moved slowly along his hands.

Killian stepped toward her. "You came back."

Her heart raced. "I—"

"Why?"

His eyes found hers and she...What was she supposed to say? Logically, he didn't need her protection. And she wasn't sure she was brave enough for honesty.

But she tried. "I wanted to make sure you're safe come tomorrow. Once the night ends, I'm leaving. For good."

A smile played at his lips. "You came back for me?"

Heat flooded her cheeks, and she turned away, still holding up the front of her dress, unable to slow her heart. "Don't think too highly of yourself, Prince."

Nova felt hot everywhere—her cheeks, her chest, her hands. She made sure Dray's heart rate stayed slow, unable to control her own. The eyes of the prince were heavy on her skin.

"Well, what should I think?" Killian moved closer, hands reaching for the ties of the dress. They latched eyes in the mirror, his filled with a question she answered with a nod.

"I don't—why are you in here?"

His fingers brushed against her skin, sending goosebumps down her spine. For a second, he was quiet. "I came to grab the gown," he said quietly, meeting her eyes again. "I didn't want anyone to discard it."

She heard him, but all she registered was the feel of his fingers brushing her skin. There were no scars, as to be expected, but she remembered pain. His touch didn't feel like that. It was only soft. Only gentle.

"I've never," she started and sighed. "I've only ever cared about one other person. And they were used against me in many ways. Maybe it was, but I've never fully trusted it was mutual. Were they kind because they needed to be safe? Or were they kind because they cared? And you..." She looked down, circling her bracelet. "You have been nothing but deserving of my help. And I couldn't stand the idea of you being hurt or vulnerable to something I could've helped stopped."

He continued lacing until he met her hair, brushing the curls out of the way to finish the threads. Every touch made her breath catch. "If you're putting yourself at risk, don't stay. You deserve to go—if that's what you want."

It was. She wanted to be free, but not if it meant leaving him to their hands.

"It is. But I want to do this, too." She turned, and his hands fell to her waist, hovering, only his fingers brushing the gown. "No one else can know I'm here. If all goes well...I'll be gone again before you know it. I only want to watch from the shadows."

"Maybe one day came a bit sooner than I expected," he said, his full lips curving up.

She reached out and ran her hands over the collar of the shirt. Multiple silver pendants were clasped around his throat, and she fought the urge to run her fingers over those as well.

"Maybe there'll be another."

"I'll look for you out there."

"You won't find me; the point is to blend in, Prince."

With a shake of his head, he let his eyes roam over every inch of her, and when they locked eyes again, his green eyes shone with warmth. "I'll find you."

Someone else might've fought her decision, but the prince knew. He could've told her as much, but she wouldn't have listened. Instead, Killian let his vines wrap around her wrist and let his lips brush against her ear as he said, "Thank you, Nova. For everything."

Nova stood there, feeling the remnants of his touch over every inch of her body. And then, a gentle thought knocked at the edges of her brain. *You look beautiful, Nova. Even the shadows will recognize that.*

And her heart settled, and her mind cleared.

It was time. One last sacrifice, and then, she would be free.

THE ORNATE THRONE room was situated on the mid-level of the castle between the widest part of the mountain ranges.

There was a wall of tall windows that folded into each other, allowing the ballroom and the large balcony to become one, while above, the entire ceiling retracted, allowing the moon and stars to shine directly overhead.

Nova stayed on the upper levels of the room, tucked under arches or beside columns, sneaking in the minds of anyone who tried to speak to her and suggesting they do otherwise. Attendants walked by with trays of small plates and flutes of various liquors, and a band played on the stage below. One by one, the ruling parties had arrived through the grand doors dressed in gowns and clothing worthy of only them.

The Farrs of Azias, the Stvans of Vydara, the Kovaci's of Lazora, the Chamber of Five of Aeledin. Then came the newly crowned Reyna of Iyvia, Syrena Savali. She'd overheard the Slaters one day talking about a new queen, and despite the loss she had suffered, she held her head high, draped in fabric of various blues.

She watched as the shadow princess, Elaia Zūne—the one that had saved her—arrived, flanked by her betrothed and two guards.

She felt the first sweep of unease as Mikel and Mireya strode into the room, immediately feeling the strangeness of their minds and off-putting beats of their hearts. The room quieted, as discomforted by their presence as she was. Ensuring she was well hidden, Nova trained her eyes on them, quickly molding the fortress of her mind to be a reflection of those around her.

Her invisibility was key.

By that point, everyone, excluding the Slaters and Killian, had arrived.

The Vahls moved around the room with glasses of wine in their hands, but their minds, though dark, were calm. Their blood was steady. She sighed, waiting. Watching. Had this been for nothing? Coming back here? Or were they only biding their time?

The doors swung open, drawing her attention again, and the Slaters moved under the light. Her heart raced.

Who had they chosen? Their daughter, out of love?

Or Killian, out of tradition and loyalty?

As they entered, all eyes, including hers, were on the space behind them.

Killian stepped forward first. There was not a crown upon his head. Even from afar, she felt the pain poisoning his threads, darkening them with sadness. Loss.

"We thank you for joining us here today to honor the decision of King Aydin and Queen Gena to step down and raise up a new leader of Eisera," the guards' voices on either side echoed through the silent room. "Please welcome your new Queen, Amala Slater."

Amala entered in a gown of silver with a crown placed delicately on her head. A shockwave went through the crowd, through the citizens of Eisera that stood here today. She could feel the surprise within them, the increase of their heartrates. They had not expected this. Not truly.

She felt the first strum of anger underneath all the discontent. Amala's smile faltered, slight, quick, but a falter all the same.

Today, in Eisera, something personal won over decades of tradition.

Honor was pushed aside for ease.

Nova hoped that was all that would grace the hall tonight.

The death of honor, instead of just death.

Time passed slowly and uneventfully.

Killian moved around the room with confidence despite his loss. She was attuned to him without trying, felt the pace of his heart and the way he steadied himself by his threads. Maybe he was not a king, but he was still the Ižavore. Still the chosen.

Still, all she did was wait.

Watching every single one of them. The shadow princess and the two guards she'd entered with. Vittoria as she tilted around the room, off kilter, with various glasses of liquor. And the Vahls, who moved slow and steady. But she noticed much of the crowd gave them a wide berth as they approached, as if they were sick.

She took a sip of water, tapping her fingers on the glass. Thoughts poured in of mindless nothingness, while the threads of those around her flashed various colors and weights, changing with every second, things that held no meaning for her but she noted anyway.

Then a thought echoed, not meant for her, but heard all the same.

Close the doors.

For a second, no one moved, then guards took their posts.

Her brows furrowed. Within the movement, there was something familiar. A familiar heartbeat, light and fast, as if always on edge. Nova swallowed. She would know the feel of that blood anywhere.

They brought Jonah.

They knew she was here.

Her legs thrummed, adrenaline rushing through her as she fought the urge to fall, to run. Instead, she curled her hand around the railing, forcing herself to still, her eyes never straying.

And then—

"Ready to enjoy the show, Witch?" An arm snaked around her waist before she could stop them, squeezing tight as flames flickered at her spine. Dray.

People muddled about, oblivious to the tension of his hold. Her skin pricked in discomfort.

"Release me, Dray. Now." She grabbed hold of his blood, twisting his fingers.

"I wouldn't do that. Wouldn't want to make a scene, would you?" His words were clear, unlike the woods, but his voice was off.

"I should've killed you when I had the chance," she snarled, but he was right. Gods, he was right.

Too many people around. A risk she wasn't ready to take. Not yet.

Around them, the guards moved as one, closing the tall windows, shutting out the air. And above, the ceiling began to close, all of it in perfect rhythm. Confusion danced over the faces of the guests, and the threads of Killian and his family grew heavy.

He looked around, eyes searching every corner, and she knew he was looking for her.

I'm here, Killian. Stay calm.

Thoughts had no direction, and yet, he seemed to look right at her. If it wasn't for the shadows, he would've seen her.

She inhaled, not letting go of Dray's blood, but not fighting. The doors clicked closed, and the guards moved to stand in front of each one, abandoning their previous posts. Her heart dropped as she spotted Jonah moving through the crowd until he stood at the center. Murmurs of confusion crawled through the room as everyone looked at him.

"Guards!"

But the guards did not answer. They did not move a muscle.

No. *No.* They couldn't have. Nova looked at the guards closest to find their eyes clouded over and hazy. She reached within and found their minds muddled.

She saw Mireya roaming the outskirts of the room with slow studious effort. Something scratched at her mind. *Nova, darling, how nice of you to join us.* Within her chest, her heart slowed, barely beating.

Bile in her stomach turned, but Dray held her still. She had nowhere to go.

Jonah fell to his knees.

No, no, no. *Will you save him, Nova? Or let him die?* Mireya's voice was a cold claw in her head.

All eyes were on Jonah. Of course, they were. No one noticed Mireya and Mikel moving calmly around them. But the red of her hair was a beacon flashing in the dark for Nova.

Just like that, Jonah began to writhe. She could feel his mind fracture and reform and fracture again, a technique she'd suffered at the hands of the Vahls before. But his blood became hot and heavy, the molecules shifting and curving under his skin.

And then, like the others she had killed, his eyes leaked.

Down his cheeks streaked tears of blood.

CHAPTER 52

MASTER OF BLOOD AND DEATH

Through a small door, more guards poured in with blank eyes, taking up every inch of the wall and blocking every exit.

Nova writhed again, trying to gain leverage that didn't require spilling blood against Dray. A guard moved blindly to Jonah, dragging a blade upon his arm and spilling his blood onto his skin.

Underneath it all, Nova could feel Mireya's nails on her own head and dragging across the minds of those in the room, far stronger than she once believed.

Silence fell as the blood from Jonah pooled on the foreign skin and began to warp, to bend, to encompass the skin. Oh, Gods, she felt sick. The blood formed around the guards' and Jonah's bodies, crawling up their arms while his eyes leaked red.

What is this? What have they done? She knew it was the Vahls —they had infected him or poisoned him or *something* and found a way to turn it into...what? A weapon?

This was her fault. She had left him for a freedom she still didn't have.

"Get off me." She threw an elbow into the heat of Dray behind her, twisting his blood so his extremities failed. He struck, his own eyes blurred and empty, with the heat of flames burning within. Nova ducked, striking him when she could.

She felt more than saw the blood spread over the floor below. More guards had joined them in the center, and the blood found each one of them.

Jonah? Jonah, can you hear me? I'm coming. His mind was blurred and weak, but she tried to speak, nonetheless.

Dray blasted her with heat, singeing her skin as he pushed her into the balcony, the stone unyielding against her spine. She grunted, clicking her bracelet and quickly clawing her own palm until beads of blood appeared. Swiftly, she let the blood fall and wind around his legs like a rope, pulling them out from under her. Threads of black swirled in his eyes like worms as he stood.

"What have they done to you?" she whispered without meaning to. What was the black in his eyes? Was it the Vahls' hold on him? Infecting him? Or was it whatever they had given Jonah?

"Follow the Witch. Follow the Witch." With every word, he struck. Even like this, his hits were sure and steady. A well-trained guard, no matter the circumstances.

But a well-trained hit was no match for her blood in anger. She made daggers of them, striking his palms with every punch until his own blood fell. She swirled it until he slipped, then wound it around his neck and choked him with it.

She crouched and removed all his weapons, taking them for herself. Her curls were wild, and she felt blood on her cheeks. She took one last look at the guard, his mind not his own and blood curled around his skin like ropes.

Around her, the people on the overhang looked horrified.

Was she a woman or a monster?

She could hear their thoughts, their questions, circling her like vultures. Her lip snarled in annoyance.

A woman or a monster. What was the difference anymore? She would be both.

Nova used her blood to sheath the weapons she stole, uncaring if she sliced herself in the process. She would heal. The crowd parted as she moved for the stairs with a claw on one hand and a dagger in the other. Sounds of chaos came up to meet her as she picked up the pace.

To be met with guards covered in blood and reaching for anyone in their grasp. Horror spun around her and landed on her shoulders like a bird, draping over her with heavy wings. Blood splattered the floors, and screams echoed against the glass as the strange black blood spread.

And at the center stood the Vahls, with Elaia and Vittoria—untouched and unflinching in the eye of the storm. Mireya found Nova immediately, cocking her head as a knowing smile formed.

"Mireya, what is this?" Aydin shouted, eyes frantically surveying the room.

Chaos was everywhere, but Nova felt frozen under the queen's heavy stare. But this had to end. She had to stop it.

Even if that meant revealing herself.

In front of her, a body fell to its knees, blood crawling up their skin as a guard grabbed everyone in their reach. Quickly drawn back into reality, Nova took a quick look around. Everyone except those at the center fought back. But whatever magic the guards themselves claimed fought back. Water trapped in air. Fire was choked by shadows.

She found Killian near the stairs of the throne, focused and deadly. He had cracked the marble stairs and turned them into shards, sending them at the others—the sick, the controlled—or *whatever* they were, but they kept coming. Through the crowd, he found her.

"Nova," he said, his voice carrying to her, "can you stop this?" In her mind, he said something else. *I'm sorry. You should've never come back.*

Blood pounded in her ears. She heard it moving and twisting and choking those it found. It felt off, weightless and heavy at once. Wrongly shaped. Dark and venomous. But she swirled her hand, and it answered to her.

It was *still* blood.

It called to her.

She was a Witch of the blood.

It answered to *her*. It always would.

She rushed forward, sending her own blood into the air as daggers. They whistled through as she tried to push those poisoned back away from the rest.

In the corner of her eye, she saw Mireya smile, as if she was playing into a hand already dealt. Dread slithered around her like a snake.

Was this what they wanted?

The blood on the floor seemed to follow her where she went, shifting toward her as she passed and retreating as she moved along. Blows were thrown her way when the guards turned their blank eyes on her, their blood-encased bodies reaching for her. Most, if not all, had tears of red on their cheeks. Their weapons were practically molded to their bodies, the blood locking them together. It leeched into their skin, making their veins dark and full.

She flipped her blade, trying to figure out where to strike when a blow to the head struck her first. Spinning, she came face-to-face with a guard with a dagger in each hand. Blood was caked onto his skin so much, she was unable to see what was his and what wasn't. A sound came from his mouth as he plunged each dagger.

Nova entered the dance, footsteps light as to not slip. For a second, she moved the blood on the floor into the guards path, trying to make him fall, to no avail. Water dripped from his fingertips before swirling back up to try and encase her. In a whirling turn, she escaped a punch and sliced the underside of his arm, tearing the muscle before dropping and doing the same behind his knee.

But he kept coming, crawling when walking wasn't an option. And the others seemed to join him.

Nova was pushed to the center, every poisoned guard locking their eyes on her. Jonah remained in the middle, bleeding out of his eyes. She could feel his pulse weakening.

Her breaths came quick as danger closed in. The rest of the party watched her, too, their eyes filled with things she didn't want to see. Horror. Confusion. Disbelief.

In a room of monsters, she was one, too.

Through them all, she found Killian, staring at her with something else. Something reverent.

Was he not afraid of her? Would that change, too?

Though time was dwindling, she let her eyes fall closed and *felt* instead. The threads of the poisoned were dismal and tangled, like Dray's. The others were colorful, stable and able to be followed. Blood of the sick moved wrong, pausing and flowing again, twisting and curling with their veins. The pulse was off and strange. When she opened her eyes, she could see it.

The sick had veins aching for relief, the blood almost black. A haze that only she could see.

And though the world had stopped—it restarted.

They came at her one after another. No thoughts, no sense, just mindless attacking. She had a hold on their blood but danced around the room, avoiding strikes and blades. She slashed left and right with a talon or blade. Blood splattered over her skin, but she felt nothing else. One by one, she took them down.

But they kept rising, their blood never quite spilling enough. And the poisoned blood grew like armor.

Pressure built in her from the ground up as blood and sweat dripped off her body. In the reprieve, she grabbed on, stronger this time, to their blood. Twisted it with an effort she'd never felt. Nova had never controlled this many people at once.

Blood streaked out of her own eyes, like those around her.

Like looking in a mirror.

With a guttural scream that crept out of her lips, she pulled and pushed until their blood began to move so fast, it heated. She fell to her knees as the effort draped over her. Pulling and pushing and expanding and contracting until there was a release.

All of them, one by one, with bruised skin and bleeding eyes, began to fall. Inch by inch, the stone floor of the ballroom became nothing but blood.

Her heart raced. Her hands shook. Exhaustion sat on her like stone as the dead fell around her. Mere images of herself with blood-streaked cheeks.

What was this? What had they done? She felt like an anomaly —it was a joke she'd been left out of. Were they mocking her?

Heaving for air, Nova spun, finding Mireya was already watching her with a crooked smile.

I hope you find peace, my friend. I will miss you.

No. No, no no—no. She had not...she had forgotten that Jonah was one of them. Her soul threatened to break when she laid her eyes upon him, his face in a puddle of blood, the light from his eyes fading with every rattled breath.

"Jonah," she whispered, but the word threatened to shatter her eardrums. His eyes found hers, slowly closing as he sent out one final thought to her.

It is not your fault, Nova. Remember that.

Panic forced her over, her hands wet with blood as she felt his pulse weaken. She tried, crawling forward and reaching for him, trying to will his heart into beating. But he was too weak, too much blood lost. His skin too scorched from the inside.

A sob leaked out of her lips.

She had left him. And now, he was dead because she killed him.

Around her, horrified looks burned her skin from those untouched as they watched her. She felt nothing as she looked at them. Within, all she knew was an aching emptiness.

Nova sat in a pool of blood, in the room full of the dead— and she was the master of them both.

CHAPTER 53

SEA OF LIES

A SLOW CLAP ECHOED IN THE BALLROOM, A SICK LAUGH joining with it.

"Do you believe us now?" Mireya's voice was a frigid breeze in the silent room. *Well done, Nova. Well done.*

She tipped her head, eyes closing. The hand had been played, and she was a pawn. No matter how hard she'd tried to run, she never moved fast enough.

With a snap of Mikel's fingers, the other guards moved forward, dragging the dead back, trailing the blood with them. Their bones were at odd angles where the blood had formed around them. She had shattered both blood and bone.

"What has been unleashed here?" Lady Anika Stvan of Vydara's words dripped with anger. "What is this, Mireya?"

"This is exactly what we warned you about at the assembly. You waved us off, told us we were foolish, old us we were falling victim to stories told in the dark," Mireya snarled. "*This* is what I have tried to tell you was spreading back in Syris. In Azias and Vilies and Ceron. *This* is what killed the Elders. *This* is what will slowly leak into all of Valora. The Witches have returned." She motioned to Nova, who raised her head slowly. "And they have brought destruction with them, a destruction they control and only they can destroy."

They were pinning this on her? She swallowed down her anger, but it went nowhere.

"And how do you know this, Mireya?" The Empress of Lazora spoke now.

Mireya walked through the blood to the center, closing in on her. "She's our daughter."

The threads of those living in the room flickered with dark distrust and confusion. Nova watched it all unfold. Every royal stood at the stairs in front of the throne, watching her.

And Killian was at the center. His face had gone stoic, his eyes unreadable.

They couldn't do this to her. Hadn't they done enough?

"We have been studying her blood and her power as long as she has been alive." Mireya huffed as she came directly next to her, placing a hand on her head, dragging her hands roughly over her curls. The touch felt like poison on her skin. "She escaped not long ago. Not long before the Elders ended up dead," Mireya said, wrapping her hand around the back of Nova's neck. "We suspected, but we couldn't be sure. But after this, we know she is the one responsible for their deaths. And we tried—we tried to warn you. But you ignored our letters, our pleas for help. And this is what you get."

Every eye in the room was turned on Nova—to where she sat surrounded by blood. They were going to believe them. Dread was heavy in her gut, like stones. Why wouldn't they? She had appeared as a monster in front of their faces. They would see nothing else.

"We tried to use her for good. Our networks would return to us with suspicions of Witch magic, of those protecting them. We sent her to stop them, to kill them. It seems our efforts may have been in vain."

Lies. It was all lies.

She didn't kill anyone because they were destroying anything or anyone. She killed them because she had to. Because they *told* her to.

They couldn't do this to her, blame her for their madness. She was supposed to be out of their reach, but instead, she'd walked right back into it. And yet she could not speak.

Nova willed herself to do anything. To fight back, to disagree, but there was nothing left. The phantom heartbeats of the dead pulsed in her palms. The blood hadn't even cooled, and Jonah's body was only steps away.

"Will you hear us now?" Mireya asked, her voice echoing.

No. No. Please, do not listen to them, Nova tried to meet their eyes, *anyone's* eyes. But it was useless. Silence had blanketed the room like the first snow of winter. Mireya had done this. Calculated every second of this.

"What is it you want from us, Mireya? What can we do to stop it?" The Empress of Lazora stepped forward, sparing a single glance of disgust in Nova's direction.

Nova felt Mireya's nails dig into her neck. "We need access to the Aether points. We believe that if we can use it to our will, we can fight this *power* that only they wield. The Aether runs free now. We must take advantage of that while we can before more Witches make themselves known, before we find out how true the history books really are."

Nova closed her eyes. "No, no, no." She tried to stand, but Mireya's grip was tight. "They are lying. I'm not—this is—it's not—"

"Do you deny it? Do you deny those you've killed? The Elders?"

"I—" She was lost, floating in a sea of lies she was now at the center of. None of these people would believe her, not after what they just witnessed her do.

Underneath, she found a steady heartbeat even in the chaos. Killian's eyes were cool, sharp. Pain splintered through her.

She was going to lose him, too.

He would never forgive her for the truth.

"Do you deny it, Nova?" Mireya bent, bringing them face-to-face. And then, her head split. *It is in your best interest to think carefully, daughter. What of the chosen son? What will happen to him should you stand against us? Would you like to watch as we slit his throat at your feet?*

The world was crumbling beneath her. Blood physically and metaphorically covered her until she no longer knew right from left. They would take him from her, even if he wasn't hers to have.

She scratched at the fortress of his head, begging him to let her in. *Killian, please. Do not believe them.*

But then, air wrapped around her throat like a hand, stealing her focus. Yet, she found him. Tenacious and unyielding. His jaw was clenched, and the vines were writhing against his skin. So unlike the person she'd come to know.

Stand with us, and he will live. Stand against us, and you will be responsible for yet another death. Even in her thoughts, Mireya was callous. She cared about nothing else except controlling Nova. With that, she could do anything.

Part of her wanted to beg him. To fall to her knees and beg him to believe *her* and not them. But the lies and the truth were so intertwined, one could not exist without the other.

Letting him hate her was the option that ensured his safety.

And what was one more person who directed their hatred at her?

She gave one more lingering glance before tipping her head. No words left her mouth. Her silence, her actions, were proof enough.

Smart girl, Mireya thought, squeezing her arm as she went. "After her disappearance, I called together the Eastern Alliance." She motioned to those with her, Vittoria and Elaia. She should've known. Her savior was a pawn, too. "We had reason to believe she would make play for power, but we had no idea it would be as drastic as it was. We've been working together, intercepting those that have arrived on our shores, watching all communications or letters sent. We know that she has been here, studying the history of the Witches, and communicating with others we have yet to find—"

Surprise struck when Killian stepped forward. Those watching flickered between him and them. "That cannot be true. She has sent no letters. Spoken to no one outside of this room. What proof do you have?" He no longer looked at her. Something sharp plucked his threads.

"Perfect timing. Dray, come." Mireya motioned to those behind her and to Dray, who approached, standing on Nova's other side. "We've been working with many. Those who have trusted us, those who have seen the truth, have joined us."

Godsdamned idiots, they all were.

"Dray here, a friend of yours, Killian, and the new personal guard to the queen, has been relaying information to us. Her movements, her findings in the Emerald library, sending everything to us. About the Aether. The Witches." Mireya eyed Killian.

She didn't understand how—she knew he had been there, but he must've been around far more than she had known. But how did he ever meet them? When? It didn't make sense. When she looked at him, she saw nothing but empty eyes. Were they controlling him?

Betrayal turned Killian's threads hot. "It makes no sense. I would've known. He never once said anything."

"Well, that's not all, Killian."

Vittoria stepped forward with a smile, moving like a twisted dancer over the floor. And Amala met her, reaching for her hand. "Your sister has been helping, too."

This time she knew the gasps came from Aydin and Gena. She was pretty sure she just felt Killian's heart break.

"Why?" The question floated in the air, directed toward Amala and Mireya, and yet, neither of them. "Why are you doing this?"

He wasn't looking at them. He was looking at her.

Though his voice did not waver and he stood steady, she could feel the threads fracturing within. She'd never felt a heart break. Never felt the blood falter in that manner, never felt pain travel through the bloodstream—until now.

All the while, in her ribs, what was left of her own broke, too.

Mireya scoffed. "We've been studying the bloodlust. She's a Witch. This is what she was made for—"

"Not her," Killian said, dragging his eyes away. "*You.*"

In the chaos, the room had shifted. Those that were drawn into Mireya's words, her *lies*, had moved incrementally closer. Though she couldn't take her eyes of Amala, who stood alone with the Vahls. Aydin and Gena had not moved from Killian's side, but she was their daughter. She was the queen. What would they decide?

Vydara had not moved an inch. They were notorious for their privacy. They had no alliances and no enemies. Would this force their hand?

As Nova looked, all she could see was a Valora split.

Killian's voice grew louder as he motioned to the room. "Why are you doing this? In this way? In this manner?"

Mireya's eyes went cold. "*We* have not done anything. She has." Mireya gripped Nova's neck even harder. "All we tried to do was make you aware. But our warnings went unheard, and now, the violence, the death, has found your home. Your people."

Nova wanted to scream. Hearing Mireya spin this as some cry for help when anyone with eyes could see all this was, and would ever be, was for power. The yearning for power dripped off Mireya like water droplets, spread off her skin like a web from a spider, and it latched on to those she could control, trapping them like flies. Bending them to her will. She wanted to scream, but she said nothing.

Just like before.

Above, the moon had fallen behind clouds, stealing its light with it. In the ruckus, many of the light orbs and lanterns had fallen, leaving them in a hazy glow.

"Who will stand with us? To help us fight this. To help us find the Witches that have returned to threaten us." Mireya raised her head, and Nova could feel the claws of her power sinking in to the room. "We must harness the Aether how we see fit now, to protect us before it is too late." The Queen of Syris walked slowly, purposefully, making eye contact with every single royal in the room. "I ask again, who will stand with us? And who will stand against us?"

It was a pointless question. The only ones that stood against them were Killian, the two remaining members of Aeledin's Chamber of Five, and Syrena Savali.

Lady Anika stepped forward, her head high. "The people of Vydara want nothing to do with this. We stand with no one but ourselves." She cast a look of pure fire over everyone. "You will let us leave, or we will be sure everyone feels the flames on their skin."

Mireya tsked. "You are making a mistake, Anika. But I cannot force you to see the error of your ways. Leave. You will need us soon enough." Mireya turned, her eyes finding the Reyna of Iyvia. "But you...we can help you. Ruling alone is a feat no one can prepare for. Stand with us against these Witches, and we will give you everything you've ever dreamed of."

The Reyna tipped her chin, her piercing blue eyes sharp against her dark skin. "I do not dream of death." The Reyna's pulse raced, but it didn't show. "Iyvia needs no help, nor do I."

"You're sure of this?" Mireya asked once more to be met with silence again. "Fine. Guards." She snapped, and the guards, once still as statues, moved quicker than Nova expected.

Aydin snarled, "Stop! You do not answer to anyone else; you answer only to your queen." Aydin looked upon their daughter, who said nothing. Nova felt her threads tangle. Her parents had chosen her to rule, but would they choose her now? As she stood on the side of death?

It didn't matter. The guards didn't stop. They moved forward, quick and swift, dodging magic thrown at them. Ice patches and vines and cracks in the floor did not stop them. Those that fell untangled and kept moving.

The others had nowhere to go.

Eventually, despite the protests and the orders that went unfollowed, Nova watched one by one as the guards kicked them to their knees and tied their hands. Those around that were still alive stood in the corners, crouched together until the guards rounded them up, too.

Amala crouched, eyes on her brother. "Killian, you can still—"

"No. You don't get to say anything to me, Amala. Not now. Maybe not ever," he said, never looking weak despite being on his knees.

"Enough of you," Mireya said, waving her hand.

Horror filled Nova's gut when Killian doubled over, unable to catch himself, as his eyes began to flutter. Amala faltered, tripping over her feet as she watched her brother in pain. Reaching forward, she felt Mireya in his head, fissuring his thoughts, making him feel and experience things that weren't real.

She tried to send the wisps of her power in, to diminish it, but Mireya spun, sending them nose to nose. "Do you want him dead, Nova?" she snarled, and because she was in his head, she felt the new wave of pain. "Do you want to be the reason he suffers? Another one you make bleed?"

On the outside, she stilled, did not let Mireya see the wound she had re-opened. But within, she felt the words slice through her, ripping through scar tissue.

She was made up of nothing more than old wounds that never healed. *Another you make bleed.*

She pulled her power back, leaving Killian to her. And for the first time, she felt fear when he collapsed. Fear of what might happen to him. To his country.

Fear not for herself, but for *him.*

He might hate her forever. He might never forgive her. He might never look at her with kindness again. But if this was what she had to do to ensure he *lived,* she would do it.

Nova would do whatever was needed if it meant he lived.

They cleared out, the guards ordered to shove them down in the castle cells, until Nova was the only one left in the ballroom. Just her and the dead. She walked through the blood where Jonah's body lay and fell to her knees again, new blood splattering over her skin.

She didn't cry. She didn't weep.

Nova sat in a pool of blood, her life once again not her own.

CHAPTER 54

FORGOTTEN DOES NOT MEAN LOST

ZAHRA MOVED IN A FRENZY AROUND THEIR CHAMBERS. Rohan and Xerxes sat on the leather chair under the window, silent.

"Zahra—"

"My Gods, what have you done, Elaia?" Her hair fanned out, framing the anger on her face clear as day. With every step, spurts of light followed over the dark wooden floor.

Elaia sat on the top of the desk, nails scratching at her hand repeatedly. "I did what I had to do."

"For whom?"

"For whom?" Her head was spinning. Her body was heavy. "For what's left of my family, for Rersa, for you—"

"No. No! Don't you dare use me as a reason for standing by and allowing *that*." She pointed in the direction of the door, referencing the ballroom. "Don't you dare use your family. Nomara would hate this. Your sisters would be ashamed." Every word out of her mouth was sharp, pointed. Zahra knew exactly where she was vulnerable. "You didn't do this for them, for us, for *me*. You did this for you. You keep saying it's to keep us safe, but you never ask us how we feel. You never ask us what safety feels like. But safety to you is control. *That's* why you did this. To have a say, to ensure you never lose control. But you have lost so much more."

Every time Elaia closed her eyes, she saw pools of blood, streaks left behind from the bodies, bones broken under armor of blood. All she saw was blood. And yet...

"And who of us have suffered? None of us are dead. None of us were used. *We* are safe." Her nail broke skin, leaving a line of blood on the top of her hand between the ink.

Zahra stopped, the jewelry around her ankles ceasing their tinkling, and hung her head. Her body shook—with tears or laughter, Elaia couldn't be sure. "What were you thinking?"

She stood, blood on her hand. "I had to make a choice."

"A choice. That's your excuse?" Zahra's hands shook. "We all have to make choices, Elaia. You made the wrong one."

But had she? If not, they would've been on the receiving end of that attack. They would've left the ballroom in chains instead of on their feet. Rohan and Xerxes remained silent, eyes flickering back and forth between the two.

"To you, it was the wrong choice. To me, it was the only one."

Zahra approached her, wrapping her delicate fingers around Elaia's wrists. "You are smarter than this, Elaia. You *know* better. There are always consequences to every choice. Good or bad or in-between. Do you know the consequences of your decision? Do you understand them?"

"I understand the consequences of *not* choosing them. That could've been us out there. Dead. Bleeding. If I stood against them, if I denied them when they came to me, do you think they would let us go peacefully? That they would not find a way to access our shores without me? Do you understand that?"

She went cold in an instant. "No, Elaia, because you never told me." Auburn eyes burned into hers. "You've isolated yourself. You don't talk to me anymore. You talk *at* me. You don't confide in me. I'm not even sure..." Zahra took a deep breath. "You have made these decisions on your own. I wanted to help, but you were too impatient. You saw the path you wanted to see, and you took it. Can you live with it?"

Elaia tipped her chin up, willing her hands to stop shaking. "Because of me, we get the chance to find out. We will live. They will not kill us in their pursuit of power. They will need us. And we will survive."

Zahra struck her with a glare that held the heat of a thousand suns. A pressure on every nerve. She turned, sticking Rohan with a glare equally as strong before disappearing into the hall, slamming the door behind her. As much as Rohan had been there for her, he had been there for Zahra, too. Coming here with no family as a girl was hard, and Rohan had made it less so. And now, because of a choice she made, he had disappointed her, too.

A consequence.

The first of many.

Elaia pulled her shoulders back, forcing herself to stand tall, even if part of her wanted to curl up in the darkness. The only sound was the wind howling against the windows from the mountains.

"Rohan, send a message home. Instruct the governors to quarantine any that show strange signs of sickness or expelling of blood. And send a message to Simon to ensure that every port is guarded. No one gets into Rersa without my knowing. The Vahls have my support, not my trust."

Rohan finally met her eyes again with a lingering spark of disappointment that threatened to ricochet off her bones until they shattered. "Yes, Your Majesty."

"Rohan," she said, but he was gone. Out of the room in seconds.

It stung more than she would've liked. Especially after her father hadn't bothered to depart the *Nomara*. After he did not introduce her as the High Shade. Desmond had not spoken a single word to her since the challenge. And now it seemed Rohan might follow in his footsteps.

Another consequence.

Only Xerxes remained. He rested his arm over the back of the couch, relaxed almost, aside from the intensity in his eyes as he looked at her. Elaia stalked forward until she stood before him and looked down at him. "And what do you think of me, Xerxes?"

He tipped his head back, loose curls brushing the collar of his leathers. The glass jewelry of Pyth he wore reflected in the low lights. The boot he wore brushed against her ankle as he placed his foot directly next to hers. "I don't envy you. I don't envy your ambitions or your goals. Or the sacrifices you believe you must make to get them."

She furrowed her brow. "The ones I believe?"

"We're different people, Elaia." He shook his head, his lips curling. "I wouldn't make the choices you have. I probably would've removed myself from the responsibility and disappeared. You have the means to do so. It's hard for me to understand that—that you care so deeply that you think you *must* remain. That you believe you owe them anything of yourself."

She studied him. All the scars and the freckles. Felt the heat emitting off of him. "Is it so hard to believe I care?"

"It's not. I can see that every day. It's hard for me to *understand.* There is no one on this planet that I would sacrifice myself for. Not a soul." Xerxes met her eyes with a heady gaze. "You have people that you care about and are willing to do anything for. As I said before, I don't know what that feels like."

"That can't be true. The Order must care for you in some ways."

Xerxes scoffed. "Above all else, the Order is about control, not love or dedication. It's about power, and power demands a loss of self. A loss of empathy. Of compassion. The search, the yearning for power, bleeds you dry. It steals parts of you day by day. And the Order has been around a long time. We are nothing but accomplices in that. They care not for me and I not for them. No one does."

He tried to hide it, but she heard the pain underneath his

words, tucked away as far as he could put them. But not far enough. Elaia hummed, her knee now brushing his. She couldn't explain it, why she was drawn to him. Maybe it was the warmth or how he did not shy away from her or her decisions. Maybe it was that she simply didn't feel obligated to him like she did the rest.

"Seems lonely."

Xerxes tracked his eyes slowly over her, taking in every detail from the top of her head to where their knees touched. "It can be."

"It also seems freeing, the not caring part," she said barely above a whisper, scared to admit something she did not quite understand.

"It can be," Xerxes repeated. "Though, I often wonder what it might feel like." He leaned forward, fingertips brushing her leg over the fabric of her dress. "To care about people that deeply. To be cared about."

Her heart rate stuttered at the feel of him touching her. "It's not that difficult." She found her shadows curling under her feet, wrapping around both of their ankles.

"That's easy for you to say," he murmured with a soft smile. "You've never known anything else."

Memories of her childhood with her dad flashed—the tests, the training, having to prove herself over and over again. Sure, it was different than what he was describing, but she knew what *that* felt like.

Xerxes stood, walking his fingers up as he went, leaving tiny bites of heat behind until he was towering over her. "I would ask you to teach me, but you've got far too much on your plate already." The words were a whisper, his lips close to her ski, yet not close enough.

She swallowed, trapped in the embrace of the Fire Elemental. He made her feel free. There was no show, no mask she had to wear. And he had turned her speechless.

He bent down, lips a breath closer. "To answer your question, what do I think of you, High Shade?" Xerxes lips brushed her cheek, making her breath catch. "I think I've never seen someone so overcome with dedication they are willing to lose themselves. So deeply protective of the ones she loves, she would stop the world from turning to save them." He moved, brushing his lips on her opposite cheek. "I'm not sure we should worship you or stop you before you run out of pieces to give away."

The thing was, she knew exactly where each piece of her had gone. Some taken when her mother and sisters left. Some taken over the years by her father. Some taken by her ambition for the crown. Each of them chased her like phantoms, waiting to remind her. When he said things like that, it made her think that he controlled all of them.

So she pivoted. "What would you have me teach you, Xerxes?"

"I can't give you all my secrets, princess, I've given you plenty," he murmured.

It was true. The idea that he had nothing to fear, no one to love, no one to care for—those were things she was unsure she would've admitted to someone. To anyone. But she wanted more. She wanted to turn him inside out to find what made him, *him*.

"Sometimes I think I've forgotten who I am. How do you seem to see it so clearly?" She inhaled as their noses touched, smelling the oil he used on the leather armor he wore.

Their lips touched. Not kissed. Just touched. "I have a knack for seeing the things people would rather forget."

She let her eyes fall closed. She wanted him to kiss her, to kiss him, even if that felt wrong. Zahra was her light. Her friend. Her lover. Her everything. But recently, it felt like they were just missing each other.

Because when she closed her eyes, she didn't see the blood or the dead, she only saw darkness. Only felt him. "Xerxes…"

"I think we recognize something in each other. Pain. Loss. An ache that we feel that others might not. That's how I see you. Because I see me, too." He pulled away, his hand cupping her chin. "You're still in there. Just because you've forgotten doesn't mean you're lost." Xerxes thumb traced the outline of her jaw, his thumb brushing just under her bottom lip.

Up close, the various shades in his eyes were visible, able to be traced separately. She could see where the brown met green and where the tiniest specks of blue melded in and every individual eyelash that protected them.

Elaia rolled up onto her tiptoes. Just a bit closer—

A loud knock on the door echoed through the room, her heart racing as she jumped back. Without looking back, she approached, only to find Rohan. He met her eyes for only a second before stepping aside. "The Vahls want you."

She stepped through the door without a single glance backward, leaving Xerxes and Rohan behind.

"You are preparing to leave, yes?" Mireya asked, bent over the desk and the notes splayed over the surface.

Behind her, Vittoria and Amala sat quietly. She spared a glance to both of them.

"Yes. Most likely tomorrow evening, if the not the following morning."

"Tomorrow then."

Behind her back, Elaia pressed her nails into her palm. "What's next?"

"We will send the members of our guard to set up an access point where the Aether is the strongest. They will need safe passage to the canyon from your shores and protection. And are there any Creators you can spare? They have proved vital for us."

Her Nightguard. Her people. Her land. "Understood. When should I expect them?"

"No later than two weeks' time when the new moon appears. We will arrive shortly after."

She watched the queen, cautious and reserved. Personally, she thought the ballroom was unnecessary. Nothing more than an overly aggressive show of power, but she said nothing of the sort.

"What should we expect now?" At that, Vittoria's eyes rose to hers in that uncomfortably wide gaze. "What will you expect of us?"

Mireya lifted her head. "We will need to send emissaries to Vydara and Lazora first. Maybe a small coalition to Pyth, Esin, and Vilies. We must make it clear that joining us is their only option for survival. To stand against us...well," Mireya said with a twisted smile, "you saw what happened. We will ensure they know that is the only fate that will await them."

"So, war then." Elaia raised a brow.

The queen hummed—a light, joyful tune, not at all like the air of the room. "I suppose, yes. To war. Or to death."

The last war that Valora had seen was the War of the Athera. A war that lasted over half a century.

Another consequence.

Elaia saw the faces of Killian, of Syrena, of the Chamber of Five, of the Witch. People she had worked with. People she betrayed. Maybe they were not the best of friends, but she had worked with them—all of them, in one way or another. And if it came to it, she would meet them in war. The worst was that she knew—had always known—that the Vahls would do this if they needed, and she'd agreed. Because if it came down to them and her, she would never chose them.

Elaia dipped her head and left, feeling the weight of their stares as she did.

And ran right into the Witch.

CHAPTER 55

HEARTS OF VALORA

NOVA STARED AT THE PRINCESS—*HIGH SHADE*—OF Rersa. Up close in the light, she really saw her this time. More than a shape in the darkness, helping her escape. Though, now she knew that was all false—nothing more than a lie.

Her lip curled in anger. "High Shade."

Elaia's golden-brown eyes sharpened. "Witch."

There was not a spec of blood on her. Not a cut or a scrape aside from a strange mark on her hand. There were no remnants of what had happened, whereas Nova still had blood caked underneath her nails.

"You've made—you are *making* a mistake. You know that?" They stood in a hall of stone, cool air wrapping around them. "Whatever the Vahls have promised you is false."

It didn't matter what they told her, Nova knew it would not be upheld. They were capable of only lies.

"Why should I listen to you?" The High Shade tilted her head. "You couldn't see the power they were wielding? You thought you would go free?" She almost laughed on the word *free*, sending indignant anger down Nova's spine.

The High Shade had found a bruise and punched her fist into it.

Because she'd replayed that night a million times. Why had she trusted Elaia? Why had she trusted that she would be free? It was weak. A weak desire for help. And she fell for it.

"And you think you will? You may as well sign over your soul. They'll never let you go. They will never let those you care for live freely."

Fear flashed in those golden-brown eyes, and Nova furrowed her brows. There was something familiar about the High Shade, beyond that night on the Elderlands. There was something there that she'd seen before. Maybe the shape of her jaw, or the jewelry on her hands, or her eyes?

Nova shook her head of the thoughts in time to see Elaia hold her chin high. "I'm not you."

"Obviously."

Elaia stepped forward, bringing them closer. "I'm not you. I'm not going to look the other way. I don't trust them. I don't believe they'll give me anything. But I will get it." She stepped around her, walking backward down the hall, shadows dancing under her feet. "I suppose I'll see you around, Witch."

"I'd sooner see you bleed."

The High Shade disappeared into the dark. After a deep breath, Nova entered the room, finding Mireya, Vittoria, and Amala. What a disgrace. A sister would so easily betray her brother, blood or not. Mikel was nowhere to be seen as the door closed behind her. The rooms were all similar in the guest wing. Stone walls and wooden floors with smaller chambers but still a living quarter and bedroom. Flowers were potted on every surface with windows showcasing various views of Izlena.

She ignored Vittoria and Amala, who were seated closely next to one another, and kept her eyes on Mireya. "You requested me?"

Mireya gave her a lazy glance. "So glad you made the right decision, Nova."

"Why did you need me here? Why couldn't you let me go?"

"We knew, thanks to Vittoria, that the coronation would be announced soon, and after the Elders, we needed a place, an event, to announce *your* return to the world. To make the others see the death that would threaten their shores. As for our needs, Nalādin is the Aether point we know the least about. No idea where it comes closest to the surface or where it is strongest. After this, only Lazora and the Godlands remain out of our hands. Something that we will soon rectify." The queen sat up, crossing her legs as the gown of shimmering gray folded around her legs. "As for you, well, my girl, you can't possibly think you were ever going to be free of us?"

Mireya continued, "You were never going to be free. Not since the beginning. You were never lost at sea. Elaia ensured you would land here, shipwrecked on the shores. We needed you for the show. We need them to fear you so they would trust us. Your freedom was never an option."

She swallowed, becoming the unreadable, unbendable girl from before.

Mireya stood, dragging a nail down the side of her cheek. "Since the moment you came back to us, we've been testing your blood. This scar," she said, running her thumb over the scar on Nova's throat, stilling her, "was because we couldn't figure out a way to make your blood work for us. Couldn't quite figure out how to keep you in line. Until we did."

Nova's skin crawled. Her scar pulsed. "What did you find?"

A smile crawled onto Mireya's face. "How about I show you instead?"

Dread settled in her blood, weighing her down. But she was going to get out of this place. No matter what it cost.

A SMALL TEAM of guards accompanied Mireya and Nova to the forest, through the winding paths out of Willowgrove and to the edge of Nalādin. In the dark, the forest looked larger than life.

Trees with thick, wide trunks towered over them. Fronds of willow danced down from the moon-streaked sky, and thick leaves of green pointed heavily toward the ground. But what Nova noticed was the stillness. The silence.

Every second she spent outside, Nalādin—the whole of Eisera, really—was alive. Plants constantly blooming, leaves crawling over the roots, birds and deer and sprites flitting among the woods.

Now, it was though all the life had left.

"Come. Let me show you this first." Mireya had two small dishes brought to her, the guard, a Light Naturalist, created just enough for them to see. One dish had blood in it, dark and thick and strange. "Your hand," she said, and before Nova could protest, she was slicing it open, letting a few drops fall into the empty dish.

The other blood was poured over top, and just like in the ballroom, it grew around her own, expanded it, hardened it—and then, it infiltrated it until it shattered. "Best you do what you're told from now on."

Nova stared at Mireya, who watched the blood in awe. Had she ever been a person to them? Or just a thing to control? She wasn't sure if it was hurt or indifference or if she felt anything at all.

"Can we get to it, Mireya?"

The queen stood and pulled them forward into the shadow of the forest's edge. Willow fronds brushed the top of Nova's shoulders like a greeting. "Dray mentioned how the forest welcomed you. Chose you even. At the same time, we've had small amounts of Aether collected, plucked from the Elderlands, and it seemed to welcome your blood, to answer its call. We've lost many trying to find the strongest points of access, but I should no longer have to."

Mireya reopened the cut sharply, and they watched as her blood sank into the soil. The heartbeat of the world was far below, and it altered just so. Seconds passed with no change until the soil seemed hollow and sink, taking her blood with it. And in mere moments, the forest came alive.

No, no, no. Nova pleaded silently, *do not let her see.* But the ground had a mind of its own. The trees shifted from willow and oak to trees of red and black wood and leaves so thick, the sky had disappeared. They were somewhere else, only the two of them. For all she knew, they could be at the furthest point of the forest or trapped somewhere in the middle or in another world. In the back of her mind, she could hear the whispering voices of the dead, the prophecies told, the weight of those gone around her.

"And how do you expect to get out of here, Mireya? How is this of any use to you?"

She laughed. "You keep missing it, dear girl. You keep underestimating me, when you, of all people, shouldn't. That blood, that *disease*, is so much more than that. You think I made something I couldn't control? I've been at this for centur—for *years*. You think I would win power with something that could fight back?" They were so close, she could see every beautiful and ugly inch of Mireya. With every word, she found it harder to breathe. "I tried to teach you that power is not brute force but a delicate, masterful show of control. Of balance. Of wit. It can be taken, sure. But if it can't be controlled, than what use is it? Power is chaos. And if chaos is left unattended, all it will do is burn."

"So, the ballroom, you controlled that?" she asked, breathless. Gods help them, she was a fool. Of course, she did. Mireya loved control more than anyone.

"For the most part, yes. Still working out some flaws in the design."

"How have you done this?"

Mireya raised a perfect brow. "What do you think I've been doing with all the bodies? Every single person you have killed has led us here. There were, of course, the ones we told you to leave on the edge of death, too. We've studied them all. At first, the disease would run its course, their immune systems clearing it out.

Then overtime, we found that if we could twist their minds, we could convince their bodies to stop fighting it."

Nova was going to be sick. Nausea rolled in her gut, and she could practically feel the blood she'd spilled on her hands. How much had they suffered beyond her?

"The *disease,* so to speak, is an extension of our abilities—"

"But if what I discovered was true, your *abilities* aren't true. You aren't....the spirit isn't real."

Mireya sighed. "Dear girl, who do you think erased the existence of soul from the history books? From the world? Who do you think orchestrated the massacre of the Witches? The spirit was stolen from the soul. We—*they*—made it into what we are now. And we have made the world as we wanted."

By the Gods.

Of course, it made sense, in a way. Where else would spirit come from? Why would it be false when the soul was true...but hearing it was a knife to the heart. Had they truly destroyed one to make themselves? Worse, was that Nova knew she was only admitting this because now, with what had been done...no one would believe a word from a Witch's mouth.

There were no words to say. Underneath them, the soil seemed to become translucent. And Mireya dropped that dark, thick blood within, and she watched it grow. It latched on to her blood and sank deep into the ground.

"How are you going to find it again once we leave?"

"Once I can control it, I can force it to open to me. I won't need you," Mireya said, a threatening air on her words. "Unless you remain useful to me."

Again, the forest changed until they seemed to be halfway between worlds—in the soil and yet not. Nova could see the roots of the trees, so old and gnarled they must've been here for centuries. Eyes blinked out of the darkness, but none came to light. But that heavy presence of the dead was potent, seemingly whispering the prophecies in her ears. As if that would save her. Save anyone.

There were stones of every color leading them down a path of sorts, weaving between the roots and between dark puddles. Above, the trees still towered, and the mountain peaks were visible but far, far away. They followed the blood as it crawled, moving slower than it did before, but moving still. Burrowing and looking for things to destroy along the way until it reached a pool of silvery water. One touch, and the blood disappeared into it. Droplets landed on both herself and the queen, and those droplets became waves, washing them under. And the whole world appeared to be alive. Around them, the air thrummed with something unseen. On the walls, threads of silver and black intertwined like vines and wrapped around every surface.

Nova felt the heartbeat of the world louder here, steadier.

In her mind, the threads, the pulsing material of silver and black, looked like veins. And the caverns they created like the heart itself. This was the heart, or one of the hearts, of Valora.

And she'd led Mireya right to it.

Light reflected over Mireya's face, which glowed with contemptuous triumph. She looked youthful, alive, bursting with the purpose to destroy. Swallowing, Nova reached out, infiltrating Mireya's blood. Feeling the odd darkness of it and just barely, twisting—

"I wouldn't do that, Nova." Mireya walked under the veins of Aether and pointed down. The ground beneath Nova's feet undulated, and that same dark blood rose, circling her legs but not yet touching. As she looked up, Mireya gripped her throat tight, her claws scratching at her mind. "Release my blood. Or everyone above will die at your hands. Everyone up there will die because of you."

Her nails dug into Nova's neck, those icy eyes unblinking as she drew them closer. "I am going to remake the world bit by bit until it is mine." Mireya's lip curled. "And you will watch."

Chapter 56

Drops of Wrath

The shores of Eisera became distant as soon as the *Namora* hit the deep sea. There were clouds of dark fury over top of the mountains that protected Izlena—an ominous view. But what became of it was not her responsibility. Not now.

Elaia watched the seas churn underneath the swift moving ship, letting the wind whip her hair around her face. Rohan hadn't looked at her for longer than a few seconds since he'd discovered her involvement, and Zahra had not returned since she stormed out. Everything she had done had been for them, for Rersa, for herself...

And still, she stood alone.

Sort of.

Xerxes was sitting on the stairs of the deck, watching her. She'd replayed that almost-kiss a million times. Even now, a day later, she could feel the heat of him and see the intensity of it in his eyes.

Looking back, she wasn't even sure she could pinpoint the moment she'd began to look at him in a different light. She knew only that she had. But she didn't love Zahra any less, she didn't want her any less.

She just wanted him, too.

Sometimes, she wished she could remove her brain and turn it all off. The emotions, the memories, the good and the bad. Somedays, one didn't make it easier to appreciate the other; somedays, it just made life hard to bear.

Every decision and every choice weighed heavier with every second she breathed. *How many consequences would there be? What if she hadn't prepared well enough? What if everything went wrong and she was at fault?*

It was constant. A loop of possibilities and answers and more possibilities that her brain churned up. It never ended. It never stopped. And the world kept on spinning.

A nose nudged the small of her back, Akiro forcing himself next to her. Usually when he knew something was wrong, he would force her onto the ground and sit on her lap as a way to ground her. But today, he whined and his tail was tucked between his legs, which she had never seen before. Not once.

Elaia bent, hands cupping his big head. "Akiro, what's wrong? What's happened?"

He yipped and spun her toward the chambers. She spared a glance to Xerxes, who'd stood as well, and began to follow the hound. Akiro's steps were erratic, forward and then circling her again to make sure she was still there.

"It's okay. I'm right here," she said, her hand on his back.

They went into the lower deck, where her and her father's chambers were. A strange sensation crawled up her spin as Akiro went right for Desmond's room. The door was cracked open, which was odd, and Akiro pushed right in, pulling her with him.

He was laid out on the bed as though he was sleeping.

But the room was stagnant. Bare. The air, the ground—there were no shadows slinking into the corners. It felt abandoned.

In a second, she felt the pieces holding her together shatter.

"Father?" she whispered, moving to where he laid unmoving. "Father?" She took his shoulders, shaking him. His skin was cold. "No, no, no," she cried, Akiro whining as he curled by her feet.

She didn't understand. Why wasn't he moving? Why wasn't

he breathing? He had been larger than life, so why couldn't she *feel* him?

A scream dug its claws into her throat and tore out of her. Shadows fell from her hands and feet, wrapping around them until there was only darkness.

"Dad?" Elaia crawled up, begging him to move, feeling like a little girl more than she had in years.

Despite their fights and their disagreements and her disillusionment of him, he was her dad. And she'd never loved him any less. Her shadows wrapped around him, extensions of herself trying to hold him close.

But he was cold. And quiet. And it was suffocatingly empty. Her tears would not stop. They kept falling one after the other until she was sure she was going to drown in them.

She dug her nails into her arms, scratching and tugging, wanting out, *out*, of her skin and out of her life. Another scream —or a sob, she wasn't sure anymore—broke free, ricocheting around the room. Akiro broke through the darkness, jumping on the bed and forcing himself into her space. His whines sounded along with her sobs until her throat ran dry. Eventually, she blinked away the tears, seeing the cold gray face of her father. The darkness subsided, her shadows growing tired as she let her head fall onto his chest.

A chest that would never feel her tears or hold her close again. A voice that would never call her his firefly again.

"Your Majesty," Rohan said, quiet and cautious as he reached for her. "You should—"

"Don't touch me." She tightened her grip. "Go! Leave me alone."

Their touch could not help her. It would not sooth the ache, it would not piece together her broken heart. All she wanted was the touch of her family—and her family was dead. She would never feel their hands again. She would never hear her father's voice again. She couldn't stand to be touched—to be reminded that somehow, she was alive.

And they were not.

The darkness returned, blanketing her. She didn't know how long she cried or laid there with her head on a chest that no longer moved. Only that she sobbed until her body ached. Until the tears felt like shards falling down her cheeks. Until there was nothing left but emptiness.

The rough seas were the thing to bring Elaia back to the present. Her eyes were puffy and her head ached like nothing else. And the body of her father was still cold.

She cleared the shadows, an orb light flickering to life in the lifeless room. *You have to stand up. Get up. Get up. Get up.* Her legs were not her own. Everything felt off kilter—the world, her heart, her body. It wasn't right. Nothing was right. Her entire family was gone. Anyone she shared blood with was *gone*.

Without feeling, Elaia forced herself to stand, hands resting on the bed. Akiro kept his eyes on her. She hadn't even examined him. There was no blood, no visible evidence that someone had done this. Maybe he'd just...died.

But there was a note on the table beside his bed, ripped but legible. It laid atop a file of parchment.

And it read: 'The Order will always find those who seek to find us."

The Order? No. What would he have known about the Order? He had ignored her mother's drawings. Why would he have been investigating? Had he been keeping things from her? More so than she feared? Had the Order used her to get to him?

With shaking hands, she began to look him over. Disturbing him when he seemed almost peaceful sent her heart twisting, but she continued. Pushing up and pulling the sleeves of his shirt back down, checking for any wounds and finding nothing.

Until she pulled his collar down, finding a mark that was burned into her brain branded on his skin. Everything went black with rage. Tears forced themselves from her eyes, but not in sadness. Instead, they fell in drops of wrath.

Elaia tore out of the room to the hall, where Rohan and Xerxes rose at her exit. More than anything, she wished Zahra was here. The thought tore through her but was eaten by her anger in seconds.

Before anyone could stop her, she was in front of Xerxes, her shadows wrapping around him and forcing him to his knees. Elaia drew her blade, pressing it against his throat. "What have you done?"

The air thrummed between them, and his eyes were wide. "What—"

"Do not play stupid with me, Xerxes. Why is the mark of the Order on my father's neck?" Her throat was raw and shredded.

"Elaia," Rohan said quietly behind her, like talking to an angry animal. "You need to—"

She spun, her blade still in place. "Do not talk to me like you're my father. I'm not stupid. I'm not a little girl in need of your protection. I need to know what happened." Her words seemed to sink into her guard, and he went quiet. Maybe she'd feel guilty later but not now.

"Explain." She forced Xerxes head back until he could only look at her. "Did you kill my father?"

"No." His throat bobbed against the blade, a small drop of blood beading on his skin. "I need to see it. Let me see it."

"Why? So you can burn it away and make me seem insane?"

Frustration sparked in his eyes, but he had no right. No godsdamned right.

"No." He inhaled, his pulse frantic in his throat. "This wasn't supposed to happen anymore—"

The world went cold.

"Anymore?" Elaia spoke sharper than the blade at his throat. Xerxes said nothing. "What exactly do you mean, Xerxes? Why is my father dead?" Before he could speak, she pressed the onyx cuff in her ear, Sacha appearing seconds later. Her face was unreadable, and she knew Rohan had told her. "Round up everyone on the decks and search for weapons. Anything. Take Akiro with you." Sacha dipped her head.

Once again, only the three of them remained. Rohan kept his hand on the hilt of his dagger, eyes flickering between the two.

"Why did the Order want him dead? And why should I believe that you didn't?"

"I had no reason to. Not anymore. I was the one to tell the Order it wasn't needed. They weren't supposed to do this."

Every word pricked her skin. It hurt more than it should coming from him.

Her skin crawled. "Stop saying *anymore.* What does that mean? How long? How *long* have you and your Order wanted my father dead?" She hated that tears pricked. But grief, old or new, did not care about who it showed itself to. "How long?" she screamed, the sound tearing her throat until it bled.

The sound was sharp with pain and so heavy that it stole all the air from the room.

Xerxes's eyes swam with emotions, and she knew he was holding back because there was no heat emitting from him. No flames dancing. This wasn't a standoff. This was a questioning. And she didn't know if any answer would suffice.

"Does it matter? Would that make a difference right now?"

"Were you involved? Now or ever?" She asked again, slower, and still, he gave nothing.

Her shadows wound around this throat. She knew. Even without him confirming, she knew. They had played her for a fool, and she'd let what she wanted cloud it. And now, he was dead like the rest of her family.

"Lock him up," Elaia whispered, lowering her knife. "Now, Rohan. Lock him up now!"

With unblinking eyes, she watched Rohan take him away, and

as soon as she was alone, she collapsed to her knees. It was too heavy. It was too strong. It was too *everything*.

Even when she thought there was nothing left, she cried again, pulling from the well that had emptied and digging even deeper. Shadows encompassed her once more, shielding her from the world that only ever took.

She wasn't sure what would give out first—her heart or her tears.

CHAPTER 57

THE OCEAN ALWAYS RISES

That was what it felt like as Syrena relived the horrors the Vahls had released as she wrestled with the knowledge of that *thing* she'd left on the ship. Was her ship even there? Still waiting for her at the port? Or was it gone? Was there any way off this godforsaken place?

She had to get out.

But she was all alone.

In the darkness of the cell, she tipped her head up to the ceiling.

"If you're somewhere listening to me, Zvon, please. Please tell me what to do," she said, her throat cracking, tears threatening to spill.

But her brother couldn't help her anymore. She spared a glance behind her, where Milana sat slumped in the corner, a lethal wound on her neck and on her gut.

Dead.

Blood was splattered on her gown. The small coalition of guards she'd brought had been killed, and she was positive it was their blood on her clothes—no one else's. Because she'd fought back, but she hadn't killed—she only held them off. In hopes—in stupid, optimistic hopes—that it would stop. That the horror would end. That the Vahls would deem they had enough, they had *shown* enough. But it didn't.

And now, everyone she came here with was dead.

Images of that woman, that *Witch*, kept replaying, and she kept failing to fathom what she had seen. She had weaved the control of the blood so flawlessly, the only one able to stop it. Were the Vahls lying? Or was this the actual truth? If they said the Witches were back and were the cause, it made sense that they would be the ones to control it, to wield it, and to end it. But the Vahls were not trustworthy people.

And Syrena didn't know what to believe.

Not anymore.

Around, from somewhere above or below, she had no concept of where she was in Willowgrove, she heard screams echoing off the mountains and the trees, almost burrowing into the ground themselves until they ricocheted off her eardrums.

"Focus."

They hadn't chained her. For whatever reason, the Vahls had not put aetherchains on her. Maybe they thought because she had not wielded a killing blow, she wasn't one to waste it on. Maybe they thought her weak. In some ways, she was, but not in the ways they thought.

Approaching Milana, she crouched, resting her palm on the guard's cheek, her skin now cold. "I'm sorry, Milana," she whispered, moving her fingers in the air, weaving the water out of the dead body.

Strands of water began to weave out of her skin, answering to the leech that Syrena was. It curled and wove through the air in a never-ending loop. The bars of the cell were strong, made of fyrestone, an almost indestructible material long ago created by the Athera and the Creators. But she only needed to move one.

She allowed the water to encase a single bar, winding around and around in swirls of blue. With a deep belly breath, she willed the water to freeze. Molecule by molecule, she watched as the water turned to ice. And again and again, she willed the water unfrozen to cover every inch of the stone. To infiltrate any cracks. Syrena froze and refroze until she was sure.

She wasn't a fighter in the sense that she would ever be sent to battle, but she had trained with her brother and Torin time and time again. Not for violence, but for stillness, for patience. It helped quiet her mind and made her ability to weave the water smoother, more powerful. It was a type of fighting arts long ago created by another water Athera, the Way of Areya.

It was hard to learn. Almost impossible to master. But Syrena was brilliant, beyond even what her brother had mastered.

She drew in a breath and let her feet become a part of the earth. Through the stone of the building and into the earth, she felt for the water of the world. She let herself become it. The small streams in a forest, the water droplets on leaves, the drops of condensation on glasses. She was the salt in the sea and the waves that answered the moon.

All of it. She was *all* of it.

And with a sweeping smoothness, she whirled and struck the frozen bar with a lethal kick and watched it shatter. Ice chips clattered against the floor, and with one final look at Milana, Syrena forced herself through the small but perfect opening. And she ran.

With the calmness of the world waters and the sureness of the ocean waves, she ran.

She was the water, and the water was her.

And she would not be leeched of life or kept captive. If they wanted to underestimate her, that was their mistake. People who didn't understand water often failed to respect it.

But she was a Reyna now, born of the ocean more than anything else.

And the ocean would always rise.

CHAPTER 58

A LAND UNKNOWN

OVER THE PEAKS OF THE MOUNTAINS, THE SUNS ROSE AS one, and the sky turned red.

Sleep had evaded her from the moment she was locked in this room after visiting the forest. All she saw was the dead. In the mirrors within her room, in the water of the tub, in the windows, and in the darkness when her eyes fell closed. And she saw Killian's face, too. How the green in his eyes went cold and his threads went blank. How all she saw was disappointment and betrayal shining back when she looked at him.

In seconds, he'd seen the truth of her, told from the lips of someone else.

The door remained locked all day, only opened once for food, which sat uneaten on the desk. Instead, Nova sat at the window and watched the bleeding suns. Birds landed on the railing of the balcony, their beady eyes looking at her. In part, she wanted to waste away. What could she do? If Mireya could control the disease and, by proxy, control whomever and whatever it touched, what could *she* do?

And yet...for the first time, she felt like she had to try. Suffering at the hands of the Vahls was not a fate she wanted the world to have to fight. It was not a fate many would win. She had lost to them time and time again. She was sick of it. So, she would try.

Daughter of the Dead will make them undone.

Nova sat and waited. They didn't know about the tunnels built into the castle. Sure, she was locked here, but she could go if she wanted. There wasn't much to be done in the light anyway, not when she could hide in the dark.

As soon as the suns fell behind the mountains, finding Killian was her first goal. Making him listen to her long enough to get him out was her second. From there...she would get them out of this place, even if it meant crawling by her fingernails. She would get them to the Witchlands, *a land unknown.*

But for now, she waited.

DARKNESS FELL, the sky shifting from crimson to blood to black. She braided her curls and slipped on the light clothing Killian had given her, hand sewn in Eisera. Most of her weapons had been taken, aside from her bracelet, but she unraveled her pack until she found a single dagger and strapped it to her thigh. The guards had maintained steady schedules all day, switching posts every few hours, but no sounds appeared outside her door.

Furrowing her brows, Nova pressed her ear against the wood. But there was only silence. A shiver went down her spine. A coolness entered the air, phantom hands touching her. *Find the others. Unravel the lies.*

Nova shook them off and made for the tunnels as the first scream echoed through the walls. *Shit.* She took off, finding the tunnel entrance in the closet quickly and entering the dark stone halls. Luckily, she didn't need light. She only felt for blood, and there was nothing alive in her path.

Her feet barely touched the ground as she moved through,

forcing the map Killian had given her to come to the front of her mind, eventually coming out under one of the many bridges. Blood dripped off and down into the lake far below.

And all she heard was screaming. Screams that seemed to go on forever and screams that were cut short. Underneath, she felt the shifting of stone, droplets in the air, Elementals fighting back. More, she felt that darkness pulsing on the threads.

The sickness.

Pulling herself up the bridge, she saw guards with lifeless eyes and blood-soaked weapons. Nova took a quick inventory. The bridge was empty, only two bodies lifeless on the ground, but there were guards everywhere—on this bridge, on the one above and below, and as far as she could see. Currently, this was the level above the ballroom. The cells were low, yes, but more so, they were built deep into the mountains.

Shit. Nova tipped her head. Had they used an Elemental to get there before? Was there a way to get there without—

A small blade whirled past her ear. Spinning, she saw a guard coming straight toward her, blood crawling up their arms. She didn't hesitate this time and watched the blood shatter, taking the guards arm with it. They fell without a sound. Clearing her head, she began moving; she could figure out the problems when they came. Carefully, she ran down the halls, looking for the shelves she knew would move. Eventually, she found her way in, running her fingers along the stone. She paused, catching her breath and reaching out—far out—and finding distant heartbeats in the mountains.

Nova followed them, trusting her powers. The tunnels were built to be a labyrinth, confusing to anyone who didn't take the time to study them. There were circular spaces that branched out, tunnels that led back into one another, and a million dead ends. But eventually, she found her way to the dark section of Willowgrove that was void of any natural life and built to withstand the worst.

The heavy door built of metal and stone had been left open,

but she saw no blood. Nova stepped in carefully. But much like the rest, the cells of Sylos were like a maze. From the ballroom, Mireya had instructed the guards to lead those who dissented here, but that was all she knew. The Reynas of Iyvia and Ceron, the Chamber of Five, Killian and the former king and queen, and a number of attendees that had survived. She took it row by row, passing empty cells and basing her movements on how the heartbeats felt.

The first row with any sign of life...well, had been void of it. Blood spilled from under the fyrestone entrapments, bodies slumped against the wall as Nova looked through the slits in the door. The mindless guards must not have been thorough because she finally found Killian.

His hands were tied with aetherchains, blood seeped from a cut on his cheek, and his eyes were closed. But she knew he sensed her by his heart rate.

She rested her hand on the stone, but he spoke first. "What are you doing here?"

"We have to go. Now."

Killian blinked his eyes open. "I'm not going anywhere with you."

"So, you'd rather sit here, trapped, than go with me?"

He exhaled, and his eyes fell. Disappointment was heavy on his threads, encompassing them in shades of gray. "You're not who I thought you were."

Those words were more painful than anything else he could've said. Hatred, anger—she could've withstood those, but this tired disenchantment was far worse.

"I know. And I know I can't change that now, but you cannot stay here. They are going to infect Nalādin. They will probably kill you and your family if you stand against them. Or worse. So, you have to come with me."

Killian kneeled, resting his elbows on one knee has he looked at her. The stare was pointed and sharp. "I don't trust you."

"You don't have to trust me right now. You just have to want to live." She rolled her eyes, shoving down the rest of her emotions. "If I wanted you dead, I wouldn't be here. Please." A scream from above or below, she couldn't be sure, echoed. "We have to go."

There was a second of nothing and then resignation. She saw how it sat on his shoulders as he stood. "Can you break these?"

"I think. But this stone can't be moved, right? If its firestone, then we need another way." Nova bent, looking at the locking mechanism on the door. She cut her palm and wove her finger, the blood floating through the air until she instructed it in the lock. It was cool and strange, but her blood seemed to find every slot, though nothing happened.

"It's a puzzle," he said. "The keys are made specially to fit in multiple sections. I can't remember—"

"Can you picture it? Can you show me?" She knew she was asking a lot. For him to let her in, even for a moment, was pushing it.

"How?"

She rested her head against the door. "Just visualize it. I only need a second." As soon as she reached out, his mind opened only an inch—enough for her to see the key, an oddly-shaped thing that she quickly formed her blood to match. But his mind was heavy, specked with pain, and though she didn't ask to feel it, she did. "Killian—"

"Out." And the forest of his mind pushed firm against her, and his anger surrounded her, trying to steal her breath.

Instead of speaking, she made quick work of the mechanism until the door came open. With her blood, she wrapped it around his chains until it encompassed all of them and congealed it and then shattered it, the chains clattering onto the stone.

In seconds, he was in front of her, looking at her as though he'd never seen her before. Maybe that was true. The version he'd known was now colliding with the truth, and she couldn't stop that. "Let's go," she said, breaking the stare.

"We have to find Aydin and Gena. And the others."

Of course, he'd want to. She could feel the time ticking away, those dark, sick threads closing in, but she followed, nonetheless. The lights on the wall flickered, some of them dark and useless, shadows leading the way. In the distance, there was a clang—a sword against stone. The guards.

"We have to hurry, Killian," she mused, picking up the pace.

The first cell they came to had been forcibly opened. Frost gleamed at the edges, water drops on the floor. One of the Reynas? She couldn't help but be impressed.

In seconds, Killian had moved ahead of her. "These are all empty. Where are they?"

She shook her head. "I don't know. I don't feel them." Pain reverberated through the prince, his eyes wide and searching. "Maybe Amala got to them first? Maybe they went with her?"

"No, they wouldn't do that. They would never do that—" He stopped abruptly, hanging his head. "Except the only time they've chosen me over her is when the forest told them so. They treated me like their son, but *she* is their daughter."

Nova stepped forward. "We have to keep moving."

"They cannot stand with them. I can't leave, Nova. Not them. Not Eisera."

"You don't have a choice. If you want there to *be* an Eisera, you need to go. If they think they can get you back, they will keep them alive." Shouts came from all around them, and she pushed him. "Go."

Most of the cells they ran past were empty of life or blood, and some were not. Along the way, she shot her blood into every lock she could, trying to figure out the puzzle of each one until a small group of people ran behind them. But none of the royals were here. No one with any power. They made it to the entrance just as the guards rounded, magic and blood dancing at their fingertips.

"Go!" she shouted, pushing them through the door, though many were dazed and unsure. Killian closed it behind them, fortifying it with stones from the surrounding wall as the guards smashed against it from the inside.

They moved quick and silent until reaching another bridge, the open air a relief from the cells that stank of despair and spilled blood. Until everyone they had taken with them suddenly halted.

The threads changed before she saw it. They went still, colorless until they begin to twist. Killian was oblivious, heading straight toward them.

"Killian, no," she said, reaching out to grab him, pulling him back as one of them swung a blade of stone. He quickly backtracked to her side.

"How do we stop this? How are they doing this?"

The guards had caught up, trapping them. She couldn't see her, but she knew Mireya was watching, somehow, someway. Every single heartbeat was in her palm. It was too loud. They were too heavy. She couldn't kill them, not this many. Not again. It would take something that she would never get back.

"Can we jump?"

He spun, meeting her eyes briefly but keeping them on the threat. "What?"

"What's below us?"

"A smaller bridge only used for passage or goods." Killian looked at the vines and pulled her toward the railing. "Come on." She was crouched, her back against the railing and hands extended, controlling the blood of many. "Shit. More guards. We can't."

An ache burrowed deep and sharp, but she stayed steady. "What do we do?" She snarled as one broke through—a guard whirling two daggers soaked with blood.

She rose, cutting her skin and swung into a kick, the blood winding around her before striking the guard down. For now.

"Here," Killian said, his vines wrapping around their midsections as he pressed his feet into the ground and the bridge began to shake.

All of the bridges were built in sections to allow for change or easy transport. And that came in handy as Killian sent the citizens to the bridge below, and with a swing of his arms, sent the stones toward the guards, leaving only a sliver for them to stand on.

"You could've done that earlier." She began pulling him along. "Where are the stables? Can we get to them from here?"

Wordlessly, he took the lead, stepping on a floating stone until he was in front as they entered the tunnels, leaving the bridge in pieces for someone else to fix. The path was clear as they wound through the halls and into the tunnels once more until they arrived at the stables—an Athera-built section of the castle that built a pasture within the mountains. Guards were sparse and easily avoided and luckily seemed to be of their own mind. They stayed to the shadows until they found Ghost and Rouge.

"Where are we going, Nova?" He stood between the horses.

"The Witchlands. We can get to the coast from the tunnels, right?" Her heart was frantic, but her words were calm. "If they can infect the Aether, we can't stop them. Not the two of us. And if what I was told in Nalādin was true, there are others. There have to be. But we can't stop them ourselves."

"You want me to abandon my country? My family?"

"Your family abandoned you. Do you see them here? Do you see Amala?" She stepped forward and tipped her chin. His green eyes were aglow with a bitter numbness. He could hate her; he could be angry, fine. But he was leaving here alive. "Do you think if you're dead, you'll be able to save them? To stop whatever is coming?"

At her words, Rouge let out a soft whinny, those big brown eyes meeting hers. Her ears flicked as though she agreed and emphasized the words with a pound of her hoof. Nova held her palm up, and Rouge approached, nudging her shoulder with her giant head.

"Are you going to lead the way, or will you let us die here?"

A blood curling scream shattered their standoff. Killian sighed. "Let's go. Now.

CHAPTER 59

ONLY ONE TO BLAME

ROHAN FOUND HER CURLED UP IN THE DARK.

She wasn't sure how much time had passed, if any. It felt like she'd been sitting there for seconds and hours all at once. The only sound was the occasional ocean wave splashing against the wood or Akiro whining on her lap. All she felt and all she knew was darkness.

"Elaia?" She blinked open her eyes to find him crouched in front of her, and luckily, despite her outbursts, he didn't look at her any differently than he always had. "They can't find her."

Her brows furrowed. "What do you mean?"

"Zahra isn't on the ship."

She was going to shroud this ship in darkness until everyone walked overboard. Was she surrounded by idiots? "Then where would she be, Rohan? Are you sure they checked every inch?"

The look in his eyes was not one of hope, and it followed her all the way to the deck. Every crew member stood in front of her, the same crew that had traveled with her time and time again. At least they had the brains to dip their heads at her arrival. The captain stepped forward and beside him, a scribe.

"We may have the answers, Your Majesty," Lyn, the captain, spoke, nudging the scribe forward. "He keeps track of every time someone leaves or boards the ship. Every journey, no matter how short or far. And it seems there has been a mistake."

Elaia narrowed her eyes. "A mistake."

The scribe swallowed. "I believed she had boarded with you. She always does. I must've marked it subconsciously during the rush. But she...she isn't here. I never checked her name off. She isn't here, Yo—Your Majesty."

She laughed something strange, bitter. Her nails bit into her skin, her shadows leaking out of her with no direction until she sent them around the scribe's throat and dragged him to her. Murmurs of discontent came from the crew, and she knew Rohan was hovering behind her.

"If you ever make a mistake again, it will be your last. If something happens to her, it will be your neck on the line."

The scribe looked upon her in horror, and around her, the rest stared at her with something she hadn't seen before. "Turn the ship around." But no one moved. "Turn. It. Around."

"We can't, Your Majesty."

She laughed again, the sound cracking. "And why is that, Captain Lyn?" The captain swallowed but pointed behind them. Dread crawled up her spine.

Turning, Elaia focused her eyes on the horizon, expecting only blue waters, but was met with the dark shapes of trailing ships. Far enough away to be lost in the distance but close enough to be menacing.

"They've followed from the moment we set sail. And they sent us a message." Lyn handed over a parchment that had previously been folded. She recognized the Vahls' handwriting immediately. They had planned this.

Her hands shook violently as she read the message. It was simple, and yet she couldn't tear her eyes away. *Safe travels, Elaia. We'll see you on the shores of Rersa and not a second before. Try not to worry too much. The light will shine—as long as you do what is expected of you.*

The shadows around the throat of the scribe tightened

without her even realizing it as the parchment floated to the deck. Sprays of salt water immediately turned it damp. In some ways, she wanted to choke the air out of him. But she knew it wasn't his fault.

It was hers. She had no one to blame but herself. Another laugh, garbled and broken. In the haze, she heard Rohan clearing the deck, but nothing made any sense. Because Zahra was in the hands of the Vahls. All because of *her*. Because Mireya wanted— needed—some type of collateral. For control. For power. All to wield over Elaia.

The light will shine—as long as you do what is expected of you.

She tipped her head up to the star-filled sky as every part of her shattered. She couldn't tell if she was crying or screaming or something in-between, but she was sure even the Gods would hear it.

If someone cared to look, they would see her heart in pieces on the floor, in tiny shards of glass, incapable of being put back together—a culmination of everyone that she had ever loved and everyone she had ever lost.

Elaia never wanted to be alone. She only ever wanted to keep the ones she loved safe. And now? Everyone in her family was dead. And the one person she'd chosen as her family was in the hands of someone twisted.

She was all alone.

And the only person to blame was herself.

CHAPTER 60

WHAT KIND OF MONSTER

Nova had known they wouldn't let up.

Underneath her, Rouge forged a path through the tunnels and into the mountains, and still, the guards followed. Before, they had only been controlled, not sick with that *disease*. But now, the wrongness of their threads and of their minds chased her through the woods. Ahead, Killian and Ghost weaved through trees and underbrush, moving confidently over rocky ground. Above, through the breaks in the leaves, the moon shone brightly, tinted red from the earlier blood suns.

She had expected to be able to catch her breath the further they got, but she only found it harder to breath. What had she missed? An unsettling sensation was hooked onto her skin, sinking into her blood as they rode toward the shore. They just needed to get out of the mountains, away from the castle, and away from the guards.

"Stay steady, girl," she whispered to Rouge before turning as far as she could to see the guards behind them.

There were a few on horseback themselves—must've taken them from the stables. But there were at least ten. Maybe more.

Reaching out, she tried to get into their minds, but that dark, sick thing met her immediately with claws of its own. It wasn't even them. She could tell. They weren't making the decision to fight her.

They weren't making any decisions at all.

She tried pushing past it, focusing on one instead of all. It was like mud and quicksand all at once, and that sickness tried to grab her and drag her down. Nova retreated. It wasn't the time to try something new and get them caught. But her intrusion had angered them. Magic danced off their fingertips and underfoot. Spinning forward, she plastered herself against Rouge's neck and stayed low.

They had to get out of here. Come on girl, Nova whispered in the horses mind, a gentle but intelligent place. Their heartbeats fell into rhythm as they moved. Luckily, these horses knew the forest, the leaves and the flowers practically bending to greet them.

"Come on, we're almost at the shore," Killian said, looking back. Sweat beaded on his forehead as he urged Ghost onward.

Almost there.

Almost free.

The horses bounded down the side of the mountains, and the waters of the Syone Channel shone black in the moonlight. The channel separated Eisera from what they now knew was the Witchlands. On the map, it was a rocky, treacherous break with waves crashing in the middle from the north and south. But it was their only choice.

As soon as the path widened, Rouge took her spot next to Ghost, their strong legs moving in time with one another. Killian turned, holding himself to Ghost with only his thighs, and sent rocks flying to the guards, the ground turning slick underneath them until they lost their step. In the distance, there was a shape, a person, moving against the sand—minuscule from their position, but a person no doubt, heading toward the water.

"Killian, do you see that? Ahead."

They locked eyes for a second, her heart stopping when he

looked at her and urged the horses on. She wasn't even sure they were even touching the ground. She felt both of their heartbeats, strong and racing. Any other day, the feeling of being on Rouge when she was in charge, racing over the world—it would've felt like flying. Today, it only felt like running. Running from things she'd had only ever failed at escaping. Monsters that were determined to make her one, too. Monsters that had succeeded.

But this was her chance. She still had one.

In the darkness, she felt the hearts of those in the forest, the guards and those who remained unseen, watching as they raced toward the shore. Large rocks were speckled in the sand, but the horses easily avoided them as they approached the figure quickly.

Killian swept out his arm, the sand moving to create a cliff of sorts, and raising the center up, trapping the person in seconds. As they moved closer, slowing to a trot, the light of the moon reflected off fabric of teal and gold. Iyvia. It had to be the *Reyna*. Syrena Savali.

"Syrena?" Killian furrowed his brows, jumping off Ghost, who nudged Rouge's neck. "I didn't realize, I apologize." The sand went back to normal. Nova eyed the blood dripping from her arm, her cheeks marred with dirt. The gown had also been ripped, the bottom half torn off and the shards of fabric fanning out around her hips. "How did you—"

"She froze the cells. And then broke them," Nova said, watching them. Behind her, the heartbeats of the guards were still far enough away.

Syrena's eyes widened as she realized who Nova was. "What are you doing with her?" She stepped back, curling her fingers. "She killed them. She killed everyone."

Nova swallowed but did not look away. "I didn't have another choice. It was them or us."

"Except you stood with them. Did you not?"

She flicked her eyes between the two royals, feeling far out of place until Rouge snapped her with her tail. She took a deep breath. "I am not with them."

"But—"

"We don't have time for this," Killian interrupted. "We need to go. We need to work together." His eyes flickered behind him as the heartbeats drew closer. "I have an idea."

Killian moved them toward the shores, the waves calm for the moment as they kissed the sands.

"We need to get out of their reach. There are lands on the other side of the channel if we can get to them."

Syrena looked at the seas. "I have to get home. But if we can get far enough away, I can get there myself."

Nova dismounted, her hands curling into Rouge's mane. Beside her, Ghost nudged her shoulder. Between the two of them, she felt protected. There was a calmness to them, an understanding that was so simple yet intelligent.

Killian let the sand fall through his hands. "If you can open the waves, I can make a path. The channel should be shallow enough."

"It is."

"Is that possible?" he asked, and Syrena nodded, stepping into the crashing waves.

"We will need to be quick."

Syrena stepped in, the water circling her dark skin, and her white-blond hair, the color of the surface of the moon, blew behind her in the wind. Nova watched as the Reyna moved with the waves, ebbing and flowing as they did until she claimed control, stopping the waves in their path. She stepped in, pushing the waves out. In perfect sync, one hand fell, pulling the waves in, and the other pushed until the water was hers. The Reyna opened a channel, the waves curling over the top but never falling.

As Killian stepped up, something shifted behind her. The air fell still, dead. The sounds of the world quieted. A pounding started in Nova's ears, the sound of heartbeats, of many. More than what there should've been all crashing against her head.

With a cry, she fell to her knees, pressing her hands against her ears. Toward the mountains, from every direction, were guards.

And not just those from Eisera under the Vahls' control or their own, but the Nightguard, too—the infamous army of Rersa. They approached quickly. Some sick, some not.

"Killian," Nova screamed, trying to stand against the ache.

She pushed, trying to fight through it, and found the talons digging into every inch of her mind, ripping her guard away. Plucking and tugging memories and emotions, forcing her to feel them. Mireya was here.

She turned, forcing her eyes open. "Go. You have to go!" she shouted at the two of them, a path of Earth rising between the waves.

She screamed into the horse's minds, but they stood over her, never moving. Pain emitted from every inch of her skin, only to circle back and stab her again. Forcing herself up, she pushed forward, walking away from the shore and toward the oncoming guard. She felt the world shift underneath her, but she couldn't tell where it was coming from—whether she was being dragged toward Killian or toward the guards.

"Nova!" His voice was a beacon in the dark, but she couldn't get to him. She would not drag him with her.

Somehow, she pushed against his head. *Go, Killian! Get out of here.*

"My dear girl, you cannot have thought you'd ever escape us?" Mireya's voice felt both near and far. Heat surrounded her, a wall of fire trapping her in, separating her from the rest.

Except when she opened her eyes again, Killian stood beside her.

"What have you done?" She sat up, her head spinning. Over the flickering fire, the wall of waves was gone. And so was Syrena. "You should've gone!" she screamed, tears streaking.

Did no one want to live? Did no one understand the Vahls would make living worse than dying? They were all fools, so blinded by a chase for power, they couldn't see the cliff in front of them, waiting for them to fall.

Killian wrapped his vines around her midsection, holding her steady, the pain still digging into her. As the fire burned, figures approached, the light reflecting on their faces. Mireya. Mikel. Dray. Amala. Vittoria.

Nova was a storm of everything and nothing.

Of anger and despair. Of broken shards and lost freedom.

Mireya bent over the flames, unafraid, and wrapped her hand around Nova's throat again, uncaring of the bloody tears that ran over her skin. "Didn't I tell you, you were going to watch? You have tried so hard to run. And all you have ever done is fail."

Out of the corner of her eye, she saw vines approaching, reaching for her, only for them to be burned. A sound of pain left Killian's mouth as he pulled them back. Before he could do more, the air was pulled from his throat, Nova forced to watch.

And his sister did nothing.

Another scream tried to crawl out, but Mireya shut it off. Destroyed it.

In the edges of her vision, she swore the earth had changed. Trees towered over her, but they were just on the sand? How was this possible? Underneath her was soil now, mixed together with rocks and sand of the shores; roots of unseen trees gnawed out of the ground, and the ocean seemed impossibly far away. From below, she felt the soil crawling up her legs.

Mireya pulled her closer, hand tight. "You are useless on your own, Nova, don't you see? You are nothing but what we have made you. And I will make you anew again."

On her throat, the scar burned, the memory playing like it was reality. Nova relived every second, so much so she wasn't sure it wasn't real. The knife against her throat. Her blood on the ground.

Black specs danced behind her eyes. Her heart weakened.

She had wanted freedom. She'd wanted Killian safe.

And she had failed.

Up and around, the dirt and soil crawled, a dark, sick thing forcing its hand as it covered them.

"Let us see what kind of monster I can make you now."

A coldness pervaded her. Soil fell into her mouth as the ground opened up and took her within its grasp. It dug beneath her nails and sank into her lungs...

Until once more, Nova was suffocating.

Thank you!

Did you enjoy **Daughter of the Dead?** Please consider leaving a review on Goodreads, Amazon, your favorite retailers, and social media.

I'd also love if you joined my newsletter (for early updates!), my discord, or follow me on social media.

Scan here to find all things *K. Jamila*!

Acknowledgments

Wow. Thank you.

I wasn't sure I'd ever make it here—the acknowledgements of a fantasy book. *My* fantasy book. For so long I thought it was a far off dream, a thing I'd always dream of doing but never actually do. But that's the thing about dreams, even if you try to push them aside, or convince yourself you aren't worthy of completing them, they never quite die.

It would be remiss of me if I didn't start with a thank you to *Avatar the Last Airbender* and specifically, the moment that Katara decides to blood bend. For so long, I've been dreaming about that ability. I hated that we villainized it and never touched it again—this story is about so much more than the violence it wields, though it is about that, too. It's about how things are not so easily black and white, but all the grey that exists between. That things that are often deemed "evil" are not always *just* evil and things that are often deemed good, often have a dark side.

At its core I think this story is about *choice*. We have the choice and the intelligence to see something in all its facets, in how things exist between the lines, not just how they are presented to us. Life and death. Love and obsession. Love and loss. Love and hatred. Good and evil. Honor and worship. I hope you see all that is unsaid, and I hope you find whatever you are looking for.

Thank you to my mom, for making this your first fantasy read (ever!) and loving it.

To Jess—for putting up with my endless voice notes and breakdowns. I hope you love the final version.

To the SGLS—I love you girls for life.

To Madison & Meaghan—Welcome to the secret club (sorry I didn't tell you sooner). Thank you for sticking around for as long as you have. I love you both.

And to everyone else for making this journey what it has been—thank you. To my author friends, to Nicole, Jessica, Kaitlyn, Brea, Victoria, Sheila, and so many more, thank you for understanding the crazy in only the ways we can. To the friends that have been here since the beginning, thank you for sticking by me. To all of you, old and new, thank you for joining me on this journey.

Thank you to everyone who helped make this book what it was. To Mitra—I will never be able to thank you enough, and I will never be able to truly express just how much I love your art. To Silver, Friel, Kayla, Tiffany, Kim, and Dewi, getting to work with so many brilliant artist and editors made this a dream.

To Juno—you were my heart and soul, my best (four-legged) friend, and in the truest sense of the word, my soul dog. I miss you every day.

And now, really, thank you, to all of *you*. For giving me and this book (and these characters) a chance. I hope we have found a home in your hearts.

www.ingramcontent.com/pod-product-compliance
Lightning Source LLC
Chambersburg PA
CBHW030328010826
48973CB00004B/917